THE
BEIGE
MAN

Also by Helene Tursten

THE BEIGE MAN

HELENE TURSTEN

Translation by Marlaine Delargy

First published in Swedish under the title *En man med litet ansikte*
Copyright © 2007 by Helene Tursten
Published in agreement with H. Samuelsson-Tursten AB, Sunne, and
Leonhardt & Høier Literary Agency, Copenhagen
English translation copyright © 2015 by Marlaine Delargy

First English translation published in 2015 by
Soho Press
853 Broadway
New York, NY 10003

Library of Congress Cataloging-in-Publication Data

Tursten, Helene.
[Man med litet ansikte. English]
The beige man / Helene Tursten ; translation by Marlaine Delargy.

First published in Swedish under the title En man med litet ansikte.

ISBN 978-1-61695-623-3
eISBN 978-1-61695-401-7
I. Delargy, Marlaine, translator. II. Title.
PT9876.3.U55M3613 2015
839.73'74—dc23   2014027670

Printed in the United States of America

10 9 8 7 6 5 4 3 2 1

To Hilmer, with all my love and gratitude
for putting up with everything this time too

THE BEIGE MAN

Chapter 1

THE NEW MOON and the stars shone as brightly as dia-
monds in the blue-black January sky. Their reflection glittered
in the rime covering Gotebörg. The car's external thermometer was already showing minus fifteen degrees. The temperature would probably drop even further during the night.
The harsh cold had managed to maintain its iron grip on the
country for almost two weeks now, although no snow had
yet fallen in the west of Sweden.

Officer Stefan Eriksson was yawning in the pleasant warmth
of the patrol car. The engine was idling, and he didn't give a
thought to any environmental concerns. When the weather
was like this, the important thing was not to let the icy cold
come creeping in. He stole a glance at the brightly lit hatch of
the kiosk that served food. Petrén, his colleague, was at the
front of the queue and was just paying. A cup of hot coffee and
a cheeseburger with all the extras would definitely hit the spot
right now, an hour before the end of their shift. A loud rumble
from Eriksson's stomach confirmed that it was high time he got
something inside him. Neither of them had eaten since they
came on duty at four o'clock in the afternoon—not because
the evening had been unusually busy, but because they had
been called to deal with a fight at a pizzeria in the Old Town
just as they were due to go back to the station for their meal
break.

Without bothering to rush, they had headed north to the

address they had been given. The arrival of the patrol car had had a calming effect on the three guys involved in the fight, and Eriksson and Petrén had soon had the situation under control. Nobody wanted to make a formal complaint; suddenly all three men were in total agreement that they had been engaged in nothing more than a lively discussion. The fact that one of them had a broken nose and was bleeding so profusely he had to be taken to Östra Hospital by ambulance was merely a regrettable accident. As were the red marks on the faces of the other two. All three of them would be sporting impressive bruises in various shades of blue and purple in a few hours. Since no one wanted the police to take any further action, Eriksson and Petrén left the pizzeria as soon as the man with the broken nose had been taken away. A report on the incident would be sufficient.

After that the officers had agreed they weren't in the mood for pizza, so they had driven to the kiosk on Delsjövägen. It was easy to park there, and the fast food was supposed to be pretty good—at least according to Petrén. He was a single guy, and more or less lived off that kind of stuff.

Eriksson was roused from his thoughts as the radio burst into life:

Calling all cars: a metallic silver BMW 630 was stolen in Stampen a few minutes ago. The owner saw two young men jump into the car and drive off along Skånegatan heading toward Liseberg. Both were wearing dark woolen hats and dark clothing. The witness thought they were of average height, slight build. The registration number of the car is . . .

Skånegatan, heading toward Liseberg. That meant they would be driving past the police station. The nerve of the bastards, Eriksson thought.

Petrén hurried toward the car with a bag of cheeseburgers in one hand and their cups of coffee in the other. He was wearing gloves, and it looked like a pretty risky balancing act; Eriksson reached across and opened the passenger door for his colleague. Petrén slid his hip into the car and bent his knee, then suddenly stopped with one foot on the floor of the car and the other on the tarmac.

Eriksson could feel the cold quickly spreading through the warm interior, and said crossly, "Get your ass in here before . . ." He broke off in the middle of the sentence and sat there open-mouthed. A car was speeding toward them along Delsjövägen, its high beams on and its engine racing. As the car passed beneath a street lamp just a few meters away, Eriksson registered the fact that it was light colored, probably silver—definitely a large BMW. It skidded sharply as the driver put his foot down and slid past the patrol car with screeching tires.

"Jesus Christ, it's the stolen BMW!" Eriksson shouted.

"What stolen BMW?" Petrén asked as he carefully slid into the passenger seat.

"The one we had a call about just now! Get on the radio and tell them we're after the bastard!"

"Can't."

"What do you mean, *can't?*"

"Hands full." Petrén held up the coffee cups and the bag by way of explanation.

"For Christ's sake, just get rid of it!" Eriksson roared.

Without a word, Petrén pushed the button to open the window with his right elbow. The discreet hum as the window slid down was drowned out by the sound of the patrol car's tires as they spun on the tarmac. Without further ado, Petrén threw out their coffee and burgers, and as the window began to close, he grabbed the microphone and called control.

"S-H-O eleven zero one by the kiosk on Delsjövägen. The

stolen BMW has just driven past us heading in the direction of Kålltorp, traveling at high speed. In pursuit. Over."

"Thank you, eleven zero one. I'll call for assistance from other patrols. Thirteen zero four is on the way from Östra Hospital and can cut across from the opposite direction. Backup is on the way."

Eriksson drove as fast as he dared. He could see the rear lights of the BMW disappearing in the direction of Swedish Television's brightly lit, box-shaped building. He put his foot down hard, and suddenly the lights in front of him glowed as brightly as two red fireworks. The BMW was swerving all over the place and looked as if it might actually go off the road.

The two police officers saw something fly up in the air, then land to one side of the car. Whatever it was, it lay motionless on the tarmac next to the sidewalk. When the driver had regained control, the BMW immediately took off again.

The patrol car slowed down and stopped.

"Shit! It's a person! Call it in!" Eriksson shouted, frantic.

Petrén once again seized the microphone with a steady hand and spoke to control in a voice that was significantly less steady, "Eleven zero one here. The BMW has hit a pedestrian outside Swedish Television. Send an ambulance and backup. We need to remain at the scene. Over."

"Understood. We'll send an ambulance and another patrol. Other teams will continue to pursue the BMW."

Stefan Eriksson was already out of the car and didn't hear the response. He reached the motionless body in a few long strides.

There was a lot of blood, and the dark pool was growing with terrifying speed. No human being could lose this much blood and survive. Deep down, Eriksson knew this person was already dead, but he cautiously moved closer to the victim's head to check for a carotid pulse. He changed his mind, however, when he saw the state of the head. In order for a person to survive, the brain needs to be inside the skull. This brain wasn't.

Eriksson had seen many traffic accident casualties during his years of service, but this one looked particularly gruesome. Because the car had been traveling so fast, the victim's unprotected limbs and head had been crushed with immense force. It wouldn't be easy to identify this person, he thought. He could hear the sound of approaching sirens in the distance. He glanced over his shoulder and saw his colleague setting out the reflective plastic screens marked POLICE. The blue flashing lights of the patrol car cast an eerie glow over the scene of the accident. A few cars had pulled up, but Petrén was managing to keep the occupants away.

The body was lying on its back, with both legs twisted in an unnatural position. The lower half of the left leg appeared to have snapped off completely, given the way it was lying in relation to the thighbone. The left arm was flung straight out to the side, but the hand was missing. When Eriksson looked around, he spotted a lump on the sidewalk that was probably the severed hand. The clothing suggested the victim was male. He was wearing some kind of black or dark blue tracksuit. His right hand lay limply on his chest. Somehow the mangled body gave an impression of peace, as if the man had realized he was going to die and had instinctively placed his hand upon his heart to feel its final beat.

The second patrol car arrived, closely followed by the ambulance. Illuminated by the flashing blue lights, something shone faintly next to the dead man's hand, just above the heart. Eriksson was careful to avoid stepping in the blood as he moved closer to take a look.

At first his brain refused to accept what he was seeing. He recognized it instantly because he had seen it countless times before. When Petrén and their newly arrived colleagues came over, Eriksson pointed at the victim's chest with a shaking hand.

A few minutes after the hit-and-run outside the TV studios, a report came in from someone who had been standing at the Lilla Torp tram stop. According to the caller, a car had turned onto Töpelsgatan and continued toward the Delsjö area at high speed. The witness thought the windshield was broken because he had seen a young man hanging out of the window on the passenger side, apparently shouting directions to the driver.

Several patrol cars had been dispatched immediately to follow up on this information. There were many, many smaller roads leading off the main route up toward the recreation and bathing area at Delsjö, and the holiday village had to be taken into account, with its countless minor roads and parking lots. There was also a chance that the car thieves had turned onto one of the bridle paths. It wouldn't be too difficult to hide a car among the trees in the darkness. The deciduous trees were bare in January, but there were dense thickets of conifers along both sides of the road.

After only ten minutes, a patrol found the abandoned BMW; the glow of the fire through the trees led them straight to it. The thieves had torched the car before taking off. The officers managed to put out the flames using the fire extinguisher in their car; the damage to the interior of the BMW was not severe, but would of course hamper the search for any traces of the perpetrators. The windshield was still in place and holding together, but had shattered into milky opaqueness. The car was parked in front of a sturdy barrier.

The other patrol cars were quickly called to the scene, and officers began searching the surrounding area, the beams of their flashlights flickering among the trees. The ground was very hilly and the dense undergrowth difficult to penetrate. On one side the ground fell away steeply toward a stream, while on the other it climbed sharply up Alfred Gärdesväg, leading to Delsjö swimming area.

There was a boarded-up brick building a few dozen meters down the slope. It wasn't very big, and had probably been used to store tools. Instead of windows and doors, all the openings were covered with thick hardboard. The whole place was in a state of advanced decay. It was probably still standing only because it hadn't yet decided in which direction to collapse. Several police officers surrounded the building, trying to move as quietly as possible. They were breathing hard, their breath misty in the cold night air. The atmosphere was tense because they had no idea whether the car thieves were armed. One officer crept forward to a damaged sheet of hardboard partly covering the doorway. She pressed her back against the wall and drew her gun. A colleague followed her, a crowbar in his hand.

"This building is surrounded!" an officer shouted from the other side. "You might as well give up right now! Come out with your hands up!"

There wasn't a sound from inside the derelict structure. The cold crackled in the branches of the trees, and the frozen grass crunched whenever one of the officers changed position. Apart from that, there was silence in the darkness. The female officer by the door nodded to her colleague, who quickly forced the crowbar under the broken board. He leaned on the shaft with all his strength and pushed as hard as he could. With a creak, the board came away and fell to the ground. The officer quickly positioned himself by the wall on the other side of the door and switched on his flashlight. Keeping his head well back, he directed the beam through the opening, moving it across the compact darkness of the interior.

No movement. Nothing.

After a while both officers slipped cautiously inside. A few tense seconds later came the sound of surprised exclamations, mixed with sniggering and slightly hysterical laughter.

"There's nothing to worry about—it's just some animal!" shouted the male officer.

"It's coming out!" his colleague added.

A small shape came waddling out through the doorway, blinking in confusion in the bright light. It raised it snout toward the cold, starry sky and sniffed suspiciously. This time, the odd burst of laughter came from the officers standing outside, and they turned away their flashlights. It was way too cold for a badger to be out and about, so it simply turned around and lumbered back inside. It almost collided with the two officers in the doorway; they stepped aside and allowed the sleepy animal to return to its winter bed, then they came out and assured everyone that there were no human beings in the building.

Meanwhile, a van arrived and parked up on the road.

"The dogs are here," the female officer stated.

"Great. Searching in the dark is impossible. They could be anywhere in the forest," her colleague said.

The sound of excited barking could be heard as soon as the back door of the van was opened and the dogs realized it was time to work.

The fact that the thieves had managed to set fire to the car turned out to be a major problem. The dogs sniffed eagerly in and around the vehicle, but neither of them seemed able to pick up a viable trail. The smell of smoke was too strong, and had eradicated every other scent inside the car. Instead, the two dog handlers began moving outward from the BMW in circles. One of the German shepherds suddenly whimpered eagerly and started up the slope leading to Alfred Gärdesväg. The tension rose among the search team, and they all headed away from the badger's house and up toward the road. The second dog had started dragging its handler in the same direction at almost the same moment. Both dogs stopped in front of an old root cellar, well concealed behind a dense thicket of small fir trees. It was furnished with a new-looking, sturdy wooden door. Fresh marks could be seen around the metal hasp; it had been broken open with such force it was hanging by only one screw. The heavy padlock lay on the ground. The dogs got very excited and started watching the door.

"They're hiding in there," the female officer whispered.

She couldn't hide the excitement in her voice. Her partner also felt the thrill of the chase. He crept over to the little door and stood to one side. Quietly he slipped the crowbar into the small gap by the broken lock. Every flashlight beam was directed at the door, and the officer in charge gave the signal to open it. The door swung wide open with a loud creak, and the light shone into the depths of the cellar.

There are moments when time simply stops. Even the dogs fell silent.

Chapter 2

DETECTIVE INSPECTOR IRENE Huss was feeling stressed as she turned into the parking lot in front of police HQ in Göteborg. She scurried in through the main door, waving a greeting to the middle-aged officer sitting behind the glass at the information desk. The waiting room was already full of people who had come, willingly or rather more reluctantly, to meet a representative of the police force. Irene hurried over to the glass door and swiped her card. The lock clicked and she stepped into the hallway. As she entered the elevator, she glanced at the clock on the wall, relieved to confirm that she still had at least five minutes to spare before morning prayer began. For that reason she was somewhat surprised when she walked into the Violent Crimes Unit to find the chief waiting impatiently outside the conference room where morning briefings usually took place.

"We've already started," Superintendent Sven Andersson said grimly.

Irene Huss knew perfectly well that she was often the last member of the team to arrive, but if you're not a morning person, there's not much you can do about it. At the same time, she made a point of never arriving late. At the last minute, perhaps, but never late. She usually had time to take off her coat, say good morning to Tommy Persson, with whom she shared an office and get herself a cup of coffee before strolling into the briefing.

"The car wouldn't start . . . it's too old for this weather," she said by way of an apology.

Which was perfectly true.

"Coffee?" she ventured, smiling at her boss.

"Later," he snapped, marching into the conference room.

Irene sighed. She had a bad feeling as she walked in and saw that the others were already there. She immediately noticed the high level of tension in the air—it was almost tangible. She could tell something extraordinary had happened. With a nod to everyone in general and no one in particular, she quickly sat down on the nearest chair and tried to look attentive.

"It's been a busy night, as I'm sure you're all aware," the superintendent began.

Irene wasn't aware of that at all, but realized this wasn't the time to say so. She leaned back in her chair, making every effort to appear totally up to speed with the night's events.

"As usual the morning paper got most things wrong, but the local radio report was more or less correct. Apart from the girl. They didn't know about her, but the evening papers have gotten a hold of that information," he went on. He peered over the top of his cheap reading glasses with a grim expression.

To Irene's relief, Tommy Persson put up his hand like a well-behaved schoolboy and asked, "What's happened? I missed the morning news. I had to scrape the ice off my windshield, then I had to ask my neighbor to help get the car started with jumper cables. I didn't even have time to look at the paper before I left."

The superintendent stuck out his lower lip and glared at Tommy, which didn't help; Persson still had no idea what had been going on. Andersson sighed loudly and continued.

"At twenty-one seventeen last night, we received a report that a car had been stolen on Stampgatan. The owner was busy loading things into his car, which was a BMW

630i. As it was so cold, he left the engine running. The car was parked approximately twenty meters from the main door of the apartment complex, where he had piled up several items he was intending to take with him. Apparently the family is in the process of moving. He had placed a folded stroller in the trunk and had just gotten back to the doorway when he heard the car doors open and close. When he turned around, he saw the car drive off."

"So he didn't see who took it?" Birgitta Moberg-Rauhala interjected.

"He did, in fact. Just after he had put the stroller in and closed the trunk, he saw two young men approaching along the sidewalk. According to the description, they were wearing dark, baggy clothes and woolen hats. He said they looked like rappers."

"Boys wearing huge pants that hang halfway down their ass," Jonny Blom said with a grin.

Irene was a little surprised. When she bumped into Jonny and his eldest son in Frölunda Square shortly before Christmas, the fifteen-year-old had been wearing baggy jeans and an oversized hoodie. Beneath his knitted hat she could see lumps and bumps that could well have been dreadlocks in the making. Irene sensed conflict within the Blom family.

Andersson pretended that he hadn't heard Jonny Blom's contribution and went on. "The witness estimated the age of the boys at between seventeen and twenty-five. They shot away along the tramlines, crossed Västra Folkunga Bridge and continued along Skånegatan. Which means the bastards drove past here a minute or so after taking the car. They headed for Liseberg, then turned off toward Örgrytemotet. They drove to Sankt Sigfridsplan, then out onto Deljsövägen. At the same time, a general call went out over the radio about the theft of the car. A patrol car was parked by the fast food kiosk on Deljsövägen and saw the BMW pass at high speed. They called it in and set off in pursuit. They gained visual contact with the suspect vehicle and saw it hit a pedestrian just outside the TV studios."

Andersson paused to clear his throat. "Of course the patrol car stopped at the scene of the accident and called for an ambulance and backup. But it was a hell of a collision. According to the medical examiner, the victim died instantly. The entire skull was crushed. And . . ." He paused again and swallowed several times before continuing. "The victim was wearing a track suit top with the police logo on it. His face was more or less gone, but . . . but it seems very likely that he was a police officer."

The silence in the room was suddenly electric. Everyone stiffened. A colleague. One of them. Someone they perhaps knew.

"Who?" asked Hannu Rauhala. He had been married to Birgitta Moberg-Rauhala for a few years now, and they had a two-year-old son. The superintendent had never gotten over the fact that they had married, but had gradually resigned himself to the situation.

"There are three colleagues who live nearby, although we were able to eliminate one straight away because Kicki Börjesson was in the backup car. Stellan Edwardsson was on duty last night, so we were able to eliminate him as well. Which leaves just one person. He retired some years ago, a little early I think. We've tried to get a hold of him on the phone, but no luck so far. He lives alone. I'm sure some of you know him . . . Torleif Sandberg."

"Muesli," Jonny said.

Andersson glared in Jonny's direction and frowned. However, he didn't contradict him; everyone had referred to Torleif as Muesli during his time as duty officer. Torleif always had a bowl of yogurt with oat muesli when the others were drinking coffee and eating Danishes. He would tirelessly hold forth to his less-knowledgeable colleagues on the health risks of the sweet pastries. No one had ever been tempted to try the dirty brown mush he recommended so heartily. His lentil soups, barley grain burgers, root vegetable stews and similar whole-food dishes were equally safe in the refrigerator. No one had ever nibbled away at the mysterious contents of his little foil containers.

"Muesl—Torleif and I started in the force at the same time," Andersson said, his voice slightly unsteady. He cleared his throat once more before continuing. "As yet we have no definite confirmation that Torleif was the victim of the hit-and-run, but we're trying to track down his family just in case . . . We'll see what happens."

Irene remembered Torleif Sandberg clearly. His unremarkable appearance with his thin, mousy hair and skinny body hadn't exactly etched itself in her memory, but she did recall his quirks. Considerate and imperturbable, but a real fanatic when it came to health. He would often talk about his favorite subject: a healthy way of life. This involved a vegetarian diet, exercise, meditation, and of course total abstinence when it came to alcohol. He didn't even drink low-alcohol beer. His enthusiastic explanations had been met by somewhat muted responses in the staff room, to put it mildly. His colleagues often would tease him gently. He hadn't liked being called Muesli, which was probably why he never managed to shake off the nickname.

And now there was a chance he might be dead. Run down by car thieves while he was out jogging in his Police Sports Association tracksuit.

Irene's thoughts were interrupted as the superintendent took a deep breath and exclaimed, "But not only did they run him down, the bastards drove off and left him! Even though the windshield was shattered. A witness saw the guy on the passenger side hanging out of the window, guiding the driver up Töpelsgatan. The car disappeared up the hill. Several patrol cars were sent to the area. At twenty-one forty-six, the glow of a fire was spotted on a side road. When the patrol arrived, the officers discovered that the little shits had torched the BMW. They managed to put out the fire with the extinguisher in their car. Other patrol teams arrived and started searching the immediate vicinity. Because of the darkness and the difficult terrain, a dog team was brought in. After just a few minutes both dogs drew attention to an old root cellar. The door had been broken open. Inside was a dead body. A girl."

Irene glanced at her colleagues. They all looked every bit as surprised as she felt.

"A girl? Could she have been one of the people in the car? If they were wearing baggy clothes, it might have been difficult to tell if one of them was a girl." The theory was put forward by Fredrik Stridh. He was thirty years old, but much to his annoyance he was still regarded as the youngest member of the team. However, he had his head screwed on, and Irene liked working with him.

Andersson shook his head. "According to the ME, she had been dead for between two and three hours before she was found. And he estimated that she was approximately twelve years old."

"Has anyone reported a girl of that age missing?" Birgitta asked.

"No. She was wearing a T-shirt, nothing else. The rest of her clothes were in a heap beside her in the cellar. The only thing we know is that she was white and blonde. The probable cause of death is strangulation."

"A sex crime?" Hannu asked.

"The ME thought that was likely. They won't get around to looking at her until this afternoon; they're short staffed, apparently."

It was a well-known fact that the medical examiner's office in Göteborg had been understaffed for a number of years. They had great difficulty in filling available posts. If anyone asked Super-intendent Andersson why that might be, he was clear about his opinion: no one in their right mind would voluntarily work for Professor Yvonne Stridner. She might be regarded as one of Europe's most skilled forensic pathologists, but he didn't care. To him she was one of the most terrifying women on the planet.

"What happened to the bastards who mowed down Muesli?" Jonny asked.

"They've gone up in smoke! We've found no trace of them, but the dog teams are carrying on with the search today. They'll be going through the holiday village with a fine-tooth comb," Andersson replied.

"Hopefully their balls will have frozen and dropped off by now," Jonny said in a voice dripping with sincerity.

"It was minus sixteen in the small hours. I'm sure several things will have frozen and dropped off."

This provided some small measure of consolation.

"Is there a connection between the car thieves and the murdered girl?" Andersson wondered aloud.

His team didn't require much time to think about that before collectively shaking their heads. Tommy Persson expressed everyone's thoughts. "It was pure chance that we found the girl so quickly. The dogs were trying to track the car thieves when they found the body. If they hadn't, she could have been lying there undiscovered for a long time."

"Exactly. And the guys in the car can't have hidden her in the root cellar. They didn't have time," Birgitta pointed out.

Tommy Persson nodded. "The girl can't have been in the trunk of the BMW because there was a folded up stroller in there. The body could have been in the back seat, but why would the two guys have bothered to move it in that case? They had every reason in the world to get away from the car as fast as possible, otherwise they wouldn't have gotten very far, and we would have found them."

"If the girl's body was in the car, then surely the owner wouldn't have reported it stolen?"

"Not necessarily. I mean, once the car was stolen, he had to report it. He might have planned on saying that he had nothing to do with the body, and putting the blame on the guys who stole the car."

"They didn't have time to move the body," Birgitta said again.

Most of the team were inclined to agree with her.

During a relatively brief period of thirty minutes, the two boys had stolen a car, driven at least five kilometers at high speed toward the lake at Delsjö, run down a pedestrian, set fire to the car and managed to get far enough away to make it impossible for the dogs to find them. No, they wouldn't have had time to conceal a body, Irene concluded.

"Have we any idea who these boys might be? Is anyone on the wanted list?" she asked.

"I thought you could look into that," Andersson said.

He glanced around his team. As usual when he was thinking, his fingertips beat a tattoo on the surface of the desk. Once he had made his decision, he slapped down the palm of his hand and said, "Irene, Tommy and Hannu will take the hit-and-run. Try to confirm the identity of the victim and check out any possible suspects for the theft of the car. Contact me as soon as you come up with anything. Birgitta, Jonny and Fredrik, you take the girl. Same thing there: contact me as soon as you know who she is."

He linked his fingers, turned his palms outward and stretched them until his knuckles cracked.

"I'll keep an eye on door-to-door inquiries and collate the witness statements that come in during the day. Not that I think we'll get very far, but one of the residents in the apartment complex on Töpelsgatan might have seen something. Then it'll be the usual goddamn puzzle as we try to sort out what goes with the hit-and-run, what goes with the murdered girl and what's totally irrelevant."

Andersson sighed deeply, and Irene could hear the whistling from his windpipe as he breathed out. This cold weather was no good for his asthma.

In five weeks he would be moving over to the cold cases team. It was a relatively new initiative, and its brief was to try to cast fresh light on old investigations before the statute of limitations ran out. Superintendent Andersson hadn't a clue when it came to computers and the latest DNA technology, but he was an excellent homicide investigator. Irene thought he would be a great asset to the cold cases team, and she also believed he would be very happy there during his final years as a police officer. But she would miss him, particularly in view of who his replacement was likely to be. There were strong indications that it would be Acting Superintendent Efva Thylqvist from the drugs squad; everyone knew she had applied for the post. Irene didn't know her, but she had heard plenty about Thylqvist and sincerely hoped that the rumors were exaggerated.

THERE WERE VERY few reports of absconders from juvenile detention centers and prisons in Västra Götaland. Most of those who had run away over Christmas and New Year were back. At this time of year it was too cold to make a bid for freedom unless you had somewhere to go. Those who were planning to make a break for it would wait until spring. Their desire for liberty increased as the temperature rose outside.

"We have seven possible suspects, all of them already on the wanted list," Irene said.

"Do any of them look particularly interesting?" Tommy asked.

Irene quickly scrolled through the list on her computer screen. "Grievous bodily harm . . . contributing to the death of another person . . . robbery . . . vandalism . . . a whole range of drug-related felonies . . . We've got the lot here. It could be any of them."

"Or none of them."

"None of them?"

"It could be two petty thieves who have never been arrested, which means they won't have a record."

Irene nodded and sighed loudly. "In that case it's going to be hard work."

"Yep. Might as well start with the names we've got."

They divided the names between them. First they would try to form a picture of the runaways using the information already available in the system. If they found anything interesting, they would go out together and start looking. It wouldn't be a good idea to meet any of these guys alone. They were often armed and hung out with like-minded associates.

Hannu was trying to establish the identity of the hit-and-run victim. He stuck his head around the door and said he still hadn't managed to get in touch with Torleif Sandberg. A patrol had been sent to his apartment, but no one had answered the door. Nor had anyone reported him or any other male missing during last night or this morning. The probability that the dead man was the retired police officer was growing stronger by the minute.

AFTER LUNCH IRENE and Tommy went through what they had found.

"We can eliminate Mijailo Janovic right away; he's one meter ninety-three and powerfully built, so he doesn't fit the description. However, his pal Janos Mijic does. They disappeared from Fagared at the same time, on New Year's Day. Mijailo is nineteen years old, and was in for grievous bodily harm and attempted murder. He sliced open the belly of a guy from a rival gang. The victim survived, but only just. It was probably a drug-related fight, but neither of them was prepared to admit to that, so Mijailo was given quite a lenient sentence: two years and three months. Janos is his trusty shadow. Wherever Mijailo is, that's where Janos is, too. They're the same age and claim to be cousins. Which isn't true, because for one thing, Mijailo is a Serb and Janos is a Croat. This fact doesn't seem to bother them. Janos is of slight build, one meter seventy-eight. He could fit the description of our rapper. Except for what I said before: wherever Mijailo is, that's where Janos is. And Mijailo was not one of our car thieves," Tommy said.

"So it's not them," Irene agreed.

"Nope. However, Tobias Karlsson could be a person of interest. He also absconded from Fagared, but only last Friday. Five days ago. He fits the description. Nineteen years old, and he already has a record as long as your arm. Serious drug offenses, grievous bodily harm, and . . . there you go! Stealing cars. Several, in fact."

"Pretty advanced for his age. Definitely of interest."

"Absolutely. His mother lives in Tynnered. Thinks the police are persecuting her son just because he holds certain strong political views. We live in a free country and everyone has the right to their own opinions: that's what she yelled out in court the first time he ended up there. The charge was extreme violence and racial harassment. The victim was a young immigrant who ended up scarred for life. Before that Karlsson had only been involved in stealing cars, but at the time he was too young to be charged."

"A Nazi," Irene said.

"Of course."

"Shaved head? Tattoos?"

"The whole package," Tommy replied smugly.

"In that case it's not him."

"What?"

"A Nazi doesn't dress like a rapper."

Tommy looked slightly put out, but had to admit she was right. Everything else had fit, and he hadn't thought about what the car thieves were wearing.

"That leaves just one name on my list: Niklas Ström.

Nineteen years old, ran away from Gräskärr exactly one week ago. According to my contact, he had problems with some of the other boys in the institution. He's gay, and that's not popular with those who sympathize with people like Tobias Karlsson. Niklas couldn't cope with the bullying."

"Why did he tell the others he was gay?"

"He didn't. It was obvious. He was charged with violent rape. The victim was a boy the same age who sustained severe injuries. In his defense, Niklas said that he was under the influence of drugs and couldn't remember a thing. He got eighteen months."

"How come the sentence is always harsher when the victim is male?" Irene broke in.

"Is it?"

"Yes."

Tommy merely shrugged in response.

Irene started to go through her list. "I also have one guy from Gräskärr and two from Fagared. The one from Gräskärr is Björn Kjellgren, known as Billy. Eighteen years old, went down for breaking into several houses and cars. A full-fledged little thief. One meter seventy-four, slight build. Strawberry blond hair that he wears in dreadlocks. Nothing unusual about that these days, but definitely worth noting, bearing in mind the rapper connection. A bit of a loner, apparently. He disappeared the day after Niklas Ström. According to the person I spoke to, he was inspired by Niklas's departure. None of the staff thinks Niklas and Billy were friends."

"But Billy is the first one we actually know is a rapper," Tommy pointed out.

Irene smiled teasingly at him.

"It's not that simple. Both of my boys from Fagared also have the hip-hop vibe."

"Did they go missing at the same time?"

"Yes, last Friday—five days ago. They're friends, and they've known each other since they were toddlers. They're both in for serious drug offenses. Perhaps it wasn't such a good idea to put them in the same institution. One is fully Swedish, the other is half-Jamaican, born in Sweden to a Swedish mother. Fredrik Svensson; he's twenty-two and has Rasta braids, but they're long and reach halfway down his back. The car owner should have noticed them."

"You'd think."

"Fredrik's pal is Daniel Lindgren. He's twenty, and he's been selling drug for years. He also went down for illegal possession of a firearm. According to the investigating officer, he's regarded as some kind of hit man for Fredrik Svensson's gang."

"So we're looking at a gang? Organized drug dealing?"

"Yes. In broad terms both of them fit the description, but when it comes to Fredrik Svensson, he's got those long Rasta braids. Plus his skin color is quite dark. Daniel Lindgren is one meter seventy. He's not well built, but is very keen on working out. I suppose he's got his image as a hit man to think of. The question is whether he could be described as slight."

"I think you ought to have a word with the owner of the BMW. He might remember things more clearly by now. I'll carry on with our absconders," Tommy said.

ON HER WAY to the elevator, Irene bumped into Hannu Rauhala, who was heading in the same direction.

"The medical examiner's office called. They found a bunch of keys in the hit-and-run victim's pocket. I thought I'd try them in Sandberg's door," Hannu said.

"Brilliant. That would save a lot of time," Irene replied.

The owner of the BMW was Alexander Hölzer. He was in his apartment on Stampgatan, just a few hundred meters from police HQ. Irene decided to walk; it would be quicker than driving around trying to find a parking space.

A large removal truck was parked in front of the building.

Two men were loading a white leather sofa into the back. Irene glanced inside and noted that Hölzer's furniture definitely hadn't come from IKEA. Not that she had expected anything else, given that the stolen car was a BMW 630i. There aren't too many families with young children driving around in those.

She found the nameplate on the third floor and rang the bell. It wasn't really necessary as the door was open, but it's always best to be polite. It's important to make a positive first impression and to create a good relationship with the witness right from the start. These basic rules in the art of interrogation would turn out to be somewhat wasted on Alexander Hölzer. Irene waited politely at the door for quite some time. Just as she was running out of patience and was reaching out to push the door, it was yanked open. She was confronted by an overweight man in his fifties, dressed in a red golf sweater with a prestigious logo on the breast, black chinos and noticeably elegant shoes.

"Yes?" he said brusquely.

"Detective Inspector Irene Huss. I'm looking for Alexander Hölzer."

"That's me. What do you want?"

At first Irene was surprised by his dismissive attitude. She made an effort not to show what she was thinking, and carried on in a pleasant tone of voice, "It's about the theft of your car yesterday. I'd just like to ask you a few more ques—"

Before Irene could finish the sentence, she saw the color rising in Hölzer's face. His voice shook with suppressed fury. "I have nothing to say to you until we get the stroller back. I've called several times, but they just keep saying they haven't finished examining it yet. What the hell are they examining the stroller for? The thieves weren't riding around in it, were they? It's just the police on some fucking power trip! It's ridiculous! I'm the one who's had my car stolen, and yet I'm being treated like some kind of—"

"In that case perhaps you'd like to accompany me to the station so that we can continue this conversation."

Hölzer's face turned purple and the words stuck in his throat; he eventually managed to force something out. "What the hell . . . ?"

Irene's expression remained impassive. "This is not just about the theft of your car. This is part of a murder inquiry."

"A murder inq—" Hölzer's eyeballs looked as if they were about to pop out of their sockets. *This guy definitely needs to check his blood pressure*, Irene thought. He simply stood staring blankly at her for a long time, not making any attempt to move from the doorway. The only sound in the stairwell was his heavy breathing. Gradually his high color began to subside; it was as if the steam were slowly hissing out of him. He shuffled backward to let Irene in, then silently led the way, lumbering through an empty hallway and into a virtually empty living room. A few packing cases stood by the wall, and a poinsettia wilted in the window.

"That's the last of the boxes. The moving guys will be back to collect them at any minute. The contract cleaners will be here tomorrow," Alexander Hölzer said wearily. He fell silent for a moment, then cleared his throat several times before going on. "What did you say about . . . about a murder inquiry?"

Irene briefly explained what had happened at the scene where Hölzer's car had been found.

"You're kidding me." Hölzer shook his head and didn't speak for a little while. He ran a hand over his hair, which was peppered with grey, and with a practiced gesture, he arranged a long strand over his incipient bald patch. "I can't cope with this. I've been told that the stroller is undamaged, and we really need it. Eleanor is five months old, and she's too heavy to be carried everywhere. I asked if I could come and pick up the stroller, and I was told that was out of the question. It cost ten thousand kronor, so I don't feel like buying a new one. And everything has been really stressful: the move, the car being stolen and . . . everything," he concluded apologetically.

That was probably the closest Irene was going to get to an actual apology, so she nodded to indicate that she understood the strain he was under.

When Hölzer mentioned that the stroller had cost ten thousand kronor, an image flickered through Irene's mind: the well-used twin stroller made of blue corduroy that she had pushed her girls around in. It had cost five hundred kronor. She could still remember how happy she had been when she and Krister could afford to buy a new one made of red and white striped nylon. That was almost twenty years ago; she presumed that strollers were more basic back then. This luxury transportation system ought to have leather-covered handles, heated rearview mirrors and side airbags, given the price.

Hölzer went over to the large living room window and looked down at the courtyard. He nipped off one of the poinsettia's shriveled leaves and crumbled it between his thumb and forefinger. With his back to the room, he asked, "Do you seriously believe that my car has something to do with the murder of this girl?"

"It's being examined carefully in order to cover every eventuality," Irene replied diplomatically.

Hölzer merely nodded at his reflection in the window.

"We'd like to know if you've come up with anything else regarding the description of the boys who took your car," Irene said.

He slowly turned around and looked at her with a frown. However, the concentration on his face suggested that he really was making an effort to try to remember any further details. Eventually he shook his head.

"No. Two boys wearing baggy pants and jackets. Woolen hats. Dark clothes. Young."

"Did you see their hair?"

"No. No hair," he said firmly.

Irene mentally crossed Fredrik Svensson off her list. Just to be on the safe side, she asked, "Did you manage to see anything of their faces?"

"I only caught a glimpse of them."

"And you didn't notice anything in particular?"

"Not that I remember."

"No scars? Skin color? Eyes?"

"They were too far away for me to see their eyes. It was dark, so it was hard to tell what color their skin might have been. And as I said, I didn't see their hair. But they were definitely two white guys. Not black. Although of course some of those Hispanics have pretty light-colored skin."

Hispanics. Irene thought about her daughter's boyfriend. Felipe was half-Swedish and half-Brazilian, and could easily be classed as both Hispanic and black by someone who was inclined to think that way.

Fredrik Svensson was definitely off the list. That left Daniel Lindgren, Fredrik's wingman, and the two boys from Gräskärr, Niklas Ström and Björn "Billy" Kjellgren. If it turned out that none of them were involved in the theft of the BMW, then the investigation was going to be tricky. There was still a chance that the perpetrators were hiding out in the Delsjö area, in which case the patrols ought to find them at some point during the day. If not, there was a significant risk that they would suffer severe frostbite, or even freeze to death. The temperature hadn't risen above minus twelve degrees so far, and as the afternoon wore on, the cold would once again intensify its grip. For several reasons, finding the two boys was a matter of urgency.

Chapter 3

"No luck so far. A helicopter equipped with a thermal imaging camera has been searching the area all afternoon, but it hasn't spotted a thing. No break-ins have been reported in the holiday village. We've found no trace whatsoever of the missing boys, but the dog teams are still out there searching. Our theory is that they've got another vehicle, but no cars have been reported stolen in the local area in the past twenty-four hours."

Detective Inspector Erik Lind, head of the search unit, was bouncing gently up and down on the soles of his sturdy boots. He had taken off the thick winter snowsuit he'd been wearing out in Delsjö all day, and he was now facing the Violent Crimes Unit team in full uniform, hands behind his back: a habit from his time spent patrolling the streets of Östra Nordstan a quarter of a century ago. With his cropped grey hair and his sharp pale blue eyes, he looked like the Hollywood template of a Nazi officer. This was far removed from the reality; he was a very likable individual who inspired great trust among his colleagues. If Lind and his team couldn't find the hit-and-run drivers, no one could.

"Could they have had a getaway car nearby?" Tommy Persson suggested.

Erik Lind considered the possibility for a moment before replying. "It's not out of the question, but taking the BMW seems to have been an opportunistic crime."

"Or they were actually looking around Stampen for a car to steal so they could get to the other car. But that seems a bit . . . far-fetched," Tommy admitted.

"If they really wanted to get to this hypothetical getaway car, they could have gone by tram," Birgitta Moberg-Rauhala pointed out.

Which was perfectly true. And Tommy was right: his suggestion was far-fetched. According to his theory, the thieves would have stolen the car on Stampgatan, then run down and killed a pedestrian outside the TV studios on Delsjövägen, shattering the windshield in the collision and making the car virtually unusable. By pure chance they must have had another car in the area where the accident happened; it had to have been parked close by so they could reach it on foot. After that they had managed to continue their flight and disappear without a trace. The theory didn't hold water, but at the same time it could explain why they had chosen Delsjövägen as their escape route. At the moment they couldn't afford to rule out any hypothesis completely, Irene realized.

"According to CSI, conditions around the side road and the root cellar are extremely challenging. They've found a whole bunch of tire tracks on the road, but it's difficult to identify them. The ground is frozen solid, and there's no snow. And a large number of police officers and dogs trampled around the place where the girl's body was found. It's fair to say that CSI isn't happy," Lind stated dryly.

"No trace of the killer?" Superintendent Andersson asked.

"Not that I've heard."

Hannu Rauhala slipped in through the door and sat down on the empty chair next to Irene. He reached into his pocket and fished out a key ring from the depths of his padded jacket.

"They fit," he whispered so that only she could hear.

Irene felt her heart give an extra beat. Their suspicions

were now confirmed: the victim of the hit-and-run was Tor-leif Sandberg. A colleague whom many people in the room had met and gotten to know. The hunt for these two car thieves would be intense. You don't get away with killing a cop. They would soon realize that.

"I'll let you know if I have any news," Erik Lind said, marching toward the door.

It very nearly smacked him in the face. Professor Yvonne Stridner rushed into the room as Erik Lind was leaving at the same high velocity. The collision was as violent as it was inevitable. Neither of the parties involved was the type to go for lengthy apologies, so the atmosphere by the door was a little tense until Lind managed to extricate himself. Professor Stridner's face was bright red by the time she reached Superintendent Andersson. No one dared smile. You just didn't smile at the Professor of Forensic Medicine.

"So rude! Crashing into people . . . !" Stridner broke off her indignant tirade and took a deep breath. "As I have to catch a train to Stockholm from Central Station in an hour, I thought I might as well swing by to give you my preliminary report on the murder victim. My colleague, Dr. Amirez, will be conducting the autopsy on the girl tomorrow afternoon. So far we have carried out only a visual examination, but I felt it was important to let you know what I have seen.

"First of all, she looks much younger than she probably is. Her exact height is one hundred and thirty-six centimeters, and her weight is twenty-eight kilos, or just over sixty-one pounds. A skinny little girl with small breasts and sparse pubic hair. Cracks at the corners of the mouth and lesions in and around the mouth indicate malnutrition and a lack of vitamins and minerals. Poor dental hygiene and several examples of untreated cavities. However, the development of the teeth suggests she is around thirteen years old. The forensic dentist was in the department on another matter, and I asked him to take a look. He noticed that her molars had come through. Tomorrow he will take X-rays of her teeth, and we will also X-ray the skeleton in order to establish her age."

The professor paused for breath and pushed up her luxuriant red hair with her fingertips. The short, light brown suede jacket looked elegant with the black pencil skirt. As usual she was wearing sky-high heels; this time it was a pair of designer leather boots in exactly the same shade as the jacket. Yvonne Stridner always dressed to make herself look taller and slimmer than she was.

"Her vagina is in a very bad state. There are clear signs of old injuries, and she was suffering from a serious infection that caused a strong odor. I've sent off samples to try to find out what kind of bacteria is involved. There is also scar tissue and severe damage around the anus. This girl has been subjected to sexual abuse over a long period. She has puncture marks of varying ages on both arms; the oldest are from several months ago. There are also puncture marks between her toes and on her inner thighs."

You could have heard a pin drop in the room as she paused once more. For a brief moment a weary, anguished expression passed across the professor's beautifully made-up face.

"I can only report on the physical abuse she has suffered. No autopsy in the world can reveal her mental torment."

With that closing statement she marched over to the door and yanked it open with the same force as when she had entered just a few minutes earlier. It seemed only logical when Detective Inspector Erik Lind stumbled in from the opposite direction. His right hand fumbled in the air for the door handle, which was no longer where it was supposed to be.

"What the hell—" he snapped, but he straightened up when he saw Stridner holding the handle on the other side.

Two steely expressions crossed like rapiers in midair.

Then something totally unexpected happened.

The corners of the professor's mouth began to twitch. Erik Lind's eyes narrowed, and he broke into a broad smile. They started to laugh, at first with a certain amount of reserve, then loud and long. Some of the other officers joined in, albeit more quietly.

Yvonne Stridner gave Erik Lind a final beaming smile before passing him in the doorway, her hips swaying. They could hear her laughter mixed with the clicking of her high heels as she headed down the corridor.

Erik Lind was still chuckling to himself as he turned to face his colleagues. He composed himself and spoke in a formal tone of voice, "I've just had a call. They've found another body."

The room fell silent. Lind realized that he needed to be more precise. "This one is old. Several months. The body is in an inaccessible rocky area. One of the dogs found it."

"What . . . who?" Andersson said in confusion. Irene could hear that he was starting to wheeze.

"Don't know. The preliminary report says that we are dealing with a body that has been dead for quite some time, judging by the condition."

"Is it a child?" Irene asked quickly.

"No. Probably an adult male, although the gender hasn't been confirmed; they're going by what was left of the clothing. Heavy boots and a Helly Hansen jacket."

That definitely sounded like a male, Irene thought with relief.

"Who's coming with me?" Lind asked.

Fredrik Stridh and Tommy Persson got to their feet and followed Lind out of the room.

Irene reported back on her efforts to establish the identity of the car thieves.

"So there are three possible suspects among the boys who are on the run right now: Daniel Lindgren, Billy Kjellgren and

Niklas Ström. If it turns out that none of them is involved, then . . . Well, then we'll just have to hope for a stroke of luck," she said.

"I think we're going to need a hell of a lot of luck if we're going to sort out the mess that has piled up over the last twenty-four hours," Jonny Blom muttered.

For once, Irene agreed with him.

Hannu Rauhala explained that he had picked up the bunch of keys from forensics, and that one of the keys fit Torleif Sandberg's front door.

"I had a quick look through the apartment. No one there. I've also traced his family. His ex-wife has moved to Stockholm, and his son lives in Umeå. I'll contact them once the identification is confirmed."

"By the forensic dentist?" Irene asked.

Hannu nodded. "Yes. We'll know for sure tomorrow."

Superintendent Andersson was frowning. There had been immense pressure on the department since yesterday evening. Journalists had virtually jammed the HQ phone lines. Andersson had promised them a press conference the following morning at ten o'clock. He had said there would be no point in holding one any earlier because they had not yet identified the girl. But tabloid journalists are full of ideas, and in the absence of information they simply use their imagination. As a consequence, the largest of the evening papers was dominated by the headline KILLER MOWED DOWN INNOCENT MAN immediately below GIRL MURDERED?

The question mark could probably be regarded as rhetorical under the circumstances. The article consisted of big photos of the side road with the barrier down, the cordoned-off root cellar, police dogs sniffing around in the undergrowth and, for further clarification, a half-page photo of a police helicopter. Since a lilac bush in full bloom could be seen in the background, it was safe to assume that the reporters had been rummaging around in the archives. There was very little text, and it contained nothing that had not already been said in the morning news reports. Apart from the reporter's own conclusion, which was that the killer had been in a hurry after murdering the girl. That was why, according to a witness, he had been driving along Delsjövägen like a bat out of hell, and had been unable to avoid the pedestrian crossing the street.

The newspaper had been lying open on Andersson's desk when they got back to the department. He pointed at the pictures and grunted something inaudible. Irene had sighed.

"For a start, the direction the car was traveling in is wrong. The BMW was heading away from town. If the driver had been involved in the murder, the car would have been going the other way. And secondly, the time doesn't fit. The girl was already dead," she'd said.

"Exactly. The two are completely unconnected," Andersson said firmly.

He had felt a certain satisfaction when he made that statement. And now they had another body on their hands. The only consolation was that it wasn't a fresh one. This body probably had nothing whatsoever to do with the murdered girl or the death of Torleif Sandberg, but it would tie up the unit's resources. Too many major investigations going on at the same time.

"I'm intending to release the information about the girl's age this afternoon," Birgitta said. "That she is probably thirteen or fourteen, and not eleven or twelve as we first thought. So far there has been no report of a missing girl who might match her description. The girls who are missing at the moment are all older, and look their age."

Irene had only seen pictures of the murder victim lying naked on the pathologist's steel table: small, skinny, with spindly arms and legs and her hair fanned out around her head. Irene's first impression was of a small, defenseless child.

The superintendent nodded, looking grim. He drummed his fingers impatiently on the desk. Then the noise stopped, and he slapped the palm of his hand down with sudden resolve.

"We need to regroup. Fredrik and Tommy will take this new case, the old body the dogs just found. Irene and Hannu will carry on with Torleif's death in the hit-and-run, and Birgitta and Jonny will stick with the murdered girl."

"ARE YOU COMING to take a look around Torleif's apartment?"

They were standing in the elevator. It was almost half past six, and Irene really wanted to go home. But there was something in Hannu's voice that made her brighten up.

"Strictly speaking, we're not allowed to go inside the apartment," she pointed out, mostly for form's sake.

"Strictly speaking," Hannu repeated with a smile.

They traveled in their own cars so they would be able to go straight home after. Birgitta had already left in the Moberg-Rauhala family's other car in order to pick up little Timo from daycare.

The rush hour traffic had started to ease off. It took little more than fifteen minutes to reach Torleif's address on Anders Zornsgatan. When they had parked their cars and met up on the sidewalk, Irene nodded toward the TV studios and said, "He was on his way home. He was only a few hundred meters from his front door."

"Strange place to get run down," Hannu said.

"Strange? The BMW was coming too fast. He didn't have time to—"

"There's a clear view in all directions. He should have seen it."

Irene had to admit he was right, but there had to be some reason Torleif Sandberg had misjudged the distance from the speeding car.

"But it was dark. He was pretty old. Maybe he had problems with his eyesight. Cataracts or something," she suggested.

"In that case, why was he out running in the dark?" Hannu countered immediately.

Irene had no comeback, and they headed toward Torleif's apartment block.

The three-story brick building had been erected in the middle of the last century. The entire area was bright and pleasant, with tall trees and lawns between the blocks. Irene knew the flowerbeds were a riot of color during the spring and summer, but right now it looked as if the frost would keep the plants underground forever. Even though it felt like a distant dream in the biting cold, she knew that winter would eventually be forced to retreat. The spring rain would soften the deep frost, and once again it would loosen its grip on bulbs and roots.

Hannu unlocked the outside door, and they walked into the warmth of the entrance hall. On the board just inside listing the names of the tenant, Irene saw that *T SANDBERG* lived on the top floor. The walls of the stairwell were freshly painted in a soft, creamy yellow shade, with a border of dark green oak leaves halfway up. They set off up the spotlessly clean stairs. On the top floor they were faced with two doors with Torleif's name on one of them.

Hannu put the key in the lock and turned it, waving Irene in ahead of him.

"He's lived here for twenty-five years," she heard Hannu's voice behind her.

"Ever since the divorce?"

"Yes."

Irene found the switch and turned on the light in the hallway. It was narrow, with space for no more than a hat stand hanging on one wall, a shoe rack and a small closet. She glanced inside and saw that it contained outdoor clothes.

Straight ahead lay the bathroom. It was half-tiled in pale green. Several of the grey tiles on the floor were cracked, and the enamel coating on both the bath and hand basin was damaged.

"Time for some renovation," Irene remarked.

"Wait till you see the kitchen," Hannu said dryly.

The bathroom and hallway might have been less than spacious, but the kitchen was almost claustrophobic. It had been the fashion to build compact kitchens in the 1950s, but this was the tiniest space imaginable. There was hardly room to boil an egg. The stove and refrigerator looked as if they were the originals. The curtains had faded slightly from the sun, but seemed to have been ironed. The forest-green stripes perfectly complemented the painted cupboard doors. Two wooden chairs and a small table covered in a green and white checked wax cloth stood by one wall; there was no room for any more. An old poster showing a healthy eating pyramid for vegetarians hung above the table. It had seeds and legumes at the top instead of meat, fish and poultry. Irene recognized it from Jenny's diet. It's important to take in enough protein when you're vegetarian.

In the larder they found boxes of dried beans and peas, bags of various kinds of flour, and—of course—several packets of Dr. Kruska's oat muesli. On one shelf a number of jars containing dried fruit were neatly arranged. The refrigerator was almost empty; the only thing inside was an open carton of soy milk and two foil trays of something unidentifiable.

They went back through the hallway and into the living room, which was surprisingly airy. A large picture window and a glass door overlooked the balcony. This room must have been lovely and light when the sun was shining. The television seemed to be the only recent purchase. Above it hung a framed poster of the sun setting over the Rocky Mountains. The sofa, armchairs, curtains, carpet and not least the combined bookcase and display cabinet clearly bore the marks of 1970s style. The bookcase housed a few paperbacks and several porcelain figurines, while the display cabinet was filled with an impressive collection of cups and trophies.

"He was very good at orienteering, and he was a fast long-distance runner. He must have won these when he was a member of the Police Sports Association," Irene said. She walked over to the cabinet. There was a small switch beside it, and when she pressed it several tiny lamps lit up inside the glass doors, the light glinting off the trophies.

"He kept them polished," Hannu stated.

Irene looked around. "Yes. He kept the whole place clean and tidy," she said.

Hannu went over to a door that was standing ajar. Cautiously he nudged it open with his foot.

The bedroom was also pretty spacious. One wall consisted of a built-in closet, and the single bed against the opposite wall was neatly made up with a pale blue coverlet. There was a colorful rag rug on the floor that looked reasonably new. The tall display cabinet at the foot of the bed had glass shelves and doors, and to Irene's surprise it was full of toy cars. The smallest was only a little bigger than a sugar lump, while the biggest was around thirty centimeters long. They were all cop cars, from every corner of the world. The largest was a blue and white 1950s model with a sheriff's star on the doors.

Next to the closed laptop on the desk lay a book entitled *Researching Your Family Tree: A Beginner's Guide*. There was also a framed photograph of a little blond-haired boy aged about three. Irene pointed to the picture and said, "That must be his son. They look alike."

Irene opened the closet; the clothes were all on hangers. In the linen cupboard, sheets and towels were folded neatly. "He lived alone. There's no sign of anyone else living here," she said.

Hannu didn't reply, but looked around the room. His gaze lingered on the bed. "Lonely," he said eventually.

The word was on the money. The entire apartment was suffused with loneliness. Perhaps they were getting completely the wrong impression. Perhaps Muesli had had a wide circle of friends in the Sports Association and pensioners' club. Irene tried to remember what he had been like when he was working with them. She hadn't really known him, but of course she had been aware of who he was. Torleif had never made much of an impression other than with his peculiar eating habits. Unremarkable appearance, although he had kept himself fit right up to retirement—he had been passionate about personal fitness. How long had it been since he had retired? Irene thought about it and realized she didn't know for sure. Somewhere between five and seven years, maybe.

"Did you know him?" she asked Hannu.

"No. I knew who he was, but I never spoke to him."

"I knew him slightly. He was a desk sergeant with the third district the last year I was working there, then he came over to HQ when the third was amalgamated with another area. But by then I'd joined the Violent Crimes Unit, and I didn't have much to do with him."

"So what was he like?" Hannu asked.

"Pretty inoffensive. The only time I saw him get excited about something was when he started talking about the importance of exercise. And eating the right food. Vegetarian, of course."

"And what was he like as a cop?"

Irene hesitated before answering. "Actually, he was . . . a bit weak. He was scared of making decisions, always had to get the nod from above. We found him quite irritating sometimes. He wasn't an outstanding colleague, but then again he wasn't the worst I've ever come across either."

"Sociable?"

"I don't know . . . not exactly. But he wasn't antisocial either. He wasn't bad-tempered or miserable, as far as I remember. There were plenty who were worse than him."

Irene could hear how evasive she sounded. She tried to sharpen up. "To tell the truth, I guess I didn't really know him at all. He was just there. One colleague among all the rest who you don't have anything in common with."

Hannu nodded, staring at the single bed. It was impossible to work out what he was thinking. The ice-blue gaze swept the room one last time before he turned on his heel and went back to the living room.

Irene found him in front of the display cabinet. The interior lights were still on.

"A collector. Trophies and cop cars," Hannu stated.

Irene had at least as many cups and trophies at home; she had won them for jiujitsu during her active years among the elite in Sweden and throughout Europe. They were tucked away on the top shelf of a closet. Undeniably a sharp contrast to the beautifully polished collection shining behind the spotless glass door of the display cabinet.

"And he was interested in his family tree, judging by the book. I suppose that's also a form of collecting. You collect members of your family as you go back through the years," Irene mused.

Hannu looked at her and gave one of his rare, fleeting smiles.

"You could be right," he said.

Chapter 4

"KATARINA'S JUST TEXTED me. They've touched down in Tenerife," Jenny yelled from upstairs.

"So when do they arrive at Landvetter?" Irene shouted back, balancing on one leg as she tried to pull down the stiff zipper on her boot.

This was by no means easy, as Sammie was winding himself around her at the same time, demanding attention. He was twelve years old, and would be thirteen in a few months. His eyesight and hearing were deteriorating. When it suited him he pretended to be stone deaf, but this was nothing new; he'd been doing it ever since he was a puppy. Otherwise he was bright and happy. If anyone had asked him what kept him young, he would no doubt have replied, "Hunting." His master could have explained that his quarry was cats and smaller dogs, but squirrels and birds were also acceptable. Just as long as they moved so that he could see them, although these days he sometimes missed them completely.

"Midnight. Felipe's dad is picking them up," Jenny replied.

Irene was relieved that she wouldn't have to drive out to the airport in the middle of the night. She was also grateful that her other daughter was safe and on her way home.

Katarina and Felipe had been in Brazil for four months. They had stayed with Felipe's relatives, studying and teaching capoeira, the dance that was also a martial art, although the description could easily be reversed: a martial art with elements of dance. To Irene's sorrow, Katarina had completely given up jiujitsu and was now putting all her efforts into capoeira.

At first Irene and Krister had been doubtful about the trip. However, the argument that Felipe had been to Brazil many times, spoke fluent Portuguese and had lots of relatives and friends in the country had finally persuaded them to agree. After all, their daughter was technically an adult.

Katarina had found a job immediately after graduating from high school at the beginning of June. She had spent the whole summer working at the Liseberg amusement park, and because she was still living at home, she had been able to save most of what she earned. She had used all her savings for the trip, and judging by her travel blog, it had been worth every single krona.

In spite of the fact that Irene had been able to follow their experiences online, she had felt anxious all the time.

She knew that Krister had been worried, too, even though he had tried not to show it. Several times she had woken up in the middle of the night and heard him wandering around the house. His insomnia had resumed in the fall, when he had been diagnosed with depression due to exhaustion. The pace of work at the exclusive restaurant where he worked was relentless, and the pressure to retain its star in the gourmet guide weighed heavily on all the staff.

As head chef, Krister had carried a considerable burden, and in the end he just couldn't cope any more. After a few months he had gone back to work, but only part-time due to ill health. Meanwhile, Glady's had appointed a new head chef who was very good, and he had taken over some of Krister's previous areas of responsibility. Irene thought Krister was getting back to his old self, although it would probably take time before he fully recovered. He was nine years older than her, but it was only during the last twelve months that she had given the age difference any thought. Something happens when you get past fifty, she often thought. Although she wasn't there yet—not by a long way.

"Evening, honey!" she heard her husband call from the kitchen.

A seductive aroma crept out into the hallway. Irene tiptoed across the kitchen floor and wrapped her arms around Krister from behind, as he was busy with various kitchen implements at the stove.

"Mmm, that smells delicious! I'm starving," she murmured into the nape of his neck.

"Roast fish soup. Well, the peppers and other vegetables have been roasted in the oven, not the fish and the shellfish. I'm cooking those separately as usual," Krister said, turning his head to try to kiss her.

It was essential to cook and serve the fish and shellfish separately because Jenny had been a vegan for several years now. These days it wasn't really a problem, but Irene had found it difficult to get used to the idea. Some days they all ate vegan food, and on other days Jenny warmed up the leftovers while the rest of the family had something different. They usually prepared vegetable dishes that could be complemented with meat or fish for those who wished to partake.

Jenny came downstairs. She had let her hair grow without coloring the roots, which were golden blonde. The rest was coal black. The band she had been in for several years had split up after the summer, and Jenny hadn't made much of an effort to find a new one; she had been fully occupied working in various daycare facilities over the fall and winter, employed on an hourly basis.

Jenny poured some of the soup into a smaller pan. She then added half the contents of a tin of butter beans in order to make it more substantial and richer in protein. She looked thoughtfully at her father as she slowly stirred the soup.

"Any chance you might be able to fix me up with a job at Glady's?" she asked.

Krister raised his eyebrows. Jenny was a good cook when it came to preparing delicious vegan meals, but she had never shown any real interest in the restaurant industry.

"Doing what?" he wondered.

She shrugged. "Don't know. Like, helping to cook maybe?"

"We have trained chefs with years of experience who are desperate to work for us. Glady's is a top-class establishment. You might possibly be able to help out as a general kitchen hand. Or as a dishwasher. Although the cleaning is contracted out to another company, so the restaurant isn't responsible for that anymore."

"Right," she said. She couldn't hide her disappointment, even though she was trying hard.

"I thought you were happy working at the daycare," Irene said.

"I am. But it doesn't feel like it's what I'm really meant to do."

"And what about your music?" Krister asked.

"I won't give that up, but right now I just feel like I want to do something different."

"Any idea what?"

"No. Well . . . I think working in a restaurant would be pretty cool."

"You mean cooking."

Jenny nodded and lifted the pan off the heat. The soup smelled delicious. She poured it into a bowl and scattered chopped fresh parsley over the top. The contrast between the bright red paprika soup and the green parsley was beautiful. Krister gazed thoughtfully at the results of her efforts.

"You've actually got a feeling for food, and an eye for what looks good. But you don't have any formal training. And the fact that you're vegan is another problem. You'd have to learn to cook meat and fish if you're going to work in a restaurant."

"Not if it's a vegetarian restaurant," Jenny shot back.

"So you'd like to learn to cook vegetarian food?"

Jenny nodded again.

"In that case you need to try to get yourself a job in a vegetarian restaurant."

"That's not easy. There are only, like, two or three in the whole of Göteborg," Jenny said.

"In that case you'll just have to get in touch with those two or three restaurants and introduce yourself. And you can tell them who your dad is," Krister said.

He smiled at Jenny, who smiled back. *They're so alike*, Irene thought, feeling a warm glow around her heart.

WHEN IRENE WENT over to the bedroom window to close the blinds, she saw that it was snowing heavily. She decided to get up early the next morning so she would have time to clear the snow off her car and wouldn't run the risk of being late for work again.

"So she wants to take up cooking—how about that!" Krister said into the darkness when they had switched off the lights. He couldn't hide the satisfaction in his voice.

"Do you think she's serious?" Irene asked.

"I hope so, I really do. I think it would suit her."

Irene felt slightly put out, somehow. She had always thought that her daughter would choose music. A vegan cook. Oh well, why not?

Chapter 5

JUST A SPOONFUL *of snow in Göteborg, and it's chaos*, Irene's mother, Gerd, always used to say. There was more than a grain of truth in her comment since she was speaking with seventy-seven years' experience.

During the night several spoonfuls of snow had fallen; almost twenty-five centimeters covered the city. There was traffic chaos everywhere. The snowplows had hardly even started clearing the streets when the morning rush hour began. As usual, the residents of Göteborg were caught off guard by the fact that heavy snow had fallen this year, too. Those who didn't have winter tires—which was a lot of people—were slithering around in the slush. Cars slid off the road and crashed into one another. Because of all the mishaps and narrow escapes, the traffic was more or less at a standstill. Irene realized she was going to be seriously late for the first time in her sixteen years with the Violent Crimes Unit. She sat there calling down the worst retribution of Judgment Day on those responsible for this pathetic attempt to clear the snow. Which didn't really help at all. She was stuck there, gridlocked along with her fellow drivers. Her only consolation was that the temperature had started to creep upward.

IRENE WAS ALMOST half an hour late when she arrived at the department, extremely stressed. She saw Fredrik Stridh further down the corridor.

He waved and called out, "Take it easy. Hannu and Birgitta aren't here yet."

It felt good to have time for her morning ritual. She hung up her coat, exchanged a few words with Tommy, then headed for the coffee machine. To be on the safe side, she took two cups of coffee into the briefing with her.

The others were sitting chatting in the meeting room. It was a little while before Irene realized that Superintendent Andersson was missing.

"Where's Sven?" she asked.

Both Jonny Blom and Fredrik Stridh looked surprised.

"Isn't he around somewhere?" Fredrik said. "He's usually the first to arrive in the mornings."

"I suppose he's stuck in the goddamn snow like everybody else," Jonny said.

"Birgitta just called. They'll be here in ten minutes," Tommy Persson relayed as he came into the room.

"Have you seen Sven?" Irene asked.

"Nope. Isn't he here?"

"No."

They sat down around the table with their coffee. Irene told them about the keys that had been found in the victim's pocket, and that one of them opened the door to Torleif Sandberg's apartment.

"Which means that it's likely that Torleif is our victim. They're doing a dental X-ray this afternoon; apparently the lower jaw is pretty much intact," she said.

There was an uncomfortable silence as they remembered the crushed head.

"Muesli was a bit of a bore—all that jogging and chewing on stuff that tasted like straw. And he didn't drink," Jonny said with his usual inability to read the atmosphere.

"I wouldn't have said he was a bore," Tommy chipped in. "But he had his . . . principles."

"Principles, exactly! The man was a big ball of principles!" Jonny said. He suddenly stared at Tommy. "Did you ever hang out with Muesli?"

"Not really. But it doesn't necessarily mean he's boring, just because—"

"Doesn't it? Do any of you know whether Muesli ever spent time with anybody at all?" He glanced at each person in turn. They all shook their heads, and Jonny said triumphantly, "Nobody hung out with him because he was so goddamn boring. Just imagine being invited to dinner at his place." He cleared his throat, then spoke in a falsetto, "Welcome to my home this Friday evening; we'll be having bean soup with water."

The others laughed at the performance until they noticed Andersson in the doorway. The look he gave Jonny was venomous.

"I used to hang out with Torleif," he said tersely.

In the silence that descended over the room, he lumbered over to his place at the head of the table. Puffing and panting, he sank down on the chair, which creaked beneath his weigh. He looked old and tired, Irene thought. Which of course he was, she reminded herself. Sixty-two, seriously overweight, high blood pressure and asthma—it was a pity his friend Torleif hadn't had more influence on his lifestyle and eating habits. But it was news to Irene that Torleif Sandberg and the superintendent had spent time together. It was difficult to think of two more different individuals. What had they had in common? It struck her that she didn't actually know anybody who hung out with Sven Andersson outside work. Irene looked at her boss as she remembered Torleif's apartment. She realized what the common denominator was: loneliness.

"I had no idea you and Muesli were friends," Jonny said, genuinely surprised. As usual he had put into words precisely what everybody else was thinking.

Andersson looked down at his hands for a little while before he spoke. "We had . . . a number of things in common. When I got divorced, he'd been through the same thing. We talked quite a lot back then." Suddenly he looked up and smiled at his colleagues around the table. "He actually invited me round for cabbage pudding once, and it was one of the tastiest things I've ever eaten."

"Cabbage pudding? But that has ground beef . . ." Jonny began.

"He used some kind of soy substitute, but it took a while before I realized it wasn't real meat."

"You'll be telling us next that he offered you a beer as well," Jonny said, rolling his eyes.

"He did, actually. Low-alcohol beer, but still."

Andersson was interrupted by the arrival of Birgitta Moberg-Rauhala. There was a brief period of confusion as she started to tell them about a pile-up on the highway outside Floda, while at the same time apologizing for her and Hannu's late arrival.

"We'll have a quick meeting before the press conference at ten," Andersson decided. Then he turned to Tommy and asked, "The body that was found yesterday—where are we on that?"

"It was found by a police dog in rough terrain behind the TV mast at Brudaremossen. It was in a crevice in the rocks in a half-sitting position. Both Fredrik and I thought it seemed like the remains of a male. He looked as if he'd been there for quite some time—several months at least," Tommy said.

"Young or old?" Andersson asked.

"Not young, judging by the clothes. Gumboots size forty-two, plus something that looked like a Helly Hansen jacket and a hat with earflaps."

"Warm clothing," Irene remarked.

"Yes, although the gumboots would suggest that the temperature wasn't below freezing. More like damp weather in the fall," Tommy speculated.

"Minus sixteen. Torleif Sandberg was wearing sneakers," Hannu suddenly said. He didn't appear to be addressing anyone in particular.

The others stared at him in surprise.

"And?" the superintendent said.

"Cold," Hannu said laconically.

Andersson, who often seemed flummoxed by their Finnish colleague, didn't reply; instead he turned to Fredrik with his next question. "Any idea how he died?"

"He definitely died where he was found. We didn't see anything suspicious at the scene: no guns or other possible weapons. And as far as we could make out, nothing about the body suggests foul play. The autopsy will clarify that, although it's likely to take a few days."

"No doubt. They're so goddamn short staffed," Andersson snorted.

He drummed a rapid solo with his fingers on the desk while pushing out his lower lip: unmistakable signs that he was thinking. Eventually he said, "Fredrik, check through missing persons for males of the right age group in the area for the past twelve months. Otherwise we'll keep that investigation on the back burner until we have the results of the autopsy. And I can tell you that door-to-door inquiries around Töpelsgatan haven't produced any results so far." He rubbed his hands together energetically and turned to Birgitta. "Any news on the girl?" he asked.

"Not really. I've spoken to colleagues in Norway, Denmark and Finland, but there are no reports of missing girls in their early teens that match, so I'm going to speak to Linda Holm in the Human Trafficking Unit today."

"Oh! Little Blondie. They couldn't use her undercover, so they had to make her the chief," Jonny said with a laugh.

"What are you talking about?" Birgitta asked.

"When they sent Little Blondie out on the streets in Rosenlund, the whole thing was a complete mess. All the johns wanted the blonde sitting in the car. The other hookers were furious and threatened to beat her up."

Jonny laughed again and seemed very pleased with his anecdote. One look at Birgitta was enough to convince him that she didn't appreciate it. She was clenching her jaw so tightly that he could see her muscles straining, and a furious flush was spreading upward from her throat to her cheeks.

"Can't you hear yourself?! You're saying the superintendent only got her job because she was no good out in the field!"

"Hey, I was just kidding . . ."

"And on top of that do you realize how misogynistic referring to her as 'Little Blondie' is?!" Birgitta was so angry that she was gasping and had to take a few deep breaths.

"Have you become a member of the Feminist Initiative or something?" Jonny sneered. He never missed an opportunity to make things worse.

Birgitta flew out of her chair and leaned across the table, her eyes flashing with rage. "Shut your mouth, Jonny! Superintendent Linda Holm is a law graduate and an excellent police officer. You could never achieve what she has, which is why you feel the need to put her down. The only thing you can actually accuse her of is being a woman!"

"That's enough, both of you!" Andersson's face was purple as he slammed his fist down on the table. He hated this kind of thing. He pointed a threatening finger at Birgitta and Jonny. "Enough!" he barked.

Birgitta sat down. She pressed her lips together and glared at an old, faded print on the wall. It showed several cranes in a harbor against an insipid grey-blue sky.

"Over-sensitive . . . nit-picking . . . no sense of humor," Jonny muttered, just loud enough to be heard.

Irene attempted to dispel the tense atmosphere by telling the late arrivals about the key that fit the door of Torleif Sandberg's apartment.

"So it seems like it really is Torleif lying there in the morgue," Andersson said.

"Yes. And we've started to check on boys who are on the run from various institutions right now. There aren't very many of them: three who fit the description, as far as we can tell."

"Try to pick them up so we can eliminate them from the investigation if nothing else," Andersson said to Irene.

She nodded and caught Tommy's eye. Time to get to grips with Daniel Lindgren, Niklas Ström and Billy Kjellgren.

Andersson turned to Birgitta. "So why are you going to speak to Superintendent Linda Holm in Human Trafficking?" he said with heavy irony.

"Such a young girl should have been reported missing if she's Swedish or from another Scandinavian country, but there's no record anywhere of such a report. There are clear signs on her body that she has been subjected to extreme sexual violence over a long period. Stridner also said that the girl was suffering from some kind of infection, and there are the needle marks on the body, indicating narcotics abuse. Putting all of this together, I think our murder victim is a sex slave who has been smuggled into the country."

Andersson nodded slowly and gazed pensively at the dark windows, the wet snow pattering against the glass. With a little imagination it was possible to sense a hint of light that just might be dawn in the miserable greyness. He started drumming his fingers again. In spite of the fact that they were prepared for it, everyone jumped when he suddenly slapped his palm down on the table.

"Irene, Fredrik and Birgitta, you work on the murdered girl. Jonny, I want you to take Irene's place in the investigation into Torleif's death, along with Tommy and Hannu. As for the guy in Brudaremossen, we'll wait for the results of the autopsy. If he's been dead for months, then he can wait a few more days," he decided.

Irene was just as surprised as everyone else, but she realized why Andersson had changed things around. There was far too much tension between Jonny and Birgitta, and it could affect the investigation. The reasons behind the toxic atmosphere went back at least seven years, to the time when Birgitta started in the unit. Almost immediately Jonny had started coming onto the blonde cutie with the sparkling brown eyes. He had gone in with his usual blunt style. At the annual Christmas party his attentions had turned physical, and Birgitta had had enough. In the middle of the dance floor she had expressed her opinions on Jonny and his groping. To the delight of her colleagues, she certainly hadn't minced her words.

The following year, when Birgitta received pornographic photos in an envelope through the internal mail with no sender's name on the envelope, Jonny immediately had become the prime suspect. Even though it later transpired that another former colleague had sent the pictures, the working relationship between Jonny and Birgitta was totally ruined. It had improved somewhat in recent years, but it was never going to recover completely.

On one occasion, suffering from an unusual desire to confide in someone, Andersson had asked Irene if she thought it would be better for Birgitta to move to another department. Irene had been furious and had snapped, "It's not Birgitta who was in the wrong! She's never groped Jonny between the legs or made inappropriate suggestions!" The superintendent had looked at her in astonishment and had left the room without a word. The matter had never been mentioned again.

"Five minutes until the press conference," Andersson informed them grimly.

He got to his feet, signaling the meeting was over.

Chapter 6

WHEN THE HUMAN Trafficking Unit in Göteborg had been formed six years earlier, it had been an experimental project. Linda Holm had been a detective inspector in the unit, working in a team of three. Over the years the unit had become a permanent fixture and had expanded; there was now a team of eight, and a year ago Linda Holm had been promoted to superintendent. The former chief was now a project leader, traveling all over the country giving talks to police officers and other groups that might come into contact with the problems associated with the increase in trafficking. Irene had found this out during the information day she and her colleagues from the Violent Crimes Unit had attended last year.

Superintendent Linda Holm was on the phone when they got to her office. As the door was open, they couldn't help overhearing parts of the conversation.

". . . that's okay. How long have the girls been here? I see. In that case, there's no time to lose."

She fell silent, listening attentively. At the same time she glanced up from her notepad and caught sight of Irene and Birgitta standing just outside the door. With a fleeting smile and an exuberant gesture, she waved them in.

"Have we got enough for a search warrant? Preferably tonight . . . Okay. In that case we'll aim for tomorrow. I'll get in touch with the prosecutor. Keep me informed. Bye now."

Linda Holm ended the call and turned her attention to her visitors. She was a few years younger than Irene. A quick appraisal of the superintendent led Irene to reflect that there might be a grain of truth in Jonny's anecdote. Nor was it particularly surprising that the superintendent, with her naturally curly hair, was referred to as Blondie.

Birgitta got straight to the point and explained why they were there. She gave a brief outline of the case and said she suspected the murdered girl was a victim of trafficking. When she had finished, Linda Holm nodded.

"I agree. It sounds as if there are grounds to suspect that trafficking is involved. Let's see if we can find her on the Internet," she said.

Superintendent Linda Holm's fingers flew over the keys, and she quickly scrolled through the pages she brought up, her brow furrowed in concentration.

"Here," she said after a while, turning the laptop around so her colleagues could see.

There was a whole page of ads. It was obvious they were advertising sex because several of them were accompanied by photographs. Naked and half-naked girls in an assortment of sexy poses, with their first name and a brief introduction.

"This week's available girls in Göteborg," Linda Holm said dryly. She pointed to the flags at the side of each text. "The flags show what languages the girls speak. Impressive, don't you think?"

Irene could see that most of them had three or four flags, and that the most common were Russian, Latvian, Estonian, German and English.

"As far as German and English are concerned, it's usually just odd words the girls picked up while being shuttled around Europe," Linda said.

Like most police officers, both Irene and Birgitta had come across various forms of trafficking during the course of their work, but Irene wanted to know more about the current situation. "How long do they stay in one country?" she asked.

"One to four weeks. And they spend only a few days in each town. A lot of the girls have been kidnapped; the family might be looking for the girl, and they might have reported her as a missing person, so the pimps don't want to stay in one place for too long. They have often bought the girl from the kidnapper, and they don't want to get rid of her until she's earned them as much money as possible. But most of the girls are bought and sold as slaves, usually by their parents or other relatives. Or by kidnappers, as I said. Organized human traffickers dazzle the girls and their families with the promise of a good job overseas because what's behind this misery is always poverty, when it comes down to it."

"Don't the girls get to keep any of the money themselves?"

"No. The pimps take their passports off them as soon as they've entered a new country. Then they threaten the girls, telling them they have to pay off the cost of getting them out of their home country. They often say that the girl's family will have to pay the price if she doesn't do as she's told. And doing as she's told means going along with any sexual demand that the pimp or the clients might make."

Linda Holm paused for a moment and took a booklet out of her desk drawer. She held it up to show them. "This is an up-to-date report from the UN. It indicates that never before in the history of the world have there been as many slaves as we have today. At least twelve million people are living in slavery; the actual number is probably significantly higher. In the past people used to be enslaved to work, but these days sex slavery is at least as common. It's more lucrative. The trade includes children and adults of both sexes, but the majority are girls and young women. The fact is that human trafficking today turns over more money than the narcotics trade."

"Why has this happened?" Birgitta asked.

"Drug-related offenses attract severe punishments all over the world. Those who are caught can risk the death penalty. Human trafficking has generally led to more lenient sentences, plus the financial gains are huge. The law isn't keeping up with the development of trafficking at all; it's like an avalanche. Even if laws do exist, the authorities aren't always interested in making use of them. And remember that the men who hold the power often have dirty pants, if you know what I mean." The expression on Linda Holm's face was grim as she uttered the last words.

"Sounds like your job is an uphill battle," Birgitta commented.

"It sometimes feels that way. Things have changed somewhat in Sweden, but overseas prostitution is viewed very differently. The law often doesn't distinguish between voluntary prostitution and trafficking. The girls are all lumped together and are regarded as whores."

"You mean none of these girls are doing this of their own free will?"

Linda gave Birgitta a long look before answering. "Six months ago we raided an apartment we'd had under surveillance. We knew there were at least two girls in there, with two pimps. Men came and went at all hours of the day and night. I was there when we went in. As usual the apartment was a complete dump, but there was something about the smell . . . it stank more than usual. I went into one room and saw a teenage girl standing there changing a diaper on a grown man. The diaper was full of shit. I still wonder where a guy weighing a hundred kilos can get a hold of a onesie like the one he was wearing. And he had a pacifier, too."

A vision of the scene flashed across Irene's mind, and she felt nauseous. "That's sick," she said.

"But not all that uncommon. Do you really think a teenage

girl would choose a life in captivity, without any chance of stepping outside the temporary brothel? Being constantly ready to supply the most humiliating sexual services to men they don't even know? Because it's these sex slaves who have to deal with the worst perversions."

"What kind of men are we talking about here?" Irene asked.

"All kinds. The age varies between seventeen and eighty. The majority are socially well-established men with families."

"Do we know why they do it?"

"You mean why they pay for sex with a sex slave?" Linda Holm clarified. She paused for a moment before answering her own question. "I've given this a great deal of thought, and I think the answer is power. The power to be able to buy the total submissiveness of another human being. I think many of them find it easier because the girl can't speak their language. She becomes nothing more than a mute object. A sex object. I believe that's an important point for this socially well-established man with a family. He hasn't really been unfaithful. He's simply used a sex object that means nothing emotionally. The fact that at the same time he's got a kick out of the power he has over the girl is something he doesn't want to admit, of course. A lot of men also convince themselves they're doing something positive by giving the girl money."

"What happens to the girls? Do they ever get away?"

Linda shook her head. "It's extremely rare. A very small number of girls manages to make it back to their home country. Things might be okay as long as the girl doesn't tell anyone what she's experienced, but the physical and mental damage is often so severe that she ends up having a complete breakdown or committing suicide."

Linda fell silent and turned the laptop back to face her. She gazed at the small images on the screen showing this week's offers on the sex market before she continued. "They're consumable goods. Most of them succumb to illness and abuse.

Some are murdered by the pimps or the clients. There's actually a separate market for that."

"A separate market? You can buy a murder victim?" Birgitta exclaimed.

"Sure. When the girl is no use to him anymore, the pimp might sell her to someone who wants to pay to kill her. Although that's expensive."

Both Irene and Birgitta remained silent for a little while.

"Are you saying this is going on in Sweden?" Birgitta asked eventually.

"Probably, although we only have two suspected cases so far, both in the Stockholm area. Plus several girls who drowned when they were thrown overboard from a ferry, likely by their pimps. A cheap and easy way to get rid of girls who are no longer any use."

"You mean the girl we have in the morgue could have been bought as a murder victim?"

"Yes. From your description, she sounds very sick and in a pretty bad way. Maybe she wasn't able to bring in money for her pimp anymore. If he could just get a hold of the right buyer, he could make some decent cash out of her one last time."

Linda Holm carried on scrolling through pages offering various sexual services. "Look at this," she said. She turned the laptop around, pointing to one of the ads with her pen. The picture showed two smiling teenage girls wearing nothing but G-strings, their arms around each other's shoulders.

"Heinz Becker has been running this ad for two years. The girls in the picture are long gone. But his clients recognize it. It tells them that Heinz is back in town, and he always has very young girls on offer. That's his specialty."

"Who is he?"

"A middle-aged ex-soldier from the former German Democratic Republic. His father was German and his mother was from Estonia, so he speaks Estonian as well. Went down for narcotics-related offenses in the early nineties. When he got out of jail he turned to trafficking. He buys young girls from the Baltic states—with the emphasis on young. Most pimps are careful. If the girls are too young, it attracts attention. The police and border guards might start asking questions, and it can be hard to claim that the girls are there voluntarily if they're underage. But Heinz is prepared to take that risk. He usually smuggles them in. He makes a huge amount of money while he's on his tours, so to speak. It's client demand that rules the market, and they're prepared to pay more for really young girls."

"And this Heinz is in Göteborg at the moment?"

"Yes. This ad has been on the net for three days. We've just located the apartment where he's installed himself and his girls. We're keeping it under surveillance, and we'll try to go in tomorrow."

"I suppose it's difficult to get these girls to talk," Irene said.

"Yes. And we always have to use interpreters. Of course the ironic thing is the only person the girl can talk to when she's in a foreign country is her pimp. Occasionally one of her sisters in misfortune might speak the same language, but there's no guarantee. The girls might well be from different countries, and the pimps often keep them apart so they don't get to know each other. This means the pimp becomes the only fixed point in the girl's existence and, as I said, the only person she can talk to."

"I imagine the pimps also tell them horror stories to make sure they're scared of the police."

"Of course. As a rule they clam up and refuse to speak. We always have a female officer present when we question them. No male officer is ever allowed to be alone with any of the girls."

Irene thought hard for a moment. The case involving the dead girl in the root cellar was just beginning to take shape. "Would it be possible for us to sit in when you're questioning Heinz Becker? It would be interesting to find out if he knows anything about our murder victim. And of course it would be helpful to speak to the girls in the apartment. They might know something."

"Sure. No problem," Linda said with a smile that never really reached her eyes. Perhaps she had seen too much human misery. It struck Irene that the weary look in Linda's eyes was pretty common among her colleagues.

It was high time for lunch after the meeting with Linda Holm, although neither Irene nor Birgitta had much of an appetite.

"How about sushi?" Irene suggested as they were riding down in the elevator.

"Um . . . no," Birgitta said, looking slightly uncomfortable.

"You usually enjoy it."

Birgitta glanced at Irene, then broke into a big smile. "Pregnant women aren't supposed to eat raw fish," she said happily.

It took a fraction of a second for Irene to make the connection. "Are you pregnant? I mean . . . congratulations!" she exclaimed in some confusion.

"Yes, I'm pregnant again. And thank you. Although somehow I don't think Sven will be congratulating me," Birgitta said, pulling a face.

No, he wouldn't. He would be furious. On the other hand, soon it wouldn't be his problem any longer since he was moving across to the Cold Cases team. But Birgitta knew that just as well as she did, so Irene didn't bother pointing it out.

Instead she asked, "When are you due?"

"In the middle of July."

They reached the ground floor and walked out through the entrance hall. Outside, the snow was falling heavily, as it had done all morning. Irene stopped and turned to Birgitta.

"July. Good thinking. You won't be pushing a stroller in the snow," she said, waving her hand to encompass all the snowy misery around them.

Chapter 7

IT WAS ONLY four o'clock, but Irene was already hurrying toward the parking lot at police HQ, battling her way through a blizzard with the wind whipping her face. Her colleagues had muttered about all the work that was piling up, but Irene had stuck to her decision to leave early for once. She had accrued a lot of paid leave, and she needed some of those hours right now. She had things to do before this evening's dinner.

Of course it would have been better if they could have had it on Friday or Saturday, but Krister was working all weekend. Waiting until the following weekend felt like too long, so it would have to be this Thursday evening. The whole family was gathering to celebrate Katarina and Felipe's safe return after four months in Brazil. Irene hadn't seen them yet because they had spent the night at Felipe's apartment, which was a small sublet on Frölunda Square. Katarina was also talking about leaving home, but she wanted to live on her own for a while before she moved in with anyone. And if she and Felipe were going to live together, she definitely didn't want to live in his one-room apartment. Her other major problem was she had yet to work out what she wanted to do with her life. Her grades were reasonable, but not good enough to enable her to train as a physiotherapist, which was her dream job. She had no desire to try to improve her grades; three years at high school was enough.

At least that had been Katarina's point of view when she set off for Brazil four months earlier. Irene was quietly wondering whether anything might have changed. She was also curious to hear more about her daughter's experiences in the vast country on the other side of the Atlantic. Neither Irene nor Krister had visited that part of the world. In fact they had never ventured outside Europe. Nowadays young people traveled all over the globe, backpacking their way through Thailand and Australia with the same nonchalance as Irene and her boyfriend at the time had cycled around the island of Gotland twenty-five years ago.

Irene had spoken to Katarina on the phone earlier in the day, and her daughter had requested the Swedish food she had been missing: her father's blinis with red onion and whitefish roe, and stuffed cannelloni with Gorgonzola sauce and smoked ham. For dessert she wanted crème brûlée. These were all among Krister's signature dishes. He laughed out loud when Irene relayed Katarina's desire for "Swedish food."

"Russian blinis and Italian cannelloni," Krister said. "And for the grand finale, a dessert with its origins in Spain's crema Catalana, which was refined in New York by the restaurant owner Sirio Maccioni. From there it was taken to Europe and France by the illustrious chef Paul Bocuse."

"Wow! Really?"

"Absolutely. Talk about globalization. Within the restaurant world it's virtually complete. We happily blend cuisine from all over the world. But the truth is we're all cosmopolitan in our everyday eating habits. Take pizza, for example. I had my first when I was about twelve years old. The whole family had been to Liseberg, then we went to one of the first real pizza restaurants in Göteborg. La Gondola is still there today. The fact is that the taste and aroma of that very first calzone made a much deeper impression on me than our visit to the amusement park. Then we went back home to Säffle, and I told all my friends about the delicious pizza I'd had in Göteborg. Only a year or so later there was a pizzeria in Säffle, too, and these days there are several. Pizza has become part of the Swedish staple diet."

This was one of Krister's favorite topics. Since Irene was at work and had a limited amount of time, she had to cut him off.

"Can you sort out the food if I get the wine?" she quickly interjected when he paused for breath.

"Sure. Jenny's usually happy with a plain tomato sauce with pasta, but I'll need to do some shopping. Mushrooms and black olives, at least. And fresh basil."

He had sounded happy, looking forward to dinner. It had been a long road back from his burnout eighteen months ago. Sometimes he could still sink down into a darker mood, but these days the episodes didn't last as long. Irene had just started to hope that he would be himself again one day. He would probably never be exactly the same, but his pleasant temperament and his sense of humor had slowly returned and were often in evidence. Their sex life was also back on track. Sometimes Irene thought that in many ways things were better now that Krister wasn't working such long hours. He usually did the shopping and cooking, and sometimes he would run the vacuum cleaner before she got home. And old Sammie didn't have to spend as much time with the dog sitter. In spite of everything, their daily life was working out pretty well, Irene thought.

IRENE DROVE HOME via Guldheden to pick up her mother. Although it was snowing heavily, Irene could see her mother from some distance away as she drove along Doktor Bex gata. Wearing a fur hat and a bright red padded coat, she was waiting outside the main door of the apartment block, leaning on her stick. Irene parked and got out of the car to help her mother, more or less carrying her over the pile of snow the plow had left on the side of the road.

They both cursed the appalling snow-clearing standards of the Göteborg sanitation department.

My mother weighs next to nothing, Irene suddenly realized. Gently she put her mother down next to the passenger door and opened it for her. Gerd laboriously edged into her seat. One hip was completely worn out, and according to Gerd's doctor, it needed to be replaced. Almost three years ago he had referred her to the hospital. A year later she had an appointment with an orthopedic specialist who had given her a thorough examination and had confirmed that surgery was required. She still hadn't been given a date for her operation.

The weight loss could be due to the fact that Gerd was worried about her partner, Sture. He would be eighty-two in May. Six months ago he'd had major heart surgery, and it had taken its toll on him. Irene had invited him to the family dinner this evening, but he had declined; he was too tired. Nor had he been well enough to stay past five o'clock on Christmas Eve. When Irene had driven him home early, he had been totally worn out, and had fallen asleep in the car. She had had to wake him when they got to his apartment. Fortunately he and Gerd lived only a couple hundred meters from one another, which was probably one of the reasons they had never moved in together.

Irene was very grateful that her mother had had Sture over the past few years. It had made her feel much less guilty about neglecting Gerd. And there was no doubt that Gerd and Sture had a lot of fun together. They had gone on a number of vacations and excursions. But now they were both starting to grow noticeably old and frail. Neither of them could walk very far. There were days when even the short distance between their apartments was too much.

Irene tried to call on her mother at least once a week, but mostly it was Krister who went to see her. He did her shopping and cleaning. This was the most practical arrangement, as

Irene worked full-time, and often more, while Krister was still only part-time. Things would become much more difficult for Irene and her mother when Krister went back to working full-time. His mother had died the previous summer, two years after her husband, almost to the day. *We've only got Mom left now*, Irene thought, glancing at the shrunken figure beside her.

"How are you doing, Mom?" she asked.

"Could be better. I can hardly sleep because of the pain."

"Don't the new tablets help?"

Gerd snorted. "They're too strong! They make me feel dizzy and confused. If I take one at night, I feel terrible all morning. I think that's why I'm having nightmares when I do happen to fall asleep."

That didn't sound good. What if her mother got up during the night and had a dizzy spell? What would happen if she fell? She could break her leg or hit her head. Irene decided it was time to tackle the subject she should have broached a long time ago. It couldn't be put off any longer. She swallowed hard and gripped the steering wheel.

"Mom, do you think maybe you should get one of those panic alarms? You know the kind of thing. You wear it around your wrist and press the button if you fall."

Gerd let out a stormy harrumph. "A panic alarm! Those are for old people! And I am not going to fall!"

Obviously it wasn't the right time for this discussion, but Irene had made a start, and she had no intention of letting it go.

IRENE WAS QUITE tense and nervous about meeting Felipe's family. The only thing she knew about them was that his father was Brazilian and had been a professional dancer. He had jumped ship when his dance troupe was on tour in Sweden almost thirty years ago, and had married Felipe's mother. He had been working for Folksam, the insurance company, for several years now. Felipe's mother, Eva, was a teacher, and that was all Irene knew about her. Like Felipe, his younger sister was also a very good dancer.

Josef Medina and his son, Felipe, were very much alike. Both men were tall and slim. But Josef's skin was slightly darker, and his hair was silver and cut in a short, neat style. His son wore his thick, dark hair woven into dozens of small braids that hung down his back. At the end of every braid were tiny wooden beads that rattled whenever he moved his head. Felipe's sister, Evita, was just sixteen, and Katarina thought the world of her.

Jenny and Katarina had pulled out both extension leaves on the large dining table, so there was plenty of space for nine people. However, the living room itself was quite small, so Gerd had to sit at one end of the table so it would be easier for her to get in and out of her chair.

The dinner went well. After only a little while the conversation was flowing. The good food and wine helped any residual tension among them to dissipate. Everyone listened with interest as Katarina and Felipe talked about everything they had experienced during their trip, and the volunteer work they had undertaken with the street children in Natal. In return for attending school every day, the children received a hot meal and free tuition in dance and capoeira. If they didn't do their schoolwork, or if they played hooky, they were removed from the capoeira group.

"School is their one chance. Knowledge is the only way out of the poverty trap," Felipe said earnestly.

Of course they had also had less pleasant experiences during their trip. Felipe told them four boys with knives had robbed him on the beach in Natal in broad daylight. No one else on the beach had even noticed what was going on. Katarina had been no more than fifty meters away, but she hadn't seen a thing.

Katarina had been horrified by the unbelievable poverty

they had encountered. Never before had she seen people who owned nothing more that the clothes on their back.

"But the worst was in Rio. We saw children and young teenagers sitting in bars or walking around in certain parks, and these men would come along and just pick one of them up. I mean, some of them didn't look any older than about ten! It was just disgusting to see those guys with a little boy or girl," Katarina said, sounding upset.

"There were also a number of older women paying for the services of young boys. Although not in the same bars," Felipe added.

"It's just as well that kind of thing doesn't happen here," Evita said.

Before Irene had time to think, she said, "But it does happen here. Although we import them. Sex slaves, I mean."

The others around the table looked at her in surprise.

Irene had to quickly think through what she was going to say before she continued. "Trafficking is a growing problem. I'm sure you've read about it. The number of sex slaves is increasing here in Sweden as well." As soon as she had spoken, she regretted it. The atmosphere around the table took a nosedive.

After a while Evita said seriously, "As long as we choose to regard sex slavery as a problem in other countries, preferably on the other side of the world, we can discuss it openly. But when we are compelled to recognize that human trafficking goes on inside our own country, then it becomes uncomfortable. Because it forces us to make a stand and act, in the name of humanity."

"Exactly," Irene agreed, with an enormous sense of relief.

"I've read about this in the paper, and I don't really see the problem. Just lock up those disgusting pimps and throw away the key, and help those poor girls to get back home. Or let them stay here if they want to," Gerd said firmly.

As usual, she thought she had the obvious solution.

Chapter 8

THE PREVIOUS EVENING, the Swedish Meteorological Office had warned of continuing snowfall. Irene had prepared herself by setting the alarm for half an hour earlier than usual.

It was horrible getting out of her lovely bed and staggering to the bathroom, dizzy with tiredness. However, as she glanced sleepily out of the window, she congratulated herself on her foresight. Another three centimeters of snow had fallen overnight.

Before she left, she tried to persuade Sammie to go outside for a pee. He didn't even open one eye but made a point of snoring loudly before rolling over onto his back with his paws in the air. If there was one thing he hated, it was cold, wet, early mornings—an opinion his mistress shared completely. Unfortunately, unlike Sammie she had no choice and had to venture out into the gloom.

"BLOND—I MEAN, LINDA Holm was looking for you," Jonny said when Irene met him in the corridor.

She glanced at her watch. Ten minutes until morning prayer. She headed for the superintendent's office. Linda Holm was standing by her desk with her back to the door, talking on the phone as she tried to shrug off a warm-looking turquoise cardigan knitted in a thick, fluffy yarn.

She ended the call and managed to extricate her arm from the sleeve. At the same time she spotted Irene in the doorway and said, "Hi. I was wondering if you and Birgitta would like to be there this afternoon when we question Heinz Becker and the girls from the brothel."

Irene thought about everything she had to do that day, and realized it was a hell of a long list. But she just had to prioritize this. So far Becker was the only lead that might help to establish the girl's identity.

"Sure. One of them might know who the murdered girl is," she replied.

"My thoughts exactly."

Linda nodded toward the computer and said, "Yesterday afternoon I went through all the girls who are currently for sale on the Internet in the Göteborg area. I also checked every town within a radius of one hundred kilometers, and I didn't find any girls as young as the one lying in the morgue. But as I said, Heinz Becker is in town, and if anyone is capable of smuggling in a really young girl, it's him. I think it's a good bet."

"In that case we'll definitely sit in on the interviews. I'll speak to Birgitta."

"I'll be in touch when we're ready."

"Okay," Irene said.

Linda nodded just as the phone started to ring again.

Irene set off along the corridor; she had just enough time to stop off at the coffee machine before the morning briefing. As she rounded the corner at speed, she bumped into Svante Malm, CSI technician.

"Oof! Oh, I'm so sorry," Irene said.

"Damn! You've got coffee all over you," Svante said.

Clumsily he tried to dab at the coffee stain spreading all over the sleeve of Irene's pale blue top, with the result that it soon covered an even wider area. Irene pushed his hand away and scurried back down the corridor to the bathroom, where she turned the cold water on all the way and stuck her arm under the stream. The water went everywhere, but thanks to the fact that she had reacted so quickly, there was no damage to her skin, although it had been painful. Svante's freckled face appeared in the doorway.

"Did you scald yourself?" he asked, sounding concerned.

"No, I'm fine. But could you get me a coffee, and I'll see you in the meeting?" Irene replied, trying to sound convincing.

A relieved smile appeared on Svante's amiable horse face. "It's cool. Everyone's waiting for me. They'll just have to be patient while I go and fetch coffee. Milk? Sugar?"

"Black. Thanks."

With a sigh she turned off the faucet and started patting the stain on her arm with some dry paper towels. It was very obvious, but there was nothing she could do about that. The question was whether it would ever come out. Irene felt slightly dejected because the thin woolen sweater was a good brand, and it was the only thing she had managed to buy in the post-Christmas sales. She glanced at her face in the mirror above the hand basin and concluded that she looked exactly the way she felt.

"WE'VE FOUND SEVERAL semen stains on the T-shirt and jacket, and we also found fresh semen in her hair," Svante Malm said. He paused and looked around the room before continuing. "The semen in her hair matched the stains on the T-shirt. The stains on the jacket are from two other men."

A deep silence followed this revelation. Birgitta whispered to Irene, "A gang bang."

Irene turned her head and briefly contemplated the picture on the whiteboard. She couldn't help shuddering as she looked at the skinny body lying on the cold metal surface of the table. In her mind's eye she saw three naked men gathering around the table. She felt sick, and pushed the image away.

Death had removed every trace of emotion from the thin face, leaving behind a seal of silence. Who was she? Where had she come from? Who had killed her? How did she end up in the root cellar?

Svante's voice penetrated her consciousness and interrupted her thoughts. "She was noticeably underdressed, given how cold it was the night she was killed. Her clothes were with her in the root cellar. It looked as if they had been thrown in, because they were on top of the body. She was wearing nothing but a polyester cotton T-shirt, extra small." Svante clicked the mouse and a picture was projected onto the screen.

An item of clothing for a child, Irene thought. But when she looked more closely, she saw that perhaps this wasn't the case. The short-sleeved top was pink, with the word SEX in big letters on the front. The neckline was very wide. Given how thin the victim had been, the top would probably have slipped down over at least one shoulder. Definitely a summer top, in Irene's opinion. She also noticed that it was dirty.

The next picture showed a pair of black skinny jeans. Once again Irene felt a stab of distaste. Children's jeans. They couldn't be any bigger than size 130.

"They've been taken in," Svante explained, pointing to the drainpipe legs. He turned back to his audience and went on. "The jeans are brand new. No semen stains."

Another picture. A pair of black boots, badly scuffed and with worn-down high heels.

"Cheap. Synthetic. Size thirty-five. Although the girl's feet were smaller; there was balled-up paper shoved into the toes. Probably bought secondhand, according to our expert. That's Emilia; she says the style is from the late nineties. No socks or tights. Presumably the girl was barefoot inside her boots."

Everyone in the room knew that Emilia was the new forensic technician at police HQ in Göteborg. She had spent many years working at SKL, the National Forensics Laboratory in Linköping, but had moved to Göteborg with her husband when he got a job at Chalmers University of Technology. She had already made an impact with her knowledge and skill, and her excellent contacts with SKL were a major advantage.

"She wasn't wearing a bra. Or at least we didn't find one. She didn't really need one either. However, we did find a G-string. Nylon."

The picture showed a few twisted bits of fabric that were supposed to represent a pair of panties.

"We also found a padded jacket, small. Far from new."

The picture showed a short pink jacket with deep knitted bands around the sleeves and waist. The band around the right sleeve was frayed and worn. The jacket was in desperate need of a wash.

"On the outside of the jacket we found a total of seven semen stains, all on the upper section at the front. This semen comes from two different men, but these stains are older than the ones on the T-shirt. At least a week old."

Irene felt an irrational sense of relief. The girl hadn't been dealing with three men at the same time. The killer had probably been alone.

"So you didn't find anything at all on the jeans?" Birgitta asked.

"No. As I said, they're brand new. There was a considerable amount of secreted matter in the crotch, but no traces of semen."

"According to Stridner, the girl had some horrible infection that stank. Presumably the johns wore condoms," Jonny said.

Svante nodded. "No doubt. But at the same time, I have a feeling that . . ." He fell silent and clicked through to the next picture, which was also the last. "Her jewelry. Very cheap. Almost the kind of thing kids get when they buy gum from a machine."

The screen showed a necklace with matching earrings in the form of small plastic flowers, and three rings with colored plastic stones. They probably constituted the girl's entire assets.

"What were you going to say just now? You said you had a feeling that . . . what?" Birgitta wondered.

Svante remained silent for a moment before he answered. "Given where we found the stains . . . I think we're looking at oral sex here. But she wasn't suffocated; she was strangled. We should find out more on that point when they've done the autopsy."

"Aren't we supposed to hear the results this afternoon?" Jonny pointed out.

Superintendent Andersson cleared his throat to indicate that he was about to speak. "I called them yesterday afternoon. The autopsy won't be finished today, but they have promised us a preliminary report on Monday afternoon. We'll also have a preliminary report on Torleif then," he informed them.

"How goddamn difficult can it be to work out what he died of?" Jonny muttered.

Andersson glared at him, but said nothing. Instead he turned back to Svante. "Do we know where the clothes were bought?"

"No. The jacket and boots are probably second hand. Possibly the T-shirt as well. The only thing we can say for sure is that the jeans were bought in Sweden, at JC. They're actually JC's own brand, Crocker. That's coming from Emilia again; her children buy that particular brand."

The superintendent pointed at Birgitta and said, "Check with every JC store in Göteborg and the surrounding area."

Irene bit her lower lip to stop herself from objecting. She hadn't yet had the chance to tell Birgitta that they would be sitting in on the interviews with Heinz Becker and the girls from the brothel.

"Needless to say we have also secured a large number of fibers and particles from her clothes. The only items of interest at the moment are some dark blue nylon fibers, approximately one centimeter in length, which we found on her T-shirt, mostly on the back. She has been lying on something fluffy, perhaps a fleece blanket, or an article of clothing made of fleece."

Those were Svante's final words. He closed his laptop and made for the door. As he was passing Irene, he asked, "How's the arm?"

"Fine," she reassured him.

It was still sore, but nothing to complain about. He gave her a consoling pat on the damp spot and smiled encouragingly as he left the room. In spite of the fact that it had been a very gentle pat, it had really hurt. She had to make an effort not to snatch her arm away and grimace from the pain.

Irene informed the team about the trafficking unit's planned raid on the apartment where Heinz Becker had established his temporary brothel. She also took the opportunity to mention Linda Holm's offer to allow the two female officers from Violent Crimes to sit in on the interviews that afternoon.

"That might be a good idea," Andersson said. "If nothing else, it could be an angle worth pursuing. But I want you to check out those JC stores first."

He turned to Hannu. "Any leads on those hoodlums who ran down Torleif?"

"There's a rumor that Daniel Lindgren was seen in Frölunda Square last Wednesday night. Our colleagues in Frölunda are keeping his mother's apartment under surveillance. No trace of the other two. We've sent out another call for Niklas Ström, Daniel Lindgren and Billy Kjellgren in every district in Västra Götaland, and at the same time we're looking into a number of other possibilities. Nothing so far," Hannu replied.

Andersson nodded. "There are five witnesses who saw the BMW driving up Töpelsgatan after it hit Torleif Sandberg. Two of the witnesses are certain there were only two people in the car. We've also had two reports of another car being driven somewhat erratically earlier that evening. Both witnesses live on Töpelsgatan. One saw the car from his window; the other was out walking his dog. They are unsure of the exact time, but both say it was around twenty thirty. The man with the dog thinks it was about twenty thirty-five. The car was traveling along Töpelsgatan at high speed. That's all the witness at the window saw. The dog owner claims that his dog was almost run over because they were about to cross the street. He shook his fist at the car, but it simply disappeared around the bend without slowing down. The witness claims there was a man and a woman in the car. I spoke to him yesterday, and he described the woman as dark haired and dressed in some kind of dark clothing. He didn't have time to get a closer look at her appearance, but he thought she was an adult rather than a child or a teenager. The man has cropped dark hair, possibly thinning on top, and he was wearing glasses. He was gesticu-lating and talking to the woman. The witness thought he looked extremely agitated. The car was a dark-colored Volvo S80, probably black or dark blue."

Andersson paused, frowning as he decided on the next step. "We'll inform the media that we're looking for the car," he said eventually. "It was in the area at around the time the girl was murdered. If nothing else, the people in the car might have seen something."

An hour before the boys in the stolen BMW had raced up the hill with a broken windshield, the dark Volvo had fol-lowed the same route at high speed. Neither the man nor the woman had contacted the police, in spite of the fact that everyone who had been in the area had been asked to do so. The relevant times had been publicized in the press. The couple in the Volvo probably had nothing to do with the murder, but it was still strange they hadn't come forward. Or perhaps they didn't want to? Were they involved in the murder after all? Irene considered various possibilities but had to give up in the end.

Fredrik Stridh spoke up. "I've had a tip about who our body

up at Brudarmossen might be," he said with an unmistakable hint of triumph in his voice.

"Who?" Andersson asked abruptly.

"I've been going through all males over the age of sixty who have gone missing in the Göteborg area during the past twelve months. Most of them have been found, but three are still unaccounted for. We can eliminate one right away because he has only one finger and the thumb on his left hand. Our body has all its digits intact. We can eliminate another because he disappeared in Majorca, and there's nothing to indicate he returned to Sweden. So that leaves just one possibility."

He looked down at his notepad and began to read aloud: "Ingvar Olsson, aged seventy-one. Reported missing in December by the property company he rented his apartment from. His last rental payment was made at the end of August, which means he disappeared during September. Olsson was a retired seaman. He lived in a one-room apartment in Kortedala, having been allowed to take over the lease after the death of his brother. There were no other living relatives, so Olsson inherited the whole thing. His brother didn't own only this apartment; he had also taken over a holiday cottage that used to belong to their parents. And guess where that cottage was?"

"Elementary. Delsjö holiday village," Birgitta answered at once.

"Exactly! As children the brothers used to run around in Delsjö during their summer vacation. Ingvar must have known the area like the back of his hand."

"Did he still own the cottage?" Birgitta asked.

"No. He sold it a few years ago. I presume old seamen don't have a financial cushion worth millions when they come ashore, and he drank pretty heavily. He was picked up several times for public intoxication over the years. And . . ." Fredrik paused dramatically, keeping his colleagues on tenterhooks for a little while. "When we moved the body, we found a rucksack that he'd been using to support his back. There was a plastic bag inside with the remains of some rotten fruit and a box of moldy sandwiches. On the ground beside him we found an almost empty bottle of Special Schnapps, and an empty bottle that had contained some kind of sleeping pills. Let me see, what were they called?" He broke off to check through his notes. "Mogadon. We don't know how many he took."

"Suicide," Andersson stated.

"It looks that way. Everything points to suicide, but we'll have to wait for the results of the autopsy before we close down the investigation."

"Good, let's do that. In the meantime you can help Irene and Birgitta to check out the JC stores. If you don't get anywhere today, contact JC headquarters in Göteborg and ask them to send out a message to all their staff. The person who sold those jeans to the girl could be off work today. Jonny and Hannu, carry on looking for the guys who killed Torleif. Tommy and I will take the witnesses from Töpelsgatan on the night of the murder. Some bastard must have seen something that can be linked to the murder. And I'd like to speak to the couple in the Volvo."

THEY GOT LUCKY with the JC store on Backaplan. The assistant clearly recalled an odd pair who had bought a pair of black Crocker jeans the previous weekend.

"I remember them because she was wearing like a short denim skirt and this really ugly pink padded jacket. Her boots must have been like a hundred years old, and she didn't have anything on her legs. I thought that was weird because it was like minus ten outside! And then her dad wanted us to take in the pant legs so she could tuck them into her boots. But this was like Saturday, so I said we couldn't do it right away, and he got real mad," the youthful voice said on the phone.

"Did he speak Swedish?" Birgitta asked.

"No, English. Like, really badly."

"And did the girl speak English, too?"

"No, she didn't say anything. She just like nodded when the old man said something to her."

"Did you recognize what language he spoke to her?"

"Not really . . . it kind of sounded like Finnish."

Estonian sounds very similar to Finnish to someone who doesn't speak either language. Birgitta was pretty sure she had found the right JC store. She asked the assistant to hang on.

"Irene. I think I've got the right store, but I need to go over to the Trafficking Unit to ask Linda Holm if she's got a photo of Heinz Becker. I also need a picture of the girl, then I'll go over to Backaplan to question the assistant and see if she recognizes either of them."

"Fantastic," Irene said, crossing out the last number she had called, although it would be premature to scrap the list of JC stores, just in case the assistant in Backaplan didn't recognize Becker or the girl.

"I'll go and see Linda and you work on a picture of the girl. The sketch we're releasing to the press should be ready by now," Irene said.

"If not I'll have to take the photo from the morgue. She looks peaceful. No injuries to her face," Birgitta mused.

Not to her face, Irene thought with a shudder.

WHEN IRENE REACHED Linda Holm's office, the superintendent was once again wrestling with her cardigan. This time she was trying to put it on while talking on the phone.

"Okay. I'm leaving right away."

She hung up and said hi to Irene, who quickly asked if there was a photo of Heinz Becker they could have. Linda Holm opened the top drawer and passed her an enlarged printout.

"There you go. A nice fresh passport photo. Taken three months ago."

Heinz Becker's eyes were narrow slits in his fleshy face. His hairline had crept up toward the top of his head, and he had slicked back the thin, greying hair and fastened it in a ponytail. At some point during his life he had broken his nose and failed to get it reset, judging by the fact that his potato nose bent to the right. He looked at least ten years older than he actually was.

"Jesus! Talk about looking like a criminal!"

"Absolutely. Listen, do you want to come with us on the raid? I'm leaving now; we're going in in just under an hour."

Irene thought fast. Birgitta could handle the interview with the store assistant; it hardly required two of them. If they could find proof that the girl lying in the morgue had been in the apartment before she died, it would save them a huge amount of time.

"Yes please. Can I bring Fredrik Stridh?"

"Sure, no problem."

Irene hurried back and gave Birgitta the picture of Heinz Becker, then asked Fredrik if he wanted to accompany her on the raid.

"Definitely," he said.

His face lit up at the prospect of getting out into the field for a while. Like Irene he loathed paperwork. He radiated a boyish happiness and energy that could easily be misinterpreted as childishness. Nothing could have been further from the truth. Irene had learned to appreciate his good humor and easy manner, and she valued his enthusiasm for his work even more. Fredrik still thought he had the best job in the world. For her part, Irene wasn't always quite so sure about that.

Chapter 9

BISKOPSGÅRDEN HAS NEVER won any prizes for its beautiful architecture or stimulating environment. Some of the older tower blocks from the late 1950s have had a minor facelift, but for the most part the buildings are just standing there slowly disintegrating. The rent money still comes in because Swedish workers and immigrants need somewhere to live now that formerly working-class blocks like Majorna, Landala and Haga have been renovated.

The eight-story, concrete-block building looked just like its neighbors. The only difference was that parts of the roof were covered with tarpaulins because there had been a fire in the attic. The building company's truck was parked outside one of the main doors. It was dark blue, with MT BYGG in white letters on the side. Both the building and the yard looked deserted. The silence was broken only by the sound of the builders working away on the roof. There were a few swings and a snow-covered sandpit in the yard, but no children playing out in the snow. Presumably it was too cold. Snow had begun falling again, and was getting heavier by the minute.

Linda Holm parked the unmarked police car in a lot that gave them a good view of the front of the building, although the increasing snowfall made it difficult to see clearly. After only a short while it was almost impossible to make out the letters on the side of the truck.

"The entrance where the truck is parked. Number thirty-three.

Fourth floor," Linda said to her colleagues in the back seat without turning her head.

Irene leaned forward cautiously and peered up at the apartment. She could see nothing but the whirling snow.

"It's a two-room apartment. The tenant has been away for a week or so, but we're trying to locate him. We are interested to find out how Heinz Becker gained access to the apartment, of course. But it's probably no coincidence that the guy who lives here chose to go away now, just when Heinz needed to borrow a place to set up his temporary brothel," Linda Holm said.

"Is that what usually happens?" Irene asked.

"We've come across it a few times. It's hard to prove who's given the pimps access to an apartment. The tenant who's gone away always professes total ignorance," Linda replied.

The door of number 33 opened and two men emerged. They were carrying a large black plastic sack between them. Hunched against the snow, they hurried over to the truck and unlocked the back door. They threw the sack inside, closed the door and quickly moved around to the cab. A few seconds later the engine roared into life. The truck jerked forward, then drove off.

Superintendent Holm took her cell phone out of her pocket and answered it. Irene hadn't heard a ringtone, and realized it must have been set to vibrate. Linda Holm made noises of agreement, then said, "Five minutes!"

She ended the call. A few minutes later the armed response unit's van slipped quietly into the yard and parked in the spot vacated by the truck.

No one in the car spoke; they were watching the numbers on the clock on Linda's cell slowly change. When exactly five minutes had passed, Linda Holm opened the car door. They didn't run, but moved quickly toward the apartment block. From a car a short distance away, two officers from the trafficking unit emerged: a man and a woman.

"The elevator and the stairs," the superintendent said when the two groups reached the main entrance at the same time.

One of the officers from the trafficking unit opened the heavy door. The pane of glass in the upper half was broken and had been replaced with a sheet of plywood. The whole thing was covered in black and blue spray paint.

Three officers ran up the stairs, and the others took the lift. One member of the armed response team was stationed by the door, while Irene ended up in the group that was detailed to block the stairs as an escape route.

She had to hurry to keep up with the other two, who had raced up the stairs. When they reached the second floor they heard a crash that reverberated through the entire stairwell. The sound of rapid footsteps indicated that the police had gained entry, but when Irene reached the fourth floor, more than a little out of breath, she was met by the grim-faced chief of the armed response unit.

"Empty. They got away," he said.

"The truck!" Irene exclaimed.

The others looked at her inquiringly.

"The one that was parked outside. It drove off just before you got here."

"We'll put out a call for it right away," the chief said. "Stensson! Get up to the top floor and ask the builders if any of their pals have just driven off in their truck. If not, get the license plate."

The officer who answered to the name of Stensson scurried out of the apartment and headed toward the elevator. A minute or so later his voice came over the radio, "None of the builders has driven off in their truck. They're furious, I can tell you. The number is . . ."

Irene didn't hear the rest; she had already started examining the apartment.

The first thing she noticed was the smell. The air was thick with cigarette smoke, but it didn't completely camouflage the oily, sweet smell of cannabis. There was also the distinct aroma of unwashed human bodies.

"CSI will be here any minute," Linda called from another room.

Irene slipped on plastic shoe covers and took out the latex gloves she had in her pocket. Then she opened a door she correctly guessed led to a bathroom and switched on the light.

The bathroom was small, and the stench was nauseating. On the floor lay a sheet that looked as if it had been used as a towel. It was stained and would no doubt give forensics plenty to work with. Some of the stains looked like blood. On the edge of the bath stood a large bottle of all-in-one shower gel and shampoo. Above the sink was a half-open mirrored cabinet. Irene gently pulled the door open. On the top shelf lay a pack of condoms, a comb, a brush and an almost empty bottle of mouthwash. At the bottom of the cabinet she could see a used syringe, with a small amount of liquid mixed with blood remaining in the needle hub. Amphetamine, Irene guessed.

"This place stinks!" Fredrik stated from the doorway.

Irene pointed to the syringe, and Fredrik nodded.

"We've found some packets of powder in the kitchen. Whoever was using this place seems to have taken off in a hurry. They've left drugs and condoms behind, and there's a box of something that looks like Viagra in the middle of the table. But so far we haven't found any passports or other papers."

Irene went into the hallway. A bare bulb was hanging from the ceiling, spreading a cold light over the officers below.

"We'll take a closer look at the apartment when CSI has finished," Linda Holm said.

Fredrik opened a closet door and peered inside. He was about to shut the door when he stopped. Irene watched as he bent down and shone his flashlight inside.

"Irene!" he said quietly.

She went across and looked over his shoulder.

Heaped on the floor of the closet was a small denim skirt.

"Do you think it's hers?" Fredrik asked, with suppressed excitement in his voice.

"I think there's a good chance," Irene said, her heart beating faster.

The girl who had bought black jeans at JC six days ago had been wearing a denim skirt, according to the assistant, and she had been bare-legged in spite of the cold. They had every reason to be optimistic about the skirt.

"If it is hers, then we're a lot closer to establishing her identity. That means we know she's been in this apartment and that Heinz Becker must know who she is and where she came from," Irene said.

She and Fredrik went into the bedroom. It was dark and gloomy; the closed blinds let in very little light. There were no pictures, rugs or curtains. The institutional grey carpet was stained and worn. The room contained a double bed with dirty sheets and two pillows, but no quilt or comforter. A waste bin stood by the bed, and a quick glance revealed that it was full of toilet paper and used condoms. The stench of human excretions was beyond obtrusive. On the two rickety bedside tables there were toilet paper rolls and an old, chipped bowl. At first glance the bowl appeared empty, but then they noticed some oval-shaped blue pills at the bottom.

"Are they popping Viagra like candy, or what?" Fredrik asked, shaking his head.

"I don't know how they dare. There could be all kinds of crap in those pills. I expect they buy them over the Internet," the chief of the armed response unit said as he came into the room. He looked around and wrinkled his nose. "We're leaving now. It's a little strange that they managed to take off right in front of you guys," he said with a teasing smile.

Neither Irene nor Fredrik bothered to tell him they weren't part of the trafficking unit. However, they had to admit that he was right: it was very strange that Heinz Becker and his sidekick had managed to disappear along with the girls. How could they know there was going to be a raid? And how had they managed to get the keys to start up the truck?

The officers went into what would normally serve as the living room, but which was currently being used as some kind of primitive dormitory. A shabby sofa and armchair had been pushed into one corner, along with some other pieces of furniture and lamps. There were two mattresses on the floor, surrounded by the same equipment as in the bedroom: toilet paper rolls, condoms and a plastic box containing more blue pills.

It looked as if the kitchen had been the pimps' domain. Along one wall there was a camp bed with a pillow and quilt. They had put the kitchen table in the middle of the floor, with a big television on top of it next to the large box of Viagra—at least that was what it said on the side of the box in blue writing. Every seat was littered with empty pizza boxes and booze bottles. A used syringe lay in the sink. The stench was revolting.

"CSI will be here any minute. We're going back to HQ," Linda Holm said, poking her head through the doorway.

"I don't suppose there's much else we can do here," Irene agreed.

"No." The superintendent didn't even try to hide the disappointment in her voice. "I just don't understand how they knew we were coming."

Fredrik looked at her pensively. When they reached the top of the stairs, he suddenly said, "I'm going to stay for a while. There's something I want to check."

Linda Holm merely nodded. She didn't really seem to have grasped what Fredrik said. She was lost in her own thoughts.

• • •

LINDA DIDN'T SAY a word as they drove back into town. In order to break the silence, Irene asked, "How did you find out where Heinz Becker was?"

"He advertised his cell number on the Internet," Linda replied.

"So one of the guys from your team called him?"

"Yes."

"And how long have you been watching the apartment?"

"Two and a half days. It takes a little while to sort out a search warrant; we have to keep the place under surveillance first, and show that we have grounds for suspicion. But we have a good working relationship with the prosecutor's office, and in this case there was no doubt. There was a constant stream of different men going in and out of the apartment."

"Do you think someone warned them so that they had time to get away?" Irene asked.

"That's the only possible explanation. They left behind valuable narcotics and aphrodisiacs. They would have taken all that with them if they'd been moving out under normal circumstances, but this makes it look like they panicked and took off. Someone tipped them off." Linda Holm's tone of voice and grim expression made it clear that if the person responsible was ever unmasked, there would be no mercy.

"How did they manage to get the truck started? I know the snow made it difficult for us to see, but it looked to me like they unlocked the back door before they threw the sack inside, and—"

"The sack!" Linda Holm interrupted Irene and slammed the steering wheel with the palm of her hand. "The girl was in the sack! Of course!"

She was gripping the wheel so tightly her knuckles had gone white. She was staring straight ahead. In spite of the fact that the windshield wipers were working at top speed, it was difficult to see out. The snowfall had turned into a blizzard.

"So they've only got one girl left," she murmured.

Irene had the distinct feeling that the superintendent was talking to herself, so she didn't say anything. The situation was probably as Linda thought: one girl was in a plastic sack in the back of a truck somewhere, and the other was lying in the refrigerator in the morgue.

"Sorry, I interrupted you. What were you saying about the truck?" Linda asked. She glanced briefly at Irene, hardly daring to take her eyes off the road for a second.

"I said it looked to me like they unlocked the back door with a key. That's what fooled me. I assumed that if they had the key, they must be builders, and . . ." Irene stopped. Suddenly she understood what Fredrik had realized.

"How did they get hold of the key?" Linda asked.

"Something tells me that's what Fredrik is trying to find out right now."

In silence they pulled into the parking lot at police HQ.

THE TRUCK WAS found an hour later, hidden behind a warehouse on the island of Ringön. A telecommunications engineer who had been working on an electrical box less than a hundred meters from the storage facility reported seeing a dark-colored station wagon, probably a Passat, stop outside. Two men and a young woman had come hurrying around from the back of the building and jumped into the Passat. It had been snowing too heavily for him to be able to give any kind of description or to see the car's license plate, but he had noticed that one of the men was tall and well-built.

"Heinz Becker," Linda Holm said gloomily.

She and Irene had grabbed a quick lunch and were now sipping coffees from the machine in the superintendent's office. The phone rang constantly, but there were nothing but negative reports. It was as if the pimps and the girl had been swallowed up by the snowstorm.

"The airports and ferry terminals have been alerted. How do you think they'll try to get out of the country?" Irene asked.

"They'll probably head south. From Skåne they can take a ferry to Estonia or Poland or Germany. Or Denmark. Then they can just carry on down through Europe. It seems like they took their passports; we didn't find any in the apartment."

"Then again, Skåne in a snowstorm is no joke."

"True. Perhaps they're lying low and waiting for a while, at least until it stops snowing."

Irene looked out of the window. The storm was raging with undiminished strength. "It looks like we're going to get snowed in here—even worse than usual," she said, smiling at Linda.

"Hi, there! We got it!" she heard from the doorway as Birgitta came in, waving the picture of Heinz Becker. "He's the guy who was at the JC store on Saturday. With our girl."

She took a folded piece of paper out of the pocket of her jeans and opened it out. She dropped it on the desk next to the picture of the pimp, grinning broadly. Irene looked at the photograph of Becker's fleshy face, which contrasted sharply with the sketch of the girl's thin features.

Birgitta's smile faded when she saw the expression on the faces of her colleagues. "What? We've got proof that the girl was part of Becker's operation, so all we have to do now is confront him with the evidence during questioning and . . . Has something happened?"

"You could say that," Linda sighed. She quickly explained what had happened during the raid out in Biskopsgården.

Birgitta remained silent for a while, then said, "Well, when we do bring them in, we've got proof that he and his associate had the girl in their power. We'll say they're wanted for homicide! I mean, until we've questioned them we don't know whether they were the ones who killed her, or whether it was a client."

"Already done," the superintendent said quietly.

Irene got to her feet. "We'll go back to our own department," she said. "But we'll be in touch if something comes up."

Linda Holm nodded and twisted her mouth into something
resembling a smile. She obviously regarded Becker and his
sidekick's escape as a personal failure. Perhaps she was particularly embarrassed because her colleagues from Violent Crimes
had been there to see her humiliation.

When Irene and Birgitta reached the corridor leading to
their offices, they saw Fredrik coming toward them, looking
very pleased with himself.

"Were you right?" Irene asked.

"Yes!"

"How many of them are there altogether?"

"Four."

"Who?"

He raised his eyebrows and looked meaningfully at his
female colleagues before replying. "All of them. Or so it
seems."

Irene nodded.

"Could you stop speaking in code and tell me what this is
all about?" Birgitta snapped.

"Okay. Let's go into my office," Fredrik said, chivalrously
holding open the door.

The women took the two chairs while Fredrik remained
standing.

"Both Irene and I saw the two guys come out of the apartment block carrying a black sack between them. One of them
got out a key and unlocked the back door of the truck so that
they could stow a sack inside, then he unlocked the driver's
cab. Then they started the engine and took off with a screech
of tires. Which is why we all assumed they were builders.
When we realized they'd gotten away by using the truck, the
question was how they'd gotten a hold of the key, of course."

"Right. So how did they?" Birgitta asked.

Fredrik couldn't hide his satisfaction as he explained, "I went up to the top floor where the builders were working. It was freezing cold and snowing hard. It's not easy to fix up tarpaulins in a snowstorm, let me tell you! They were uneasy when I turned up and introduced myself. None of them were particularly keen on talking to me, but I insisted. Told them I'd be happy to give them a lift down to HQ if they'd prefer. They were even less keen on that idea!"

He grinned happily at the memory.

"Then I spoke to them one by one, starting with the foreman. It turns out they've been working up there for four days. The fire was on Sunday night/Monday morning. At first he denied all knowledge of the brothel on the fourth floor, but at the same time he couldn't explain where the key to the truck had gone. He tried to tell me he must have dropped it, or someone had stolen it out of his pocket. That didn't get him very far, because there's no changing room up there. They go and sit on the stairs when they need to warm up a bit. They're warmly dressed in plenty of clothes while they're working, but they keep their work clothes on all day. Eventually he'd tied himself in so many knots with his lies that there was no way out. I threatened him with formal questioning down here, and he folded. He'd visited the brothel during the morning, and he reckoned that either Heinz or the other guy must have taken the key out of his pocket while he was having sex with the girl."

There was silence in the room while all three of them thought through the scenario.

"But you don't believe him," Irene said eventually.

"No. I spoke to the other three as well. When I asked them if they'd been down to the fourth floor, they became incredibly nervous. It was obvious that they all knew what was going on there. They came up with a range of answers: "I was just kind of curious," "All the others were going," and "I've never done anything like that before"—a whole load of crap! Two of them are married and one lives with his partner. The fourth is engaged, but doesn't live with his fiancée. He's the youngest. They're all shit-scared the fact they've been to a brothel will come out."

"I can't believe they didn't just deny it!" Birgitta exclaimed.

Fredrik smiled mischievously. "I have to admit that I went for the man-to-man option. Just guys talking. Lulled them into a false sense of security. They told me in confidence, so to speak."

"We definitely need to bring in the foreman, the one who admitted he'd had sex with the girl this morning," Irene said firmly.

"I promised he wouldn't have to come here . . ." Fredrik began, but Irene interrupted him.

"We have to question him, and the other three! They can give us a description of the girl. One of them might know which country she's from. They're witnesses to the fact that Becker and his associate were in the apartment at the same time."

"Okay. I'll make sure they're all brought in," Fredrik said.

"Thanks. We have to make them realize the pimps could be killers. We're investigating a homicide here; we're not interested in any crimes involving prostitution that they might have committed."

"So the foreman is married," Birgitta said.

"Yes," Fredrik replied. He moved toward the door. "I'll go back out to Biskopsgården with a patrol," he said. "That'll be the quickest way."

"Just make sure you don't get stuck in the snow," Irene said before she could stop herself. *As if Fredrik needs a mother*, she thought crossly, although he didn't seem to mind.

"There's always that risk, but I think it's letting up a little."

A quick glance out of the window showed he was right. The

storm had abated, and was now a pretty normal snowfall. Perhaps they might even stand a chance of getting home later in
the evening. *If the snow plows would just get going* . . . Irene's
thoughts were interrupted by the sound of Fredrik's phone
ringing. He was already in the doorway but turned back to his
desk to answer.

"Fredrik Stridh . . . Yes, that's right . . . A Toyota, you say?"
He stood in silence for quite some time, listening to the voice
on the other end of the line. He stiffened and eventually
exclaimed, "Both of them! But she made it . . . okay . . ."

He started to relay the information before he had even put
down the receiver. "Things are starting to happen! That was the
Varberg police. A white Toyota, which turns out to have been
stolen in Heden here in Göteborg less than two hours ago, came
off the road just north of Varberg an hour ago. There were three
people in the car who matched the descriptions we sent out.
The vehicle overturned and went down a slope. Both men were
pronounced dead on arrival at the hospital. The young woman
is very badly injured and in a coma. Serious concussion. She's
being operated on right now for a damaged spleen. She also has
a fractured pelvis and spine and God knows what else. Her condition is described as extremely critical."

Both Birgitta and Irene were lost for words at first, but eventually Irene managed to pull herself together. "That's just . . .
suddenly everything's happening at once!" she burst out.

"To say the least," Birgitta murmured.

Fredrik sank down to his chair, considering the next step.
"What do we do now? Do you still want me to go out to Biskopsgården to question the builders again?" he asked.

"Absolutely!" Irene answered immediately. "It's essential
that we establish the connection between Heinz Becker and
the girl who's lying in a coma. And you might even be able to
get one of them to admit that he's seen the girl from the root
cellar in the apartment. That would confirm that link, too."

"Particularly as Heinz Becker is dead, so we're not going to get a confession from him," Birgitta commented dryly.

"I'll let Sven know what's going on. There's no point in driving over to Varberg in this weather. The girl will probably be unconscious for quite some time, and then she'll need to get her strength back before we can question her. And we need to know what language she speaks so that we can arrange an interpreter," Irene said.

"Sounds good to me," Birgitta agreed. "I'll go and write up my report on the positive ID from the assistant in the JC store. It's a strong link between Becker and the dead girl."

"And if there's DNA on the denim skirt we found in the apartment, that will also provide solid evidence that she was there," Fredrik pointed out.

"Exactly. Even if Linda Holm wasn't too happy about the way things turned out from the Trafficking Unit's point of view, I have to say that we've made quite a lot of progress in the investigation into the girl's death. We're significantly closer to identifying her than we were this morning, and possibly her killer as well. We can take DNA samples from Becker and his associate and compare them with the semen we found in her hair," Irene said.

"Do you think it was one of them?" Birgitta asked skeptically.

"Not really. We can't ignore the possibility, although to be honest I don't think either of them killed her."

"Why not?"

"The place where she was found. How would Heinz Becker and his sidekick know about an old, hidden root cellar? It would have been much easier for them to dump her in a ditch by the side of some road. Or in the forest somewhere. The root cellar required local knowledge, which I don't believe Becker or his companion had."

"So we're still looking for the perpetrator," Birgitta concluded.

Chapter 10

IRENE HAD A free weekend, so she devoted Saturday morning to two intensive training sessions in the dojo. During the first one she had been the trainer for a group of female police officers. Several of them had started working toward their blue belt. They were keen and had worked hard. Irene was very proud of them. The second group was mixed, but was mostly made up of male participants. A spar against Irene was always popular, as she was a former European champion. It might have been more than twenty years ago, but she still had the moves.

IRENE SPENT THE rest of Saturday shoveling piles of snow outside the house and trying to reduce the piles of laundry inside. The washing machine was working overtime. It was a mystery: how could four people produce so much dirty laundry? Strangely enough, Irene thought the mountain of washing was growing as the girls got older. *We don't wear our clothes out any more; we wash them to death,* she thought. But she didn't say anything because both girls were busy cleaning the house. It was time for the monthly "Huss attack." Irene had introduced the idea several years ago, and it worked very well. Once a month the whole family pitched in and helped clean the house. Krister had been excused this time because he had done more or less all of the pre-Christmas housework himself; he had even put up Christmas curtains in the kitchen. If he hadn't, it wouldn't have happened. Curtains just weren't Irene's thing, as the twins would have put it. In any case, Krister was working this weekend, and wouldn't be home until midnight.

It was high time that Sammie had a haircut, but it was far too cold outside. It was best to let him keep his long coat for a while. By March he would look like a mountain sheep if she didn't get him to the dog groomer before then. Not that he cared. He loathed everything to do with grooming, and had throughout his entire twelve years of life. It's not for nothing that the breed is called an Irish soft-coated wheaten terrier. It was a perfect description of Sammie. He had glorious curly hair and didn't molt, but he did need to be carefully brushed and regularly clipped. And this coat that demanded so much attention was on a terrier! Irene had often wondered how anyone came up with the idea of breeding such a creature.

She just had to groom him, otherwise his coat would get too knotted to deal with. She lifted him onto the table in the utility room. He realized what was about to happen and immediately started acting up, turning around and around in circles on the table with his tail down. *It was like trying to shoe a galloping horse*, as Irene's mother used to say. Irene had had plenty of practice and knew exactly how to get hold of him. She took a gentle but firm grip on his neck and started to brush his soft fur. She kept the palm of her hand on his neck behind one ear while she brushed him with the other hand.

She could feel it very clearly under her fingers: a hard lump the size of a walnut. *It's just a cyst, nothing to worry about*, Irene immediately tried to convince herself. At the same time, she knew perfectly well what soft, fatty cysts felt like. They lay just beneath the skin and could easily be moved against the underlying musculature. This lump didn't move. She ran her fingers over Sammie's body. There was a lump almost as big in his right groin. And she found a third right in the middle of his throat, about the size of a hazelnut.

Irene went cold all over. She realized right away what this could mean. Sammie would be thirteen in April, which was a respectable age for a dog. If there's only one tumor, then it might be possible to remove it. But if the cancer has spread, the prognosis is not good. And she had found three lumps in different parts of his body.

Krister will have to take him to the vet on Monday, she thought. Her eyes filled with tears, and she could hardly see. *Let's not worry before we know what we're dealing with*, she told herself, trying hard to swallow. It was pointless; she had a huge lump in her throat.

Tenderly she held Sammie's head against her face, pressing her cheek to his. At first he was confused, but quickly realized she was upset. He gently butted her with his nose and gave her a little lick. Even if she wasn't in his good books at the moment—like anyone who attempted to groom him—she was still his beloved mistress.

SUNDAY MORNING DAWNED with a clear blue sky and not a breath of wind. Irene ambled slowly down to Fiskebäck marina with a sleepy Sammie. She was warmly dressed, and Sammie's thick fur protected him from the cold.

The view was stunning when they got down to the sea. She was dazzled by the sun sparkling on the virgin snow covering the ice. The extreme cold over the past few weeks meant that the waters off the Swedish coastline had frozen unusually early. If this carried on, it would soon be possible to drive out to the islands in the archipelago.

Irene let Sammie off the leash and he dashed ecstatically into the snow and started rolling around. He loved snow, and the cold didn't bother him at all. She was happy to let him run free for a little while; there were no other dogs in sight, and with his increasing age and deteriorating eyesight, he had become less inclined to run away. He came bounding toward

Irene, covered in snow. He looked so happy, the way only a terrier running free can do. There was no sign of old age or illness, but Irene realized with a stab of pain that they were there. It was only a matter of time.

SAMMIE FLOPPED DOWN on the rug in the living room when they got home, and within minutes he was snoring loudly. He hadn't even bothered to beg for a liver paste sandwich, in spite of the fact Krister was having his breakfast. Irene kissed her husband on the cheek. There was a pot of coffee on the table, and she poured herself a mug, filling it right to the brim. She buttered a roll and told Krister about Sammie's lumps.

"So I was thinking: you're not working tomorrow. Could you call the vet and book an appointment?"

"Sure. As you said, I'm not working."

Irene couldn't miss the bitter note in his voice, but she didn't understand what the problem was.

"Sorry, did you have other plans?" she asked.

He sighed loudly. "No. I'll contact Blue Star."

"Is that okay?" she asked uncertainly.

"It's fine."

He gave her a wan smile over the top of the morning paper. He had said it was okay, but Irene didn't think it sounded that way. She decided not to push it. No doubt she would find out what was wrong eventually. Perhaps Krister was just tired; the weekend shifts were long. Today he would finish at five and should be back just after six. Irene decided that she and the twins would surprise him with a delicious dinner; it would be on the table when he got home.

THE PHONE RANG at about four o'clock, and when Irene answered she heard Fredrik's cheerful voice trumpeting down the line.

"I think we might have found the Passat," he began, bursting with enthusiasm.

"What Passat?" she asked before she had time to think.

"The station wagon that picked up the late Heinz Becker and his equally late associate and the girl who's lying unconscious in Varberg hospital."

"Sorry. I mean . . ."

"A guy was picked up for drunk driving last night. He was driving a dark blue Passat station wagon, and he's a known villain: Anders Pettersson."

Irene knew all about Anders Pettersson. He was a big-time dealer, infamous for indiscriminately supplying narcotics to children and teenagers. He was unscrupulous and always demanded sexual favors from his young customers once he had them hooked. Some of them hadn't even lived long enough to become teenagers. Nor did he care if they were girls or boys. He had been arrested for sexual activity with a minor and drug-related offenses on a number of occasions, but often didn't get as far as court. It had never been possible to prove that he had threatened witnesses or his accusers, but those who might constitute a threat usually withdrew their accusations and witness statements. Pettersson was protected by a notorious gang of bikers, and for many years he had been their coordinator when it came to supplying the schools in Göteborg. The underage addicts didn't have a chance.

"So the bastard has been arrested for drunk driving?" Irene said.

"Yes. An armed response unit was on the way back to HQ when they saw a car weaving from lane to lane on Södra Vägen. They stopped the car; the driver was alone in the vehicle, and it was Pettersson. He was drunk out of his mind, slumped over the wheel. He was clutching his cell, and he just kept on repeating the same sentence. The officer in charge became interested when he finally worked out what he was slurring. It sounded like, 'Gotta call Heinz.' I wonder if you can guess who that officer was?"

"The guy who was involved in the raid at Biskopsgården," Irene ventured. It wasn't really a guess; it was sheer logic.

"Yes! His name is Lennart Lundstedt, by the way. Smart guy. He thought there couldn't be that many people called Heinz out there, so he confiscated Pettersson's cell. When he checked the last number called, it turned out to be Heinz Becker's, of course."

"The one listed on the Internet ad?"

"Yep. And as I'm on call this weekend, Lundstedt contacted me this morning. He'd had an idea. I did as he suggested, and I hit the jackpot!"

"What do you mean, you hit the jackpot?" Irene asked, feeling slightly irritated. At the same time, she could feel her interest rising.

"I got in touch with our colleagues in Varberg and asked them to get out Heinz Becker's cell. I called the number in Pettersson's cell, and guess which phone started to ring?"

"The one in Varberg," Irene answered obediently.

"That's right. And they found Pettersson's number in Becker's cell. We've got watertight proof of a connection between Becker and Pettersson!"

"Neat," Irene said with genuine admiration.

"The guys in Varberg also said they're searching for passports and anything else that might provide a clue to the identity of the girl and Becker's associate."

"But they haven't found anything?"

"Not yet. But they are looking. Apparently the car is a real mess; I presume it's difficult to find bags and so on."

"So we'll just have to be satisfied with the knowledge that there's a link between Becker and Pettersson."

"Satisfied! We've got a winning hand here! But we need to act fast. Like now!"

"Why the hurry?"

"Pettersson has been sleeping like the dead in the drunk tank all day. He had two point three mill of alcohol in his blood, but there's also a suspicion that he was under the influence of drugs."

"So what do you mean by a winning hand?" Irene wasn't usually slow, but right now she couldn't work out what her enthusiastic colleague was getting at.

"Pettersson doesn't know that Heinz Becker is dead."

It took a while for the significance of Fredrik's words to sink in. "You're right. We need to talk to him before he finds out," she said.

"I think it would be best if there were two of us."

"Absolutely. I'll be there in half an hour."

"Great. I'll get everything ready."

IRENE AND FREDRIK were already waiting in the interview room when Anders Pettersson was brought in by two well-built custody officers. According to the record, Pettersson was thirty-six, but he looked older. He had eyebrow piercings and was covered in tattoos, but that didn't help; he still looked older. It looked like several days had passed since he had shaved his head, and the stubble mercilessly exposed a well-developed bald patch. Once upon a time he had probably been pretty fit—after a long stretch in jail, perhaps—but now he was hauling around many surplus kilos. He looked like exactly what he was: a middle-aged villain who had had a hard life.

He slumped down opposite them, the chair groaning under his weight. He raised his hands in the air and waved them around demonstratively. "No shackles?" he asked hoarsely.

The comment triggered a wheezing fit of coughing that sounded as if it had its epicenter in the inferior lobes of his lungs. At the same time, a distinct smell of morning-after-breath spread through the interview room. Pettersson's puffy face was glistening with sweat, and his bloodshot eyes suggested that he wasn't feeling at all well.

"Not this time. We just want to ask you a few questions," Fredrik replied when the coughing had subsided. He introduced himself and Irene.

"What fucking questions? I want my lawyer here! I'm not saying a fucking—"

"Calm down. This isn't about you."

Pettersson looked at Fredrik in surprise. Slowly his drug-addled brain processed this information. "No?" was the only response he managed to come up with.

"No. This is about . . ."

Clumsily Pettersson started to get to his feet. "In that case I'm not fucking staying here."

"Sit down!" Fredrik bellowed.

"Why the fuck should I? If it's not about me, then—"

"This is about a murder."

Pettersson hesitated, his substantial posterior hovering above the chair. He stared at Fredrik, openmouthed. "What the fuck," he muttered, sinking feebly back onto his seat.

For a fraction of a second Irene was afraid that he might end up on the floor, but he landed safely. She took the opportunity to interject, "I can get you a cup of coffee if you'd like."

Pettersson attempted to focus his bloodshot eyes on her and grunted something. It seemed as if he was in dire need of something to stimulate his central nervous system.

"Milk? Sugar?" Irene asked.

"Sugar. Lots of sugar."

She got up and opened the door. With one hand she waved to the guard in the corridor. They had agreed on the signal beforehand, and he nodded and smiled conspiratorially before heading off toward the coffee machine.

"One with sugar, one with milk and one black," she called after his broad back.

She slid back into her seat as unobtrusively as possible, although it was completely unnecessary, as Pettersson's undivided attention was on Fredrik.

"What . . . what murder? I haven't—"

"We know," Fredrik broke in. "But you have a pal who is a prime suspect."

Pettersson tried to stare at him but failed. His eyeballs kept rolling around, reminding Irene of a slot machine; Pettersson's red eyes could easily serve as two cherries. Although you need three in a row to win the jackpot. All Pettersson was going to end up with was a humdinger of a hangover.

He glowered unsuccessfully at Fredrik until their coffee arrived. He didn't speak until the guard had left the room and closed the door.

"Who?"

Fredrik pretended not to hear the question. "What were you doing last Friday afternoon at approximately one thirty?"

Instead of answering, Pettersson attempted to sip his steaming coffee.

"Answer the question! Otherwise you will remain in custody for protecting a known criminal."

Pettersson merely shrugged.

"I'm sure you're not aware of this, but we put out a call for your car on Friday afternoon just after three o'clock. Every single police officer in Västra Götaland was looking for it, and you decided to drive drunk, and you got picked up by the armed response team."

Pettersson took a few small sips of his coffee; he didn't appear to be listening to Fredrik, but Irene could see the confused thoughts ricocheting around in his woolly head. She almost felt sorry for him.

"What the fuck," he mumbled eventually. "Why were you looking for my car?"

"A witness spotted your car when you picked up Heinz

Becker and the others on Ringön. In the same place where we found the truck they'd stolen. After the murder."

"What fucking murder?" he groaned.

"The murder of the little blonde girl Becker had with him. What was her name . . ."

Fredrik pretended to be searching his memory. Irene watched Pettersson, taking care not to reveal the tension she felt as she waited for his reaction. He had knitted his enormous pierced eyebrows. He seemed to be really trying to understand what Fredrik had just said.

"Has Heinz iced the little Russian?" He looked every bit as surprised as he sounded.

"Didn't you notice she was missing when you picked them up yesterday?" Fredrik asked quickly.

"Yeah . . . but Heinz said she'd already gone to Tenerife . . ."

"On her own?"

"No . . . no . . ."

"So who was with her?"

"Sergei," he replied with a weary sigh.

"What's his surname?"

Pettersson shook his round head.

"You don't know?"

"No . . . they just called him Sergei."

"So Sergei was supposed to have gone off to Tenerife with the blonde girl? Is that what Heinz said?"

"Yeah."

Irene had a strong feeling that Pettersson was telling the truth. She could understand why he didn't want to get dragged into Becker's dirty trade, given the nature of his own shady activities. However, it was obvious that they had worked together in some capacity since Becker had called on Pettersson in an emergency. What was their point of contact? Irene thought she knew, and decided to test her hypothesis.

"She didn't go to Tenerife with Sergei," she said calmly, placing the photograph of the dead girl in front of Pettersson.

He glanced distractedly at the picture, but gave a start when he saw who it was.

"You recognize her. Heinz supplied the girls and you supplied the drugs," Irene stated.

With a weary gesture Pettersson pushed the photograph away with one hand. He clenched the other hand and shook it under Fredrik's nose. "You're not going to fucking frame me for this! I want my lawyer! I've got nothing to do with that girl, you hear me?" he shouted.

Irene could almost hear the hangover starting to pound inside his head. "I can get you another coffee if you'd like one," she said in a friendly tone.

"Yes," he said, calming down slightly.

"I know you take sugar, but can I get you a Danish or a sandwich to go with it?"

"Danish," he decided after lengthy consideration.

She repeated the ordering process with the guard. Behind her she could hear Fredrik asking, "Do you remember the name of the Russian girl?"

"No . . . was it Tanya? Or Katya? It's no good, I can't remember," Pettersson said, slowly shaking his head.

"What about the other girl, then? What was her name?"

"No idea." The answer came quickly.

"Is she Russian too?"

"Don't know."

"You never heard her speaking to anyone, or anyone speaking to her?"

"No."

"But Tanya was Russian. You know that for sure," Fredrik pressed him.

Pettersson gave a short nod and clamped his lips together.

He had no intention of saying another word about the dead girl. At least they now knew she was Russian.

"So who's the other guy you picked up along with Heinz Becker?" Fredrik went on.

"Don't know."

"You've never seen him before?"

"Nope."

"And Heinz didn't mention his name in the car?"

"Nope."

There was a brief interruption as Pettersson's coffee and Danish arrived. He dipped the cinnamon whirl into the hot coffee, then devoured the soft pastry with a great deal of loud slurping. Revived by caffeine and fast carbs, he leaned back in his chair and folded his hands over his belly. *He looks as if he's ready for a nap*, Irene thought. *That's all we need.* But there was nothing to worry about; Fredrik intended to keep Pettersson awake for a while yet.

"How long have you and Heinz known each other?"

Pettersson stiffened. They could hear the wariness in his voice as he answered, "Not long . . . since last week."

"You've never had any contact in the past?"

"No."

He evidently had no intention of telling the truth. Both Irene and Fredrik knew that he was lying, but pushing him would get them nowhere. He was used to being questioned by the police, and knew when to lie and when to keep his mouth shut.

"Have you ever seen this Russian girl before . . . Tanya or Katya?"

"No."

"When did you see her for the first time?"

Pettersson remained silent for a long time, swirling the last of his coffee around in the bottom of the cup. Eventually he knocked it back and put down the cup with a firm gesture. "Saturday. Last Saturday . . ."

Fredrik looked down at the picture of the dead girl. "What was she like?" he asked abruptly.

"Do you want the details, you pervert?" Pettersson asked.

"You had sex with her," Fredrik stated.

Pettersson didn't answer; he just sat there grinning. Irene had to stop herself from slapping him across the face. "The girl was a minor," she said instead.

He still didn't answer, but the grin faded away. He yawned and said, "I've told you everything I know. And now I need to go and get some sleep." In order to further emphasize the truth of this assertion, he produced another jaw-cracking yawn.

Fredrik and Irene exchanged a quick glance and nodded at each other. They weren't going to get any more out of Pettersson. He had been unexpectedly talkative, which was probably due to the high level of alcohol still in his blood.

The custody officer escorted Pettersson back to his cell.

"I'll put in my report that Lennart Lundstedt realized that Anders Pettersson and Heinz Becker knew each other when Pettersson was babbling to himself on the way in. And that I took the opportunity to speak to Pettersson as I'm on call this weekend. The most important thing is the proof that Becker and Pettersson were in touch via their cell phones. And I'll put that he gave us some important information about the girl: she came from Russia, and her name was Tanya or Katya," Fredrik said.

"And that according to Pettersson, some guy called Sergei is involved."

"That should be enough to have him arrested."

"Pettersson isn't exactly the most reliable source I've encountered over the years, but he's all we've got right now. We'll have to go with what he's told us. I'll speak to Linda Holm tomorrow and find out if she knows this Sergei."

• • •

IRENE PARKED THE car in the lot back home at just after eight o'clock. Krister and the girls had made Sunday dinner. Irene had to heat up the leftovers in the microwave, as on so many occasions in the past.

Chapter 11

As usual Irene was out of breath as she dashed into the department, desperately hoping she would have time to grab a cup of coffee to bring to morning prayer. She hurtled around the corner at top speed and kicked open the door of her office, trying to wriggle out of her bulky winter coat at the same time. The young man waiting inside was very nearly smacked in the face by the door as it flew open. He looked just as surprised as Irene; she stopped dead in the doorway, staring at her unexpected visitor.

"Oh . . . sorry. I didn't know there was anyone in here," she eventually managed to stammer.

The man was between twenty-five and thirty, medium height, with thick dark brown hair and amber-colored eyes. He was stocky but looked as if he worked out. He was attractive, and she knew she'd never seen him before. A thick Canada Goose jacket was hanging neatly over the back of one of the visitor chairs. He was wearing sturdy boots, and the rest of his clothing—blue jeans and a dark blue sweater over a thin white cotton polo turtleneck—gave no clue to his identity. A faint aroma of a spicy aftershave hovered in the air.

Irene pulled herself together and held out her hand. "Good morning. Detective Inspector Irene Huss."

He took her hand in a firm grip and answered, "Morning. Stefan Sandberg."

Irene was taken aback. This must be Torleif Sandberg's son.

But there was no way this could be the little boy in the photo she had seen in Muesli's apartment. That little boy had been blond and fair skinned.

"I'm very sorry for your loss; your father's death was a real tragedy . . ." she began, but stopped when she saw the expression on his face.

"Thank you," he replied stiffly.

Tommy stuck his head around the door, "Morning! Are you joining us? We're starting . . . oh, you've got a visitor at this early hour! Or is this gentleman here to see me?"

Tommy came into the room, smiling at the unexpected visitor. Irene quickly made the introductions.

"If you're here about the investigation into your father's death, you really need to speak to DI Hannu Rauhala again; he's in charge of that particular inquiry," Irene informed Stefan Sandberg.

She still hadn't given up hope of that trip to the coffee machine.

"I know. But he's off sick today. The winter stomach bug, according to an older guy who I assume is some kind of chief around here. He sent me to you because I have something to report," he said, his expression serious.

"And what's that?" Irene asked. She had to make a real effort to hide her impatience.

"Torleif's car has been stolen."

Both Irene and Tommy were lost for words.

"Stolen?" Irene repeated eventually.

"Yes. The car has been stolen. It's not in his parking space."

All three of them jumped as the internal phone rang at that moment, and the superintendent's hoarse voice bellowed through the speaker. "Get yourselves in here right now!"

"Okay, okay!" Tommy called out.

Irene turned to Stefan. "As I'm sure you realize, we're short-staffed today. But we'd really like to talk to you. Would it be possible for you to come back after lunch, say around one o'clock or one thirty?"

"Sure, no problem," Stefan Sandberg said with a nod, picking up his jacket from the back of the chair.

"HANNU AND BIRGITTA are at home throwing up. The winter stomach bug has hit their kid's daycare facility," Superintendent Andersson informed his team by way of opening the new working week.

Several people looked anxious, and he hastened to reassure them. "Their little boy got sick on Friday, and Hannu and Birgitta yesterday. I called the health service information line and spoke to a nurse. There's a good chance we've escaped because this goddamn stomach bug strikes fast, and nobody else got sick over the weekend, so let's hope she's right."

In spite of this, Andersson looked worried.

"This is going to mean a significant workload increase for the rest of us because Hannu and Birgitta are unlikely to be back before the end of the week at the earliest. I've got a guy on loan from the main office; he's pretty new, but he can help Jonny with the search for the hit-and-run driver and his pal. Any luck yet?"

Andersson turned to Jonny Blom, who was slumped in his chair and looked half-asleep. Jonny gave a start and tried to sound alert. "Yes, absolutely! A patrol out in Tynnered saw Daniel Lindgren outside the house where his mother lives at around eleven o'clock yesterday morning. It was pure coincidence that they happened to be driving past just then, but they're certain it was him. He spotted them, too, and ran off into the forest behind the house. Obviously he knew the area well, so he managed to disappear. But we know he's in the area; we're stepping up the surveillance, and we'll soon pick him up."

Jonny sounded sure of himself, and Andersson contented

himself with a nod of approval. At last there was some progress on one front.

Fredrik started to go through the developments during and after Friday's raid in Biskopsgården, and he also reported back on what had happened over the weekend. Since this was news to everyone except Irene, he could hardly complain about a lack of interest among his audience.

"So Anders Pettersson and Heinz Becker had a mutual exchange of services. Pettersson probably got a supply of young girls, while Heinz got drugs and Viagra. The bikers aren't necessarily involved in the brothel side of the operation, although of course they could have set up the apartment, and possibly the drugs. I spoke to Pettersson yesterday, and he said he saw the little Russian girl last Saturday night, which is nine days ago. I asked if he was sure she was Russian, and he insisted that she was."

"But the assistant in the JC store said Heinz Becker spoke to the girl in a language that sounded like Finnish. We assumed it was Estonian; Becker spoke the language because his mother came from Estonia, but the question is, did he speak Russian? We need to find out," Irene interjected.

"You do that," Andersson said.

Irene ignored his comment and continued. "Pettersson thought the girl was called Tanya or Katya; he couldn't remember which. The only trace of her we found in the apartment was a denim skirt. According to the witness in the JC store, the girl was wearing a short denim skirt when she and Becker went in to buy the black jeans. Forensics are working on the skirt right now," Irene concluded.

Andersson's brow was furrowed as he drummed his fingers on the desk, irritatingly out of time. "Pettersson has met the little Russian. Who is dead. He's also met Becker. Who is dead. He's met Becker's sidekick. Who is dead. And he's met the other girl. Who is in a coma and might die. As I see it,

Pettersson is the only thing we have that links the whole thing together. And he's still alive. We need to question him again," he said firmly.

As the meeting started to break up, Andersson suddenly remembered something. "Irene, what did that guy want, the one who was looking for someone who was in charge of the investigation into Torleif's death? I sent him along to see you and Tommy since Hannu wasn't here."

"His name is Stefan, and he's Torleif's son. We didn't have time to speak to him, but he's coming back after lunch. He said his father's car had been stolen."

"Torleif's car has been stolen?" Andersson repeated in surprise.

"That's what he said. I'll find out more this afternoon."

"Good," the superintended muttered.

He suddenly looked very old and tired.

IMMEDIATELY AFTER THE meeting, Irene went along to see Linda Holm. The superintendent of the Human Trafficking Unit was deeply absorbed in something on her computer screen and didn't notice her at first. Irene knocked gently on the doorframe. Linda's face lit up when she saw Irene, and she immediately waved her inside.

"Hi! There have certainly been some strange developments since Friday. Both Becker and his associate are dead, and the girl is still unconscious. They've promised to call me from the hospital in Varberg as soon as she wakes up."

Linda Holm shook her blonde hair and moved her head around in a way that's supposed to be good for people who spend a lot of time working at the computer. Irene didn't sit down because she was in a hurry. Instead she quickly went through what had emerged during the previous day's conversation with Anders Pettersson. Linda Holm listened attentively.

"That's interesting. Russian. She could have been, of

course, but there's also a large Russian population in Estonia. She could easily have come from there and spoken both Estonian and Russian. There are many children and young people who disappear from the slums of Russia and the Baltic countries. Not least from children's homes; often there's a member of staff involved. And it's almost impossible for us to establish a child's identity if they can't tell us themselves. Which our little Russian can't do, of course."

"So that doesn't really help us to find out where she's from," Irene said, finding it difficult to hide her disappointment. "Perhaps the other girl will be able to tell us something when she comes round," she added hopefully.

"Perhaps. Since it was Heinz Becker who brought the girls here, I suspect he made them a few years older in their passports than they actually are, and I'm sure he gave them false names."

"Sven Andersson has asked the police in Varberg to send over any papers and passports found in the wreckage of the car. I'll make sure you get copies right away."

As she was about to leave, Irene remembered something she had forgotten to pass on to Linda. "According to Anders Pettersson, Heinz Becker told him that the little Russian and Sergei had already gone to Tenerife. Do you know of anyone called Sergei?" she asked.

Linda Holm thought for a moment before replying. "Sergei is a common Russian name. And there are plenty of Russians involved in trafficking. Tenerife is definitely a lead; I'll see what I can find out."

"Do you really think they were intending to go on to Tenerife?" Irene asked.

"More than likely. Where there's money, there's prostitution. The clients are the most important thing. Wherever they are, the sex trade will flourish."

"Yes, but I mean . . . Tenerife is a tourist destination. Families go there on vacation, and—"

"Sure. That's the image the tourist industry wants us to see. But the fact is there's a huge sex industry in the Canaries, both legal and not so legal. The East European mafia have established themselves very firmly on the islands. They provide whatever the clients want. As I said, the demand from the clients rules the market. If they're ready to pay, then everything is for sale, and I mean everything."

Irene stared at Linda Holm, not really knowing what to say. No doubt Linda was hardened and cynical after all her years with the Trafficking Unit, but on the other hand she knew what she was talking about.

Irene thanked her for her help and headed for the door. When she glanced back over her shoulder, Linda was once again absorbed in her computer screen.

"VARBERG CALLED," ANDERSSON said. "They've found three passports in a bag in the car. One was in the name of Heinz Becker, and everything matches the information we already have. It looks like he was traveling under his genuine passport. The other guy who died was called Andres Tamm, according to his documentation. An Estonian citizen aged forty-two. The third passport is also Estonian, and is in the name of Leili Tamm; she's allegedly eighteen years old. They were presumably meant to look like they were father and daughter. I've asked our colleagues in Varberg to send over everything they found in the car." Andersson was walking around the room rubbing his hands with satisfaction.

"I've spoken to Linda Holm, and she's going to help us find out whether this Sergei really exists, so she'd like copies of all the documents and passports when they come through," Irene explained.

"Sure. I'll take care of that as soon as they arrive," the superintendent promised.

• • •

AT EXACTLY ONE o'clock the officer at reception informed Irene that she had a visitor by the name of Stefan Sandberg. She went down in the elevator to collect him. When they reached the department she asked if he'd like a coffee.

"Yes, please. I had a hamburger at McDonald's for lunch, and I could do with something to wash it down."

"A veggie burger?"

"A veggie . . . ? No, an ordinary cheeseburger."

"So you're not a vegetarian like your dad?" Irene asked. She couldn't help noticing the shadow that passed over his face. She didn't say anything, but pressed the buttons on the machine to produce two cups of coffee.

They went into her office and sat down. Tommy's desk was unoccupied; he had gone over to pathology to see if he could find out anything about the autopsy on the girl from the root cellar. Neither of them had started referring to the dead girl as either Katya or Tanya; "the little Russian" was too well established.

"There's something I ought to clarify. I'm Torleif's heir; he has no other close relatives. However, he wasn't my biological father. When he and my mother got married, she was pregnant. I was born a month later, and he adopted me."

"Right," was the best Irene could come up with.

That explained why Stefan and Torleif bore no resemblance to each other. It was probably a picture of Torleif himself as a child that Irene had seen on his desk. Something was nagging away at the back of her mind, and eventually it managed to force its way into the light: why hadn't there been a single photograph or anything else in the apartment to indicate that Stefan even existed? Her curiosity had been aroused, but she had no intention of asking him questions on that point just yet. He was here to report a stolen car, first and foremost.

"Am I correct in assuming you didn't realize the car had been stolen until this weekend?" she asked instead.

"Yesterday, to be precise. I'm a doctor, and I live in Umeå. I was informed of Torleif's death last Thursday, but I wasn't able to fly down until Saturday. I arrived late in the afternoon; it was already dark, and I didn't even think about the car. There was so much else . . ." He fell silent, looking uncomfortable.

Irene decided to follow her instincts. "Were you close?"

He shuffled even more awkwardly, and quite some time passed before he answered. "No. I wouldn't say that. We had very little contact over the last few years."

He looked tense, and Irene decided to leave what was clearly a very sensitive topic for the time being.

"But you're sure he had a car? I mean if you had very little contact . . ." she said, deliberately leaving the question hanging in the air.

"He had a car. It was his only indulgence, really. A good car and one foreign vacation every year. And I happen to know he had a two-year-old Opel Astra. A white one."

Stefan seemed very sure of his facts, but Irene would check with the vehicle licensing authority.

"How do you know that? The year and the make, I mean."

"He told me. We spoke on the phone. He called me a few days before Christmas Eve, two years ago. As I said, we didn't have much in common, so he spent most of the time talking about his new car. And these are the spare keys; I found them in the drawer of his desk."

Two keys on a ring landed on Irene's desk with a jangle. She noticed that the Police Sports Association emblem was on the key ring.

"Did you speak to each other after that conversation?" Irene went on, looking at the gold crown glistening on the emblem.

Stefan sighed heavily and shook his head. "No. It was the same old thing. We . . . quarreled and hung up on each other."

A flush spread up toward his right cheekbone. Irene caught

herself thinking how good-looking he was. The fact that Muesli wasn't his biological father wasn't exactly a disadvantage; quite the reverse, in her opinion. But she kept that to herself.

"What did you quarrel about?" she asked.

"The usual. My mother . . . he was always trying to pump me for information about her. And then he started talking crap about her, like he always did."

"So what did he say?"

"Like I said . . . the usual. That she's disloyal. That she should never have been allowed to have children. Same old same old."

Stefan looked troubled as he talked about his last conversation with Torleif. Irene would have liked to probe further into the toxic relationship between Stefan and his adoptive father, but they were supposed to be talking about the stolen car.

Suddenly Stefan braced his shoulders and looked Irene straight in the eye. He said firmly, "No doubt you think it was unreasonable of me to break off contact with Torleif. He had no close relatives left, and he was something of a recluse. But he could be so nasty. For example, two years ago I told him I was going to be a dad. I thought he'd be happy, but instead he started going on about my mom and her bad genes, and saying that my dad—my biological father—was probably the same."

His voice clearly revealed how difficult it was for him to talk about his fractured relationship with Torleif.

"Do you know who your real father is?" Irene asked.

He nodded. "Yes. Mom told me everything when I was fifteen. We lived in Warsaw for the first six years after the divorce. Mom thought my biological father was still living there, but it turned out that he had died the year before we moved back. It was the usual story: he was much older than her, and married. She was working as an office clerk, and he was her boss. She got pregnant. Her whole family is Catholic, so she refused to have an abortion. My biological father fired her because he was scared that she would start to show and people would guess. Her situation was desperate. She didn't dare tell anyone in the family she was pregnant, so she answered an advertisement from someone who was looking for a wife. A Swedish man. Torleif."

He grimaced slightly as he spoke his adoptive father's name. Irene didn't know what to say. Torleif had advertised for a wife in Poland, and he wasn't the boy's father! *I wonder if Andersson knows about this*, she thought. She would have to ask him.

"How old are you?" she asked.

"Twenty-nine. I'll be thirty in April. And Amanda will be two. In April, I mean." His face lit up when he mentioned his daughter, and the sorrowful look in his eye disappeared for a moment.

"My twin daughters will be twenty in March, but my dog will be thirteen in April," Irene said.

They smiled at each other, and the atmosphere in the room lightened. Which was just as well because Irene realized that things could soon get tricky again. She had started to "poke her nose in," as Andersson usually put it, so she might as well see it through.

"How long were Torleif and your mother married?" she asked.

"Four years. According to Mom, that was four years too long."

His attractive smile faded, and the sadness returned to his eyes. There was a hint of something else too. Hatred? Anger? Fear? It was difficult to decide, but it was definitely there.

"Why did she say that? Was he abusive?"

"No . . . well, not physically. But mentally. The age gap was pretty wide: fourteen years. She was only twenty when I was born. He almost broke her with his controlling behavior. He gave her hardly any money, but he still insisted that it was her job to run the household. *Buy food and clothes for nothing*, as she used to say. She prefers not to talk about Torleif these days."

"Do you remember anything about those years with Torleif?"

He thought for a long time before replying. "Virtually nothing. Except he beat me when he found out I'd been playing with his cars. He collected miniature police cars. But that was probably the only time he hit me; it was the final straw for Mom. She packed up her things, which included me, and we went back home to Warsaw. She told me later that she'd had to borrow money from my grandmother to pay for the journey. I'm sure my grandmother had realized that Mom wasn't happy in her marriage over in Sweden, but even today none of my relatives in Poland knows that Torleif isn't my real father."

"Did you have any contact with Torleif while you were living in Poland?"

"No. None at all. Mom got a good job because she could speak and write Swedish pretty well. She worked for a Polish company, and after a few years she became their Swedish representative, which was why we moved to Stockholm. She met someone new, a Swede, and remarried. I have a half-sister who's sixteen. And Mom is still married to the same man, still living in Stockholm. But for those first few years after we came back, she was scared. I didn't really understand much at the time, but since then I've realized . . . she was afraid Torleif would contact us again. That he would make trouble. Which he did."

To Irene's surprise, he started to laugh. He could probably see what she was thinking because he quickly became serious once more.

"It's pretty funny, thinking back on it now, but it certainly wasn't funny at the time. He found out somehow that Mom and I had moved back to Sweden, and he managed to get a hold of her telephone number. I suppose he made use of his position as a police officer. You know more than I do about the methods of tracking people down."

Irene nodded but didn't say anything. She wanted him to carry on talking.

"He insisted on seeing me; he claimed he had access rights. But Mom was no longer the vulnerable little Polish girl he had taken pity on, as he used to put it. She came right back at him, told him that in that case he could pay her all those years of alimony that he owed her. And then she told him to go to hell. They argued until I said I wanted to see Torleif. I was fifteen at the time, and I still thought he was my real dad. I suppose I was yearning for a father, somewhere deep inside. I'd never really had another male role model. Except . . . I guess there was my grandfather and Uncle Jan, but they were back in Warsaw. And Mom's second husband has always been good to me. But still . . . I suppose every child has an idealized picture of the parent who isn't around. If only we could get to know each other, then everything would be terrific."

He smiled and raised his eyebrows, a wry expression on his face.

"I guess you know what happened. I caught the train from Stockholm to Göteborg, all by myself. Full of anticipation. It was the beginning of July, and all the way there I dreamed about what a great time we were going to have. Me and my dad. We'd go to the amusement park at Liseberg. Get a hamburger. Drive out to the sea and go swimming. Go to a soccer match. That particular weekend an English league team was playing against IFK Göteborg at Ullevi. I was desperately hoping he'd bought tickets for the game because I'd told him about it when we spoke on the phone the previous day. Eventually I managed to convince myself he'd definitely gotten those tickets."

He stopped for a moment, and Irene thought his eyes

looked suspiciously shiny, and it wasn't with happiness or laughter. She could tell that from his voice as he went on.

"He met me at the main train station. No hug to welcome me. Just a formal handshake. Then we went to his apartment and he cooked some kind of lentil burger. I nearly threw up. Do I need to say that there was no soccer game, no trip to Liseberg? We did go up to Delsjö for a swim, but that was all. I remember it was lovely up there, and I bought three hot dogs from a guy who was selling them from a little kiosk. I bought them in secret, when Torleif was in the water. Fortunately Mom had given me some money; after all, she knew Torleif, and she had a good idea how things would be."

He paused again, then continued. "When I got back to Stockholm I tried to keep up appearances and said it had been great to see my dad. But Mom saw right through me, of course. She took me to one side and told me the truth. She showed me the adoption papers. Father unknown, it says. She's never told anyone who my real father is; only she and I know. Even today she still says she regrets having let me go through with that visit to Göteborg, not telling me before I left. But the fact is, I was relieved when I found out the truth—that Torleif wasn't my biological father, and that I never had to see him again if I didn't want to. And I certainly didn't want to!" He looked very determined as he finished speaking.

"Did you never see each other again?" Irene asked.

"Yes. Just once, when I came down to Göteborg to see Bruce Springsteen a few years ago. My girlfriend, who is now my wife, was traveling from Malmö, where she lived, and we'd arranged to meet at the central station. I had a few hours to spare, and I called Torleif on a whim. We met in a coffee bar, and the first thing I did was to tell him I knew he wasn't my father. He didn't seem to care. And I think we both realized we didn't have anything else to say to each other. He used to call me occasionally after that; the last time was just before Christmas two years ago, as I said. And we quarreled as usual."

Stefan leaned back in his chair and took a deep breath. The amber-colored eyes gazed steadily at Irene.

"I know I don't have to tell you all this crap, but somehow I have a feeling that it's important for you to know how things were. And perhaps it was important for me to be able to tell you. Maybe I should have spoken to a therapist before I became a father myself, but this is much cheaper."

He grinned to show that he was joking, but those amber eyes told the truth. They revealed a little boy who had had a really tough time when he was growing up. In spite of that he had survived and succeeded in building a future for himself and his family. Irene had come across many children like that over the years: survivors in spite of everything.

"I really appreciate the fact that you've confided in me. I knew who Torleif was when he worked in the third district, but I never got to know him on a personal level. I suppose the age difference had something to do with that," she said, smiling back at Stefan.

He nodded, but didn't say anything.

"How long are you staying?" Irene asked to break the silence.

"Until Thursday. I spoke to a funeral director this morning, and I've made all the necessary arrangements. Now I need to deal with his estate and put the apartment on the market. All those practical things that have to be done when someone dies. The funeral is in three weeks; I'll come back down then."

"I'll put out a call for the car. I can get the license plate number from records."

They both got to their feet at the same time and shook hands as they said goodbye. Irene gave him her card in case he needed to contact her.

• • •

"THAT'S VERY STRANGE," was the superintendent's response when Irene had finished a brief summary of her conversation with Stefan Sandberg.

"So you didn't know that Torleif wasn't the boy's real father?"

Andersson shook his head. "No. Quite the opposite. He used to boast about the fact that he'd already gotten her pregnant before they were married. He always claimed they had to get married. When they split up he said it wasn't right, that she'd run off back to Poland so he didn't get to see his son. I remember telling him to go over there and visit the boy. I mean, Warsaw isn't exactly on the other side of the world. But then he complained about how expensive it was to travel. He could be a real miser, to be honest. I don't like to speak ill of the dead, but it's true. I suppose that's one of the reasons why we gradually lost touch . . ."

Andersson left the sentence hanging in the air as he stared blankly out of the window. Outside there was nothing but a compact darkness, broken only by the lights of the city. The weather forecast had promised rising temperatures, but there was also the risk of further snow or rain. Irene loved clean, white snow, but in the city it soon became black and filthy. The thought of rain on top of all that snow made her shudder. The whole lot would turn into a black, slushy mess.

Andersson glanced wearily at her. "What do you think about this business of the stolen car?" he asked.

"Presumably some thief was keeping an eye on the area and noticed that the car hadn't moved from its parking space. It is pretty new, after all."

The superintendent nodded, but didn't really seem to be listening to her answer. His mind was clearly elsewhere. What was wrong?

As if he'd noticed her concern, he said, "I'll be in a little later than usual tomorrow. After ten. I've got a check up."

His curt tone left no scope for questions. Irene was worried, with good reason. Andersson wasn't exactly blessed with an iron constitution. He was overweight, and suffered from asthma, high blood pressure and vascular cramps, among other things. Had one of his ailments gotten worse in some way? Or had he developed something new? The questions were on the tip of her tongue, but she was sensible enough to hold back. He wouldn't like it if she asked. She might find out eventually.

"We'll have a meeting after lunch tomorrow. By then we should have the autopsy report on the little Russian. Can you let the others know, please?" He waved his hand as if to indicate that the audience was over. It wasn't like him to be distracted and dismissive. There was obviously something on his mind.

Chapter 12

THE MOOD AROUND the table was subdued. Before dinner Krister had told them what had happened when he took Sammie to the vet. Irene pushed her food around her plate, unable to eat. Her worst fears had been realized: the hard lumps were probably tumors. The vet couldn't say for certain what kind of cancer it was, but the fact that the tumors were spread all over Sammie's body, more or less, meant that the prognosis wasn't good.

"According to the vet, the only course of treatment is to carry out a biopsy on one of the lumps, and then to prescribe an appropriate form of chemotherapy," Krister explained.

"Chemo makes you sick. And you lose your hair . . . or fur." Jenny sighed gloomily.

"He's happy and as bright as a button. Maybe he's a little more tired than he used to be, but after all he is almost thirteen," Irene said.

"Thirteen's old for a dog," Jenny said.

Both Krister and Irene looked at her. It was Krister who eventually spoke. "You don't think he should have any treatment?"

"No. That would just make the time he has left miserable. It's better to let him be himself for as long as he's feeling okay."

On top of being a committed vegan, Jenny was also opposed to all forms of pharmaceutical drugs. She abruptly got to her feet and went into the living room. Sammie was lying under the coffee table snoring contentedly. He woke up when Jenny lay down beside him and buried her face in his soft fur. Still half-asleep, he noticed that she was crying and did his duty as he had done so many times before. Gently he nudged her hair with his nose before licking away her tears. They were salty and delicious. He had done the same thing through all the years, whenever one of the twins had been upset. Eventually he could turn their tears into giggles and laughter. It always worked. But not this time. Instead Jenny sobbed as if her heart would break. Sammie grew more and more unhappy. He looked at his beloved young mistress in confusion as she lay there beside him, sobbing away. His troubled gaze met the eyes of his master and mistress. Krister and Irene were standing in the doorway, at a loss in the face of Jenny's grief.

Krister leaned against Irene and whispered, "I think Sammie knows best when it comes to consoling her."

They went back to the table. Katarina's place was empty; she wouldn't be home until later. At which point no doubt a similar scene would be played out.

"I don't think we should grieve before we have to. After all, we know that dogs live for around ten years. Some live longer, some less. I think Jenny is right. We should let Sammie have a good life for whatever time he has left. He doesn't seem to be in pain, or to be suffering in any way. That day might come, and if it does, we'll have to deal with it. But until then we should appreciate every day we still have him," Krister said firmly.

Irene nodded, but was incapable of answering him. She didn't think her voice would hold.

DURING THE NIGHT the weather had changed. The temperature was around freezing, and a thick fog came sweeping in off the sea, enveloping the entire coastal area. The dampness penetrated the dry snow, and the snowdrifts had begun to collapse since the previous day. Irene was glad she had cleared away the snow as it fell.

The curtain of fog meant that visibility was down to just a meter or so. The traffic edged along slowly, each car following the taillights of the vehicle in front.

It was the kind of morning that was likely to mark a distinct peak in the suicide statistics, and Tommy looked as if he were seriously considering adding one more to the count.

Irene was taken aback when she saw the gloomy expression on his face. It wasn't like him at all. He was usually annoyingly cheerful first thing in the morning. She had a bad feeling as she greeted him and hung her jacket on the hook behind the door.

"Has something happened?" she asked.

"Sit down," Tommy said, waving toward her desk.

When she had done as she was told, he said, "Hannu called. Birgitta is in hospital. Apparently she almost had a miscarriage."

"Oh my God! She told me on Friday that she was pregnant again . . ."

The worrying news was entirely in keeping with recent events, she thought pessimistically. Sammie's lumps, and now this. The fog lay draped over all this tragedy like a thick, grey blanket.

"According to Hannu, the doctors are hopeful that everything will turn out okay, but Birgitta is going to be off work for quite some time. Two weeks at least."

"Two weeks! I need a coffee," Irene said with a sigh.

"Of course you do," Tommy replied with just a glimmer of a smile.

Out in the corridor they bumped into Linda Holm. Her face brightened when she saw them.

"Hi. Just the people I was looking for. I've had a reply from our colleagues in Tenerife. From some Comandante something-or-other with the Policía Nacional. They—"

Tommy interrupted her. "Grab yourself a coffee and come along to our office," he said.

With a certain amount of satisfaction Irene noticed that for once he actually sounded a little tired.

"THAT COMANDANTE-WHATEVER ASKED if I could put him through to the person in charge of the Trafficking Unit. When I told him it was me, he went very quiet." Linda couldn't hide a smile of satisfaction before she went on. "The guy spoke terrible English, but I did manage to understand that they'd picked up my query as to whether they knew of anyone named Sergei within the trafficking industry, and they reacted right away. They've got problems with a Sergei who has disappeared. Sergei Petrov. But then it all got messy. Someone was shot dead because this Sergei has gone missing. The Comandante wasn't too happy when I explained that all we had was the name Sergei, and the fact that he was supposed to have traveled from Sweden to Tenerife with a young girl. I told him we'd found the girl dead, and that she'd been murdered. And that we have no idea who this Sergei is. To be honest, I don't know if he understood what I said. He wants to speak to the person who questioned the witness who gave you the name Sergei."

"That was Fredrik, but he's not too happy at the moment," Irene said. "Svanér, Anders Pettersson's hotshot lawyer, came steaming in this morning and managed to get his client released. Fredrik has been to see the prosecutor and raised hell; he's persuaded them to let us pick Pettersson up again."

She went to see if Fredrik was in his office. When she opened the door and peeped in, she could see that everything looked the same as usual—as if a minor tornado had swept through the room. Fredrik insisted that he could put his hand on whatever he needed in the middle of all the mess; it was just that no one else had managed to crack his system.

"He's already out, probably looking for Pettersson," Irene informed the other two when she got back to her office.

"I'll leave a note on his desk with the Comandante's phone number so that he can give him a call when he gets back," Linda said, getting up to leave.

In her mind's eye Irene saw the piles of paper on Fredrik's desk. He wouldn't even notice Linda's note. It could end up lying there for weeks. Or months.

"Actually it would be much better to shoot him an email," she said.

"An email? Okay." Linda Holm looked a little surprised, but didn't ask why. Presumably she had heard stranger things in her life.

SUPERINTENDENT ANDERSSON RETURNED just after ten. Hot on his heels came Fredrik, carrying a big bag from the bakery store. He opened the bag and dropped it on the table; the tempting aroma of fresh cinnamon buns revealed the contents.

"To brighten up a miserable Tuesday," Fredrik explained.

Irene had called him on his cell to tell him they would be two colleagues down for the next few days.

For once Fredrik had sounded seriously downcast. Pettersson hadn't been at the address where he was registered. Nor anywhere else, apparently.

"Mmmm. Smells fantastic! Thank goodness there's one bright spot on a day like this," Tommy said, looking a little more cheerful at the thought of freshly baked buns with his coffee.

Fredrik put the warm cinnamon buns on a plate and passed them around. Everyone took one. Everyone except Andersson.

It was a while before Irene realized that the plate had passed the superintendent by. This was extremely surprising. Usually he was more than happy to help himself to something delicious at coffee time, but now he was looking sideways at the plate without indulging. Jonny had noticed, too.

"On a diet?" he said with a smirk.

"That's none of your fucking business!" Andersson snapped.

Jonny's smirk faded and was replaced by a surprised expression. The language used between the two of them was often pretty caustic, and they would often enjoy a joke that might have seemed to others to go a little too far. But this time Jonny had obviously ventured into forbidden territory. Even he realized that. During the silence that followed, Andersson got to his feet, picked up his coffee and left the room.

"He's kind of oversensitive today," Jonny said when the door had closed behind the superintendent.

"He went for a check-up this morning. I expect the doctor has told him he needs to lose some weight," Irene said.

"Probably. That won't be easy for him," Tommy agreed.

They all ate their buns in silence. When Irene got up to top off her coffee, she turned to Fredrik and asked, "Are you going to call that guy in Tenerife?"

"Sí, sí!" he said with a grin.

"And then you're going to go back to looking for Pettersson," she went on.

"Sí, again."

"And Tommy . . ." She left the question hanging in the air, unsure of his plans.

"I'm going to contact pathology. They promised the report on the little Russian, but nothing has come through yet. I'll give them a kick in the ass, get them moving," Tommy replied.

"Good. Ask if they've had time to take a look at Torleif as well," Irene said.

"Jesper and I will carry on trying to find those guys who ran him down," Jonny hurried to announce. Clearly he had no intention of letting some woman tell him what to do.

A few seconds passed before Irene remembered that Jesper

Tobiasson was the new guy who would be working with Jonny while Hannu and Birgitta were sick.

"And Andersson is going to pursue inquiries in the area around Töpelsgatan. Have we had any luck finding the couple who went racing up the hill around the time of the murder?" Irene asked.

Both Jonny and Tommy shook their heads.

"That's strange. We went to the media, asking them to contact us. They can hardly have missed it," Irene mused aloud.

"And how are you going to pass the day?" Jonny asked.

"I'm going to concentrate on Heinz Becker and his associate. I need to follow up on the passports; I called Varberg yesterday and asked them to make sure they were sent over. I'll try to check whether Andres and Leili Tamm were their real names. I also need to see if there's any possibility of finding out the little Russian's real name. And I'll see if we've gotten anywhere with the search for Torleif's car. And—"

She was interrupted by a call from reception over the intercom.

"Messenger from Varberg for Irene Huss."

"I'll be right down."

IRENE ALREADY KNEW that Heinz Becker's passport was genuine, but she needed to check on the other two. She sent off an inquiry to the Estonian police authority regarding Andres and Leili Tamm. With a bit of luck she might get an answer at some point during the day.

The three passports lay open on the desk in front of her. She was already familiar with Heinz Becker's fleshy face, so she concentrated on the other two.

According to the details on his passport, Andres Tamm was forty-two years old, 177 centimeters tall and had very pale blue eyes and blond hair. In the photograph he was wearing modern rimless glasses. His fair hair was quite long and carefully styled.

At the bottom of the picture she could just see a white shirt collar, held together by a shiny tie that looked like silk. He was also wearing a dark jacket. Even in the passport photograph it was obvious that he had a tan. If he hadn't been in the company of Becker and the girl when he died, Irene would have guessed that he was a successful businessman.

Leili Tamm could probably have passed as his daughter. According to her details she was eighteen years old, 163 centimeters tall, blonde, and her eyes were classed as "mixed color." In spite of heavy makeup, she didn't look a day over fourteen, possibly because of the childish roundness in her cheeks or the sullen, pouting lips. Irene was taken aback when she looked more closely at the girl's eyes. That dead expression didn't belong to a young teenager. A very old woman, more like. Or was she heavily drugged? It was by no means unlikely. Part of a low-cut T-shirt was visible in the photograph; around her neck she wore a thin chain with a trinket on it. Irene recognized the little plastic flower. It was very similar to the cheap jewelry the little Russian had been wearing.

Irene called the Varberg police and managed to reach the officer who had investigated the car accident. After a few introductory remarks, she asked, "Do you know if any trace of drugs was found in the men's bodies?"

"No, but I do know that samples were taken. We won't hear anything before the end of the week at the earliest."

"Do you know if the girl was tested for drugs?"

"No. You'll have to check with the hospital. Do you suspect this is also to do with narcotics?"

"Possibly. We found a lot in the apartment," Irene replied evasively.

Of course the Varberg police knew about the abortive raid, at least in broad terms, and they also knew that the case involved trafficking.

"Well, I guess that's pretty common. If they're up to their

necks in one kind of crap, they're probably up to something else as well. And the whole thing turns into a nightmare!"

You're certainly not wrong there, Irene thought, but she didn't say it out loud. Instead she thanked her colleague and hung up.

Her next call was to the Intensive Care Unit at Varberg hospital. She spoke to a very busy doctor who asked if he could call her back. Of course the safety of the patient was paramount, but it was still annoying to have to wait almost ten minutes for the doctor to call. He did apologize, and said that he had conferred with a senior colleague with regard to what they could tell the police.

"As you know, we haven't yet been able to confirm her identity," Irene told him. "The same applies to the man who was allegedly her father, according to his passport. The other deceased male is a notorious human trafficker. He bought and sold young women and forced them into prostitution."

"I see," the doctor said warily.

"We suspect that Leili is not the girl's real name and that she is a victim of trafficking."

"I understand."

"We found a large quantity of narcotics in the apartment where the men were keeping Leili imprisoned. I'd like to know whether you've tested the girl for drugs."

There was a long silence at the other end of the line before he answered. "We have. She had several fresh needle marks on her body, and she tested positive for morphine and amphetamine. She'd probably been injected with both heroin and amphetamine, but she'd also been taking amphetamines orally. We found a number of tablets in the pocket of her jeans."

"How is she at the moment?"

"Her condition is unchanged. She has a large number of serious fractures, but it's the injuries to her skull that are causing the most concern. She's in a coma. She doesn't react when we turn her, but we are giving her analgesics anyway. We don't know if the dose is sufficient for her to be pain-free. It's difficult to assess the correct dosage for a person who is a habitual user."

"How long do you think she's been on drugs?"

"A few months at most. She still has a sound basic physique, and she isn't particularly emaciated."

"How old would you say she is?"

"Well . . . yesterday we were told that she's eighteen, according to her passport. But I think all of us felt she was younger. And now you're telling me the passport could be false, so . . . No more than fifteen, in my view."

The doctor's assessment fit perfectly with Irene's own. If Leili Tamm wasn't the girl's name, and she might not even be Estonian, then who was she? And who was the man who claimed to be her father?

"Could you possibly take a DNA sample from Leili?" Irene asked.

"For what reason?"

"We need to check whether the dead man—Andres Tamm, according to his passport—is actually her father."

"I understand. No problem. This falls under patient confidentiality, but you ought to know that the girl is pregnant. The pregnancy is at a relatively early stage: week thirteen or fourteen."

"What are you going to do?"

"We will probably have to carry out a termination. The girl can't cope with a pregnancy in her current condition. And we don't even know if she's going to come round. As she's been injected with narcotics, we've sent off samples to be tested for blood infections. She doesn't have hepatitis A or B, but we don't know about HIV yet."

Irene felt something like sorrow growing inside her. Perhaps there was also a real sense of powerlessness. These young girls are condemned to such a terrible existence by their unscrupulous pimps, she thought. They're sold like consumable goods, always following the same pattern: sold, exploited, used up. Eventually they are dumped like the sex industry's waste product. But who cares about industrial waste? They're only human beings, after all.

When she had finished her conversation with the doctor, Irene called Svante Malm and asked him to keep an eye open for Andres and Leili's DNA profiles. As always he was happy to oblige, and promised to call her as soon as he had the results.

Irene decided to sneak out for some food. It looked as if this was going to be a long day.

WHEN SHE GOT back to her office after a quick lunch, she had received an email from the Estonian police. They had no missing persons matching the information Irene had provided in her query. Nor had they received any reports of missing persons that matched the photographs. She wasn't particularly surprised as she concluded that both passports were false. But the question remained: What were the real identities of Andres and Leili?

Chapter 13

"THE AUTOPSY REPORT on the little Russian confirms that the primary cause of death is strangulation. She was strangled from the front. The killer put both hands around her throat and squeezed with his thumbs. It seems likely that a limited amount of strength was required, but she did put up something of a struggle. There were fragments of skin under her nails, which means we have the killer's DNA profile. And it matches the semen we found in her hair."

Tommy Persson sounded optimistic as he finished speaking. DNA always provides better evidence when it comes to catching a perpetrator. All they had to do now was find the man who had left his DNA on the victim.

Irene, Fredrik Stridh, Jonny Blom and Superintendent Andersson were listening to Tommy's report. Jesper Tobiasson, Jonny's new colleague, was in the office they shared, working indefatigably on the search for the two absconders involved in the hit-and-run outside the TV studios.

"The little Russian had several injuries to her vagina and rectum. She also had a very serious infection, caused by antibiotic-resistant gonorrhea. The infection was so advanced that the girl was showing signs of blood poisoning. Or 'sepsis,' as it says in the report. The gonorrhea bacteria got into her bloodstream through the wounds in her vagina and were present in her lungs and kidneys. She must have been very sick at the time of the murder. Not that it's any consolation, but if she hadn't been killed she probably would have died as a result of the infection."

"So Heinz Becker or Andres Tamm might have decided to get rid of a girl who was no longer of any use to them," Irene stated flatly.

"That's certainly a possibility. We'll compare their DNA with the profile we already have from the skin fragments and the semen."

"I've requested their DNA. It should be here in a few days," Irene informed him.

"Good. In that case we'll wait until then. Apart from that, the autopsy confirmed what we already knew: the girl was badly undernourished and tested positive for both morphine and amphetamine. A lethal mixture of uppers and downers that would be dangerous for anybody, particularly a girl in such poor health. Stridner says she was also suffering from some kind of hormonal imbalance. She was producing too few growth and sex hormones; this is evidently a genetic condition which can be treated if it's discovered in time. According to the forensic odontologist, the development of her teeth indicates that she was between thirteen and a half and fourteen and a half. However, she is physically underdeveloped and looks pre-pubertal. Most of us guessed that she was around ten years old, twelve at the most, when we found her."

Irene couldn't help turning her head to look at the picture on the wall. The blonde hair fanned out around the thin face . . . She didn't look a day older than eleven.

"The stomach contents consisted of a small amount of white bread and a little coleslaw: the kind of salad you get with pizza. Her last meal was consumed at least six hours before she died. She was probably too ill to eat or drink much."

Tommy concluded his summary of the autopsy report and put down the papers on the desk in front of him.

"But she obviously wasn't too ill to be exploited. She was

expected to oblige right to the very end!" Irene couldn't hide the bitterness in her voice.

"Yes," Tommy began, "but after all it was the killer who—"

Irene interrupted him. "He forced a dying child to perform a sex act. We know that the semen in her hair got there at around the time of her death. The skin fragments under her nails suggest that she tried to defend herself. Presumably he lost his temper and ejaculated all over her hair. Perhaps he strangled her at the same time!"

Irene realized she was glaring at the men around the table, an angry flush staining her cheeks red.

"Calm down. None of us killed the girl," Jonny said nastily.

Irene could feel her pulse rate increasing, but she tried to suppress her anger. He was right. At the same time, Linda Holm's word's echoed in her mind: *the majority are socially well-established men with families.*

It could be anybody. Even one of her colleagues. She made a huge effort to try to push away her gloomy thoughts. It wasn't entirely successful. Suddenly she said, "This is exactly what makes me so . . . furious. Swedish men know these girls are slaves. They know that the girls live in appalling conditions. In spite of that, they support the trade in human trafficking by paying for sex. I just don't get it! You're men. Can someone explain it to me?!"

There was silence around the table. Four pairs of eyes gazed uncomprehendingly at her. Eventually the superintendent spoke.

"So you're getting all feminist, like those women who run around saying that all men are monsters," he said acidly.

"I just don't understand how a man can have sex with a person he knows has been forced into slavery," Irene retorted.

Tommy was the first to respond. "I know what you mean. The places where the girls conduct their business are so disgusting that I don't even know how anyone can get it up in the first place. The stench, and those bastards hanging around . . . no, I just don't understand it. But it's important to remember that most men wouldn't dream of having sex with a girl under those circumstances."

"But there are still those who do," Irene insisted.

Fredrik looked as if he was giving serious consideration to Irene's question. "The girls supplied through trafficking are often cheaper than ordinary hookers," he said eventually.

"So you're telling me it's down to financial reasons? I don't believe . . ." Irene began, but she was interrupted by Jonny.

"Oh for fuck's sake! Your normal john is a guy sitting on his own in his hotel room feeling horny. Or he's sitting at home while his wife is off doing something else. What does he do? He gets out his laptop and opens an Internet browser. Checks out the girls that are available in town right now. Then he makes contact. If things work out he gets his rocks off, the girl gets her money, and that's the end of that. It doesn't do anybody any harm!"

"But what if one of those johns had sex with the little Russian a few weeks ago? Without using a condom? By now he will have infected his wife or partner with gonorrhea. Or possibly HIV. Or pubic lice."

"Nice souvenirs you get from those ladies." Jonny grinned.

"Can we please stop bullshitting and get back to work?" Andersson exploded.

None of the others had noticed the chief's rising frustration, which was why his outburst was met with astonished silence.

"This nonsense has no relevance to our investigation," the superintendent added firmly.

Irene could tell he was trying to bring his blood pressure down by taking deep breaths. He had learned this technique from a training course on crisis management a few years ago. It was more or less the only thing he remembered about the course.

Irene would have liked to contradict him, but she realized there was no point in pursuing the discussion. The problem remained; she still couldn't for the life of her understand how men could support the existence of slavery in today's enlightened society.

There was a knock on the door and Superintendent Linda Holm walked in before anyone had the chance to speak. She stopped dead as she picked up on the tense atmosphere, then continued into the room as if she hadn't noticed anything.

"Sorry to disturb you, but apparently someone else has been shot. That Comandante from Tenerife has just called again. He seems a little shaken, to say the least," she said with a grimace.

"What the hell does he expect us to do about crime in the Canaries?" Jonny asked.

"I'm not really sure. His English is terrible. Now he wants to speak to the person in charge of the homicide investigation. Which would be you, I guess," she said, nodding to Andersson.

The superintendent squirmed uncomfortably on his chair. "What? Oh . . . well . . . yes, I suppose it would," he said.

If there was one thing Andersson couldn't stand, it was talking to foreigners on the phone. It didn't matter if they were Danes, Germans or Spaniards. The main problem was that he didn't speak very good English, but the other major issue was his hearing, which was gradually deteriorating. Over the past few years it had affected him more and more. In a large group of people he found it very difficult to make out what people were saying. Everything just merged into a hum of conversation.

"Is there anyone in the department who speaks Spanish?" he asked.

Everyone shook their heads. Suddenly Fredrik's face lit up. "Birgitta speaks Spanish!" he exclaimed.

"She's in the hospital. She won't be back for at least a couple of weeks," Tommy reminded him.

There was a brief silence, then Andersson fixed his gaze on Irene. "You talk to him."

"Me? Why me? I can't speak a word of Spanish, and I'm not in charge of the investigation," she protested.

"But you can speak English on the phone," Andersson countered.

It was true that she had spoken quite a lot of English during the Schyttelius homicide case a few years earlier. She had talked to British colleagues, both on the phone and in person in London. She was still in touch with Glen Thomsen, the superintendent at Scotland Yard. The Huss and Thomsen families had visited each other's countries and had a very enjoyable time together.

An agitated Spanish commanding officer was something else entirely, particularly if his English wasn't good.

"Okay. But it's late afternoon now. I'll call him tomorrow," Irene said with a sigh.

"Excellent," Linda said, passing her a yellow Post-it note.

Without looking at it Irene stuck it inside her folder. As she flicked through to find her most recent notes, the yellow scrap of paper was forgotten.

Linda Holm had only just left the room when the door flew open again. This time the visitor didn't even bother knocking, let alone apologizing for the intrusion. It was Jonny's temporary assistant, Jesper Tobiasson, who hurtled in looking extremely excited.

"They've picked up Daniel Lindgren!" he announced jubilantly.

Jonny leapt to his feet. "Where?"

"At his mom's place in Tynnered."

"Is he already here?"

"I don't know, but they're supposed to be bringing him straight in."

"Okay. We'll question him as soon as possible, ask him what

he's been doing since he took off. If it's too late he can sit and stew in a custody cell until tomorrow," Jonny decided.

Andersson rubbed his hands with satisfaction. "Good! At least we should be able to link him to the hit-and-run or eliminate him from our inquiries," he said, standing up to indicate that the meeting was over.

HEAVY SLEET LASHED against the windshield as Irene drove home. The snow that had already fallen was quickly turning into thick slush. Several drains were completely blocked, and pools of melting slush had quickly formed on the streets. In some of them the water was above the hubcaps on Irene's car. Even though rush hour was over it was impossible to maintain the speed limit because of the flooded roads.

Irene was tired by the time she put the key in the front door. She was looking forward to an excellent dinner. Krister had been off work today; he usually took the opportunity to go into town and do some shopping at the main indoor market or the fish market. If he was inspired the result could be something really special, even though it was the middle of the week.

The wonderful aroma of fried chicken and garlic drifted toward her as she opened the door. Her mouth watered as she thought about the delights to come. She quickly shrugged off her coat and hung it up.

Jenny came into the hallway with a steaming cup of tea in one hand and a cress and tomato sandwich on a plate in the other. She stopped with one foot on the bottom step and beamed at her mother.

"Hi! I went over to Grodden today, and they have a job for me!" she informed Irene.

"Fantastic. Where's Grodden?"

"Redbergsplatsen."

"But why do you have to work so far away? Isn't there a day

care center in the western part of the city that would want you? And why can't you stay at Tomtebo?"

Jenny rolled her eyes and sighed. "Grodden isn't a day care center, it's a vegetarian restaurant. I'm going to be cooking! I can start at the beginning of March. And guess what the best thing is?"

She paused for effect, her eyes sparkling with anticipation. Irene shook her head wearily.

"There's an apartment I can rent in the same building! A two-room apartment! It's a sublet, but the tenancy agreement will be for a year!"

A lot of overwhelming good news had been delivered all at the same time. Irene went over to her daughter and kissed her on the cheek. She didn't dare risk a hug because the hot cup of tea was balancing precariously on a saucer in Jenny's hand.

"Congratulations, sweetheart! That's so cool!"

Jenny beamed at her again before disappearing up the stairs.

In the kitchen Krister was busy straining freshly cooked tagliatelle, which he was planning to serve with a tasty Italian chicken casserole. It was absolutely delicious and one of Irene's favorite dishes.

She threw her arms around him and buried her nose in the back of his neck. He smelled of garlic and the hot stove.

"So our little bundle of joy is leaving home. Imagine that," she murmured into his neck.

He turned around and wrapped her in his arms. They stood there for a long time, holding each other close and feeling the warmth of each other's bodies. Irene turned up her face and found his mouth. It had been a while since they had kissed so passionately—in the middle of the kitchen, on an ordinary weekday evening, stone-cold sober.

"Get a room, you two!"

Irene and Krister stopped in the middle of a kiss and

instinctively stepped apart. Katarina was standing in the doorway, laughing at them.

"I was only teasing. You're so sweet! At your age . . . !" She wagged her finger jokingly at them.

"What do you mean, at our age? From a purely statistical point of view, I expect to live for another thirty years or so, and your mother will be around for at least forty-five," Krister said.

He demonstratively pulled Irene close and gave her another burning kiss. Then he turned to his daughter and said, "What makes you think you stop loving someone just because you reach a certain age? Love is timeless, and age is irrelevant."

"Oh, please. I'm starving. Something smells amazing!"

Katarina strolled in and sat down at the kitchen table. Irene sat down beside her and scooped a large portion of pasta and chicken onto each plate.

"How did Jenny manage to get that apartment?" she asked Katarina.

"Stoffe, the guy she's covering for, owns the place. He's going to work in London for a year or so—in an ordinary restaurant, but they want someone who can cook good vegetarian food. Stoffe's girlfriend is a waitress, and she's fixed up a job, too, so they're leaving in two weeks. And Jenny's asked if I want to share the apartment with her until I find somewhere of my own. I think I will. For, like, six months anyway."

Irene paused with the fork halfway to her mouth. "So you're moving out at the same time as Jenny."

"I think so, yeah."

Irene could see that this came as a surprise to Krister as well. He didn't say anything, but nodded silently to himself several times, as if something he had long suspected had just been confirmed.

Katarina was as tall as Irene, slender and fit. A beautiful grown woman. Who would soon be leaving home. And Sammie was old, and in the not-too-distant future he too would be gone. Suddenly there would be only Irene and Krister once more. They had known each other for just eighteen months when the twins were born, and the girls had been a part of their life together for almost twenty years.

A new phase would soon begin, with more disposable income and the chance to travel and indulge themselves with material possessions. It was a tempting prospect. At the same time, there would no longer be any kind of buffer between them. It would be just the two of them for the rest of their lives.

HANNU WAS QUIETER than usual. He had answered in monosyllables when Irene asked how Birgitta was. It was obvious he wasn't feeling too well. Birgitta's mother had moved in temporarily to help out with little Timo. Irene had met her once, and knew that she was a determined woman with firm views on most things. She had raised Birgitta alone, while at the same time pursuing a brilliant career in banking. She had retired at the age of sixty-five after many years as a bank director, and these days she spent most of her recently acquired free time at Alingsås golf club. But now it was the middle of winter, and she could devote all of her energy to her daughter's family. Hannu was grateful for her help, of course, but Irene knew that his relationship with his mother-in-law wasn't always smooth sailing.

Irene tactfully refrained from asking any more questions about the family, and instead started to tell him about Stefan Sandberg's visit two days earlier and Torleif's stolen car.

"I checked the vehicle register, but I didn't have time to go and see if the Opel was in its parking space. I should have done it on Monday," Hannu said gloomily.

Irene understood perfectly why he hadn't had time. She glimpsed a spark of interest in his unusually dull expression when she revealed that Torleif was Stefan's adoptive father.

"Do you know if they've done the autopsy yet?" Hannu asked.

"I'm not sure, but they hadn't got around to it yesterday when Tommy got the report on the little Russian."

"Are you getting anywhere?"

"It's a slow process," Irene admitted.

"As usual."

He gave her a wan smile that failed to reach his eyes.

ON THE WAY back to her office, Irene was stopped in the corridor by the sound of Fredrik's voice.

"They've found the car!"

She spun around, realizing at once which car he meant. Fredrik hurried toward her, waving a piece of paper.

"Where?" she asked.

"In a dilapidated barn outside Olofstorp. The roof collapsed yesterday under the weight of the snow. The farmer went over there this morning to check on the damage, and discovered the car. He immediately suspected that it was stolen, so he called the Angered police. They checked the license plates and saw we were looking for the car, so they called us. It's on its way here."

"Have forensics examined it?"

"No, but they know it's being brought in."

"Excellent. Are you going to go and take a look at it today?"

Fredrik glanced at his watch. "No, I want to check out an address. Anders Pettersson's."

"No trace of him yet?"

"No, but rumor has it that he was in a pub on Järntorget on Monday night. He managed to get wasted and get himself thrown out. Since then no one has seen him."

"Where does he live?"

"Slottsskogsgatan. A beautiful, recently renovated four-room apartment in a nineteenth century building. He's not short on money, that guy. Although it took me two days to track him down—that's not the address he's registered at. I wonder if his neighbors know what he actually does."

"Shouldn't we have the place under surveillance?"

"We should, but we don't have enough staff at the moment to watch it twenty-four seven. Andersson is working on it. They've finished going through all the information received from the public about the incident on Töpelsgatan—nothing new there, by the way. So some of the people who were working on that can help watch Pettersson's apartment. We probably won't get that set up until tomorrow, so right now it's just me; I'm dropping by several times today, just to check out the situation."

"Have you rung the bell to see if he's home?"

"Of course. He might be inside, but he hasn't bothered to answer the door. I haven't seen any lights in the windows after dark."

"Perhaps he's sitting there in the shadows, thinking about the meaning of life," Irene suggested ironically.

"More than likely. Particularly if he's got some good stuff to smoke."

They both smiled, but realized at the same time that there could be a great deal of truth in the joke. It was obvious that Pettersson had a serious drug problem of his own.

"Will you talk to Hannu about the car, or do you want me to do it?" Irene asked.

"I'll do it. We have to fill in our card for the trotting races anyway," Fredrik informed her.

"Good luck," Irene said with a smile.

Tommy, Fredrik, Jonny and Hannu had started filling in their cards together for the V75 trotting races almost two years ago. None of them had asked whether Birgitta or Irene would like to join in, so the two female detectives would sometimes buy a 100-kronor Saturday lucky dip. The computer in the newsagent's would fill in their cards, and there was no doubt that it knew considerably more about the lottery and football than either Birgitta or Irene. They had been over the moon last October when the football pools brought them a win of nearly four thousand kronor. They had celebrated with a very good lunch at a top restaurant on Götaplatsen, and still had plenty of money left over to share between them. The gentlemen had congratulated them on their win with forced smiles. Their carefully considered trotting cards had never won them more than 370 kronor. As Birgitta had said encouragingly: just enough for a takeaway pizza and a low-alcohol beer each.

The paperwork was piling up on Irene's desk. With a sigh she sank down onto her chair. She hated paperwork, but knew that it was a necessary evil. She might as well get down to writing some reports. The longer she put it off, the more she would have to do.

She caught herself wishing that something would happen to interrupt her, and for once her wish came true.

"Hi there!"

Linda Holm's blonde curls appeared in the doorway. She walked in before Irene had the chance to say anything. Linda was carrying a blue plastic folder; she took out a sheet of paper and placed it on the desk in front of Irene.

"This arrived just a minute ago," she said.

It was a printout of a faxed "Wanted" poster. The text below the picture was in Spanish. The man in the photograph had cropped hair, but Irene could see that it was dark. Several gold hoops glinted in each ear. The eyes were pale, and he was glaring straight at the camera. The full lips were framed by a neat, thin beard. His septum was pierced by a heavy gold nose ring. He was wearing a wifebeater, and Irene could see the muscles of his neck were over-developed, as were the parts of his shoulders and chest visible in the picture. A gold chain as thick as a well-fed boa constrictor snaked around his neck.

"There's something familiar about him," Irene murmured to herself.

"Picture him five years older. Not quite as heavy. Without the beard and the gold jewelry. Glasses. Longer hair, bleached blond, and—"

"Andres Tamm!"

"Yes! And check out the name on the poster."

Irene skimmed through the incomprehensible text and immediately spotted the letters in larger, bold print: Sergei Petrov.

"So Andres's real name is Sergei," Irene concluded.

"Yes again. And my esteemed colleague El Comandante has also produced a picture of the girl, which is why he's so shaken up. Surprise!"

With the air of a magician conjuring up whole colonies of rabbits out of a top hat, Linda whipped another sheet of paper out of the plastic folder.

The girl in the image was half-turned away with her back to the camera, glancing into the lens over her shoulder. Her hair hung down over one eye like a blonde curtain. She had pulled up her skirt with the hand nearest the camera to show that she wasn't wearing any panties. Her buttocks were small and firm. A child's buttocks. She was naked from the waist up. It was just possible to make out a negligible breast in half-profile; it was hardly more than a faint curve on the skinny chest. You could count the vertebrae on her thin back. Her spindly legs were shoved into black boots.

The picture could have been sexy except for the girl's age and the expression on her face. Fear shone from the one visible eye. The photograph had probably been taken several months earlier, because she didn't look as emaciated as in the shot from the ME. Perhaps the big stainless steel autopsy table made her look even smaller after her death.

The text was in German, but Irene could read the name

"Tanya" and some numbers that she understood: "10 bis 03 Uhr" and "€130." The little Russian finally had a name, even if it probably wasn't the name she'd been given at birth. Tanya's services were available between ten o'clock at night and three in the morning, at the modest price of 130 Euro.

Irene recognized both the skirt and the boots. She had been wearing those same boots on the night she was killed, and the skirt was identical to the denim skirt they had found in the apartment in Biskopsgården.

"Tanya. She was in Germany during the fall. Did our Spanish colleague say where he got the picture?" Irene asked.

"No. Well, if he did, I didn't understand him. But I did grasp that he's going to suggest that one of us goes over to Tenerife to assist them with the murder inquiry. Or possibly several murder inquiries. I couldn't work out whether he was dealing with two or three bodies. He said he's intending to speak to 'highest Comandante for Policía Nacional in Göteborg.' It sounds like he's completely desperate. He yelled 'No gang war!' at me several times over the phone. And 'Murder bad for tourists!'"

They laughed heartily at the Spanish police chief's problems. Homicide on an island off the coast of North Africa felt like police work at a safe distance. Their own investigations were more than enough to deal with right now.

"He did actually say they would pay for travel and accommodation if we could send someone over," Linda said when she had straightened her face.

"In that case you'd better go."

"Impossible. For a start, the homicide investigation has nothing to do with me. That's your area of responsibility. And secondly, we're planning another raid. Tomorrow. Believe it or not, this time it's a café in Trollhättan."

"A café?"

"Yes. A pimp accompanied by several girls has turned up

there a number of times over the last few months. They rent a kind of storeroom next door to the café for a week at a time. It was a neighbor who tipped us off. He thought there was a noticeable increase in the number of male customers visiting the café at certain periods. We've been keeping the place under surveillance, and now we're ready to go in."

"Young girls?"

"Not as young as Tanya and Leili."

Irene felt an irrational surge of relief. It was terrible when women were forced into prostitution, irrespective of age, but those very young girls were so desperately lost, somehow. Their lives were over before they'd even begun.

AFTER LUNCH IRENE went back to writing her reports. Tommy came in when she had almost finished the last one, which was about the fax from Tenerife and the identification of Andres Tamm as Sergei Petrov. It consisted of just a few lines because she had requested translations of the Spanish and German text. Irene felt optimistic about the prospect of revealing Tanya's true identity. The question was whether they would also succeed in revealing the identity of her killer.

Irene showed Tommy the faxed picture of Tanya. He raised his eyebrows when he saw it.

"Well how about that. Tanya. So the little Russian has a name. Although obviously it's not her real name. But it might make it slightly easier to track her down."

"Let's hope so."

"Where did the fax come from?"

"Linda Holm got it from her Comandante in Tenerife. Apparently he's in a real mess; he sounds pretty desperate."

Irene told Tommy what he had said to Linda over the phone, and they both laughed, partly with relief at not having an ongoing gang war on their patch. They knew from experience how difficult that could be from a purely investigative point of view, and they also knew that dealing with gangs swallowed up resources on a huge scale. As a rule they just went on until the majority of the combatants were either dead or behind bars. "A kind of natural selection," as Jonny put it.

"Have you spoken to Hannu?" Irene asked.

"Only in passing. He was going over to the ME's office. They've finished the autopsy on Torleif."

"You heard that the car's been found?"

"Yes. It's a remarkable coincidence that his car was stolen, although I would go with the theory that the thief had been keeping an eye on the parking lot and noticed the car hadn't been used for a few days."

"You're probably right. I mean, Stefan doesn't know when it was stolen. He didn't notice if it was there when he arrived on Saturday evening because it was already dark."

"We'll see what forensics have to say tomorrow. They might find prints belonging to one of the star names on our records."

"That would be way too simple. Every single petty thief knows that you need to wear gloves. Or wipe every surface. Or torch the car. Bearing in mind how cold it was, I'm sure the thief had something on his hands."

"Let's hope you're wrong. Maybe his hands were freezing and he took the car so that his fingers wouldn't fall off with frostbite."

When Tommy finished speaking, Irene realized she was sitting staring at him without saying a word.

"What is it?" he said with a curious look.

"You said something that triggered a thought in the back of my mind. But it's gone."

"What did I say? That he took the car so that his fingers wouldn't fall off?" Tommy ventured helpfully.

Irene shook her head sadly. "It's no good; it's gone."

She knew there was no point in trying to force the issue. Whatever it was would float to the surface eventually. But it was incredibly irritating, like walking around with a popcorn husk stuck between your teeth and not being able to get rid of it.

"THE LITTLE BASTARD has a watertight alibi," Jonny informed his colleagues over coffee that afternoon.

He both looked and sounded angry, and Jesper Tobiasson was slumped gloomily in the chair next to him.

Daniel Lindgren had cooperated fully when confronted with the accusation that he was suspected of having been involved in a hit-and-run incident in which a retired police officer had died. In spite of his age, he was no greenhorn when it came to criminal activities, and he was well aware of how the police regarded crimes against one of their own. He immediately admitted that he and his friend Fredrik Svensson had caught a bus to Göteborg's central station after escaping from the juvenile detention center. From there they had traveled by train to Copenhagen; when they arrived in the city a few hours later, they had headed straight for Christiania, where they already knew quite a few people. These friends had apparently taken good care of them and provided them with a roof over their heads. The police had suddenly turned up out of the blue and taken them into custody. According to Daniel, this was all a misunderstanding, and he and Fredrik had been released after two days.

The Copenhagen police had a rather different version. A notorious narcotics dealer had been found murdered in Nyhavn. His body was almost frozen solid in the slushy ice just below the quayside. The cause of death was repeated blows to the head, delivered with extreme force. The autopsy had shown that he was likely dead before he was thrown into the water, since there was no water in his lungs. Daniel Lindgren's friends from Christiania were the only people who had been seen with the dealer during the last few hours of his life. They had been in a pub in Nyhavn, and the dealer had been with them. According to a witness, the victim had argued loudly with some of the group, although there was no physical violence. Everything seemed to have calmed down by the time they left the pub at around midnight, but the following day the dealer's body had been found by a man walking his dog along the quay early in the morning.

The whole group of friends from Christiania had been picked up, including Daniel Lindgren and Fredrik Svensson. They had all flatly denied any knowledge of the dealer's death, and insisted that he had been very much alive when they parted company outside the pub. There were no witnesses, and no trace of forensic evidence that could link any of them to what had happened. After two days they were all released.

So at the time when Torleif Sandberg was run down by two young car thieves in Göteborg, Daniel and Fredrik were spending their second night in the cells in Copenhagen.

Daniel had gotten cold feet and come running home to Göteborg, but he didn't have an apartment of his own in the city, so he had had to go and stay with his mom. Which was where he had been picked up.

"Well, at least that means we can definitely cross those two off our list. So that just leaves Björn Kjellgren, alias Billy, and Niklas Ström," Irene said in an attempt to lighten the atmosphere.

The baleful look she got from Jonny said it all. He was obviously frustrated at the thought of having to start all over again.

"Irene is right. Even though it didn't look as if those two guys knew each other, there is one thing that suggests it might be them. They both absconded from Gräskärr," Tommy pointed out.

"Billy Kjellgren is a loner and Niklas Ström is a crazy homosexual rapist. According to the staff, they both kept to themselves, and none of the other guys would hang out with them. Hardly surprising in Niklas Ström's case. Obviously you want to know that your ass is safe when you go for a shower." Jonny snickered at his own joke.

Jesper joined in, but stopped abruptly when he realized that no one else was laughing.

"Of course it could be that only one of them was involved," Tommy said, ignoring Jonny's last comment. "Or neither. The nightmare scenario as far as we're concerned is that we might be dealing with two guys who are completely unknown to us. But for the time being we have to go with the two names we have left: Niklas Ström and Billy Kjellgren."

"Am I disturbing you?" came a woman's voice from the doorway.

Everyone in the room recognized the voice and turned their heads. Marianne Wärme, the Acting Chief of Police, was standing there. She was a small, plump, middle-aged woman with short greying hair and glasses. Her bright, nut-brown eyes twinkled behind the thick lenses, and she often smiled warmly at the person she was talking to. When she wasn't in uniform she usually wore a skirt suit and pumps and carried a matching purse. Anyone who didn't know better could easily have taken her for a harmless old biddy, but she wasn't nicknamed "The Iron Lady" for nothing. While climbing the career ladder, she had developed a reputation for incorruptible honesty, uncompromising toughness, and a will of steel. Whatever task she set for herself, she carried to its conclusion. Nobody could question her ability or her leadership skills—at least not within earshot of Marianne Wärme. Most people liked her because she gave clear, straight answers, and at the same time they had the greatest respect for her. Women with power and authority tend to intimidate people far more than men with the same qualities, particularly if those women deserve the position they have achieved. Acting Chief of Police Marianne Wärme was one of those women.

She walked into the room in her sensible low-heeled shoes and refused the offer of a cup of coffee.

"I'm in a rush. I'll be brief. The commissioner of the Policía Nacional in Spain has contacted me. He's received a request from the Chief of Police in Tenerife that a colleague from the Violent Crimes Unit in Göteborg go over there to help with an investigation into a series of homicides. There are four victims in total. Apparently these homicides are directly linked to the murder of the Russian girl who was found out at Delsjön."

She paused, her sharp gaze scanning her audience. They all looked completely at a loss for words. Eventually Andersson managed to pull himself together, and protested feebly. "I don't think we can send anyone over. We've already got a couple of colleagues off sick, and this is a complex case, and—"

"Yes, it certainly does seem very complex. Which is why I think it's a good idea if one of you goes to Tenerife. You can be there in the sunshine in five or six hours, which is no longer than it takes to drive to Stockholm. And the Spanish authorities will pay, as they've already said. We're talking about two days, one overnight stay. That should give both sides plenty of time to exchange information. It could well benefit our investigation here in Göteborg, if the Spaniards are privy to information we don't have."

She definitely had a point. There were still major question marks within the investigation.

"It also fosters goodwill if we facilitate this kind of information exchange between countries within the EU," the Acting Chief of Police said with a smile.

That smile fooled no one. If Marianne Wärme said that one of them was going to Tenerife, then one of them would soon be sitting on a plane.

"I HAVEN'T GOT time to go," Irene said firmly.

The main reason was they were snowed under with work. The

other reason was the Huss family had planned a ski trip at the cottage in Värmland. Irene had booked two days of leave, Friday and Monday, and wanted to clear her desk before the weekend. Krister was free for the long weekend, and the twins were coming too. On the way up to Sunne, they were going to stop off in Säffle and have lunch with Krister's sister; they hadn't gotten together since the funeral of Irene's mother-in-law in August.

"You're the only one who can go," Andersson said.

"What do you mean? Am I the only person who's dispensable in this department? We're up to our ears in work! And you're saying you can spare me?" Irene didn't often flare up, but right now she was deeply hurt.

"You're going to Tenerife to work. Not to sunbathe and see the sights. You have experience working with colleagues in different countries," the superintendent said.

Irene detected more than a hint of flattery, but there was some truth in what he said. She had traveled to Copenhagen, London and Paris in the line of duty, and in each city she had worked with the local police. Not always with great success, admittedly, but at least it had given her a skill set her colleagues in the department lacked. And for the most part she had found it both productive and interesting.

"Hannu can't go because of the situation with Birgitta. And we need Tommy to carry on looking for Torleif's killers. That knocks out Jonny, too, and that new guy . . . Jonathan."

"Jesper," Irene corrected him.

"That new guy Jesper. And Fredrik is trying to track down Anders Pettersson. I don't know how we lost him! We need to find the bastard."

Andersson paused for breath, then went on. "Which leaves you. You're looking into the girl's death on your own now that Birgitta isn't here, so I think it would be a wise move to go down to Tenerife. Plenty of people will be green with envy when they hear you've headed south to the sunshine."

"Right. Two days' traveling, one after the other. I'll get to spend around twelve hours on the island," Irene protested.

As she spoke she looked over at the window. The sleet was lashing against the glass, leaving wet snail trails as it slid down toward the sill. The temperature was just above freezing, and the wind was howling. Perhaps a day or two somewhere warm wouldn't be such a bad thing after all. Although she had no intention of letting Andersson know what she was thinking. And then there was the problem of the ski trip to Sunne.

"Okay then. Although I really don't have time," she said with a theatrical sigh.

Andersson's face lit up. "Terrific! You can go tomorrow, or the day after at the latest. I'll let you contact the Spaniards yourself to tell them the good news," he said with a smile, handing her a crumpled scrap of paper. He was reaching for the phone before she got to the door. He wanted to be the one to inform the Acting Chief of Police that a Detective Inspector was already on the way to support the Policía Nacional in their complex investigation.

LINDA HOLM WAS right: Miguel de Viera did indeed speak English poorly. He didn't seem particularly thrilled at the prospect of meeting a female colleague from Sweden. Irene thought she had heard him sigh: "Only women *policía?*"

After a few minutes they had reached a state of complete mutual confusion, and Irene was beginning to feel quite exhausted. She gave a start when de Viera suddenly yelled into the phone. It took a few bewildering seconds before she realized that he wasn't shouting at her, but at someone in his office. He dropped the receiver with a thud, and she could hear him gibbering agitatedly. After a while the receiver was picked up again, and a calm male voice said, "Detective Inspector Juan Rejón speaking."

Irene explained who she was, and that she was intending to come to Tenerife at his colleague's request either the next day or on Friday.

"Excellent. In that case we will book your tickets and accommodation."

He spoke good English with a noticeable Spanish accent. Since Irene's own English was only serviceable, she was very relieved when he went on.

"I will contact you again, Inspector Huss, when I have found out the flight times. And I will pick you up at the airport."

"Thank you very much," Irene said with heartfelt gratitude. She was very happy to avoid dealing with all the practical aspects of her journey since she had a lot of other things to sort out before she left.

"We are the ones who should be thanking you, Inspector. We are very grateful that you have agreed to come to Tenerife. Our situation is . . . desperate."

He uttered the final word with a certain amount of hesitation, but Irene had no doubt that he was speaking the truth. If they hadn't been desperate, they would hardly have requested the assistance of a colleague from the distant frozen North. And they were paying for everything without so much as a murmur.

INSPECTOR JUAN REJÓN called back just as Irene was about to go home for the day. He explained that there were no seats available on flights to Tenerife the following day, and that every flight to Göteborg from Tenerife on the Saturday was also full. He therefore hoped that Inspector Huss would not object to staying for two nights. She would be leaving from Landvetter at 7:15 on Friday morning, returning at 1:00 P.M. on Sunday. As her ski trip was ruined anyway, Irene was quite happy at the thought of an extra day in the sun. A room had been booked at the Golden Sun Club Hotel. Rejón had commented somewhat cryptically that this was a strategic choice of hotel, but Irene didn't want to ask him what he meant.

Chapter 14

THE FAMILY'S REACTION to the news of Irene's weekend trip to the Canaries could best be described as a resigned acceptance. They were used to the fact that she often had to work overtime, including weekends when she should have been free. Krister had struggled to hide his disappointment. He had a long weekend off work every five weeks, and he had been looking forward to a trip to the cottage in Värmland to go skiing and snowboarding. However, his mood lightened when Katarina said firmly that they ought to go anyway. Felipe could take Irene's place. Before Felipe met Katarina he had never been anywhere near a ski slope, but they had been up to Ski Sunne several times the previous winter. Thanks to his training as a dancer his balance was good, and he had quickly learned to master the snowboard. These days he was an enthusiastic practitioner.

Irene couldn't help the fleeting thought that passed through her mind: she was dispensable within her family. Resolutely she pushed the foolish thought aside. She was being replaced by Felipe purely because of her work.

"Two days! I don't begrudge you a single hour!"

Tommy smiled as he spoke, but the little sigh that escaped him gave away the truth. He would have loved to doze off on a plane flying south to the sun on Friday morning. The discussions with their Spanish colleagues could be dealt with that afternoon, leaving Saturday free to spend by the pool. Irene was thinking along much the same lines.

Jonny merely glared at her, then said, "*You're* going? Haven't those poor Spaniards got enough problems already?" He wasn't smiling as he spoke.

They were all in the conference room waiting for Hannu. He had called on his cell from a traffic jam outside Lerum. One section of the freeway was flooded, and the traffic had been diverted along a series of smaller roads. He was going to be at least thirty minutes late.

Irene had finished her reports and scanned all the relevant pictures into her laptop. To be on the safe side she had also made hard copies of everything, just in case the technology let her down. That had happened all too often in the past.

When Hannu arrived he seemed perfectly normal at first glance. He sat down opposite Irene, which gave her the opportunity to take a closer look at him. His ash-blond hair had been cut fairly recently, and he was wearing jeans and a sweater as always. But when Irene happened to meet his gaze, she felt very uneasy. The blue eyes were bloodshot and did not reflect his usual serenity. Had he been crying? He certainly didn't look as if he'd slept much. Irene had never noticed any lines on his face before, but now they were clearly visible in the harsh fluorescent light. Admittedly that particular light didn't flatter anyone, but Hannu looked unusually worn out and whey-faced.

Irene got to her feet and said, "I'll get you a coffee. I need a top-off anyway."

Hannu nodded gratefully at her.

"Coffee: Irene's universal panacea," Tommy said, smiling warmly at Hannu.

He, too, had realized that something wasn't right. They had worked with Hannu for many years now, and they knew him well by this stage. Or at least as well as Hannu allowed any of his colleagues to get to know him. Something was definitely wrong. Did it have to do with Birgitta? Irene felt a vague anxiety begin to churn away in her stomach as she hurried off to the coffee machine. She realized how worried she was when she couldn't remember whether or not Hannu took milk. Everyone in the department knew how everyone else liked their coffee. She took a chance and pressed the MILK button.

"Thanks. I don't mind it with milk."

Hannu gave her a wan smile. Damn! It was Birgitta who usually took milk. Irene offered to swap with him, but he refused.

"I'll top it off with black in a minute," he said.

He took a deep swig of his coffee, unconsciously pulling a face before putting the cup down.

"First of all I need to tell you that Birgitta . . . that we . . . lost the baby last night," he said, his voice trembling.

Nobody knew what to say. The room went very quiet. Superintendent Andersson cleared his throat and made a few uncoordinated movements with his mouth as if he was working up to saying something, but no audible sounds emerged.

It was Hannu himself who went on. "Birgitta isn't feeling too bad, under the circumstances, but her blood pressure is still high. She won't be back at work until it comes down."

Blood pressure still high? Irene couldn't remember Birgitta mentioning high blood pressure. On the contrary, she had seemed so happy and full of confidence. The only consolation was that the pregnancy hadn't been very far along; Irene assumed that would make it slightly easier for Birgitta to recover, both physically and mentally. And no doubt she and Hannu would soon have a new sibling for little Timo.

Hannu knocked back the remaining contents of his coffee cup in one gulp. "I picked up the autopsy report on Torleif Sandberg yesterday," he said.

He was speaking in his usual calm tone, and his colleagues

immediately relaxed. That half-strangled voice with its under-lying black despair had made them uneasy. Grief is difficult to handle if it comes too close. It's always easier if a professional distance can be maintained.

"The skull was shattered. Death was instantaneous. Exten-sive injuries to the rest of the body. The aorta was severed and he bled to death very quickly. Professor Stridner sees nothing unusual in the injuries; they are exactly as she would have expected. However, she did make a number of other discov-eries."

He glanced up from the document he had placed in front of him on the table. When no one showed any sign of wanting to speak, he looked down again and continued. "She pointed out that he was wearing very insubstantial clothing, given that the temperature was minus fifteen when he went out for a run. Nothing on his head. No mittens or gloves. No thermal pants. Ordinary sneakers and short sports socks. Short-sleeved T-shirt and underpants and an ordinary track suit. Admittedly it was a lined police-issue tracksuit in cotton poplin, but people usually wear those when it's several degrees above freezing. They're not particularly warm."

No gloves. It was the image from the scene of the accident that had flickered through Irene's subconscious: the severed hand lying on the pavement, with no glove or mitten on it.

"So he was dressed for a run in a temperature of five degrees above zero or higher," Fredrik concluded.

"Exactly. Stridner thought that was worth noting, particu-larly as he was showing signs of damage due to frostbite in several parts of his body: fingers, toes, cheeks, nose, ears and chin. According to Stridner, he must have been out in the cold for at least an hour in order to have sustained such extensive damage."

"Frostbite? So why the hell wasn't he dressed properly? Tor-leif has been going out running in all weather for at least forty years!" Andersson was clearly finding it difficult to control his indignation.

"He was an outstanding member of the police orienteering team for many years. He had lots of prizes in his cabinet," Irene said.

"How do you know that?" Andersson said suspiciously.

Since Andersson wasn't supposed to know about the unofficial visit she and Hannu had made to Torleif's apartment, she said glibly, "Stefan mentioned it. His adoptive son."

"I know who he is," the superintendent snapped. He still found it difficult to deal with the thought that Torleif had lied to his face about being the boy's father. Perhaps Torleif had been too embarrassed to tell his colleagues he was marrying a woman who was carrying another man's child. But then it was never easy to understand what motivated other people. That was something Irene had learned during her years as a police officer.

"Why would someone who obviously knew better go out in such cold weather dressed like that? And why did he run so far? He must have gone a long way if he was out for at least an hour. And why did he go out so late at night? I mean, it was pitch dark," Tommy said, rattling out a barrage of both questions and answers.

"Could he have been a bit gaga?" Jonny suggested.

"Possibly, but there's nothing to indicate that," Hannu replied.

Irene thought about the clean, tidy apartment. The décor might have been dull and old-fashioned, but everything had been in perfect order. Spotless. It hadn't looked as if a person with dementia had been living there. Torleif Sandberg had been sixty-four years old when he died, and she knew that it was relatively rare for dementia to strike at such an early age. Although she had wondered about herself occasionally. Only last week she had put the milk away in the microwave; she had found it there the following morning. She had simply poured it down the sink without telling anyone else in the family. But it had given her pause.

"Could it be connected to the stolen car?" Fredrik said.

"In what way?" Andersson said.

Fredrik thought for a moment before outlining his theory. "If he happened to look out the window and saw someone stealing his car, perhaps he rushed outside in what he happened to be wearing. He probably wouldn't have given a thought to how cold it was. By the time he got outside, the thief had already started the car and was driving off. Torleif ran after him—Irene says he was fast. And then . . . what happened next? Maybe he got lost?" Fredrik looked around, hoping to find support among his colleagues.

"Lost? I hardly think so," Andersson said. "He'd lived in the area for at least twenty-five years, and went running around there virtually every day."

"And he couldn't have seen the car being stolen. His apartment doesn't have a window overlooking the street where it was parked," Hannu pointed out.

Irene was thinking the same thing. The entrance to Torleif's apartment was at the far side of the building, while his car had been parked at the opposite end. There was no chance that he could have seen the car from his windows.

"So then why was he outside dressed like that when it was so cold?" Tommy repeated.

It was difficult to come up with a reasonable explanation as to why Torleif had been out in the cold for at least an hour. No experienced runner exposes himself to the dangers of temperatures well below freezing. The risk of damage to muscles and tendons increases significantly in the cold, particularly for older people, which is why runners usually prefer to wear too much rather than too little. It's easier to remove an item of clothing if you get too hot than to try to run faster when you start to stiffen up.

"What about the toxicology?" Irene asked.

"No trace of narcotics or pharmaceutical drugs," Hannu confirmed.

"That would have been all we needed," Andersson muttered to himself. He was drumming his fingers on the table, looking pensive. "Tommy, can you give us a summary of where we are in the investigation? We might come up with something while we're listening to you," he said eventually.

"Okay. So to begin with we have Torleif, who—according to the witnesses waiting at the tram stop—comes running along at high speed past the entrance of the TV studios. Without showing any sign of slowing down or looking around, he runs straight out into Delsjövägen. At that point a BMW comes racing up the road, driven by a car thief with his pal sitting next to him in the passenger seat. The stolen car is being followed by a patrol car at a distance of approximately 150 meters. The cops see the stolen car hit someone; the body is thrown up in the air. They stop and call an ambulance. The witnesses see the BMW, with a shattered windshield, turn onto Töpelsgatan and disappear up the hill. When—"

Andersson waved his hands and interrupted Tommy. "Stop! We know exactly what happened after Torleif was run down. The problem is that we have no idea what happened before! Why the hell was he out running in the dark and the cold? The more I think about it, the less sense it makes."

Everyone in the room agreed with him. No one had a decent theory—not after Fredrik's had gone down in flames.

"The question is whether we need to look into why he was out running. Maybe he'd just misjudged how far he was going to go. Or maybe he just took out the trash, then spotted something and set off," Tommy said.

"He was on his way home," Irene pointed out quietly.

"What? How the hell do you know that?" Andersson demanded.

"He was running straight across Delsjövägen, toward Anders Zornsgatan where he lived. Which means it's likely that he ran across the street in the opposite direction earlier in the evening. Where had he been in the period in between? Did he spend an hour running along marked tracks? Or was he indoors somewhere? If so, where?"

"Perhaps he was in a car," Fredrik suggested.

"Possibly. There's a big parking lot outside the TV studios," Irene said.

"The frostbite damage," Hannu reminded her.

"That proves he was outdoors," Tommy said. "Not in a car. And even if he was only going to the parking lot at the TV studios, surely he would have put on a jacket at least. It's still a few hundred meters from his apartment, and it really was freezing."

"Perhaps he ran there," Fredrik tried again.

"Or maybe he was running around looking for his missing car," Jonny said.

"This is getting us nowhere. And the important thing isn't whatever the hell Torleif was doing before he was run down. The important thing is to catch the bastards who killed him!" Andersson said.

Irene and Hannu exchanged a glance. They both knew the superintendent was right. There was no point in channeling their limited resources into something that wasn't relevant to the investigation. But at the same time they were both experienced officers, and they were intrigued by all the odd, unexpected details that had begun to emerge as they looked into Torleif Sandberg's life and death.

Everyone jumped as the intercom suddenly crackled into life. "Hello! Are you there?" came Svante Malm's voice.

Tommy, who was sitting nearest, leaned over and pressed the button. "Yes, we're here," he answered cheerfully.

"Good. I've just run a check on the fingerprints we found in Torleif Sandberg's car. They were in our records, and they belong to two guys named Niklas Ström and Björn Kjellgren. Their ID numbers are—"

"Thanks, Svante. We've already got their details," Tommy managed to say with some difficulty.

"Okay, I'll be in touch if I find anything else."

When the connection was broken you could have heard a pin drop in the room. They sat there motionless, hardly even blinking. Some of their heads were full of thoughts, buzzing around like a swarm of bees, while others' brains had stopped working completely.

"What the hell does this mean?" Jonny said eventually.

"I have no idea. This can't be right," Tommy said in confusion.

"Jesper and I have been working our asses off trying to find the bastards who had absconded from various institutions," Jonny said. "There were a few to choose from at the beginning; we've gradually been able to eliminate them from our inquiries, one by one. Which only leaves Billy and Niklas. But we've been looking for them as the suspects who stole the BMW that ran down and killed Muesli. And now it turns out that they stole *his* car! How the hell is that possible?" His frustration was obvious, and it was shared by everyone in the room.

"It does seem pretty unlikely," Tommy agreed.

"Unlikely! It's fucking impossible!" the superintendent exploded. His face was a worrying shade of bright red.

"I don't suppose there's any chance it could be a mistake?" Irene said.

"More like a bad joke," Tommy said wearily.

"So Billy's hooked up with the gay rapist! Maybe little Billy is similarly inclined. I bet he likes it rough." Jonny grinned. He was obviously recovering from the initial shock, and was well on the way to being his usual self again.

"It's slightly surprising, but then again, perhaps not. They were both in Gräskärr. According to the staff they didn't have much close contact, but they must have had some. They took off within twenty-four hours of each other, Niklas first and then Billy. Everybody assumed that Billy had been inspired by Niklas's escape; nobody thought they'd planned it together," Irene said. She was the one who had collated the information about the absconders at an early stage of the investigation. It felt like a long time ago.

"There's no point in sitting here speculating! Get out there and find the little bastards!" Andersson snapped.

He got to his feet, indicating that the meeting was over. Irene noticed that he hadn't taken a cookie out of the open packet lying on the table. She was starting to get seriously worried about him.

Hannu came over to Irene and stood beside her. He waited until they were alone in the room.

"Could you help me with something?" he said quietly.

His facial expression was now completely under control. It must have taken an enormous toll on him to reveal his grief over the tragedy that had befallen his family, and in front of all his colleagues, too. Irene knew he wouldn't say any more unless she asked. If then.

"Of course. What do you want me to do?"

"You seemed to get on well with Stefan Sandberg. I got the impression that he trusted you. He told you a lot more than he needed to."

Irene nodded.

"Could you give him a call and tell him that the car has been found?"

"He doesn't know yet?" Irene exclaimed.

"No. Nobody thought about it yesterday."

Irene opened her mouth to say something, then thought better of it. She knew better than anyone that they were overwhelmed with work. A stolen car wasn't exactly a high priority, at least not until inexplicable connections started popping up.

The two boys who they suspected of having run down and killed Torleif turned out instead to be the ones who had stolen his car. Admittedly this had happened just a few hundred meters from the spot where Torleif had died, but there was still no rhyme or reason to it. Why were they even in the area? How could they have got hold of Torleif's car keys? Did they know it was his car when they stole it?

"Tell Stefan Sandberg about the fingerprints. Ask him if he can think of any possible connection between Torleif and the two boys," Hannu went on.

"Where are you going with this?" She realized there must be a point to his questions.

"Niklas Ström is gay. We don't know anything about Billy Kjellgren's inclinations, but he ran away with Niklas. I'm just wondering whether Torleif might have been gay. Niklas and Billy could have lured Torleif out to his car, perhaps by promising him sex. Torleif could have been threatened and managed to get out of the car. Obviously his instinct was to run straight home. They could have been some distance away, which would explain the frostbite damage. That would also explain why we haven't found his car keys, just the spare keys that he had in the apartment. Niklas and Billy hung onto the keys and the car."

Irene realized she was sitting staring at Hannu. That was probably the longest single speech she had ever heard from him. And his theory was absolutely credible. It would explain the link between the two boys, Torleif and his car.

"That's an excellent theory! So you want me to try and find out if Stefan knows whether Torleif was gay?"

"Yes."

"I'll get on it right away."

Irene went straight to her office. Hannu had definitely come up with a theory where no one else had been able to. Of course, the big question still remained: Who had killed Torleif?

• • •

Stefan Sandberg answered his cell when she called. He said he would be going home to Umeå that afternoon. He had managed to sort out most things, and wouldn't be coming back until the funeral. He didn't show much interest when she told him that the stolen car had been found.

"Outside Olofstorp? Does that mean the thieves are there?" he asked.

"Not necessarily. The car had run out of gas. They might have had another car nearby. At any rate they didn't steal another car in the area, at least not as far as we know," Irene said.

She wondered feverishly how she could introduce the subject of Torleif's sexual inclinations. There wasn't a natural segue in the conversation, so she decided the best thing was to go straight to the point. Stefan was a doctor, after all.

"There is one thing that's puzzling us. Forensics found the fingerprints of the two car thieves. They're on our records, so we know who they are."

"But surely that's a good thing? What's the problem?"

"The problem is the link between Torleif and these two guys. We can't work out how the whole thing hangs together, which is why I have to ask you a very delicate question." Irene paused, wondering how to phrase her query.

"What do you mean, delicate?" She could hear that Stefan was a little wary.

"At least one of the two guys was homosexual. Do you happen to know whether Torleif might have been gay?" She had decided it was best to be frank.

There was such a long silence that Irene began to think Stefan wasn't going to answer.

To her relief he spoke at last. "I'm just trying to think . . . Mom never said anything to suggest that. If he was gay, then he probably hid it from her. Or perhaps he didn't acknowledge that side of himself until after the divorce."

Irene couldn't help feeling a pang of disappointment.

"I guess the problem is I didn't know Torleif well. I have virtually no memories from my first four years, when I lived with him and Mom here in Göteborg. Are you sure he had a connection with the guys who took his car?"

"They had the keys," Irene informed him.

"In that case they must have gotten a hold of them somehow. It's very strange. But I have come across another mystery," Stefan said.

"A mystery? Sounds interesting."

"It is. I had a meeting with Torleif's personal banking adviser yesterday afternoon. There's a lot of stuff to sort out with the bank after someone dies. I discovered that Torleif had only eighty-three thousand kronor in his account. That was all."

"That's not too bad, is it?"

Irene thought about her own account. She would have been delighted if Torleif's money had found its way there by some miracle.

"No, it's a reasonable amount. But Torleif has always lived so . . . carefully. I expected there to be more money. And his adviser told me exactly what Torleif had done with it all. He showed me the paperwork. Torleif had just bought a house in Thailand!"

Irene was astonished. "Thailand?" she repeated.

"Yes. A big house that cost eight hundred thousand kronor. Apparently it's a luxury villa, and it would cost many times that amount in Sweden. It's got a pool and everything."

"Did you have any idea that he was planning to move to Thailand?"

"No, but I know he's been there. He told me the last time I saw him, three years ago. He said he treated himself to a good car and one trip abroad each year, and the previous year he'd been to Thailand."

"Unbelievable!"

Possibly not the most inspired comment, Irene thought, but it expressed exactly how she was feeling right now.

"You could say that. Now I'm stuck with a house in Thailand, which is an unexpected problem. Speaking of problems, did you find Torleif's cell after he'd been hit?"

"No. He didn't have a cell with him—just the keys to his apartment. And there was a flashlight lying next to him," Irene said.

"That's odd. A bill has just arrived for a brand new contract with Telenor and a new Nokia. I've searched the whole apartment, but there's no sign of his cell."

Did this have any relevance to the investigation into Torleif's death?

"I'll check with forensics, see if they've found a Nokia in the car," she said.

"Good. I need to contact Telenor and cancel the contract; they might want the phone back. I don't really know what their policy is in the case of a sudden death."

"I have no idea," Irene answered honestly.

"You have my cell number if you need to contact me once I'm back home," Stefan said.

Irene was suddenly struck by a thought. "I've got your number, but was Torleif's number on the paperwork from Telenor?"

"Absolutely. Both his number and pin code, along with the cell phone's ID number. It's all here."

He gave Irene the details and she jotted them down.

When she had finished talking to Stefan, she called Svante Malm on his direct line. He wasn't available because he was out on a job. Irene sent him an email, asking if they had found a Nokia in Torleif Sandberg's car. She also included all the numbers Stefan had given her.

Then she picked up her laptop and her bag containing all the case notes, and said goodbye to her colleagues. Following a barrage of jokes and good wishes with varying degrees of sincerity, she left the department and pressed the elevator button. She was going straight home to pack.

Chapter 15

IRENE WASN'T PARTICULARLY well traveled. In the past she had had neither the time nor the money to venture far afield. The house she and Krister had bought when the twins were four had always been a heavy financial burden. They had thought it was worth the sacrifice so the girls could grow up close to nature and the sea. In recent years they had treated themselves to two package holidays to Greece, just the two of them. They were planning to go again toward the end of the summer, in exactly six months' time. They just had to hang on until then.

To be fair, they had actually traveled overseas last Easter as well. They had gone to London to visit Irene's colleague, Glen Thomsen, and his lively family. That was when she had found out that Superintendent Andersson's little romance with Donna, Glen's Brazilian mother, was over. She had turned out to be a little too fiery for Andersson in the long run. She had found a new man much closer to home, but she and Andersson were still in touch by phone and letter. Glen had brought Irene up to date, while Andersson went around imagining that no one knew about his little fling in London. Irene hadn't seen any signs of a broken heart.

Glen and Irene had become good friends a few years earlier during her second work-related overseas trip. The first had been to Copenhagen; Irene still shuddered when she thought about the case of the dismembered bodies. The whole investigation was something she tried to erase from her memory, but she couldn't do anything about the horrific images that still sometimes haunted her dreams.

The weekend visit to Tenerife was first and foremost a working trip, and secondly, a break from the bitter cold. King Bore, the god of winter, still hadn't slackened his grip on Scandinavia, nor was he likely to do so for another month or so. During the night the temperature had started to drop again, and it was now several degrees below freezing. All the meltwater that had caused floods in the west of Sweden during the thaw of the previous twenty-four hours had now frozen once again.

When the cab picked Irene up just after five, the whole of Göteborg was encased in a carapace of ice. It wasn't only tiredness that made her unsteady on her feet as she covered the short distance between her front door and the parking lot. The pavement was like glass, and the gritting truck hadn't been out this early in the morning. She had to take tiny steps to avoid falling over, and sighed with relief when she managed to make it safely and sank into the back seat of her cab. The journey to the airport at Landvetter would be pretty expensive, but the Spaniards could pay. That was her last conscious thought before she fell asleep.

THERE WAS ONE thing about flying that sometimes made Irene think it wasn't worth it: the departure times are always so early in the morning. She had very little luggage, just her laptop case and a small rucksack. She was able to take them both on board with her, but she still needed to check in an hour before departure. Which was why she was wandering around the terminal, half-asleep, at twenty past six in the morning. More by instinct than judgment she followed the aroma of coffee and ended up in a café. After three cups of coffee and a fresh minibaguette with egg and anchovies, she began to feel a little more positive about life.

Gazing into the darkness outside the enormous windows of the terminal building, Irene could see the runway lights and the flashing warning lights of the utility vehicles out on the airfield. There were buses transporting passengers between the terminals and the planes, and small shuttle trucks delivering airline food. Irene decided to buy another baguette to take on board with her.

She went into a duty-free shop to look for the items on the list the girls had given her. She also bought herself new mascara and a small bottle of SPF 15 sun lotion. She didn't want to get home looking like a freshly boiled lobster, or she would be getting "sympathetic" comments from her colleagues for weeks.

As she headed for the checkout to pay, she passed a display labeled THIS MONTH'S SPECIAL OFFERS. Duty free plus a special offer must be really cheap, Irene thought as she stopped to take a closer look. Above all the creams and lotions was a mirror. A quick glance at her face confirmed that she needed all the help she could get. Everything that could possibly droop was drooping: the corners of her mouth, her eyelids, her cheeks. There were lines around her eyes and between her eyebrows. And since when did she have bags under her eyes? She could blame a certain amount on the fact that it was so early in the morning and she wasn't wearing any makeup, but there was no denying it: she was definitely on the wrong side of forty. She discreetly dug her reading glasses out of her rucksack; these days she couldn't make out small print without them. She started examining the beautifully designed packages, each and every one promising smoother skin, fewer wrinkles and a reduction in ugly pigmentation. She also found the miracle she needed: a tube of eye cream especially for bags and dark circles under the eyes. Perfect! Above the shelf a sign proclaimed: BUY ONE GET ONE FREE. How good was that? Resolutely she picked up two tubes of eye cream, a day cream that promised to make the skin look twenty years younger and the accompanying night cream. Satisfied with her haul, she went to the checkout to pay.

The assistant asked to see her boarding card, then scanned her purchases.

"Two thousand nine hundred and forty kronor," she said.

Irene's immediate reaction was that she must have misheard. Almost three thousand kronor for cosmetics? At that very moment her flight was called.

"This is the final call for Spanair flight three-one-two-one to Tenerife, departing at seven fifteen. Please proceed to gate twelve," a voice announced brightly over the loudspeaker.

Irene feebly handed her credit card to the assistant, who yawned without a trace of embarrassment as she asked Irene to enter her pin number. Irene realized there was no time to ask if she could put something back; besides which, she needed the whole lot. The face in the mirror had been in dire need of an emergency extreme makeover.

IRENE STOWED HER thin poplin coat and knitted cotton cardigan in the overhead locker, then slid her laptop underneath them. The outside pockets of the laptop case contained all the paperwork relating to the investigation. She wanted to be prepared for every eventuality. She checked to make sure that the case and all its pockets were securely closed, then settled down in her seat. She was wearing stretch jeans that could cope with a long journey without getting creased, and a thin woolen polo neck sweater with a short-sleeved top underneath. She had dressed according to the onion principle. On her feet were ordinary deck shoes, with knee-high socks made of the finest wool. When they landed she would take off the socks and go barefoot in her shoes. Before that she would probably have already removed the polo neck. In her rucksack she had packed her toilet bag, her newly acquired rejuvenating creams, clean underwear, a bikini, two T-shirts, a pair of light sandals and a nice pair of shorts. In the outer pocket were her passport, e-ticket and wallet. She would need to withdraw some money at the airport when she arrived, but in spite of the short notice, she thought she had everything under control.

A couple in their seventies arrived and sat down beside her; they said hello, but didn't introduce themselves. As soon as they were settled they both produced sleep masks made of dark blue silk. They were obviously waiting for the plane to take off so that they could recline their seats and go back to sleep, which suited Irene perfectly. She wasn't in the mood for polite small talk this early in the morning and intended to follow her neighbors' example, minus the sleep mask.

A family with three children ended up in the row in front of them. Even before the plane took off everyone knew that the boys were called Lukas, Simon and Natan. Lukas had evidently started school because he kept teasing his brothers about the fact that it was *his* half-term break. The two younger boys got more and more annoyed with their big brother, who triumphantly proclaimed that little kids shouldn't really be allowed to go away during the traditional winter sports' break since they didn't go to school and therefore didn't actually have a break. The logic sounded convincing, and the little ones retaliated by starting to punch their brother while yelling at the tops of their voices.

Their mother was slightly plump with bleached blonde hair, but she had a sweet face. She could have been anywhere between thirty and forty. In spite of the fact that she wasn't wearing a coat when they boarded the plane, she was already sweating profusely. She had squeezed her generous curves into a sleeveless calf-length denim dress, with a low-cut pink T-shirt underneath. She tried to shut up her offspring, first by pleading with them and then by threatening to revoke certain privileges. There would be no swimming in the pool, no ice cream, no new inflatable toys unless they behaved themselves. Her sons ignored her completely; the noise level became virtually unbearable. Their father was sitting on the other side of the aisle reading the morning paper.

When the illuminated seat belt sign went off, the children finally settled down. Irene heard a sigh of relief from her neighbors.

IRENE SPOTTED DETECTIVE Inspector Juan Rejón right away. And she wasn't the only one. Most of the women in the Arrivals hall—and quite a few men—noticed the police officer holding up a small sign on which someone had written MS. HUSS with a red marker. He seemed unaware of the attention, or perhaps he was just used to it and didn't care. He stood there with his legs slightly apart, calmly observing the stream of people emerging from customs. The dark blue shirt hugged his muscular upper body. The gold stripes on his shoulders drew the eye. On his head he wore a dark blue cap with a glinting gold badge. As Irene came closer she could make out the letters PN: Policía Nacional. His body language made it clear that he was no ordinary beat cop. She also noticed his face, with its high cheekbones and well-shaped mouth. The cheeks and chin bore the shadow of dark stubble. The eyes were very dark, with long eyelashes and strong eyebrows arching over them. The thick brown hair visible under the cap curled at the back of the neck. Good Lord, was she going to be escorted around the island by some kind of male model? Given his rank he ought to be around thirty, but he looked younger. Inspector Juan Rejón was a very stylish man.

Irene was smiling as she walked over to him. His face lit up, and he held out his hand. They introduced themselves, and both noticed that she was a few centimeters taller than him. She couldn't help laughing when she saw the envious looks of the women around them.

"I'll drive you to the Golden Sun Club Hotel first; you can have some lunch and a little rest. I'll pick you up at four," he said, offering to carry one of her bags.

She declined politely because both the laptop case over her shoulder and the rucksack on her back were light. He led the way through the automatic glass doors. According to the thermometer inside the terminal the temperature outside was supposed to be twenty-five degrees Celsius. As she walked through the doors, a wave of heat suddenly struck her. She almost gasped for breath. The thirty-degree difference in temperature had hit her hard. It was a little while before she realized there was actually a light breeze ruffling her hair, which was very pleasant. Tall palm trees were growing on the other side of the street; the breeze was stirring the leaves and making them rustle. She suddenly felt more like a tourist than a police officer.

"What was the temperature in Göteborg when you left?" Inspector Rejón asked, with the hint of a smile at one corner of his mouth.

He had noticed that his tall colleague from Sweden had stopped dead outside the terminal doors and taken several deep breaths. She had then closed her eyes and instinctively turned her face up to the sun.

"Minus five. And the slush that had thawed over the past few days froze again overnight," she said, still with her eyes closed and her face upturned.

She started fumbling in her jacket pocket, found her sunglasses and put them on. If nothing else, at least they would hide the worst of the bags and dark circles. Once she got to the hotel, she would take a shower and apply the miracle creams.

Inspector Rejón shook his head. "How can anyone live in such a climate? Terrible! Although it's lucky for us, of course. All those frozen Scandinavians come here during the winter to find some sunshine and get warm. Not to mention the rest of

Northern Europe," he said, his white teeth flashing in a big smile.

"As I understand it, that's part of the reason I'm here. Your chief, de Viera, told my superintendent that he was worried that these murders would damage the tourist industry," Irene said, keeping her tone casual.

Inspector Rejón didn't answer, but simply carried on walking toward the police car parked in a reserved bay marked POLICÍA. Irene glanced at him sideways and saw that his face had stiffened into an inscrutable mask. Had she said something wrong? And if so, what was it?

He held open the passenger door, then slammed it shut once she was safely inside. Unnecessarily hard, in Irene's opinion. His reaction could hardly be down to her comment. There was something else behind his behavior; after all, she had only repeated exactly what de Viera had said with regard to the need for her visit. She was determined to find out what was behind Rejón's sudden change of mood.

They sat in silence for a few minutes as they left the comparatively bare airport complex. After a while, more palm trees and tall cacti began to appear along the side of the highway.

"It would be very helpful if you could tell me about the murders. All I know is that three people are dead, killed in some kind of gangland dispute," she said in a pleasant tone, as if she hadn't noticed the rapid deterioration in her colleague's attitude.

Inspector Rejón had just pulled onto the freeway that led to Los Cristianos and Playa de las Américas, according to the sign. He didn't say anything for a long time, but eventually he spoke. "There has been a great deal in the press here, of course. As far as we can make out, the whole thing started when Jesus Gomez, who is a gangster and a nightclub owner, began to have financial problems. Among other things, he had invested in a big casino that failed and a hotel that was never finished.

We know he was desperate and borrowed a lot of money from different people, including a restaurant and nightclub owner by the name of Lembit Saar. Gomez repaid Saar with a number of . . . services. Gomez helps girls come over here and work. Illegal girls, if you know what I mean." He glanced at Irene out of the corner of his eye.

"Trafficking. The trade in sex slaves," she said, nodding.

"Slaves?" He considered the choice of word for a few seconds before he went on. "At any rate, Jesus Gomez was supposed to find two new girls for Lembit Saar. A business arrangement instead of the money Gomez didn't have. Gomez has employed strippers and lap dancers and waitresses in his club for many years, so he knows people in the industry. We also suspect that he has been involved in narcotics and a whole lot of other stuff. But Saar wanted young blondes to attract clients to his newly opened casino and nightclub. A very exclusive place. It's in a prime location very close to your hotel. I'll show you when we get there. Jesus Gomez used an old contact who promised to provide him with two young blondes, but it would be up to Gomez to get them over here from Sweden. Gomez's right-hand man, Sergei Petrov, would go and fetch them. Petrov is well known to us; he's been in jail several times. He left here on Thursday, the nineteenth of January, and was due back with the girls the following day. But none of them turned up."

No, because one of the girls was seriously ill and then she was murdered, Irene thought. And the other is hovering between life and death in a Swedish hospital. But instead of saying anything, she asked, "Where does Lembit Saar come from?"

"Estonia. Which is another reason Gomez didn't like him." He gave her a meaningful look, then continued. "Last Friday one of Jesus Gomez's closest associates contacted Lembit Saar. They arranged to meet in a bar outside the main tourist areas.

The village is some distance away, up in the mountains. Saar didn't have time to go and sent two of his most trusted men instead. On the way, their car was forced off the road. One of them escaped with minor injuries, but the other died. There were no witnesses to the incident apart from the man who survived, and he didn't see anything."

Inspector Juan Rejón paused briefly to catch his breath.

"At midnight the same day, Lembit Saar turned up without warning at Jesus Gomez's nightclub, Casablanca. According to witnesses, Saar and two of his men went into the office. After a while the witnesses heard a loud argument, followed by several shots. Someone called the police, and when they arrived on the scene they found Jesus Gomez and Saar's two heavies dead. Shot, of course. Saar himself was seriously hurt, but his injuries weren't life threatening. He'll be out of the hospital soon. Needless to say this has made headlines overseas as well: four dead within twenty-four hours! Under normal circumstances Tenerife has very little serious crime to speak of, but when something like this happens . . ."

Inspector Rejón shrugged as if to say that it would have been impossible to avoid the publicity.

The police car whizzed along the road, which was steadily descending. The countryside was beautiful, with steep, crumbling hillsides on the right-hand side. They were covered with creeping vegetation, clinging to the rock. Colorful flowers of many different varieties bloomed everywhere, but Irene had no idea what they were called. Newly built houses with a fantastic view of the sea lined the other side of the road. Irene was wearing her pale blue T-shirt and her deck shoes with no socks; she felt like a tourist, in spite of the fact that she and Inspector Rejón were talking about four murders.

They were approaching a built-up area, and there was more traffic. They drove past the sign for Los Cristianos and carried on toward Playa de las Américas.

"Ballistic tests show that Saar and his bodyguards were shot with Jesus Gomez's .357 Magnum Smith and Wesson 340PD, which was found next to Gomez in the room. Gomez was a skilled marksman, and the revolver is a highly accurate weapon, particularly at such close quarters. Saar survived due to the fact that Gomez had probably already been hit and didn't have time to take aim properly. The bullet entered at the side of the abdomen, but didn't damage any vital organs. Gomez was hit by two shots, one from each of the bodyguards' P226 Sig Sauer," Rejón said.

The gangsters on Tenerife aren't exactly using peashooters, Irene thought.

After a while Rejón said matter-of-factly, "The current situation is that we are right in the middle of a blood vendetta. At the same time, everyone has been wondering why Sergei Petrov disappeared with the two girls. And then we get an inquiry from a superintendent in Göteborg, asking whether the Policía Nacional has any information about Sergei in connection with Tenerife and the sex trade. De Viera literally exploded! I saw it myself. I was there when he got the fax."

He smiled at the memory without taking his eyes off the road and the stream of traffic. Irene merely nodded, without asking any questions. She felt like Rejón had more on his mind.

"There's one thing I think you ought to know—de Viera is a blood relation to Jesus Gomez. He has always protected Gomez. And vice versa."

It took a few seconds before Irene grasped the implications of what Rejón had said. So that was why Miguel de Viera had been so stubborn, refusing to give up until the police in Göteborg had agreed to send over an investigator. This wasn't just an ordinary homicide case; this was first and foremost a matter of the chief of police saving his own skin. And in spite of Irene's limited knowledge of vendettas in Southern Europe, she realized that it could ultimately cost him his life. If he had protected Jesus Gomez, who was now dead, he could well be the next target.

"So this isn't about tourism, which is what he told my boss. He wants to put a stop to any further escalation of the violence between the Gomez and Saar gangs. His last chance is to find out the truth about what happened in Sweden," Irene said.

"Yes."

"He must be pretty desperate."

Inspector Rejón nodded. The fleeting expression that crossed his handsome face told Irene that she had just delivered the understatement of the year.

Inspector Rejón parked outside the flamboyant entrance of the Golden Sun Club Hotel. When they stepped out of the car, he pointed diagonally across the wide avenue. "Over there is Lembit Saar's newly opened casino and nightclub, Casino Royal de Tenerife. It's the biggest and most exclusive club on the island," he said.

Irene could see the façade of the casino between the palms lining both sides of the avenue. It looked like a palace, which was no doubt the intention. Replicas of classical Greek statues adorned the wide steps leading up to the entrance. The building itself was made of golden yellow sandstone, shimmering in the bright sunshine. On one wall a little waterfall tumbled between bronze statues representing sea gods and mythical sea monsters. The splash as the water cascaded freely into a pool at the bottom could be heard all the way to the hotel where Irene was standing.

"So tacky," as her beloved father-in-law from Säffle would have said.

It would surely be easy to find women who would be happy to work in such an extravagant establishment. Why had Saar asked Gomez for two girls through the sex trafficking channel? Irene thought she knew the answer: he hadn't been looking for ordinary girls. What he had wanted, what he had demanded, were two young blonde sex slaves.

Inspector Rejón accompanied her into the elegant hotel lobby. He spoke to the female receptionist in rapid Spanish; he evidently wanted to make sure that Irene was properly checked in. The young woman handed Irene a small envelope containing the key card; the room number was written on the outside in green ink.

"Room three twelve. I hope you enjoy your stay with us," she recited in a monotone, unable to take her eyes off Juan Rejón.

He seemed oblivious to the receptionist's doe-eyed attentions and turned his back on her to speak to Irene.

"I'll pick you up at four o'clock on the dot," he said, firing off a smile that would have floored the receptionist behind him if she had been able to see it.

Irene nodded and headed for the elevator, her rubber-soled shoes squeaking faintly on the polished pale-grey marble floor. Huge white lilies arranged in tall red glass vases filled the air with a wonderful perfume. Next to the elevator a sign indicated the way to the pool bar and restaurant, which was where Irene intended to go as soon as she had dumped her bags in her room. Lunch on the plane had been a joke. The wrapped baguette she had bought at the airport had been a godsend, but now she was ravenous.

The room was large and airy, with grey-blue and white as the dominant colors. The pale-grey tiled floor felt pleasantly cool beneath her bare feet. One wall consisted entirely of glass sliding doors, leading out onto a generous balcony. She had a view of the leafy garden and the bathing area; there were two large pools and a children's pool, arranged like a clover leaf with the bar in the middle. Irene could see people eating at small tables. Most of them were dressed in swimwear, and there were large glasses of beer in front of several diners. Suddenly

Irene realized how dry her mouth was. An ice-cold beer was exactly what she needed.

She made an instant decision, then got undressed and took a quick shower before applying plenty of sun lotion and putting on her bikini. She slipped her pale blue T-shirt and shorts over the top. She grabbed a white towel from the bathroom and put it in her rucksack, and slid her feet into her sandals. A quick glance at the time told her that she had exactly two hours for lunch and a swim before Juan Rejón came to pick her up.

Chapter 16

THE TOMATO SALAD with a chicken kebab had tasted delicious. The fried potato wedges and a large glass of beer had significantly raised the GI-index of the meal, but what the hell; it wasn't every day that she had lunch by a pool, wearing nothing but a bikini. And it was definitely a special occasion at the beginning of February.

Irene's rucksack occupied the chair beside her, her clothes neatly folded on top. The swim could wait; there were too many people in the pool. She ordered dessert: three scoops of differently flavored ice creams, along with a double espresso. When the ice cream dish and the coffee cup were empty, she leaned back on the plastic chair and observed the lively activity around the pool.

It was clear that the school vacation had begun in Sweden. Several of the children jumping up and down in the water were yelling at each other in Swedish. Irene was a little taken aback to see Lukas and Simon come hurtling along, each with an inflatable ring around their tummies. To be on the safe side, Simon was also kitted out with inflatable armbands. In their wake came their parents, pulling Natan along in a little cart. He was fast asleep. His mother was wearing black bikini bottoms and a low-cut top that generously exposed the deep cleft between her heavy breasts. His father wore only swimming trunks in a hallucinogenic tropical pattern of apricot and pea-green. Irene couldn't help smiling to herself as she pictured what Krister's face would look like if she were to present him with something similar.

She looked at her watch and realized it was time to head back to her room to get ready for her meeting with de Viera. She still wasn't sure of his correct title. Was he the chief of police for the whole of Tenerife, or just Playa de las Américas? Or was he the equivalent of a superintendent?

"WHAT IS DE Viera's actual rank?" Irene asked Inspector Rejón.

"He's the head of the Policía Nacional in Playa de las Américas and Los Cristianos. It's not very big in geographical terms, but this is where most of the tourists are, which means that he has a very important area of responsibility."

They chatted easily during the short trip to the police station, a large two-story limestone building not far from the freeway exit ramp. It was obviously old, but well maintained. The blue emblem of the Policía Nacional was displayed above the entrance. The entire place, including the large paved yard at the front, was surrounded by a high barbed-wire fence. They drove in through the open gates, which were made of heavy wrought iron, and parked in the shade of a large palm tree.

Inspector Rejón tapped a series of numbers into the keypad next to the sturdy oak door. A click revealed that it was unlocked. He pushed the heavy door and politely held it open for Irene, who jokingly saluted him as she walked past. The entrance hall was cool and completely deserted. Their footsteps echoed between the bare, pale grey walls. In spite of the fact that Irene was wearing her sandals, it sounded as if she were tap dancing across the floor.

They went up a worn limestone staircase and along a dark corridor with several closed doors. There was a strong smell of wax polish and detergent. Fat, iridescent bluebottles buzzed lazily in the windows. Juan Rejón stopped outside the only set of double doors in the corridor and knocked. A few words in Spanish came from inside the room; Inspector Rejón opened the door and held it for Irene.

Chief of Police Miguel de Viera got to his feet with some difficulty on the far side of the polished conference table and waited for Irene and Rejón to come to him. He was in uniform and looked exactly as Irene had imagined: just like Superintendent Andersson, but shorter. De Viera was probably a few years younger than his counterpart in the north, but otherwise they were very much alike: overweight, with thinning hair and high color. The latter could be due to the temperature in the room; an air-conditioning unit protruded from the wall, rattling like a threshing machine.

The entire over-furnished room gave Irene the feeling that a point was being made. It was hardly likely to be an office, not even for a Spanish chief of police who should at least have a computer on his desk. The only modern thing in this room was an ordinary black push-button telephone in the middle of the table.

Inspector Rejón introduced Irene to de Viera, who gave her a charming smile, revealing nicotine-stained teeth, and said a few words in Spanish. Irene didn't understand a thing, so she simply murmured in agreement. With an extravagant gesture, de Viera indicated that she should sit down on one of the carved chairs along the wall. The old leather creaked ominously as she complied. The chief of police then signaled to Inspector Rejón that he wished to speak to him out in the corridor. In his left hand, de Viera was holding a rolled-up newspaper, which he had been clutching when Irene and Rejón came into the room.

Irene felt a little foolish, perched on the edge of the chair with her laptop case balanced on her knee. It was almost like sitting in an empty waiting room before an unpleasant procedure. And there were no old gossip magazines to read.

What happened next made her forget such thoughts.

Through the door came the sound of an increasingly heated exchange of words, which soon turned into a full-blown argument. The main protagonist appeared to be de Viera, whose hoarse barking dominated the quarrel. He really was incensed with poor Rejón, who spoke up for himself as best he could when de Viera paused to catch his breath. The respite lasted only a few seconds, and soon the chief of police was sounding off once more. Irene didn't need to understand a word of Spanish to realize that Rejón was in deep shit.

Suddenly there was silence outside the door. They're throttling each other, Irene thought. She slid forward a fraction on her chair so she could leap up and save her colleague. Although she wasn't sure which one, she had to admit.

Before she had to make a decision, the door flew open and de Viera came barreling in as fast as his bulk would allow. His face was even more purple than before. A small, anemic-looking middle-aged woman came bobbing along in his wake. She looked around the room with big eyes, and Irene realized this was the first time she had ever been in there. Eventually her gaze settled on Irene. The brown eyes were the only element of color in her entire appearance. She looked like an ancient, faded sepia photograph.

De Viera slapped the highly polished surface of the table with the newspaper as he growled, "She *habla ingles*."

He jerked his thumb over his shoulder at the pale woman, who nodded mutely at Irene. She evidently had no name, or at least not one that was worth mentioning.

"Should we wait for Inspector Rejón?" Irene dared to ask.

She was trying to look as if she hadn't heard the row in the corridor. De Viera glared at her before answering curtly in Spanish. Irene looked inquiringly at the interpreter, who translated what the chief of police had said, her voice shaking:

"Inspector Rejón has been removed from the case. His position was . . . compromised."

Her voice was barely audible in the large room, but her English was perfect. Only then did Irene realize that the woman was in fact English, not Spanish.

"Compromised in what way?" Irene asked, looking straight at de Viera. He understood perfectly without any need for the interpreter to translate. He kept his eyes fixed on her as he raised the newspaper, which was still tightly furled in his hand. Slowly he began to unroll it, then he held it out to Irene, pointing with his fat index finger at a picture on the lower half of the front page. He tapped the picture peremptorily with his nail, demanding that Irene take a closer look. The old chair pad made a sucking sound as she got up and went over to him. Today's date was at the top of the page. She leaned forward and peered at the image.

There were two people in the photograph. One was an attractive blonde in her early twenties. The other was Inspector Juan Rejón. Both of them were smiling at the camera, and they had just gotten out of a limousine. They were a very good-looking couple. She was wearing a close-fitting silver evening dress, and he was dazzlingly stylish in a dark suit. Once again Irene thought he could make a fortune as a model, but apparently he was intending to make a fortune in a different way. The headline proclaimed: NUEVO BOYFRIEND, and even Irene could guess what that meant. Underneath the picture were the names Juan Rejón and Julia Saar.

"Is Julia Saar related to Lembit Saar?" she asked, although she suspected that she already knew the answer.

"Sí," de Viera replied grimly.

"His daughter," the interpreter piped up boldly.

De Viera gave no indication that he had heard her. Instead he cast a final glance of loathing at the picture before screwing it up and throwing it in the waste bin. He then spat out a few brief comments, which the interpreter quickly translated.

"As Rejón is now off the case, you are to report directly to the chief of police," she said.

"Only to him?" Irene asked, feeling somewhat surprised.

"*Sí*," de Viera said before the interpreter had the chance to ask him.

Irene took out her laptop. When she asked if there was a projector so that she could give a PowerPoint presentation, both de Viera and the interpreter looked blankly at her. Irene suppressed a sigh, while at the same time blessing her foresight in bringing hard copies of all the case notes. It was a substantial bundle. She passed the top sheet of paper to de Viera and began:

"We were actually looking for two young men who had run down and killed a retired police officer. We knew which direction the car had taken after the accident. When our teams were searching the area, they found the body of a very young girl . . ."

THE LONG AFTERNOON had turned to evening by the time they had finished. Irene's mouth was as dry as a desert after all that talking, but de Viera had hardly moved a muscle during her report. He certainly hadn't asked for anything to drink. Only when she had finished did he pick up the phone, hit speed dial and bark out brief orders. When he had put down the receiver he stared straight at Irene and fired off a lengthy harangue.

The interpreter looked as if she was seriously considering whether to faint rather than translating what he had just said. With a huge effort she pulled herself together and managed to speak. "Refreshments are on the way. Then we'll go through it all again in front of the other police officers."

Irene couldn't believe her ears. It was a while before she

realized he wasn't joking. At the same time, she thought she knew why he had asked her to deliver her report to him before allowing her to address a larger audience. He wanted to make sure that there was nothing that would compromise him—or rather the Gomez gang—in the investigation. This is all about saving de Viera's skin, she reminded herself. She felt a surge of anger. Could she refuse to cooperate? After a rapid analysis she decided such a course of action would be impossible. De Viera was paying for her trip and all her expenses. At least on paper. Perhaps it wasn't the Policía Nacional who were paying at all. She was beginning to have her doubts. Perhaps one of the gangster syndicates had brought her to Tenerife. Paranoid thoughts, but not entirely unreasonable.

On the other hand, the commissioner of the Policía Nacional had contacted Acting Chief of Police Marianne Wärme; the gangsters couldn't have had any influence on that. Or could they? Irene had some knowledge of the mafia in Europe, and she knew that their tentacles reached the upper echelons of the hierarchy of power. However, she decided that the commissioner was unlikely to be directly involved. This seemed to be an internal arrangement on the island. Perhaps de Viera had conned the commissioner into requesting assistance. Whatever the truth of the matter was, the fact remained that she had to make the best of a bad situation.

The door opened and a young woman in a blue uniform came in carrying a small tray with three bottles and three glasses. In the middle of the tray was a plate of sliced melon. De Viera grabbed the ice-cold—and only—bottle of beer and left the room without further comment.

In silence Irene and the interpreter ate pieces of melon and drank a small bottle of Perrier each. They were both resigned to their fate. All they could do was grit their teeth and go through the whole thing all over again. Resolutely Irene wiped her fingers on a thin paper napkin, then held out her hand to

the interpreter and introduced herself. The pale woman hesi-
tantly placed a frozen hand in Irene's and said, "Josephine
Baxter."

Irene blinked in surprise. Josephine? The sepia-lady struck
her as more of an Edith or Vera.

IT WAS ALREADY dark outside the windows when five male
police officers joined them for the second briefing, which
started just after seven. They all smiled at Irene, shook hands
and introduced themselves. This was a complete waste of time,
because it was impossible for Irene to remember the Spanish
names. They disappeared from her memory as soon as she tried
to fix them. When de Viera returned he was followed by the
young female officer, who was now carrying a projector.
Without a word de Viera placed a thin piece of Styrofoam on
the polished surface of the table, and the woman placed the
projector on top of it. Irene saw one of her male colleagues
place his hand on her bottom, as if by accident. The young
woman gave no indication that she was aware of his touch, but
left the room as quickly as she had crept in.

De Viera tucked the hard copy of the case notes, which
Irene had just gone through with him, under his arm. The
glance he gave her contained a trace of triumph. The Swedish
text would be of no use whatsoever to him, but she realized
that he wanted the DNA profile that proved that Sergei
Petrov had not killed the little Russian. It was of the utmost
importance for the Gomez gang—and consequently de Viera—
to be able to prove that the failed attempt to deliver the two
girls was the result of an unfortunate series of events. There
must not be the least suspicion that the Gomez phalanx—
through Petrov—had tried to deceive Saar and his associates.
The financial discrepancy would still remain, of course, but no
doubt that could be sorted out. Or perhaps it was about the
money after all. Saar wanted recompense for the girls who

hadn't turned up, and Gomez had been unable or unwilling to pay up. Irene wondered what kind of money was involved. A substantial amount, she supposed, given that four men had already lost their lives.

Irene plugged her laptop into the projector as de Viera left the room with the printout securely clamped under his arm. When he returned a few minutes later, he was empty-handed. Presumably he had locked it away somewhere.

Irene was able to deliver her report more quickly the second time. This was partly because it was easier to see the pictures when they were enlarged on the wall, and partly because she and the interpreter had already been through everything once. It went better than she could have expected. De Viera thanked her politely for coming all the way from Sweden to support her colleagues in Tenerife with the difficult investigation in which they were currently involved. Her assistance had made things significantly easier for them. Everyone present nodded in agreement, then as if on a given signal, they all got up and left the room.

Through Josephine Baxter, de Viera asked Irene if she would like to have dinner with him. She declined politely, making the excuse that she had a headache and intended to go straight back to her hotel to rest. He couldn't quite hide his relief. No doubt he also thought it would have been horrific to spend the evening trying to communicate through sign language and poor English with an unwelcome dinner companion.

Josephine Baxter drove Irene back to the hotel in her little Fiat. They didn't say much because they were both tired after talking for several hours. However, Irene did learn Josephine had been living in Tenerife for ten years.

Josephine dropped her off outside the hotel. Irene waved goodbye to the rear lights of the Fiat as it disappeared down the avenue, and suddenly realized how hungry and thirsty she was. Her stomach was in knots. Her tongue rasped against her dry palate. She decided to go straight to her room to freshen up, then she would go out and look for a decent restaurant.

She quickly crossed the lobby and took the elevator up to her room. She stepped inside with a huge sense of relief and headed for the bathroom. Her bladder was full to bursting, and she had to empty it. After that she took a quick shower. A dab of perfume here and there made her feel fresh once more. The pool bar was still open, and the prospect of a meal in the near future cheered her up considerably.

Chapter 17

THE MAN HAD his legs crossed, one elegant shoe bobbing up and down. Irene noticed that he had unusually small feet. To her surprise he smiled at her and got up from the armchair as she emerged from the elevator. He trotted toward her across the marble floor of the hotel lobby.

"My name is Günter Schmidt," he said, holding out his hand.

The handshake was brief and damp. He was quite short and was wearing a white shirt and a tailored dark suit. His tie was made of pale blue silk, and was held in place by a gold tie pin. His hair was thick and almost pure white, but his face was youthful. He looked like he might be in his mid-fifties. His English was flawless, but his accent suggested that he was probably German.

As if he had read her mind, he said, "I am Austrian, but I have spent the last thirty years living in different parts of the world. I am now managing director of Casino Royal de Tenerife. Lembit Saar is my highly respected boss. All of his employees have been deeply worried since the attempt on his life and the murder of two of our most valued colleagues."

He assumed a suitably grief-stricken expression.

The attempt on the life of Lembit Saar and the murder of two of . . . ? Did he really think she had no idea what was going on? As far as she understood it, Lembit Saar and his goons had turned up at Jesus Gomez's nightclub Casablanca and shot Gomez dead.

Günter Schmidt gestured toward a thin man in a dark uniform who was standing a few meters away. "This is my chauffeur. He will drive us to the casino. I would very much like to invite you to dinner, so we can chat about our mutual interests."

Suddenly Irene felt a surge of pure rage. "I am a Swedish police officer, and I am here at the invitation of the Chief of the Policía Nacional, Miguel de Viera. I have no authority whatsoever to discuss any aspect of an ongoing investigation with members of the public," she said formally.

In order to further underline her position, she straightened up to her full 180 centimeters and looked down on the man in front of her.

As if he hadn't heard a word she'd said, Günter Schmidt grabbed her elbow and started pushing her toward the door. The skinny chauffeur materialized at her other side.

"I usually get on well with people," Schmidt said. The grip on her elbow tightened, although his friendly tone of voice remained the same. "It will be a pleasure to have the honor of welcoming you as our guest at Casino Royal this evening," he said.

Irene's mind raced. What could she do? She realized that the reason for Schmidt's visit was that Inspector Juan Rejón had not been allowed to attend her presentation at police HQ. If he had been there, then the Saar gang would have received a direct report from their man on the inside, and she would have been spared this unwanted dinner invitation.

At the same time, she realized this wasn't personal. The gangsters wanted the information she had, that was all. Oh well, if one gang had heard everything, she might as well talk to the others.

"In that case I need my laptop," she said with an air of resignation.

"If you will give your key card to my chauffeur, he will go up to your room and collect the computer," Schmidt said politely.

Irene stopped dead and opened her mouth to protest, but thought better of it when she saw the look in his eyes. This was not a thoughtful gesture to save her the trouble of going upstairs; this was a direct order to hand over her key.

With a deliberately exaggerated gesture she took the key card out of her pocket and gave it to the uniformed chauffeur. His face remained impassive as he took it and headed for the elevators. A short while later he returned with her laptop and key card.

Irene shouldn't have been surprised to find a black limousine waiting for them outside the hotel, but she was. The windows were also black, apart from the windshield and the side window on the driver's side, which were tinted. It was impossible to see who was in the car. She climbed in with great reluctance. The interior carried the residual aroma of cigarette smoke and perfume left behind by previous passengers. Combined with the smell of the white leather seats, they formed a heavy odor that made Irene feel sick, probably because she was hungry. She was grateful that they were only traveling a short distance along the avenue, otherwise she would definitely have been car sick.

Casino Royal de Tenerife glittered like a magnificent palace, outshining every other building in sight. The artistically arranged lighting made the façade look like a baroque monument rather than the gigantic travesty it actually was. The statues appeared to be made of marble and bronze; they could of course be molded plastic, but it was hard to tell in the artificial light. The babbling waterfall cascading down the wall and into the pool tempted many passersby to stop and admire the lavish sight.

Smartly dressed guests were walking up the broad steps in a steady stream, passing two stony-faced doormen in tuxedos, one at each side of the entrance. This wasn't the kind of place for shorts and a T-shirt. Which was exactly what Irene was wearing.

Günter Schmidt had noticed her clothing, and said, "I suggest we go in the back way; it's more discreet."

They walked toward the side of the building. Irene hadn't noticed the red and yellow flashing neon sign that covered the entire wall because that part of Casino Royal de Tenerife couldn't be seen from her hotel. The sign informed everyone in large red letters that there was a club right here called RED LIGHT DISTRICT DE TENERIFE, and underneath it proclaimed STRIPTEASE and SEX SHOW in yellow. Irene realized this was where the little Russian would have ended up working. According to a smaller neon sign in blue, the establishment was open from six in the evening until six in the morning. Even if the guests were greeted by a spectacular stage show, there were probably a number of smaller rooms in the innermost recesses of the club where young women provided sexual services twelve hours a day.

She followed Günter Schmidt up an unprepossessing staircase, wishing she were somewhere else. He keyed a series of numbers into a keypad; the door opened, and they were admitted by a tall well-built guard. He was wearing an earpiece, with a wire leading down to his lapel. No doubt the Saar gang was on full alert.

They continued up another flight of stairs and reached a smooth oak door. Irene recognized a security door when she saw one. Once again Günther Schmidt keyed in a code, and the lock clicked. He opened the door and gestured to Irene to step inside, where another guard was on duty. The room felt very warm and stuffy; Irene noticed that there were no windows.

The décor was light and Scandinavian, with modern furniture in a combination of birch and white leather and a thick pale blue carpet. The walls were covered in rough plaster in the Spanish style. On one wall hung a large portrait of a blonde woman. At first glance Irene thought it was the actress Grace

Kelly, who later became Princess Grace of Monaco, but then she realized that the woman in the picture merely looked very similar to the beautiful American. Irene could just make out a small brass plaque on the frame: ELISABETH SAAR, B.TANNER, 1953-2002.

A man had folded his gangly frame into one of the compact armchairs, and there was a woman standing beside him who Irene recognized. According to the newspaper headline, Inspector Juan Rejón was this young woman's new boyfriend.

The man in the armchair was about thirty years old. His white linen pants suggested that he had an expensive tailor. He was the Scandinavian type of man whose hair begins to thin at an early age; it was quite sparse, and had already begun to recede significantly at the temples. His features were finely drawn, dominated by an aristocratic aquiline nose. His sharp eyes were the same color as the carpet. He got to his feet as Irene walked in with her escort. An almost imperceptible smile played around his lips as he held out his hand.

"I do apologize for taking up yet more of your time. Unfortunately we had no alternative but to ask you to come here to share the information the Swedish police have acquired," he said politely. He inclined his head. "My name is Nicholas Saar, and this is my sister, Julia."

He gestured toward the young woman, who didn't even bother looking at Irene. She took a long, thin cigarette out of her spectacular white handbag and lit it with a small gold lighter.

"Please don't smoke in here, Julia!" her brother said sharply.

She gave him a dirty look with her sapphire-blue eyes, but stubbed out the cigarette in the ashtray on the coffee table.

"We're having problems with the air-conditioning. Thank God it's only the offices that are affected; the casino and the clubs are fine," Nicholas Saar said apologetically.

Irene stood there awkwardly with her laptop case hanging

over one shoulder. She noticed that she was pressing it hard against the side of her body, as if it would give her strength.

"As you can see we have already made preparations for your presentation, and the projector is all set up. However, you must be hungry after your long session with Miguel de Viera. He isn't exactly known for his generosity or hospitality. Any funding available for that kind of thing disappears into his own pocket," Saar went on in a casual tone of voice, as if he really were chatting to an invited guest.

There might well have been a certain amount of truth in his comment, at least judging by the reception Irene had been given by the chief of police. With the best will in the world, it couldn't be described as hospitable.

Irene was still standing there in silence, allowing Nicholas Saar to dominate the conversation, which seemed to suit him perfectly. His English pronunciation was impeccable and could have belonged to an upper-class character in a BBC television series. English boarding school, Irene thought.

"What would you like to eat?" Nicholas asked.

Irene's appetite had disappeared. However, she was aware of the headache that was starting to make its presence felt just behind her forehead. She needed to get something inside her.

"I'd like a cold bottle of Carlsberg, a large glass of iced water and a cheese sandwich."

She deliberately refrained from saying "please" or "thank you." She didn't think she was under any obligation to do so since she had practically been abducted. She had expected to be sitting by the pool at her hotel now, enjoying a delicious hot meal, but she had no desire to have dinner in front of present company. She could drink beer and eat a sandwich while running through the key points of the investigation.

Nicholas Saar raised one eyebrow ironically when she had placed her order, then nodded without further comment. He said something in Spanish to the guard, who immediately went over to the internal telephone on the wall by the door. A few brief words and everyone looked satisfied.

Irene plugged her laptop into the projector and adjusted the focus. The first picture on the white wall showed the outside of the root cellar where the little Russian had been found. Irene felt as if it had happened in another life, several years ago. She was astonished to realize that only three and a half weeks had passed since then.

The sound of discreet tapping came from the door; Irene heard four rapid knocks, followed by two more with a pause of a second or so in between. The guard didn't move until the signal was repeated. The gang members were nervous, bordering on paranoid. There were guards on both the inside and the outside of the building. There were keypads on every door. Who would be able to gain access to this fortress?

A waiter.

First of all he shot the guard between the eyes. In spite of the shock as the report from the revolver filled the room, Irene had just enough time to see Nicholas Saar's gangly body being hurled backward. At the same moment she felt a violent blow against her shoulder. She threw herself on the floor and rolled under the table, thanking her lucky stars it wasn't made of glass. Logic told her that the killer was after the Saar gang, not her, but the voice of reason grew fainter and fainter as she lay there defenseless on the floor. Fear sent the adrenaline surging as the sound of repeated shots hammered against her eardrums.

She could see Nicholas Saar's motionless body from her position under the table; a dark patch of blood was quickly spreading across his dazzling white shirt. His sister jerked and spun around in a half circle before collapsing beside him. Shots echoed around the room, and the whole thing became a confused tangle of gunpowder smoke and dust.

The walls closed in and began to spin around, faster and faster. Her field of vision shrank until she was looking down a tunnel. It was like staring into the wrong end of a telescope. At the end of the tunnel she could see the motionless bodies of Nicholas and Julia Saar.

Then everything went black.

Chapter 18

SOMEONE WAS TALKING. Or whispering.

"*Señora Huss? Señora Huss?*"

This was followed by a lengthy torrent of words, of which she understood not one. Irene felt a strong desire not to wake up. There would be nothing but trouble. She decided not to open her eyes. Staying in the dark was the safest thing to do.

She heard rapid footsteps walking away. Cautiously she raised one eyelid, just a fraction. A snow-covered field. She was so surprised that she blinked several times. The snow-covered field was still there, but somewhere deep inside her befuddled brain she began to realize that she was looking up at a white ceiling. And that she was lying in a bed.

Her left hand hurt. Slowly she raised it in the air. It was a while before she managed to focus. A big needle. Taped to the back of her hand. That was what was hurting. Her hand felt cold and swollen. There was a drip stand next to the bed. A half-full plastic bag containing clear fluid hung on the stand. A tube connected the plastic bag to the needle in her hand. She was on a drip.

Therefore, she must be in a hospital.

"*Señora Huss? Cómo está usted?*"

She must still be asleep and dreaming. Having a nightmare. Because she recognized the voice; it belonged to Chief of Police Miguel de Viera.

Suddenly the curtains in her mind were brutally ripped

apart and the images came surging forward: the hours at police HQ, the men who had come to her hotel, the guards, the keypads, the windowless room. The shots. She remembered the shots and the gunpowder smoke.

De Viera's puffy red face suddenly came into view. A woman's face appeared beside him, and she said something to him. He was obviously trying to protest, but she pushed him away, gently but firmly. Well done, girl, get him out of my room, Irene thought before she lost consciousness once more.

"THE CHIEF OF Police was wondering if you might be well enough to answer a few questions."

Josephine Baxter had been brought in again to assist de Viera. She was wearing a kind of mustard yellow suit that completely drained her already colorless complexion. Under the jacket was a pale grey-green sweater, which completed the disaster. The woman looked like the very personification of seasickness.

"Of course. No problem," Irene replied.

She was propped up in bed with pillows behind her back. The morning sun was shining in through the Venetian blinds. Beside her on the bedside table was her breakfast tray. She had managed two sandwiches and two cups of coffee. The drip had been removed, and she was gradually beginning to feel human again, although her hand still ached from the intravenous. It was just before eight o'clock on Saturday morning; her second day in Tenerife had begun.

Apart from the interpreter and de Viera, there were two more colleagues from Policía Nacional in the room. She recognized them from her second briefing the previous evening, but she couldn't remember their names. The three officers took turns asking questions, and Irene answered as best she could. She noticed that de Viera asked for a description of the killer several times. Irene told the truth: she never saw him properly.

She had been busy with her laptop and the projector. The table had been at the opposite end of the room from the door. Because of her position, she couldn't be seen from the doorway. The only thing she remembered was that the hand holding the heavy revolver had been perfectly steady, and that the arm appeared to be in the sleeve of a white waiter's jacket.

As the interview was coming to an end, Irene took the opportunity to ask her colleagues how they had managed to gain access to the hermetically sealed room and what had happened to the others who had been there.

De Viera explained and Ms. Baxter translated. All those who had a key to the locked security door had been on the inside, which was a problem until one of the head waiters remembered that Lembit Saar was still in the hospital. The police had been called, and the officer in charge contacted the hospital. Lembit Saar had a key, of course, and he also gave them the code for the lock. It was necessary to have both in order to open it from the outside.

Less than half an hour after the shooting, the police managed to get into the room. Fortunately the door opened outward, because a guard was lying dead just inside. To make a long story short, Irene and Arvo Piirsalou were the only people in the room who had escaped with their lives intact. After some confusion Irene realized that the chauffeur actually had a name. It seemed he was also from Estonia.

It had been an upsetting stay in the holiday paradise of Tenerife to say the least. All she wanted to do now was go home.

Before her colleagues left, they returned her laptop. They didn't need it. De Viera had copies of all the case notes, Irene thought. She tactfully refrained from pointing this out, and merely thanked them politely.

AN HOUR LATER she left the hospital in a cab. The doctor had told her to take it easy before the journey home the following day, and reminded her to drink lots of water. The bullet wound to her shoulder was superficial and would heal within a week. Her loss of consciousness had been due to a combination of shock and severe dehydration. They had given her a sedative when she was brought in after the drama, which was why she had felt so drowsy and confused during the morning.

Two liters of fluid and a good night's sleep had worked wonders. She felt wide awake when she got back to her hotel room. Almost exactly thirteen hours ago she had walked in through that same door and gone straight to the bathroom.

She stood in the shower for a long time, letting the water cascade over her body. She soaped herself over and over again with the hotel shower gel, then rinsed away the scented bubbles. She didn't feel clean however hard she scrubbed.

Her thoughts kept returning to scenes from the locked room in the casino. With a huge effort of willpower she decided this was her last shower for now. It was time to move on.

She applied sun lotion all over her body, then put on her bikini and a thin camisole. The shorts from the previous evening were stained with blood and dirt. Disgusted, she threw them in the waste bin, along with the fine sweater she had been wearing. Now she only had one clean T-shirt left. She would save that for the journey home. The bikini and the thin top would have to do; she had no intention of leaving the hotel. She slipped her money, cell phone and sunglasses into her rucksack and went down to the pool.

There was a small kiosk where you could borrow a beach towel if you gave your hotel room number. Irene spread the soft thick fabric over one of the last vacant sun loungers and got out the paperback she had brought with her. Jenny had bought it in an antiquarian bookshop and given it to her for Christmas. It was an Ed McBain detective novel: *Give the Boys a Great Big Hand*. Irene had asked for books in English because she wanted to improve her knowledge of the language. She had also brought with her a thick bilingual pocket dictionary.

Several guests were already sitting around the pool having lunch. She was beginning to feel hungry, and took that as a positive sign. It was definitely time for something to eat. Almost twenty-four hours had passed since her last hot meal.

SHE LAY IN the sun trying to read her book as she digested her lunch, but she found it difficult to concentrate. She kept thinking about everything that had happened. Irene began to feel restless, so she decided to take a walk along the esplanade. On the map it looked around fifteen kilometers long; it followed the coastline from the ferry port in Los Cristianos, past Playa de Fañabé and up to the small village of La Caleta. Since Irene's hotel lay almost exactly in the middle, she decided to head north toward La Caleta. She quickly gathered up her things and pushed them into her rucksack, leaving the towel behind to save her place. At least she had learned something from her two package trips to Crete: it was probably a good idea to keep the sun lounger in case she felt like a dip in the pool and a rest after her walk.

THE WIDE ESPLANADE was bursting with life and color. People of various nationalities wandered happily among the stalls, trying to avoid the restaurants touting loudly for business. The outdoor seating areas were all full. Irene wasn't hungry, but decided to have a cold beer a little later. After all, the doctor had told her to drink plenty. Although he had specified water.

The waves rose high in the air as they rolled toward the shore. Out on the water the surfers lay on their boards in their wetsuits, bobbing up and down as they waited for the perfect wave.

The fresh breeze felt warm against her skin and gently rustled the leaves of the palm trees. For the first time since she landed on the island, Irene felt a sense of freedom. Out here she was just one among the thousands of other tourists. Nobody knew that she had been involved in the incident described by the newspaper placards as "*Masacre!*" She intended to enjoy a lovely outing along the coast and to try to forget the unpleasant memories that kept trying to surface.

She walked at a steady pace past pebbled beaches, noisy bars, beautifully constructed sandy beaches and lavish hotels. When she reached the end of Playa de Fañabé, she turned and strolled back to the hotel.

She saw him as soon as she walked in. He was sitting in the same armchair that had been occupied by Günther Schmidt the previous evening. Inspector Juan Rejón broke into a smile and got to his feet. The same receptionist who had checked Irene in the previous day also noticed his smile and gave Irene a dirty look.

After making a few introductory remarks and asking how she was feeling, Rejón asked if he could buy her a beer at the pool bar. Irene was happy to accept; she also had the impression he had something on his mind.

When they were both sitting at the bar with large ice-cold beers, he raised his glass to her. "Here's to the happy outcome of yesterday's terrible events."

They each took a long drink.

"It wasn't a happy outcome for the other people in the room," Irene said after they had put down their glasses.

A dark shadow passed over Rejón's face. "No. You are in danger. You are the only survivor. You are a police officer. In other words, you are a reliable witness with no connection to either of the opposing sides," he said seriously.

It occurred to Irene that she was probably the only police officer in Playa de Las Américas who had no connection to any of the gangs on the island, but she decided to keep that thought to herself.

"But the Estonian . . . the chauffeur, he survived as well," she protested.

"Arvo Piirsalou. He's never going to say anything. Not to the police, at any rate." His face suddenly broke into a broad grin. "You need a bodyguard!"

"A bodyguard!" Irene exclaimed.

An elderly couple at a nearby table looked at her in surprise. She was far more surprised than they could possibly be, but anger immediately took over.

"I most certainly do not need a bodyguard!" she snapped.

He laughed mischievously and held up his hands in a defensive gesture. "No, probably not. But you must be careful. You're a witness."

Irene was somewhat mollified by his disarming smile, but still said icily, "As I have informed your colleagues, I didn't see the killer. Only his arm in the doorway. And the gun."

"The people who hired the gunman can't be sure you're telling the truth. They might think you're recovering from shock and will eventually remember what he looked like. They could decide that you need to be silenced, just to be on the safe side."

Every trace of mischief had vanished from his face. Irene realized he was speaking with absolute conviction. A chill spread through her bones. It had never occurred to her that her own life could still be in danger. The thought left her badly shaken.

"My injury was caused by a ricochet. I was standing in a dead corner. I never saw him. And he didn't see me either. That's probably why I'm still alive," she said.

"You may be right. But in that case you must also realize that if the killer had seen you in that room, he would have tried to shoot you, too. This guy didn't intend to leave any witnesses behind."

Irene took a long drink of her beer and tried to digest what

Rejón had said. She felt her heart rate increase as her unease grew. Images from the sealed room were trying to break through into the light. No, she couldn't allow that to happen. Not right now. She forced herself to sound calmer than she actually was.

"Any ideas as to the identity of the killer?" she asked.

"Without doubt a contract killer, someone who's been brought in from outside. We don't have anyone like that here in Tenerife."

"My condolences on the tragic death of your fiancée, of course," Irene said quietly.

She deliberately used the word fiancée, even though the newspaper headlines had referred to Juan Rejón only as Julia Saar's new boyfriend.

He quickly glanced up from his beer and met her gaze. "Fiancée? No. Julia was not my fiancée. And I wasn't her boyfriend. You're referring to that picture in the paper." He fell silent. His voice was totally under control when he went on. "I don't . . . didn't know her. But I knew her brother well. I'm a surfing instructor, and I teach him and his friends. He asked me to escort Julia to that party. I didn't want to at first, but he talked me into it. She wanted to make some other guy jealous. She . . . Julia was used to getting what she wanted, and this guy had dumped her. She was furious. She spent the entire time in the car just bad-mouthing him." He smiled faintly at the memory.

"Do you know who he was?"

"No idea. Julia changed her boyfriends about as often as I change my shirt. She's a celebrity here on the island because she's a famous model, and she's also appeared in a film. It was only a minor role, but still. So she wasn't just Lembit Saar's daughter."

"But de Viera said your position was compromised," Irene said sharply.

Juan Rejón rolled his eyes. "Of course! That paparazzi picture gave him the perfect excuse to get me off the case," he said.

"Why would he want to do that?"

"He didn't want anyone involved in the investigation who might have the slightest contact with the Saar family. The fact is he's related to Jesus Gomez. They're cousins."

Irene thought over everything she had learned from Rejón. He seemed trustworthy, but was he really telling the truth? She decided to be direct, see if she could work out where he was coming from.

"What do you think is the reason behind yesterday's murders?"

He lowered his eyes and started to draw shapes in the condensation on his beer glass. Irene didn't break the silence, but continued to stare at him, challenging him to respond. She wanted to try to get an honest answer out of him, but it didn't look as if he was ready to provide it.

"There are many reasons behind the murders," he said slowly.

"So this isn't just about the failure to deliver the two girls from Sweden to Tenerife; nor is it about Sergei Petrov," she concluded.

He shook his head. "No. This is about a whole lot more."

"Like what?" she pressed him implacably.

He met her gaze and said slowly, emphasizing every syllable, "It is definitely not healthy to know everything."

His voice had a sharp edge, and Irene realized he was deadly serious. Once again she felt a hair-raising chill spread through her body. And she knew he was right. It wasn't always healthy to know everything. Strictly speaking, none of this had anything to do with her own investigation into Tanya's death. The gang murders were part of a significantly wider case that was the responsibility of the Policía Nacional. In her opinion, they were unlikely to be able to solve it. They might need reinforcements from the mainland, but that wasn't her call. Her job was to try to get home without getting herself killed.

"You're right. What do you think I should do?"

"To be safe?"

"Yes."

"Stay in the hotel. Don't leave the building. Have an early dinner and go up to your room. Don't open the door if anyone knocks. Don't speak to anyone. Even if they say they're guests or hotel staff, they could easily be something else altogether."

Irene opened her mouth to protest, then thought better of it. "Okay," she said.

For the second time during their conversation he favored her with that beautiful smile. "I have something I wanted to give you."

He reached into the pocket of his tight jeans and, with a triumphant gesture, produced a folded piece of paper, which he handed over to Irene.

"Sergei Petrov's, alias Andres Tamm's, flight reservations between Tenerife and Scandinavia. He left here alone early on Thursday morning and flew direct to Landvetter airport in Gota . . . Gote—"

"Göteborg," Irene supplied.

"Thank you. Apparently he managed to get a last-minute deal on a charter flight. He had booked a return trip on Friday evening, on the last plane from Kastrup, but that reservation was for Anne and Leili Tamm as well. A one-way ticket for all three of them."

Irene's heart was beating faster. So that was why Heinz Becker and Andres Tamm had left Göteborg and driven south along the west coast, in spite of the bad weather. They had obviously intended to try to get over to Copenhagen and Kastrup. Even if the flight was delayed because of the snow, they would have been on the spot for a quick getaway as soon as flights resumed.

They knew who Leili was. They had found her passport. Anne must have been Tanya. Her passport was still missing.

Heinz Becker had probably decided to get out of Göteborg fast because things were getting a bit too hot after the raid on the brothel in Biskopsgården. And once Leili had been handed over to Andres and Tanya was dead, he no longer had a source of income, so it was time for him to travel back to the Baltic states to find some new girls. It would have suited Becker to get to Copenhagen; from there he could travel on to Germany. The combination of the drugs in his system and the onslaught of bad weather had finally put a stop to all their plans. The girl known as Leili might not survive either.

"Thank you. This is really very kind of—" Irene began, but Rejón interrupted her.

"No problem. I knew it would be difficult for you to get this information. It wouldn't surprise me if it had mysteriously disappeared from the computer. Human error, a computer error . . . there are many ways of waving a magic wand to get rid of information you don't want to hand over."

He smiled again and raised his eyebrows. Irene nodded. She understood perfectly that Rejón hadn't given her this information simply out of the goodness of his heart. It was also one in the eye for the Gomez gang—and indirectly de Viera.

Irene read through the sheet of paper several times before putting it away in the pocket of her shorts. It showed how the human traffickers had planned to transport the girls across Europe.

IRENE FOLLOWED JUAN Rejón's advice to the letter, but first she slipped into a little store near the hotel and bought a bottle of red wine that looked pretty good and a large packet of mixed salted nuts. She spent what was left of the afternoon on the balcony with her book. She might be overdoing the suntan a little, but she thought it was a good idea to make the most of the opportunity. It might be a very long time before she had so much sun on her body again.

She tried to call Krister and the girls several times, but without success. Angrily she cursed their new cell phone operator's poor coverage outside densely populated areas. Then again, the plan had been cheap and had included a new cell that Jenny had immediately grabbed.

She had dinner in the hotel restaurant, then spent the rest of the evening locked in her room with the bottle of wine and her colleagues from the 87th Precinct to keep her company.

Chapter 19

THERE WERE BIG problems when Irene flew back to Landvetter. The steward explained over the intercom that snowfall had created chaos in Göteborg. The snow itself had eased, but there were still strong winds. The passengers had to wear their seatbelts for the last hour due to severe turbulence.

When Irene emerged from the plane, the temperature was several degrees below freezing, and the wind nearly blew her over. She almost slipped and fell several times, but she was glad to have solid ground underfoot. The ice from Friday's cold snap was still there, lurking treacherously under the fresh covering of snow.

Irene was lucky, and managed to get a cab right away. All she wanted as she sank into the back seat was to get home.

THE HOUSE WAS in darkness. The rest of the family wouldn't be back until the following day. Her footsteps echoed desolately as she walked up the stairs in the silent house. She quickly unpacked her rucksack and threw the clothes she had worn on the trip into the laundry basket. She ran herself a bath and added a generous handful of rose-scented salts. With a sigh of pleasure she lowered herself into the bubbles and relaxed in the hot water. She reminded herself that she must keep the dressing on her left shoulder dry. The doctor at the Hospital del Sur had told her very firmly that she wasn't to touch it for five days.

She must have fallen asleep, because she suddenly became aware of the distant sound of a telephone ringing. Just as she was about to leap up and answer it, she heard the answering machine kick in. She was disappointed to hear that the caller didn't leave a message.

The water had cooled, so she got out of the bath and briskly toweled herself dry to get her circulation going. She rubbed some of the expensive cream she had bought at the airport into her face, then she wrapped herself in the soft robe Krister had given her for Christmas a few years ago and slid her feet into her sheepskin slippers.

Feeling somewhat better in both body and soul, she went down to the kitchen to fix herself something to eat. It was almost ten o'clock, and she was ravenous. Dinner on the plane had been served in something that looked like a medium-sized matchbox, with a tiny plastic knife and fork. There were already signs of turbulence at that stage, and Irene had managed only the small dry bread roll, washed down with mineral water.

The refrigerator was depressingly empty. There weren't even any leftovers she could heat up in the microwave. She was going to have to cook something. After briefly considering what little there was, she decided on a mushroom omelet. She added crisp bread topped with Kalles caviar; a couple of forgotten clementines in the vegetable rack would have to serve as both dessert and a source of vitamin C.

Irene tried to ring Krister and the girls once again. The only place in the cottage with any network coverage was upstairs by the window at the eastern gable end. With a sigh she concluded that none of them happened to be standing in that particular spot. She would just have to wait until they tried to call her.

She felt a pang of sadness as she thought about her family and what she was missing. They usually ate very well when they were up at the cottage, which was why the refrigerator in Göteborg had been ransacked. They had taken everything that could be used; the only other option was to drive twenty kilometers to Sunne to buy whatever they didn't have with them.

While she was eating, she glanced through the mail and the weekend papers. A short item in Sunday's paper caught her eye: the police had picked up two young men for questioning. Both were eighteen years old and had escaped from Gräskärr juvenile detention center in January. They had been found at an address registered to the grandmother of one of the fugitives, just outside Gråbo. There wasn't much more information, but Irene immediately suspected that this was about Niklas Ström and Björn "Billy" Kjellgren. They both had a lot of explaining to do: how they had managed to steal Torleif Sandberg's car, for example.

Her eyes were beginning to feel heavy with tiredness. Before she went up to bed, the image of which was hovering temptingly on the edge of her consciousness, she made another vain attempt to reach Krister on his cell. She cursed their parsimony in refusing to have a land line in the cottage. Then she remembered to check the answering machine; they might have called and left her a welcome home message. She pressed the display, and when she saw the number that came up, she was suddenly wide-awake. Twenty-two messages since Friday! She had a really bad feeling as she pressed PLAY. The first four messages were for the twins. The rest were from Sahlgrenska Hospital.

With fumbling fingers Irene keyed in the number. A cheerful female voice answered, giving a ward number and her name, Sister Anna. Irene introduced herself and explained that she had been away all weekend.

"That's what I thought. We've been trying to reach you since yesterday afternoon," the nurse explained in a pleasant tone of voice.

"What's this about?" Irene asked, dreading the answer.

"Your mother slipped and fell on the sidewalk outside her apartment yesterday. It was extremely treacherous! Unfortunately Gerd hit her head and was a little disorientated when she came in here. It took a while before we could get the name and phone number of her next of kin, and she didn't remember your cell number until today. We tried to call you, but your phone was switched off."

That must have been during the flight back from Tenerife.

"So she's got a head injury. Is it serious?"

"No, no. It was just a mild concussion. The real problem is her hip."

"Her hip?" Irene echoed in horror.

"Yes. She's broken the femur and damaged the joint itself. She needs surgery as soon as possible; she's booked for this Tuesday."

"Will she . . . will she get through it?"

"The doctors don't foresee any problem. Her vitals are good, and her heart and blood pressure are fine. Mentally she's stable and fully alert."

"What about after the operation? Will she be able to walk properly?"

"Absolutely. She might even be better than she was before. She's had problems with that hip for quite some time. She told us how long she's been on the waiting list for surgery. But there is a lengthy rehabilitation phase after an operation like this."

"Will she be able to go up and down stairs?"

"No. Not at first, anyway."

Irene remained silent for a moment, then said, "She lives on the second floor of an apartment block with no elevator."

"Oh dear."

Yes indeed. Oh dear. Irene decided to deal with one problem at a time. They would have to try to sort out the practical details eventually, but not right now.

"Can I come up and see her tonight?" she asked.

"No, it's too late. She's already asleep. She's on quite a heavy dose of analgesics. She's relatively pain free, but of course she gets extremely tired."

"When can I visit?"

"Tomorrow, once the doctors have done their rounds. After ten o'clock."

When Irene had thanked the friendly nurse and ended the call, she was overwhelmed by a feeling of weakness. *Not this as well! I can't cope!* she thought. Which didn't really help.

The phone rang again, and she quickly grabbed the receiver and answered.

"Hi, honey! I hope you're missing me as much as I'm missing you," Krister's soft voice said, and he really sounded like he meant it.

"Yes . . . I . . . yes," was all Irene could manage.

To her horror she burst into tears. Soon she was weeping helplessly. Everything that had happened during the weekend had caught up with her, and she couldn't stop. Krister tried to console her, but she had to put the phone down. She sobbed her way into the kitchen and tore off a length of paper towel. She wiped her face and blew her nose.

Feeling a little calmer, she went back to the phone. It was the longest telephone conversation they had ever had in the twenty-two years they had been together. Irene talked nonstop, getting the events of the last two days off her chest. When she eventually paused to catch her breath, Krister quietly asked if it was all really true, and not some American gangster movie that had been shown on the plane. He meant it as a joke, but she almost started crying again.

Afterward she felt completely exhausted, but at the same time she was considerably calmer. She fell into bed just before midnight.

She didn't wake up until the alarm went off; she discovered she had spent the night in her robe. Presumably she had felt the need to be wrapped in something that reminded her of a safe embrace.

Chapter 20

"MORNING! YOU'VE GONE a bit overboard with the sunbathing!" Jonny greeted her with a grin.

Irene didn't even have the strength to reply; she merely glared wearily at him.

"Oh, come on! We taxpayers foot the bill for your weekend in the sun, and you walk in and give me a dirty look!"

Irene stopped dead in front of him in the corridor. Without taking her eyes off him she began to remove her clothes. First of all she took off her jacket, then the thin cotton polo neck. Eventually she was standing there in nothing but her bra and camisole. She pointed to the white dressing which contrasted sharply with her red, sunburnt shoulder.

"This is a bullet wound from a Smith and Wesson 357 Magnum. I was lucky to survive. One other person made it, but he's seriously injured. The other four people who were in the room with us are all dead. And the Spaniards are paying for the whole trip. Not one öre is coming from the Swedish police authority or from taxpayers in any other way."

The truth was that she couldn't remember the exact make and caliber of the gun the killer had used, but a Magnum sounded good. And she had no intention of telling Jonny that she had been hit by a ricochet. To her annoyance she realized that her voice was unsteady as she delivered her dramatic riposte. Jonny didn't notice; he was too busy staring at the dressing with grudging fascination. When Irene saw his eyes start to move toward her décolletage, she slipped her polo-neck back on. At least her unexpected outburst had shut him up for a while.

When she turned around to head for the coffee machine, she found herself face-to-face with the chief.

"What are you two up to?" the superintendent said, sounding extremely confused.

"Irene was just showing me the fantastic tan she got in Tenerife. She's been sunbathing topless," Jonny replied before Irene had the chance to speak.

He had recovered remarkably quickly after her performance.

"I was actually showing him my bullet wound," she said with an air of assumed nonchalance as she skirted the superintendent before he had time to block her retreat.

Behind her back she could hear him yelping. "Topless? Bullet wound? What the hell is going on here?"

"If you go into the meeting room I'll be along shortly, and I'll explain everything," Irene said without turning around.

IRENE HAD HAD the foresight to bring home a copy of the newspaper with MASACRE! in thick black letters on the front page. She used it as her starting point when she began to report back on the dramatic events of the weekend. She spoke for over an hour without being interrupted once.

In conclusion, she said, "As far as I can make out, this gang war is about far more than the fact that the transportation of two girls from Sweden to Tenerife went wrong. The girls can always be replaced, but there's a lot of money involved in human trafficking. A source within the local police also told me there are drugs in the mix. 'Obviously,' I almost said. After all, drugs are the basis of all organized crime these days."

Andersson gazed thoughtfully at Irene. Eventually he said, "Okay. So we sent you down there at the Spaniards' request. By the time you left Tenerife, the body count in the case had risen by one hundred percent. Instead of four homicides, they now have eight. I suspect that wasn't exactly what they were hoping for." He frowned and went on. "My question is: What did they actually want from us? And did we find out anything useful as far as our investigation into the murder of the little Russian goes?"

Irene felt quite upset that Andersson was making it sound as if it was her fault that another four people had been shot dead. She decided to ignore his sarcastic summary of her visit and answered his question with apparent unconcern. "They found proof that Sergei Petrov hadn't disappeared with Tanya. It was important for Jesus Gomez's gang to be able to prove that Petrov hadn't killed her, and it was vital for one of our colleagues within the Policía Nacional to be able to show that the Gomez gang couldn't be blamed for Tanya's death. This has nothing to do with concern for the girl's well-being; she was worth a lot of money. Gomez is in debt to Saar, and Tanya was supposed to pay off part of that debt. Lembit Saar has no scruples when it comes to exploiting these girls. He was just angry because Tanya went missing. All the cash she would have made in the back rooms of the sex club would have gone straight into Lembit Saar's pocket. And now that wasn't going to happen."

"And what did we get out of it?" Andersson persisted.

"We know that Tanya and Leili were due to be taken to Tenerife. We know where they were going to be kept when they reached the island. We also know that neither of them had a passport of their own. Both were going to be smuggled out of Sweden by Sergei Petrov. The little Russian was found dead late on Tuesday night. The Swedish press didn't get the news until Wednesday. The interesting thing is that Petrov flew out of Tenerife early on the following Thursday as Andres Tamm, so it seems like the human traffickers over there didn't know that Tanya was no longer with Becker. The question is whether Heinz Becker and Sergei Petrov knew even on Friday that Tanya was dead. Neither of them could read a Swedish newspaper or understand a Swedish news broadcast. And the overseas media were hardly likely to carry the story of an unknown young girl found dead in Göteborg."

"How was Petrov intending to get the girls to Tenerife?" Andersson asked.

"He was booked on a late flight from Kastrup the following day, that Friday, together with Anne and Leili Tamm. We can assume that he brought his own passport and the girls' fake passports with him. We've found Andres and Leili Tamm's passports, but not Anne's. It's highly likely that Anne is Tanya, our little Russian," Irene said.

"And that's not her real name either," Andersson sighed.

"No. And I don't suppose Leili is called Leili. Has she regained consciousness, by the way?" Irene directed the question to Tommy, who shook his head.

"I called just before the meeting. Her condition has deteriorated," he informed the team.

"That's strange. Irene hasn't been anywhere near her," Jonny said.

He is definitely in top form this grey Monday morning, Irene thought.

"In that case perhaps I could get an update on what's been happening on the home front," she said.

"Sure. Shoot!" Fredrik said cheerfully.

"Did you manage to track down Anders Pettersson?" she asked.

"I did. He's safely under lock and key."

"Has he said anything?"

"Not a word. I picked him up on Friday night. He was lying flat on the floor in a pub on Linnégatan; all I had to do was scoop him up. I tried to talk to him twice over the weekend, but he refused to say anything. I'll have another go this after-noon."

Fredrik sounded optimistic, but Irene knew Pettersson was a hard nut to crack. Perhaps a little female cunning was needed in order to pierce his shell.

"I'd like to sit in, if you don't mind."

"Sure." He nodded.

"And I saw in the paper that Billy and Niklas have been found. Have you questioned them yet?" she asked Jonny.

"No. I thought the little bastards could sit and sweat for a while longer," he said.

The truth is you couldn't be bothered to come in and interview them over the weekend, Irene thought.

"Tommy and I are going to speak to them as soon as we're done here," Jonny added, glancing over at Andersson.

The superintendent's face brightened and he nodded approvingly. He looked at Irene over the top of his reading glasses, his eyes twinkling. "You've got a busy morning writing a report on all your adventures down south. And this after-noon you're in with Fredrik, questioning Pettersson. I've said it before, and I'll say it again: give him hell! He's up to his ears in this whole goddamn mess!"

The last comment was delivered with grim determination. Irene agreed with him on every point, apart from the first one.

"I can't write my report today. I have to go to the hospital."

Andersson opened his mouth and looked as if he were about to object, but when he met Irene's gaze he immediately closed it again.

"Stay away from that place! They're bound to amputate your arm. That's a serious injury you've got there! It must be so painful," Jonny said spitefully.

"The only thing that hurts is your jokes," Irene snapped.

She hurried out of the room so she wouldn't have to listen to any more.

• • •

THE ROOM WAS meant for two patients, but there was only one bed in it at the moment. The space by the window was empty. Gerd looked so tiny in the neatly made hospital bed. Her eyes were closed, and she looked as if she were sleeping. Her pale face almost matched the white pillowcase. For the first time in her life, Irene thought of her mother as old. She had aged so quickly over the past few days. Irene edged closer to the bed, not wanting to wake her. As if she sensed her daughter's presence, Gerd opened her eyes and looked straight at Irene.

"Hi, Mom. How are you feeling?"

Gerd licked her chapped lips several times before she spoke, "I'm fine. Can you get me some water please?" With a trembling hand she pointed to the empty glass on the bedside table.

Irene leaned over and gave her mother a gentle hug and a kiss on the cheek. Perhaps she was being a little too cautious, but Gerd looked more fragile since her accident. Or maybe it was just Irene's imagination. She picked up the glass and went over to the sink. It took forever before the stream of water even began to feel cool against her fingers.

"To think you have to throw yourself down on the sidewalk and break your hip to get to the top of the waiting list for surgery!" Gerd said behind her.

When Irene turned around, her mother's eyes were twinkling and she was smiling mischievously.

"Wasn't that a bit drastic?" Irene said.

"Maybe. But I'm having my operation. On Tuesday."

Gerd sounded very pleased with herself and seemed to be in good spirits. Irene realized how relieved she was feeling. She had been worried that the concussion and painkillers would leave her mother feeling depressed or confused, but she was reassured to find that Gerd appeared to be her usual self. Irene went over to the bed and gave her the water.

Gerd took several sips and put down the almost-empty glass on the bedside table. "Could you get in touch with Sture? That's where I was going when . . . when this happened. He called me. He wasn't feeling too good."

"Was it his heart?"

"Yes. His keys are in my purse. Could you take them and go see him? He's only got me; there's no one else. Actually, you can take my keys as well so that you can water my plants, pick up the mail and . . ."

"Mom, we've already got a spare key to your apartment. I promise we'll take care of everything. And I promise I'll speak to Sture and make sure he's okay."

Gerd's hand was resting on the covers. Irene squeezed it gently. It was so thin. *Why haven't I noticed that Mom has lost weight recently?* she thought. *Or did I just not want to see it?* Irene blamed her lack of time. As usual.

"How's your head feeling? Sister Anna said you had a mild concussion," Irene said, trying to push away all thoughts of self-reproach.

"I was dizzy for the first day or so, but I'm much better now. The pain in my leg and hip is worse. And I'm in some kind of frame so I can't turn over. But they're giving me strong pain-killers, which is good. The only thing is I feel a bit disorientated. What time is it?"

"Almost ten thirty."

"Is it Monday or Tuesday?"

"Monday," Irene said.

Now she was worried again. Gerd had tried to give the impression that her mind was clear, but this obviously wasn't the case. Irene hoped it was because of the strong medication.

"Good. I'm glad it's only Monday, otherwise they would have missed my operation. I'm first on the list on Tuesday morning," Gerd said.

"I'm pleased to hear that you seem convinced you'll be fine before too long," Irene said.

"Of course! The pain I've had in this goddamn hip over the past year . . . you have no idea. I'm so pleased to be having surgery at long last. Even if I can't walk afterward, at least the pain will be gone."

"But Mom, of course you'll be able to walk!" Irene protested.

"Maybe. We'll just have to see what happens," Gerd murmured.

Her eyelids were beginning to droop. When Irene thought she had fallen asleep, she quietly got to her feet. At which point Gerd's eyes flew open and she fixed her daughter with a sharp stare.

"And a panic alarm wouldn't have helped at all! They only work inside the apartment!"

She closed her eyes again before Irene had time to respond.

Indomitable and stubborn; thank you for passing on those qualities to me, my darling Mom.

Irene turned around in the doorway and looked back at her mother. The covers rose and fell with her steady breathing. *You're going to get through this,* she thought tenderly.

THE APARTMENT COMPLEX had been built in the 1950s, just like the one that housed the three-bedroom apartment Gerd had occupied for almost forty years. The only difference was that Sture's place had only two rooms. He had bought it after the death of his wife fifteen years earlier, when he sold their house and moved into the city. He and Gerd had met at the grocery store on Doktor Fries Square, where they were both regular customers. They had often bumped into each other and started chatting. After a year or so a genuine affection had developed between them, and they had been together for almost ten years. Neither of them had been interested in moving in together. As Gerd had put it, "I've spent my whole life developing good and bad habits, and I have absolutely no desire to change now."

Sture and Gerd had had a very happy relationship over the years, and Irene had often blessed the day they met. She and her family had always been very fond of Sture, who was a kind, quiet man.

Irene called him on her cell, but there was no reply. She began to feel the faint stirrings of anxiety and unconsciously tried to put her foot down, which was impossible in the lunch-time traffic.

There was an empty parking space right next to the main entrance. She unlocked the outside door and hurried up to the first floor. She rang the bell and heard it echo peremptorily through the apartment, but there were no sounds of movement from inside. She used the key Gerd had given her to let herself in.

"Sture! It's me, Irene!"

Her voice reached into every room, but there was no reply. The faint smell of an elderly gentleman hovered in the air. Not at all unpleasant, but very distinctive.

The living room was furnished with items that must have dated from the time when Sture and his wife were newly married. The only modern features were a large flat-screen TV on the wall and an impressive music system. The bookshelves were mainly filled with hundreds of CDs and vinyl LPs; Sture was a great music lover. He did have a small number of books: mainly biographies and travel writing.

The compact kitchen was clean and tidy as usual. It had been renovated at some stage in the 1970s, and was starting to look as if it needed doing again. The stove definitely needed replacing, as did the old refrigerator, which was humming loudly to itself. Outside the window some blue tits were fighting over a suet ball that Sture had hung up. The poor things needed all the help they could get in this harsh winter.

In the bedroom the bed was neatly made. There were some folded items of clothing on a chair, and freshly ironed shirts hung on the closet door. The ironing board was still standing in the middle of the floor. Irene checked to make sure that the iron was unplugged, which it was. The Christmas cactus in the window was wilting, and she decided to water it before she left the apartment.

She found him on the tiled floor in the bathroom. It looked as if he had been on his way toward the hand basin or the small cabinet above it, because he had pitched forward and was lying with his head under the basin. She had seen enough bodies over the past twenty years to be certain that he had been dead for some time. The body was cold. Nothing feels as cold as a dead person.

If what Gerd had said was correct, he could have been lying on the floor for almost forty-eight hours. Why had he called her instead of an ambulance?

Irene sat down in a small high-backed armchair in the living room while she waited for the ambulance and the police. Her throat closed up, choked with tears that couldn't quite break through. Or perhaps she didn't want to let them break through; she didn't really know. It felt as if everything was suddenly too much. Too many bodies. She couldn't cope anymore. But she had to, for Gerd's sake.

The ambulance arrived. She heard the sound of the gurney being taken out, then the back doors slamming shut. At that moment she made a decision.

Death is never convenient. It is non-negotiable. It is inexorable and definitive.

But you don't have to tell everyone that it's happened.

Chapter 21

"INTERVIEW WITH ANDERS Pettersson . . ."

Irene walked into the room just as Fredrik had begun. She breathlessly apologized for her late arrival and sank down onto a chair at the end of the table.

". . . Detective Inspector Irene Huss has just entered the room," Fredrik added for the benefit of the recording.

Pettersson was leaning back in his chair, apparently completely uninterested in what was going on in the room.

"Okay, Anders . . . I've asked Inspector Huss to have a word with you. She has a significant amount of fresh information," Fredrik began.

Pettersson glanced distractedly at Irene. Beneath the apparent lack of engagement she sensed watchful tension. No one knew better than Pettersson how many shady dealings he had been mixed up in. Being questioned by the police definitely wasn't one of his interests.

Irene started off with a little small talk to break the ice, then suddenly she said, "We now know more about Tanya, the Russian girl who was murdered, and Sergei Petrov."

Pettersson couldn't hide his surprise when she used Sergei's full name, and he visibly twitched in his seat. The look in his eyes was unmistakably sharper now. He knew they had walked straight into a minefield. In order to hide his anxiety, he smiled scornfully and shook his head.

"We know that Sergei traveled to Göteborg under a false

identity. As Andres Tamm. Did you meet him after he had made contact with Heinz Becker?" Irene went on.

"I have no idea what you're talking about."

Irene took out the Spanish wanted poster featuring Sergei Petrov and the enlarged passport photograph of Andres Tamm.

"So you've never met this man? Neither under the name of Sergei Petrov, nor as Andres Tamm?"

After an indifferent glance at both pictures, Pettersson shook his shaven head once more. Irene couldn't see any sign of recognition, in spite of the fact that they knew it must have been Pettersson who picked up Sergei Petrov, together with Heinz Becker and the other girl, after they had fled from the raid on the brothel in Biskopsgården.

The interview continued in the same way; it was a real struggle. Pettersson denied everything he had said previously. When Fredrik confronted him with the fact that he was the one who had given them the names of Tanya and Sergei, he claimed that he had no memory of such a thing. He insisted he had never heard the names before. Perhaps he had heard something somewhere when he'd been drinking, and simply regurgitated it when he was confused and under the influence. And he wanted his lawyer present at all future interviews. Joar Svanér was well-known—or rather notorious—at police HQ. Somehow he usually managed to pull off a balancing act just within the boundaries of the law, and he was undeniably skillful. He had become very wealthy over the years, and was one of the most famous legal representatives in Göteborg. Celebrity parties, women and fast cars were his hallmark. He had just one piece of advice for his clients: keep your mouth shut!

It was obvious that Pettersson had been paying attention and had no intention of saying a word.

After spending an hour going around and around in circles, Irene gave Fredrik a discreet signal. He ended the interview.

When Pettersson had left the room with a final smirk, Fredrik said gloomily, "He's never going to talk."

"He will. We just have to find something that will scare him into opening his mouth. What is he most frightened of?"

"He's afraid the gang will beat him up if he squeals. They might even kill him."

"He has good reason to be scared about that, but it seems to me that as soon as we start talking about his own activities, he gets nervous. I think he's worried that we'll find something that could send him back to jail. Something tells me he's not very happy in the slammer."

"I don't suppose anyone is."

"No, but maybe Pettersson has a really tough time in there. Pedophiles usually do. And there's something he's afraid we'll find out. We just have to work out what it is. And be able to prove it."

Fredrik nodded, lost in thought. Suddenly he said, "I spoke to the carpenters who were working at Biskopsgården, and I took DNA samples. None of them matched the semen we found on Tanya's jacket or in her hair. Maybe we should check Pettersson's DNA?"

"Why not? We've already got his DNA profile from previous investigations into the sexual exploitation of minors."

"Although I have a feeling he didn't kill Tanya," Fredrik said.

"No, maybe not. But he knows something about the murder. He knew the people who were involved much better than he's prepared to admit."

ACCORDING TO HIS ID, Björn "Billy" Kjellgren had just turned eighteen. He looked younger. The baggy pants and hoodie hung loosely on his skinny body. His angular shoulders protruded sharply under his top. To tell the truth, he looked almost undernourished. Clumps of red-blond hair stuck out from beneath his dark blue woolen hat. His face was fine-featured, but his skin was marred by severe acne. He sat slumped on his chair, his gaze fixed on the toes of his scruffy boots.

Irene was standing behind the two-way mirror in the interview room, watching Jonny's struggle to get Billy to start talking. It was a waste of time.

Billy was doing very well, from his point of view. He didn't make a single sound during the entire interview. Every question from the increasingly frustrated Jonny was met with total silence. Even when Jonny pointed out that the probable sentences for the crimes of which Billy was accused would put him behind bars for several years, his face remained impassive.

Eventually Jonny gave up. It was a rare occurrence, but this time he had met his match: a skinny little eighteen-year-old who was accused of absconding from juvie, stealing a car, leaving the scene of an accident, and manslaughter.

"The little shit seems to have had a frontal lobotomy," Jonny said with a sigh as he and Irene were having coffee after the interview. He needed to recharge his batteries before speaking to Niklas Ström.

"Is it okay if I sit in?" Irene asked.

Jonny shrugged. "Sure. But aren't you busy with your own investigation?"

"Yes, but I'm not due to meet Linda Holm until four o'clock. I can sit in with you until then."

Jonny gave her a searching look. "Why?"

Irene was prepared for the question. "I want to know whether he or Billy saw anything on the night Tanya was murdered, the night Torleif Sandberg was run down. They must have been somewhere nearby, even if they weren't the ones who hit Torleif."

"Who else would it have been?"

"Exactly. There's a lot to suggest it was these two, but I can't for the life of me work out how they managed to get the keys and steal Torleif's car, which was parked outside his apartment block several hundred meters away."

"You're right. It doesn't make sense," Jonny agreed.

NIKLAS STRÖM WAS slightly taller and stronger than Billy, but otherwise they were surprisingly alike, and easily could have passed for brothers. The big difference was their body language. Billy was inert and expressionless, while Niklas couldn't sit still for a second. His body twitched uncontrollably all the time. He was the very manifestation of the phrase "ants in his pants."

Even if Niklas wasn't prepared to answer any questions, he was far from quiet. He kept up a constant stream of throat-clearing and small snorting noises.

After the usual introductory phrases, Jonny said, "As I understand it, you and Billy got together and decided to get out of Gräskärr. To be honest, I don't care how you planned it or how you got away. What interests me is what you did when you reached Göteborg."

Niklas snorted several times, drumming his fingers rapidly on the table.

"Tell me about the first few days after you took off."

Niklas shook his head and emitted a series of loud groans in quick succession. No response emerged through his tightly compressed lips.

"It was freezing cold. You needed a place to stay. And you needed a car," Jonny tried again.

The only reaction from Niklas was a strange whistling sound through his nostrils. Irene was becoming increasingly convinced that there was something wrong with him. Did it have something to do with his drug habit? Was he suffering withdrawal symptoms?

When it became clear that Niklas had no intention of answering Jonny's questions, Irene took the opportunity to ask one of her own. "Have you and Billy taken any drugs while you've been out?"

Niklas looked at her and shook his head firmly. "I've given all that up," he answered, much to her surprise.

"So neither of you has taken anything?" she repeated, just to make sure.

He cleared his throat several times. "Billy's never used, and I've stopped."

"That's good. Why did you stop?"

After another bout of coughing and spluttering, he said, "I couldn't handle it. That was why I . . . although I don't really remember . . . everything was kind of spinning around, then everything went black . . ."

"You mean when you raped that guy," Jonny said brutally.

Niklas delivered a rapid volley of coughs before managing to get out, "Yeah."

"So you're telling us that deep down you're a sweet little gay boy? The rape was just an accident that happened because you'd used too much crack? It wasn't your fault that the victim sustained serious injuries and ended up in hospital for several weeks?"

Irene saw Niklas's eyes darken, and she realized that the interview had taken a disastrous wrong turn. Jonny was wasting his sarcasm on an offense for which Niklas had already been convicted. She quickly tried to get back to those fateful days in January.

"Where did you and Billy stay for the first few nights after you left Gräskärr?"

Another bout of throat clearing, but no reply. Niklas also refused to answer any subsequent questions. Jonny's provocative comments about the rape had made him clam up completely. Irene cursed her colleague's stupidity but realized there wasn't much they could do about it now. The damage was done. There was no point in carrying on; they would just have to try again the next day. So far they hadn't even come close to asking how the boys had gotten Torleif's keys and his car.

WHEN IRENE GOT home, the whole family was there. She hadn't even realized how stressed she was feeling, but as she hugged them she felt the tension leave her body. They had already dropped Felipe off at his apartment. He had enjoyed the skiing trip, apart from a sprained thumb. Krister and the girls had a healthy glow after spending several hours each day outdoors. Superficially the whole family looked fine, but they had a lot to talk about. Krister had done some food shopping in Mellerud, and he quickly made hamburgers with plenty of onion, which was one of Irene's favorite dishes. Jenny was happy with veggie burgers from the freezer.

Sammie had been fed and was snoring happily under the kitchen table. The Huss family had dinner and discussed everything that had happened over the weekend. Irene did most of the talking. Once again she went over the story of the shooting at the casino. Krister had told the girls about it, but they wanted to hear it from their mom. The experience was therapeutic for Irene; she felt better after going through the details one more time. It was also good to shed a few tears and be comforted by those she loved most in the world.

They sat there for a long time working out how they could best help Gerd when she came home. All four were convinced that she would get through the surgery without any major problems, but the aftermath was a worry.

"She won't be able to manage in the apartment. Two floors up and no elevator," Irene said gloomily.

"Can't she come and live here?" Katarina suggested.

"Of course. But you know what she's like—as stubborn as a mule. She's going to want to live in her own apartment."

"So that's where you get it from," Katarina teased.

"Oh yes. And you didn't exactly miss out on that particular quality either," Irene came right back at her.

"Come on, ladies, this is about Gerd. We need to make sure she can get back into her apartment. Surely the ambulance driver or whoever transports patients home from hospital will help out," Krister said firmly.

"The home care service usually deals with medical needs, but as far as anything else goes . . ." Irene left the sentence unfinished, and sighed.

"We'll have to work out a schedule, take it in turns to go in and see her every day," Jenny said.

Eventually Irene felt ready to tell them about Sture's death. Krister and the girls were shocked, the atmosphere around the table was suffused with grief for a long time. They all agreed that this was all a bit too much to take in at once.

"I don't think we should tell Mom about Sture yet. She needs to recover from the operation first," Irene said.

Krister gazed at her thoughtfully. "Is that wise? What if she finds out?"

"If we don't say anything, she won't find out."

"And when do you think we should tell her?" Krister asked.

"In a few days," Irene replied evasively.

She had no idea when it would be a good time. Of course there was never a good time for news like that. All she knew was she just couldn't tell her mother right now.

Chapter 22

FREDRIK POKED HIS head around the door to Irene and Tommy's shared office.

"Irene, there's a guy who wants to speak to the person responsible for investigating the murder of the little Russian," he said.

At the moment Irene was the only one still working actively on the case, so there weren't many officers to choose from.

"Okay. Put him through," she answered distractedly. Her attention was focused on the computer screen as she laboriously tried to summarize what had happened in Tenerife. Even if she kept it brief, the report still gave the impression that she spent at least a week on the island. And made up most of the events.

"He's not on the phone. He's here."

"Oh, right . . . I just want to . . ."

Before she had time to finish the sentence, Fredrik had shown the man into the room. Or perhaps he had pushed his way in. He was dressed in a thick, dark blue sailing jacket with a hood, which was a practical choice given the freezing rain that was hammering against the windowpane.

"Good afternoon. My name is Martin Wallström. I have some important information regarding the place where you found the girl."

His whole attitude made it clear he was a man who was

accustomed to being listened to. Irene guessed that he was around forty-five years old. The hair on top of his head was thinning, but at the sides it was dark and cut very short. He looked like he was in good shape. His features were sharply defined, his expression alert and intelligent behind the rimless glasses.

Irene introduced herself and asked him to sit down opposite her. Martin Wallström slipped off the expensive jacket and hung it over the back of the chair. Underneath he was wearing a thin pale grey woolen sweater over a dark grey polo shirt. Together with his black chinos and sturdy black shoes, his clothing made a sober but relaxed impression.

However, what made him interesting was the fact that he seemed to have information regarding the investigation into the death of the little Russian. No one else had come forward since they started looking into Tanya's murder.

"I'd appreciate hearing what you have to say," she said with an encouraging smile.

He nodded, then gazed at her appraisingly. He said abruptly, "You have to understand that this is rather . . . delicate."

Irene nodded in return, as if she understood completely, but wondering what the hell this was all about. She said nothing, just waited.

"The evening when that little girl was killed . . . I was in the spot where she was found. Not in the cellar, of course, but on the narrow road leading to the canoe club. I parked a little way along that road."

Irene could feel her pulse rate increasing. This could be very interesting. She made an effort not to show how hopeful she was. "What time did you get there?" she asked calmly.

"Half past eight—I think that's pretty accurate. Possibly a few minutes later," he answered promptly.

"What kind of car do you have?"

"A dark blue Volvo S80. Last year's model."

That could be the car that had screeched up Töpelsgatan at

high speed. The time and the model of the car fit with the witness reports. Which would mean that Martin Wallström hadn't been alone in the car. According to the man with the dog that had almost been run over, there had been a woman in the car as well.

"Why did you go up there? I mean, it was late at night and extremely cold . . ."

Irene left the sentence hanging in the air, hoping he would latch onto it and keep talking.

"We needed a place where we could talk without being disturbed. I knew the road because I often go jogging in the area. I live in Örgryte."

You don't say, Irene thought sarcastically as she nodded encouragement.

"I wasn't alone in the car. There was a woman with me. We had . . . important matters to discuss." He fell silent and took a deep breath as if to gather strength before he went on. "We've been involved for several months. Neither of us expected this to happen, but . . . the situation was starting to become untenable, so we drove up toward the canoe club to talk about what we were going to do. Should we end the relationship, or should we leave our respective partners? Another problem is we live practically next door to each other. People had started . . . talking. Some of the neighbors had seen us."

Martin Wallström looked troubled as he finished speaking. Irene wondered which he thought was worse: the fact that he was screwing the neighbor's wife or the knowledge that people were beginning to gossip.

"As you will understand, we were talking about some very critical issues. It was cold, and we left the engine running so we wouldn't freeze. I should think we were there for almost an hour. Longer than forty-five minutes, at any rate. Then we had to leave because it was getting late. We still hadn't reached a final decision. Neither of us wanted to end things, but we both have children. Hers are younger than mine . . . it's complicated."

For the first time he looked away and gazed at the rain-spattered window. He swallowed hard several times.

"What I wanted to tell you is that all the time we were sitting in the car, there was another car parked a short distance away. A little closer to the barrier."

And the root cellar, Irene thought. "Was there anyone in the car?"

"No, it was empty. I think. I mean, it was very dark; some of the nearby street lamps were out. But I didn't notice anything to suggest that there was anyone around."

"What kind of car was it?"

"I don't know. I think it was a pale color, and a pretty big model. I don't know what make it was. It was parked facing toward us."

Martin Wallström fell silent and stared almost defiantly at Irene. When he didn't show any signs of continuing, she asked, "Why didn't you contact us until now?"

He shuffled uncomfortably. "I should think that's obvious," he snapped.

"No. Please explain," Irene said politely.

"We hadn't decided what to do about the future and . . . everything. But now my wife has found out about us. From a friend who had seen us. So there's no turning back. We're both going to get a divorce and try to build a new life together."

Irene almost asked whether he had actually discussed this with his new woman, but she managed to stop herself. Instead she said, "But you must have realized that what you had seen was important."

"Well, yes. But for the reasons I've already given, I didn't want to speak to you. There was a risk that our respective partners would find out that we'd been sitting there in the car . . .

they'd want to know what we'd been doing and why . . . you understand what I mean."

Irene decided to let it go, in spite of her annoyance. "So you didn't see anyone in the vicinity of the light-colored car?"

"No. But when we were driving back down Delsjövägen, we heard a siren in the distance. It was coming from the direction of the city, and we could see the flashing blue lights. We didn't want to be held up, so we turned onto Bögatan and headed down to Sankt Sigfridsplan. Then we drove straight home along Sankt Sigfridsgatan," Wallström explained.

The siren they had heard was probably the police car pursuing the stolen BMW. Wallström and his squeeze had missed the accident in which Torleif Sandberg was killed by just a few seconds. Or maybe they just hadn't noticed it.

"You didn't see a car coming along Delsjövägen from the opposite direction? I'm thinking about the vehicle the police were pursuing," Irene said.

"No. I've tried to think, but I don't remember a car coming the other way. Although of course I was upset . . . as I said, we'd been talking about some life-changing stuff . . . I probably wasn't paying much attention. My only thought when I saw the blue lights and heard the siren was that I didn't want to get stuck. We had to get home before it got too late."

Irene nodded to show she understood. "I'll need to speak to the woman who was with you," she said.

He glanced over at the window again. "It's not that simple. Her husband has taken this very badly. She's moved back home to her parents'. Only temporarily, until we can move into the new house I've bought. The children are still with him, but that's probably not such a good . . ." His voice tailed away, and he looked tormented.

"Does she have a name?"

The question sounded more acidic than Irene had intended.

"What? Who? Oh . . . sure. Marika. Marika Lager." He took

out a business card and scribbled something on the back before handing it to Irene. "That's her cell number. She's out sick from work at the moment. My number is on the card as well. It's best to call my cell."

He got to his feet, suddenly looking as energetic and decisive as he had when he walked in.

"You'll have to excuse me, but I need to get back to work. I have a meeting."

He held out his hand and pumped Irene's hand up and down several times, then quickly left the room.

"I CALLED MARIKA Lager and she confirmed what Martin Wallström said. She didn't have anything to add; quite the reverse, in fact. She recalled seeing the parked car, but nothing else. She couldn't even remember whether it was a dark or light color."

Andersson nodded and folded his hands over his belly. "So the only thing we know for sure is that there was a car parked up by the barrier," he said.

"Yes. Just below the slope where the root cellar is," Irene confirmed.

"The bastard could have been hiding in the car. He might have already stowed the little Russian in the cellar, but didn't have time to get away before Wallström and his girlfriend turned up. Or maybe he dumped her in there as fast as he could once the turtledoves had left," Jonny said.

"We don't even know if it was the killer's car, but I think we can safely assume that it was since the driver hasn't come forward," Irene said.

"Even if he dumped the body quickly after they'd left, he didn't have much time to play with. If Wallström drove off at around half past nine, that means the murderer had something like ten minutes to carry the little Russian up the slope to the cellar, break open the door and put the body inside. And he must have gotten away before the BMW arrived, otherwise it would have blocked him in," Fredrik said.

"What if he didn't get away? What if our two little hit-and-run drivers actually arrived before he had time to get away?" Tommy said thoughtfully.

Irene considered what he had just said, and realized where he was going with this.

"You mean in that case they know who he is, or at least what he looks like," she said.

"Yep."

Everyone turned to Jonny. "Okay, I'll try the little shits again. And that particular spot seems to be a popular spot for lovers," he said with a smirk.

"Although there wasn't a lot of lovemaking going on in this case," Irene said sharply.

"Enough! Get back to the interviews," Andersson said in a voice that brooked no contradictions.

"YEP!" TOMMY SAID with the phone pressed to his ear. He grinned at Irene and gave her a thumbs-up sign. "You'll email it to me right away? Great!"

He put down the phone with a flourish. He was still smiling as he said, "I think you and Fredrik have the ammunition you need against Anders Pettersson." He paused dramatically, his eyes twinkling teasingly as he made her wait.

"Out with it!" she said impatiently, since that was clearly what was expected of her.

"The lab has compared the DNA from the semen we found on Tanya with Pettersson's DNA profile. And they've found a match!"

Irene stared at him, lost for words. "In her hair . . . and the skin fragments under her nails?" she managed eventually.

"No. Not the killer's DNA. But one of the stains on her jacket!"

The grubby pink jacket had had several semen stains that pre-dated the murder. And one of them matched Pettersson's DNA. Slowly Irene began to see the opportunities this presented.

"So one of the semen stains comes from our good friend Pettersson. We can prove it, and he can't get away from that fact. We know it's not the killer's DNA. But Pettersson has no idea that we know that," she said, her smile as broad as Tommy's.

"Exactly." He got up and headed for the door, but stopped halfway and turned back to Irene. "And Svante said we forgot to cancel the DNA comparison between Andres and Leili Tamm. It confirms what we already knew: they're not related."

ANDERS PETTERSSON HAD been deeply shaken when he was re-arrested, this time on suspicion of murder. His lawyer, Joar Svanér, had shown up right away, insisting that his client be released immediately. However, when faced with the fact that Pettersson's DNA had been found on the dead girl's jacket, even Svanér had realized the gravity of the situation. He had demanded and been granted time alone with his client; immediately following their meeting, Svanér informed the police that Anders Pettersson was prepared to talk.

Irene and Fredrik were already waiting in the interview room. As on the previous occasion, Pettersson was accompanied by two custody officers. This time the escort also included Svanér.

Irene had always thought he looked more like a superannuated disco dancer than a lawyer. The mid-length hair was colored dark brown and slicked back with generous amounts of gel. Today he was wearing a black leather jacket over a pink shirt with no tie. A wide black belt with a shiny silver buckle rested on his hips. Given the size of the buckle, it was a wonder it wasn't weighing down the elegantly tailored black pants rather than holding them up. In spite of the current fashion for drainpipes, there was definitely the hint of a flare at the bottom. On his feet he was wearing heeled cowboy boots, which were every bit as impractical in the pouring rain as the brown suede coat he was carrying over one arm. He hung the coat over the back of a chair in the interview room. It would have been easy to dismiss Joar Svanér as over the top and foolish had it not been for the look in the eyes behind the yellow-tinted glasses.

Irene had once seen a nature program about the role of scavengers in the wild. The cameraman had filmed a huge Egyptian vulture as it sat watching the death throes of an injured goat. From time to time the vulture lifted its wings threateningly to scare off smaller birds and other predators. Otherwise it sat there motionless, its gaze fixed on its prospective meal. Only the indifferent eyes moved when it became necessary to monitor some approaching competitor. Irene remembered that look: it registered everything and missed nothing. It revealed no emotion whatsoever.

Joar Svanér had exactly the same look in his eyes.

"My client is prepared to tell the truth about his association with the homicide victim," Sanér stated without preamble.

"Good. Start talking," Irene said, nodding to Anders Pettersson.

He looked haggard, and had made no attempt to hide it. His expensive designer top stank of sweat, and his baggy jeans were filthy. The stubble on his chin was slightly longer than the emerging hairs on his shaven head. His bloodshot eyes peered out from his puffy face. He looked like a mental and physical wreck. His dealings had finally caught up with him. This was probably what he had feared most: the discovery that he had been associated with Heinz Becker and his shady dealings.

Narcotics offenses attract severe sentencing. Human trafficking has also caught the attention of the media in recent times, but the sentences handed down are still relatively lenient compared with those for drug crimes. Pettersson's activities were mainly drug-related, and he was acutely aware of the lengthy jail sentence that awaited him if he was convicted.

"I . . . I had a . . . I'm not sure how to put this . . . I had contact with the girl."

Pettersson fell silent and stared down at the table. His face was beaded with sweat even though the room wasn't especially warm. He was confessing to a crime as far as the law regarding prostitution was concerned, but it wasn't going to land him behind bars. However, he was noticeably tense and uncomfortable.

"Start from the beginning. How did you get in touch with Heinz Becker?" Irene asked.

"I called when I saw the advertisement. The one about the girls."

"And where did you see this advertisement?"

"In . . . in a newspaper," he answered evasively.

"Which newspaper?"

"I don't remember."

"What did the ad look like?"

Pettersson looked completely bewildered. "What kind of a stupid fucking question is—"

"It's important for our investigation," Irene interrupted.

Not least because he had already come out with the first lie. Heinz Becker had advertised only on the Internet. Pettersson had no reason to know this since Becker had probably contacted him directly for narcotics and aphrodisiacs.

"I don't remember," Pettersson replied truculently.

"So you had never had any contact with Heinz Becker in the past?"

"No."

"So why did he get in touch with you now?"

"You misunderstand, Detective Inspector," Joar Svanér interjected. "My client called a telephone number that was given in an advertisement for willing girls."

"That's right." Pettersson nodded.

Irene pretended she hadn't heard, and carried on. "When was this?"

"I've already fucking told you! The Saturday before . . . before you picked me up for drunk driving! I mean the Saturday of the week before. That's what I mean."

So you remember the first interview, Irene thought. *And you remember the date when you met Tanya. Not bad, considering how much of a drug-induced fog you've been in over the past few weeks.* Irene suspected that Anders Pettersson and Joar Svanér had carefully worked out exactly what he was going to say. And what he was definitely not going to say.

"So you called the number in the ad," Irene said.

"Yes. If you're horny, you're horny!" He was trying to act like his usual bumptious self, but even he could hear how ridiculous it sounded. Irene gave him an icy stare. His attempt to play the ordinary john who just happened to end up in the brothel in Biskopsgården was utterly pathetic.

"Then what happened?"

"When I got there he said . . . Becker . . . that the little whore had an infected pussy. She'd caught something disgusting, so she was only doing blow jobs. There were guys already waiting for the other hooker, so I said what the hell, let's go for the blow job."

He sounded a little more sure of himself, and Irene had a feeling that he was suddenly telling the truth.

"How did Tanya seem when you met her?"

"How did she . . . I don't . . . she was cold, so she kept that fucking jacket on. That's how she got my spunk on her. And I had nothing to do with her death, for fuck's sake!"

It was probably true that Pettersson had had oral sex with

Tanya, and Saturday could well fit in with what they already knew. Forensics had already established that the stains on the jacket were a couple of days older than the semen in her hair, so Pettersson was probably telling the truth about his encounter with Tanya.

"So Tanya kept her jacket on. Weren't you indoors?" Irene asked.

"Yes."

"Where were you?"

"In . . . in Biskopsgården."

"And did you think it was cold in the apartment?"

"No. But she must have thought it was fucking freezing."

"Why do you say she must have thought it was freezing?"

Both Pettersson and his lawyer looked confused. Even Fredrik gave her a sideways glance as he wondered where she was going with this.

"How the fuck should I know?" Pettersson exploded.

"How was Tanya feeling?"

"How was . . . Why should I have a fucking clue?" He glanced uncertainly at her with his bloodshot eyes, but immediately looked away. Perhaps he was beginning to sense where this was heading.

"Did she seem healthy?"

"May I point out that my client is not a medical practitioner," Svanér protested. "It is impossible for him to ascertain whether a person he has only just met is healthy or not."

"But he can answer a simple question as to whether this person he had only just met looked healthy and behaved like a healthy individual," Irene said coldly.

Pettersson's gaze flicked from Irene to Svanér and back again. With a final sideways look at his lawyer, he said uncertainly, "Maybe she wasn't a hundred per cent. I mean . . . she seemed really . . . listless. How else can I put it . . . yes, really listless."

"So you forced a seriously ill underage girl to perform oral sex on you," Irene stated.

He swallowed several times before answering. "Forced . . . no fucking way . . . it was business. She got paid."

"Did you give the money to her?"

"Sure I did!" Pettersson said with a grin.

They both knew that wasn't what had happened, but Irene couldn't prove it.

"How come Heinz Becker had your cell number in his phone?"

"He said he'd contact me when the little whore's pussy was better," Pettersson replied, his face expressionless.

He and Svanér must have spent a while polishing up that lie. They had known the question would come. They knew the police already had evidence that Pettersson and Becker had been in touch with each other via their cell phones, and Pettersson certainly had no intention of revealing that they had been discussing the supply of drugs and other items.

During the rest of the interview Irene tried several times to get him to admit that he had had dealings with Heinz Becker in the past, but he remained unshakeable. He was definitely following his lawyer's strict instructions to the letter; he would not confirm any link to Heinz Becker beyond the transaction involving Tanya.

"We've traced a number of calls between your cell and Heinz Becker's. You called each other several times during the week he was here with the girls. How do you explain that?"

"He was keeping me informed. About the progress of the little pussy," Pettersson said with a scornful grin.

"Is that why he called you when they needed a ride from Ringön? To tell you about the progress of the little pussy?"

Pettersson once again glanced at his lawyer, but answered quickly, "I was very surprised, but I was happy to help out. They paid me well because they had a plane to catch from Kastrup."

"They?"

"That guy and the other girl."

"Did you ask what had happened to Tanya?"

Pettersson remained silent for a long time. "Yes. They said she'd already left."

"Alone?"

"No."

"Who was she with?"

"With . . . some guy called Sergei."

He obviously remembered that he had mentioned Sergei's name during his first interview, and in order to make himself appear more trustworthy, he had decided to mention it again. Perhaps he knew about the disastrous events in Tenerife. That wasn't out of the question, if he really was involved in human trafficking. His gang had their dirty fingers in that pie as well, and in every other criminal activity that generated money.

"When you picked up Heinz Becker and Leili, there was another man with them. Do you know who he was?"

"No, they just said he was taking that girl—Leili, is that what you called her?—to Tenerife."

"So she was going to Tenerife as well?"

"Yes. That's what Heinz told me."

"Were she and Tanya going to the same place?"

"How the fuck should I know? I just drove them to the parking lot at Heden. I had nothing to do with their fucking travel arrangements!"

I'm sure you know more than you're prepared to tell me, Irene thought. However, she also realized that there was no point in pushing him any further.

Instead she went on. "So you asked Becker where Tanya was. What did he say?"

"I've already told you! He said she'd gone on ahead. With that Sergei guy."

"Did he say anything about her illness?"

Pettersson rubbed his hands several times over his stubbly scalp, as if he was trying to stimulate some kind of internal activity through massage. Suddenly he lowered his hands and looked Irene straight in the eye.

"They said some guy had taken her to the doctor. And she got better—well enough to travel to Tenerife."

The immovable eye of the vulture blinked so fast that Irene only just registered it. For a fraction of a second Joar Svanér's inscrutable façade cracked. In that nanosecond Irene could see that he was completely unprepared for Pettersson's revelation.

"Who took her to the doctor?" Irene asked immediately.

"Don't know. Some fucking john."

Now it was Irene's turn to almost let the mask slip. This could be important, if it was true. And right now it did seem as if Pettersson had decided to tell the truth. The explanation was probably very simple: he wanted to divert the interest of the police and point them in a completely different direction.

"What makes you think it was a john?"

"He said something in the car . . . what was it . . . something about a john he trusted."

"You don't remember exactly what he said?"

"For fuck's sake! It's a long time ago! You can't expect me to . . ."

A glance at his lawyer shut him up. Svanér had also realized that the tactic of introducing a new angle that led away from Pettersson's activities might be quite useful. Particularly as the police seemed to be interested in what he had to say.

"Jesus Christ . . . Becker's English was crap. But he said he '*trusted this man*,'" Pettersson said, switching to English to quote Becker, "and that he was a '*good customer*.'" Pettersson's English pronunciation was surprisingly good.

According to what Pettersson was trying to get them to believe, a trusted client had been asked to take Tanya to the doctor. Instead of driving her to the surgery, he had forced her to perform oral sex on him. His semen was in her hair when her body was found several hours later.

Therefore, this unknown, trusted customer was in all probability her killer.

Bearing in mind what the police knew and Pettersson didn't, what he had just told them could very well be true.

As soon as the interview was over, Irene went to her office and called the hospital. The duty nurse on the orthopedic ward informed her that Gerd was still in recovery. She would probably be brought up to the ward toward evening if there was no cause for concern. But Gerd had undergone major surgery, so Irene shouldn't worry if they decided to keep her under observation overnight. The nurse asked Irene to call back after five o'clock, by which time they would know what the situation was.

With a sigh Irene went back to her report on the events in Tenerife. She found it difficult to concentrate, and her progress was slow.

Chapter 23

GERD HAD BEEN kept under observation overnight, and wouldn't be back on the ward until lunchtime. The nurse recommended that Irene wait until the evening to visit.

Irene put the phone down and stared unseeingly at the wall for a little while. She was bone weary after a virtually sleepless night. Worrying about her mother and thinking about Sture's death had kept her awake.

The insistent sound of the telephone brought her back to reality, disturbing her thoughts. Before she even had time to answer properly, she heard Svante Malm's voice on the other end of the line:

"Hi! I can't get hold of Hannu. Can you come down? I've got something you're going to find interesting."

He ended the call before she had time to ask any questions. She had no choice but to head down to forensics.

"I HAD AN idea, and I checked it out with lost property. This was handed in on January eighteenth, the day after the girl was killed."

With a knowing smile he handed the item to Irene. It was a brand new black Nokia with a wide matte silver border. Irene flipped it open and saw that it was switched off.

"Torleif Sandberg's?" she asked.

"Yes. I got his cell phone's ID number from you, and it's a

match. The battery has run out, but I had the pin code from you as well, so I checked the SIM card in another cell."

"Where was it found?"

"On the bridle path that runs just above the TV studios. A riding instructor found it when she was out exercising the horses."

"But hadn't it started snowing? How come she could see it?"

"It was lying right in the middle of the path. And it didn't snow until the following day. The path was clear."

To think that Muesli, who had been so careful with his money, had treated himself to such an expensive phone! Irene looked at the neat little cell that fit so comfortably in her hand. She flipped it open and admired the smart design. It was high time she upgraded her old cell, which was the size of a brick. Perhaps she should get one like this, with a built-in camera.

"I thought it might be interesting to see what kind of pictures he's saved," Svante said, as if he had read her mind.

"Do you know what to do? I think you just have to plug the cell into a computer . . ."

"I'm a chemist. I'm useless when it comes to technology. This is one of the latest models. The easiest thing would be to take out the photo chip or whatever it's called, but to be honest I have no idea how to do it. Or even if it's possible on this kind of phone. How about you?"

"Haven't a clue."

Svante gave her a relieved smile. It was good to know that both of them were at a loss when it came to the latest technology.

"Taking the memory card out of a digital camera is no problem, but how a phone like this works . . . I'm scared of messing up. And Jens, who knows all about this kind of thing, is in the mountains this week. He won't be back until Monday. I'll try charging the cell, then we should be able to see his photographs, if there are any. I'll have to find the right charger though; I'll need a new model to match the phone. Should be sorted out by tomorrow," Svante said.

It was bad luck that their IT genius happened to be on holiday this week. He looked like a teenage skateboarder as he ambled along the corridors, but he was almost thirty. He could work magic when it came to everything related to computers. Thanks to his skill they had succeeded in solving a very tricky case where the only clue had been a few photographs of major fires, with people in the foreground silhouetted against the flames. He had managed to bring out their facial features and other important details that would have been impossible to see without his expertise.

"So what did Torleif have on his SIM card?" Irene asked with interest.

"Just one number. I checked it out, and it went straight to a banker. Did Torleif need a personal banker to deal with major financial affairs?"

"I don't know . . . He'd bought a house in Thailand. Scrimped and saved for several years. It came as a complete surprise to his son. It sounds like a real luxury pad, with a swimming pool and so on."

"Hmm. And his son didn't know about it?"

Irene didn't really want to pass on what Stefan Sandberg had told her about his relationship with Torleif. "They haven't seen much of one another over the past few years. He's a doctor up in Norrland," she said.

Svante seemed to accept her explanation and dropped the subject. "Coffee?" he asked.

"No thanks. I've got to get back to my computer." The coffee in forensics was the worst in the entire building, at least when Svante made it.

"Okay. In that case I'll call you when we can look at the pictures," he said with a smile.

• • •

A PALE FEBRUARY sun was shining down on the city, hidden only occasionally by thin veils of cloud. People in the street were blinking up at the sky like small creatures newly awakened from hibernation, unaccustomed to the strange light. Nobody was fooled; there would be plenty more rain and snow before spring arrived, but the sun allowed them to hope there would actually be a spring this year, too. The winter had been unusually depressing. The wind was still strong, with sudden fierce gusts, but that was a good thing; it would dry up the meltwater from the streets more quickly. The ground was frozen solid, so there was nowhere for the water to go.

Irene splashed energetically through the slush to her mother's apartment. She had dashed out during her lunch break to pick up a few things that Gerd had asked her to take to the hospital. It would probably be a few days before she started asking for them, but it was a good idea to have them ready for when they were needed.

When Irene opened the door, the memories came flooding toward her. She had spent the first nineteen years of her life in this apartment. Gerd had lived there for almost forty-three years.

It was a small three-room apartment, or perhaps two rooms and a tiny box room just off the kitchen, which had been Irene's for all those years. She had just managed to squeeze in a bed, a chest of drawers and a tiny desk with a shelf above. The wallpaper had originally boasted a pattern of little pink rosebuds; when she was about fourteen Irene had painted the walls a heathery purple. The first thing her father had done when she moved out was to repaint the whole room, this time beige. The purple rug and bedspread had been allowed to stay, as had the furniture. Everything was just the same. Her parents had used it as a guestroom. When the twins had stayed over with their grandmother after she was widowed, Gerd had given the girls her double bed while she moved into the little room.

Irene picked up the mail and newspapers in the hallway and went into the kitchen to fetch the watering can. Unlike her daughter, Gerd had a green thumb and loved her flowers. The windowsills were filled with beautiful potted plants. Even during the darkest time of the year, she managed to cultivate flowers to brighten the place up. Right now two glorious cerise-pink orchids were holding court in the living room window.

In the doorway of the galley kitchen she stopped and gazed at the familiar interior. Her father had painted the cupboard doors white at the same time as he had redone the walls in her room; he had redecorated the rest of the apartment too, and since then nothing had changed in her childhood home, although the cooker and refrigerator had been replaced in the mid-1980s when the newly formed residents' association had secured a good deal with a supplier and had replaced all the white goods in the building. The stairwells and the yard had been renovated, and the general maintenance had been contracted out to a service company. Since then the snow simply lay where it fell, unless one of the council plows happened to end up in Guldheden by mistake. Irene sighed; things had been better in the past. She filled up the watering can and added a generous dose of plant food. None of Gerd's plants was going to die of thirst during her absence. Irene was determined to make sure of that.

When she had finished she suddenly thought about Sture's plants. Who was looking after his apartment? He had no children, and Irene hadn't heard of any close relatives. And when should she tell her mother about Sture's death? She reminded herself of her earlier thoughts: there was never a good time to deliver news like that. She ought to tell her as soon as possible.

"WHERE THE HELL have you been? I've been looking for you," Jonny said accusingly.

"Good to see you too," Irene replied. She had no intention of telling him where she'd been. It had nothing to do with him.

Jonny glared at her, shifting uncomfortably from one foot to the other before he reluctantly came out with it. "You seemed to get on well with that little shirt-lifter Niklas Ström. Tommy and I had another go at Billy, but it's a waste of time. He's as silent as a fucking freemason!"

Irene thought that was probably because the two police officers represented everything Billy had learned to distrust: middle-aged men, authority figures and homophobes. The latter applied primarily to Jonny.

"I'm happy to sit in when you speak to Niklas. I'll just take off my coat," she said, heading into her office.

"Interview room two in half an hour," she heard Jonny's voice behind her.

Tommy wasn't there. It occurred to her that it had been a while since she had spoken to him. It wasn't that she had anything in particular on her mind, but it was good to chat with old friends and colleagues from time to time. As she was hanging up her coat, the intercom crackled into life.

"Hi, Tommy. I'm on my way down."

Irene recognized Superintendent Linda Holm's voice, and all her instincts as an investigator kicked in. Where were Tommy and Linda Holm going? Together? She decided to find out, from sheer curiosity.

She quickly slipped into the corridor and strolled along to the exit, which was the door leading to the elevators. She could hear the sound of Linda Holm's high-heeled boots approaching along the corridor. A few meters ahead of Irene, the superintendent of the trafficking unit swung around the corner, making for the elevators. She seemed to be in a hurry, and obviously hadn't noticed Irene, who continued walking calmly toward the glass door. As Irene opened the door she saw

Linda step into an elevator. The display showed that she had stopped on the second floor; presumably she was going to the cafeteria. Wild horses couldn't have stopped Irene from going to the same place. It's a free country, she thought. If I want a cup of coffee, then I want a cup of coffee, and I'm perfectly entitled to go to the cafeteria.

She spotted Tommy right in the corner. He was already sitting at a table, and he was waving. Not at Irene, but at Linda, who was holding a steaming cup in one hand and a cellophane-wrapped sandwich in the other. Irene decided to follow her example. She hadn't had time for lunch because she'd spent her break in Gerd's apartment.

Nonchalantly she strolled over to the counter and picked up a coffee and a cheese roll. After a brief hesitation she grabbed a liver paste sandwich as well, then she stood there holding her little tray and gazing around the way you do when you're hoping to see someone you know. As if by chance, she glanced over toward the corner. There wasn't much point in joining Tommy and Linda, who were already sitting opposite each other deep in conversation, maintaining eye contact. She would only be intruding.

Fortunately she spotted Hannu sitting on his own.

"Mind if I join you?"

"Not at all."

His attempt at a smile was more of a feeble grimace. She had never seen Hannu looking so . . . devastated. That was the word that came into her mind. Devastated.

"How's it going?" she asked.

"Okay."

It wasn't much of a response, so she tried again.

"When is Birgitta coming home?"

"Tomorrow."

"Is your mother-in-law still here?"

"Yes."

She had grown used to Hannu and his taciturnity, but this was pushing it even for him.

"When is Birgitta coming back to work?"

"Don't know. A week maybe."

Things were looking up. Two sentences in a row!

"How is she?"

"Better."

"Good."

You're known by the company you keep, as Gerd used to say. A glance at Hannu's haggard face made her ashamed of her thoughts. It was hardly surprising if he didn't feel like chatting. He had more than enough to deal with right now. The look he gave her as he put down his coffee cup was dull and weary. He rubbed one eye with his index finger.

"I've been thinking," Hannu said. "He wasn't warmly dressed."

It took a few seconds for Irene to work out who he was talking about. "You mean Torleif."

"Yes. He had frostbite. Because he had never intended to be outdoors."

Irene didn't answer, but took a bite of her cheese roll while she thought about what he had said. He would get to the point eventually.

"He knew exactly how to dress when it's very cold. But he was forced out. And they took his car."

"The guys who escaped from Gräskärr? Niklas and Billy?"

"Yes. That's what must have happened."

"I've been thinking along those lines as well . . ."

"But there's a problem." Hannu caught her eye. "Why didn't he call the police?"

Irene opened her mouth to speak, then closed it again. Good question. Why didn't he call the police when someone stole his car?

"He had a cell phone. It's been found, by the way," she said.

"I heard."

Irene thought out loud. "Maybe he couldn't use his cell. It's the latest model. Perhaps he hadn't learned how it works," she hypothesized.

"Possibly. But . . ."

"Look at you two, having a cozy little chat!" came a familiar voice behind Irene.

She turned around with a sarcastic comment aimed at Tommy and his companion on the tip of her tongue, but quickly swallowed it. He was standing there all alone, smiling at her. There was no sign of Linda Holm.

THE TIME SPENT in custody was beginning to take its toll on Niklas Ström. There were dark circles under his eyes, suggesting a severe lack of sleep. His entire body constantly twitched and jerked uncontrollably, and it was completely impossible for him to sit still. The frequency of involuntary snorts and inarticulate noises also seemed to have increased. Irene noticed that his nails were bitten down to the quick.

Jonny started the interview, but soon handed over to Irene. He couldn't get Niklas to answer a single question properly. Irene had carefully considered her approach.

"Niklas, are you scared of ending up back in jail with an extended sentence?" she asked.

He immediately looked up from his frantically drumming fingers and met her gaze. "What the fuck do you think?" he snapped.

"Let me explain something. At the moment you and Billy are suspected of murder, or involvement in a murder. And I'm not talking about running down a guy who later died of his injuries. I'm talking about the murder of a young girl."

"What the fuck are you talking about? Are you fucking crazy, you . . ."

Niklas tried to get up from his chair, but was stopped dead

by Irene's voice, which sliced through the air like the crack of a whip, "Sit down! Listen to me!"

He slumped back down on the chair and stared defiantly at her. Irene noticed he had beautiful aquamarine eyes.

"This is something we have to look into because we have evidence that you and Billy were in the area when the murder was committed. We found your fingerprints in the car that belonged to the man who was run down. The car must have been stolen on the day he died. And the girl was also killed that same evening."

She paused and looked searchingly at him. He refused to meet her eye and sat with his head down, grunting repeatedly. His upper body rocked back and forth as if an invisible person were gently shaking him.

"It's going to take us a long time to investigate the girl's death. You and Billy will be held in custody for a lengthy period. There is also a risk that the officers concerned will draw the wrong conclusions. The court may do the same. This means that you might be given a considerably longer sentence than you really deserve. In order to avoid this, we need your help. We have to know the truth."

She fell silent again to see whether he was listening and had understood what she was saying. His face was twitching violently, and loud groans were forcing their way out of his mouth. The prospect of spending an unspecified amount of time in custody was clearly causing him great distress. The risk of a longer sentence wasn't exactly appealing either.

"Niklas. Tell me exactly what happened on the night of January seventeenth. You will save both yourself and Billy a whole lot of grief. You've done what you've done, and you'll go down for that. But surely it's unnecessary to put yourselves through the lengthy process of a homicide inquiry? Is there anything you'd like to tell me about the girl?"

"What fucking girl? I don't know nothing about no fucking

girl! We . . ." He stopped and looked insolently at her. "I didn't see no fucking girl!"

"So what did you see?"

By now he was writhing around on the chair so violently that he was in danger of falling off. His anguish was clear.

"Sit still, for God's sake!" Jonny yelled.

Irene had almost forgotten that he was there. The effect on Niklas was instantaneous. His movements grew even more pronounced, and he glared at Jonny, his beautiful eyes burning with hatred. Something told Irene that Niklas had often heard those particular words.

"Niklas, listen to me. I am trying to help you. I am trying to explain to you what is going on," she said.

The important thing was to sound calm and trustworthy. She felt as if she and the hyperactive boy on the other side of the table had managed to establish some kind of fragile contact, and then Jonny came trampling in and shattered a trust that was thinner than sheet ice that had formed overnight. She threw him an irritated look before turning her attention back to Niklas.

"We are investigating two crimes. Both crimes took place at virtually the same time. First of all there is the hit-and-run, which had a fatal outcome. The witnesses saw two guys in a BMW that had been stolen on Stampgatan. Outside the TV studios they hit a man who died immediately from the injuries he sustained. We will be arranging a lineup for the witnesses with you and Billy. You both fit the descriptions we have been given. Stealing cars and running people down are serious offenses. But they are nowhere near as serious as premeditated murder. And that's the second crime we are looking into. That will lead to a lengthy jail term."

She paused to let her words sink in. Niklas didn't say anything, but Irene had a strong feeling that he was listening.

"When we found the BMW in flames on the road leading

down to the canoe club, we naturally carried out a detailed search of the area. Lots of police officers and dogs—you know how it goes. And we found the body of a young girl. She had been killed at approximately the time when the BMW drove onto that road, and her body was hidden close by."

Irene sent up a silent prayer that Jonny would have the sense to keep quiet. For once it seemed as if her prayer had been answered. Niklas twitched and looked sharply at her.

"You mean the girl in that cellar? Like some kind of root cellar? It has to be, right? Are you crazy? We were . . ." He broke off, staring at Irene.

She took no notice, and calmly continued. "So you've read and heard about the murder. Yes, it's the girl in the root cellar. You have to understand that we cannot simply dismiss any suspicion that you were involved. You were there. You had the opportunity. And—"

"That's a fucking lie! We never . . ." Niklas was breathing heavily and seemed to be in danger of hyperventilating.

"I can understand that you don't want to be linked to a premeditated murder. But in order for us to remove that suspicion, you have to tell the truth. You have to tell us what really happened that night."

Niklas remained silent for a long time, chewing on a bloody fingertip. Both knees bobbed up and down as he rapidly flexed his toes. His breathing was shallow and audible.

"I need to . . . think. And I want my lawyer!" he said firmly.

"Of course. We'll contact your legal representative right away, then we can meet again this evening or tomorrow," Irene said.

She had to make a real effort to hide her disappointment. Naturally Niklas had every right to have his lawyer present, but she felt as if he had been on the point of starting to talk.

She switched off the tape recorder and got ready to leave. Niklas was on his feet.

"We didn't see nothing! There was no one there! Just the car," he said suddenly.

Irene stiffened and her mouth went dry. She mustn't say the wrong thing now!

"What car? You mean the BMW?" she said almost indifferently as she put her notepad and pen away in her shoulder bag.

"No, not the BMW! The Opel! The white Opel!"

For a few seconds Irene completely lost focus. Behind her she heard Jonny's sharp intake of breath.

"You mean the Opel that you and Billy later drove out to Olofstorp?" she managed to say when she had more or less pulled herself together.

After another bout of head twitching, Niklas replied, "Yes."

"So you and Billy abandoned the stolen BMW and torched it. Then you took the car that was parked by the barrier. How did you get it started?"

"The keys were in the ignition." Suddenly he looked completely calm. His finger had started bleeding, and there was blood on his lips. He licked them and gazed thoughtfully at his finger.

"The keys were in the ignition," Irene said, frantically trying to think.

"Did you know the Opel was going to be there?" Jonny asked.

At first it looked like Niklas wasn't going to answer, but then he shrugged. "How the fuck would we know that? It was just there, okay?"

He moved over to the door to wait patiently for his escort back to the custody cell. Irene was completely at a loss.

Torleif Sandberg's car had been parked on the side road leading down to the canoe club. Unlocked and with the keys in the ignition. Why had the car been there? And why had he abandoned it and gone running off into the cold winter night?

That was why Niklas and Billy had been able to disappear

so quickly. They had already been far away by the time the helicopters were brought in the following morning.

"How did you manage to get past the roadblocks?" Irene asked Niklas.

"Side roads. There are plenty of them up around Delsjö," he said.

For the first time Irene saw the hint of a smile on his face. He was probably quite pleased with the way he and Billy had gotten away.

When the door closed behind Niklas and the guards, Irene heard Jonny mutter, "What the hell . . ."

She couldn't help but agree with him.

ANDERSSON LOOKED FAR from happy by the time Irene had finished reporting back on the interview with Niklas Ström. The only reason he didn't protest was Jonny was sitting next to her and confirmed everything she had said.

"What the hell was Torleif doing there?" the superintendent asked.

"I have no idea. But it's very odd. He had serious frostbite injuries, which suggests that he didn't try to run straight home. And according to Wallström's witness statement, the Opel was already there when he and his girlfriend arrived at about eight thirty."

"So you're saying the idiot must have been rambling around for over an hour before he was run down on Delsjövägen," Jonny said dubiously.

"Hardly. As I said before, he knew the area like the back of his hand," Andersson said firmly.

"Could he have seen the killer come along and dump Tanya in the root cellar? And then maybe he tried to follow whoever it was? I mean, Torleif was a good runner. If the killer left on foot, then . . ."

Irene broke off. The idea that struck her almost knocked her off her chair.

"Oh my God! Excuse me," she said as she got to her feet.

When she got to the door, she turned around and said, "Svante!"

Then she was gone.

Andersson frowned at Jonny. They both shook their heads and exchanged a look of mutual sympathy.

Chapter 24

BEFORE IRENE WENT home for the day, she called the hospital to see how her mother was. The nurse informed her that Gerd was feeling a little tired, but by and large she was recovering well.

"She had an intertrochanteric fracture, which is the most common hip fracture in older people; it occurs at the neck of the femur. Because the ball joint itself was in a poor condition, we've removed it, so Gerd has a new prosthetic hip. One slight problem is that she also has a small crack in her coccyx," the pleasant professional voice explained.

"And what can be done about that?" Irene asked anxiously.

"Not much, unfortunately. It is causing her pain, and that could go on for quite some time."

"Can I come up and see her in a little while?"

"Of course."

SHE HAD EVIDENTLY arrived in the middle of the rush hour when it came to visiting, because it was almost impossible to find a parking space. Eventually she spotted one and slammed the Volvo in right in front of a VW Polo. The driver of the smaller car reacted with a series of long, angry blasts on the horn, but Irene pretended not to notice. She bestowed a sweet smile on her furious fellow driver and hurried off to the ticket machine.

Up on the ward there was a lot of activity in the corridor. A male auxiliary was maneuvering a huge stainless steel container, rattling toward the elevators as he transported the dinner trays back to the central kitchen.

Gerd was no longer alone in her room. The occupant of the bed by the window was snoring loudly. Judging by the shape under the blanket, it was a very well-built woman. There was a frame at the end of the bed to stop the bedclothes from touching her feet.

Gerd was lying there with her eyes closed. A lump came into Irene's throat as she gazed at her mother; she looked like a pale, fragile china doll. Irene edged toward the bed and bent down to stroke her mother's white hair. Gerd opened her eyes and smiled.

"You don't imagine I can sleep with this racket going on, do you?" she said.

Irene was relieved to find that her mother hadn't lost her sense of humor.

"How are you feeling?" she asked.

"Well, I know I've had surgery, but I thought it would be worse. I'm starting physical therapy tomorrow."

"Tomorrow? Isn't that a bit soon?"

"It's to minimize the risk of blood clots."

Irene was suddenly aware that she had turned up empty-handed. "I didn't know if you were allowed flowers on this ward. And I didn't know if you were eating yet. So tomorrow I'll—"

"Don't bother. Bring me a few magazines instead. And one of those things you can play talking books on. Then I can plug in my earphones, and I won't have to listen to . . ." She gestured toward her neighbor who had just taken a deep breath culminating in a huge snore, after a period of total silence. It sounded as if she was swallowing her tongue and choking.

"Sleep apnea. It's dangerous. It can lead to a stroke," Gerd said knowledgeably. She always read medical articles with great interest. You have to know more than the doctors if you're going to cope with being ill, she always said.

All at once she looked sharply at Irene. "Did you get hold of Sture?"

This was the moment Irene had been dreading. She took one of Gerd's hands in both of her own. It was ice-cold.

"Mom . . . Sture . . . He . . ."

"He's dead."

Gerd was looking straight at her as she spoke. Her eyes shone with tears which slowly rolled down her cheeks and onto the pillow.

"Yes. I found him when . . . when I went over there," Irene said, her voice breaking.

Gerd nodded, as if Irene had confirmed something that she had already suspected. For a long time Irene sat there holding her mother's hand.

The tears were still flowing when Gerd suddenly said, "He had a feeling he was going to die. He called me on Saturday to say goodbye. That was why I went out even though I knew it was icy, and I shouldn't have . . . I wanted to see him before . . ." She waved her free hand toward the bedside table, where there was a pile of paper napkins. Irene passed her a handful.

"Why didn't he call an ambulance?" Irene asked.

Gerd blew her nose on the crackly napkin before she answered. "That's exactly what I told him to do . . . he said he would, just as soon as we'd hung up. But he obviously decided not to, or else he didn't have time."

"I don't think he had time. It must have happened very quickly."

"Where . . . how did you find him?"

There was no point in lying and saying that he'd been in bed. One of Sture's neighbors was bound to know what had happened; he or she would mention it to an acquaintance in the grocery store, who in turn would speak to someone who happened to live near Gerd, and that person would . . . She was bound to find out one way or another.

"He was lying on the bathroom floor. But he hadn't hurt himself. It looked like he had just decided to lie down. Peaceful. He looked peaceful," Irene said.

Gerd squeezed her hand. "Thank you. Thank you," was all she said.

Irene stayed with her mother for over an hour. By the time she left, Gerd had fallen asleep—or at least she was lying there with her eyes closed, in spite of the deafening snores from the other bed.

THE ENTIRE HALLWAY was strewn with boxes. The twins had obviously decided to start packing; they would be moving in a couple of weeks.

The house would be empty.

That was the disadvantage of having twins; they always hit the various stages of life simultaneously despite the fact that they were so different in terms of character. It was entirely logical for them both to move out at the same time, which doubled the sense of loss. On the other hand, it meant that Irene would need to work through empty-nest syndrome only once. But perhaps it never went away completely?

"Mom! I'm taking my bed!" Jenny yelled from upstairs.

Irene hadn't even taken off her coat. She called back, "Okay!"

"Great! In that case I'll take the curtains as well. We bought them to match the bedspread," her daughter replied happily.

Really? Irene couldn't remember, but perhaps Jenny was right. They had definitely bought the bedspread with stripes in every color of the rainbow at IKEA because she had been there. But as for the curtains . . .

"I'm taking the bedroom and there's already a lovely double bed, so mine can stay here," Katarina said, emerging from the bathroom with a pile of fluffy white bath towels. Also from IKEA. Brand new. Not even used.

"Those are mine," Irene said.

"Ours. Me and Jenny need one each."

"One each. You've got four there. At least," Irene pointed out sourly.

"Yes, but we need spares. Our mom raised us to be good clean girls," Katarina countered with a smile.

"I said you could take some towels from the linen closet. Not the new ones!" Krister called out from the kitchen.

Katarina sighed and rolled her eyes. "Surely we can have one each."

Irene's heart softened. "Okay. One each of the new ones and two of the old ones. Take the red ones. You can put the rest on your birthday wish list."

"Cool!" Katarina said.

"How's Grandma?" Jenny shouted down the stairs.

"We'll find out over dinner, which is ready *now*!" Krister yelled before Irene had the chance to answer.

She went into the kitchen and smiled at him. There was an appetizing smell of boiled fish—or poached, as her husband would have said. An aromatic symphony of dill, lemon and prawns rose from the largest pan on the stove. The potatoes were bubbling along beside it. Irene suddenly realized how hungry she was and how much she appreciated her lively, loving family.

It wouldn't just be empty when the twins moved out. It would also be extremely quiet.

THE TEMPERATURE REMAINED above freezing, and the wind blew steadily. Most of the slush had disappeared by the time Irene drove into the city center on Thursday morning. The weather was supposed to stay more or less the same until Saturday, and then it would get colder. Irene hoped that by then there wouldn't be much water left on the streets to turn into ice. Healthcare costs for the number of broken arms and legs this winter had already surpassed all records, according to the front page headline in *Göteborgs Posten* that morning. And spring was still a long way off, as the song said. So Gerd was just another statistic. It's not easy getting old, Irene thought with a sigh.

Chapter 25

"IT'S NOT EASY getting old," the superintendent said with a sigh.

"I promise we'll sort this out," the assistant at Lindén's bakery said.

Andersson had been buying bread and cakes there ever since he moved to Partille almost thirty years ago. The woman behind the counter had worked there for almost as long. They had gotten to know one another pretty well, or at least as well as a regular customer and a pleasant shop assistant usually get to know each other. She was the one he chose to confess his secret to, the secret he had carried alone for several weeks. He had noticed the others exchanging glances at coffee time, but he hadn't said anything. It was none of their business.

"My mother had type two diabetes as well," he admitted in a burst of total honesty.

"It's so common these days, and not only among older people; young kids can develop diabetes as well. But I can easily put together a box of assorted treats. I'll show you which ones are sugar-free, and you choose from those. It's worked before," she said with a smile and a conspiratorial wink.

She had a lovely smile, he had always thought so. And she had the ability to spread warmth and a sense of security—yes, that was the word!—around her. If the store wasn't too busy he would often linger for a little chat, inhaling the aroma of freshly brewed coffee and delicious cakes as a bonus.

She was cheerful and easygoing, curvaceous and pretty; why had he never taken a chance before? The thought suddenly occurred to him, and he was completely taken by surprise.

". . . so you can pick them up in the morning," she interrupted his train of thought.

"What? I mean . . . sorry," he said in confusion.

She laughed out loud, and he almost thought she might be flirting with him. Maybe she was? He smiled back, and all at once his heart felt warm and lighter.

"I said I'd sort out the box this evening and put it in the refrigerator, then you can pick it up on your way to work in the morning. We open at seven, but you'll have to knock on the back door. It's probably best if you pay me now, then it's all taken care of."

"Sure! That's terrific." He took out a number of one hundred-kronor notes and placed them on the palm of her well-shaped hand.

As she was ringing up the prices of the cakes, she said without taking her eyes off the cash register, "So are you going to leave work? Retire?"

"No, not at all! I'm moving to the cold cases team. You know, investigating old homicides before the statute of limitations runs . . ."

"Oh, I've seen the TV series! I love it! Although it's a young girl and her associates who solve the crimes," she said cheerfully.

Andersson arranged his features into a regretful smile. "Unfortunately there's no young girl on the team. Just old men. Like me," he said.

"Nonsense. You're not old! We must be more or less the same age, you and I. And that would mean that I'm old, too. Or maybe that's what you think?" she said, pretending to be affronted.

"Absolutely not! You're . . . you're . . . lovely!"

Andersson blushed, feeling like a teenager on his first date. They both laughed, dispelling the slightly awkward atmosphere. The wonderful feeling in the superintendent's chest was starting to spread right through his body. Cupid must have flown past Lindén's bakery on this grey, miserable February morning and shot his arrow straight into Andersson's heart.

IRENE AND JONNY got the day off to a brisk start by questioning Niklas Ström again. This time his lawyer was present. Irene's first thought when she saw Michaela Lackbergh was that the well-known firm of Lemberg, Lemberg & Anjou had sent an intern. She certainly looked very young, although she had to be between twenty-five and thirty if she was a qualified lawyer. Perhaps it was her almost ethereal appearance that fooled people into thinking she was younger than she actually was. She was a dainty creature, and so pale she was almost transparent. "Albino," Jonny had hissed in Irene's ear. "She hasn't got red eyes," Irene had whispered back. The woman's eyes were anything but red; they were steel blue and laser sharp. The platinum blonde hair was pulled back into a ponytail. She was wearing a light tweed jacket over a white shirt and skinny jeans tucked into a pair of white cowboy boots. In spite of the high heels she didn't even come up to Irene's shoulder. Her extraordinarily long nails made it difficult for her to grasp her papers as she attempted to get them out and put them on the table. The bundle of documents wasn't especially thick, but it was in a blue plastic folder, and the shiny pale lilac nails scrabbled against the surface of the folder as she tried once more to get a hold of them. Never underestimate an apparently harmless kitten because it always has claws, Irene thought.

Niklas Ström looked more or less the same as the day before. He was getting virtually no sleep in his cell, judging by the circles under his eyes. Irene had gone through his case notes and discovered the reason behind his odd behavior and the restlessness that seemed to possess his body. According to the limited assessment carried out by the forensic psychiatrist the previous year when Niklas was arrested for the rape, he was suffering from Tourette's, which can cause symptoms such as involuntary noises and an inability to keep still.

They began the interview with some neutral questions in the hope that Niklas would feel comfortable and relaxed, at least to a certain extent. As before, Irene was leading.

"I'm not really interested in why you and Billy took off from Gräskärr. You can discuss that with other officers. Here in the Violent Crimes Unit, we are primarily interested in what happened on the night of January seventeenth. As I told you yesterday, we are investigating the homicide of a young girl. On the night she died, you and Billy were in the vicinity of where she was found, so I would like you to tell me what happened. Hopefully we will then be able to eliminate both of you from the murder inquiry, and things will be much easier for all of us."

Niklas was shifting uneasily on his chair and emitting brief snorts at regular intervals. He glanced inquiringly at his lawyer, who nodded without giving him an encouraging smile. Irene provided the smile instead. Niklas looked as if he was thinking things over. Eventually, after a series of loud groans, he took a deep breath and began.

"We had nothing to do with that girl, for fuck's sake! We didn't see anybody!"

"Do you mean when you and Billy drove the BMW with the shattered windshield along the side road leading to the Göteborg Canoe Club?" Irene quickly interposed.

"How the fuck am I supposed to know if there was a canoe club down there? We had other stuff to think about!"

"Like what?"

He gave her a long look before he answered. "Like how we

were going to get the hell out of there as fast as possible," he muttered.

"But not because you'd killed the girl."

"Of course not!"

He was getting agitated and let out yet more loud groans. His whole body jerked uncontrollably when he tried to sit still.

"Just before you left this room yesterday, you mentioned that there was a car parked not far from where you pulled up in the BMW. Can you remember what make of car it was?"

"An Opel Astra."

"Color?"

"White."

"What did you do after you got out of the BMW?"

"We torched it."

"Why?"

"Because we weren't wearing gloves."

"So you were afraid of leaving fingerprints in the car?"

"Mm hmm."

"So you set fire to it. Forensics found traces of a flammable liquid in the car. They think alcohol was used. Is that correct?"

Niklas nodded. "Billy found an unopened bottle of Absolut vodka under the seat. So we had a little. I mean it was fucking freezing! Then we poured some into the car and set fire to it. There was a little left, and we took it with us."

"You took the bottle with you when you changed cars and got into the white Opel?"

"Yes."

"Did you have to hot wire it?"

Niklas looked quite animated as he leaned across the table, looking directly at Irene. "No! The keys were in the ignition!" He laughed out loud at the recollection of how easily they had gotten away from their pursuers.

"So you didn't drive back down toward Delsjövägen, if I've understood you correctly?"

"No. We drove around up there using all the little roads—even, like, footpaths. Eventually we came out in Härlanda, and we just took off."

"Where did you go?"

"To Billy's gran. She is one cool lady."

"And you've been there all the time."

"Yes."

Irene gazed thoughtfully at Niklas. The twitching and the noises had diminished now that he had spoken to her. Perhaps he had spent the night thinking about the previous day's conversation.

"Niklas, I'd like you to think back to that evening when you got into the Opel. Do you remember whether it was warm or cold inside the car?"

He considered the question carefully before he replied. "Cold."

"Like a refrigerator, or just a little chilly?" Irene said.

"Kind of like a refrigerator, but not like a freezer," Niklas said, smiling at his own ingenuity.

"Good. The outside temperature was minus sixteen, but you're telling me it wasn't that cold inside the car?"

"No way. But I think it had been there for a while."

"Do you remember any particular smells inside the car? Cigarette smoke or alcohol or—"

"No."

"Did you or Billy take anything from the car when you got to Olofstorp?"

"No. At first we were going to take the blanket, but we decided not to. We'd have looked like the Indians in those old cowboy films if we'd gone around wrapped in blankets. People notice that kind of thing. But . . . we did take the vodka bottle, like I said. There was a drop left," he said happily.

"I thought you and Billy were off the drugs and booze?" Irene said quietly.

"Oh . . . that was later. Billy's grandma said we couldn't stay there if we were using. And we couldn't get a hold of anything anyway." He shrugged and snorted vigorously several times. Irene couldn't help smiling as she thought about the way Billy and Niklas had made a virtue out of a necessity. They couldn't get their hands on any drugs, so that meant they were clean. No doubt it had done them some good, but at the same time it showed how scared they must have been. They had lain low in Billy's grandmother's house, not even daring to go out to score drugs. They were smart enough to realize that there was a major police search underway.

"Did you follow the investigation into the accident you had caused, either on TV or in the newspapers?"

"Both. Annika . . . Billy's grandma . . . gets *Göteborgs Posten*. And we watched the local news on TV."

"And you just sat there hiding out. How long did you think you could carry on like that?"

Niklas shrugged again. "Don't know. Until things had calmed down. We were thinking of taking off somewhere . . . but neither of us had any cash. We didn't even have enough to fill up the fucking car."

"The Opel?"

"Yes."

"Was that why you hid it in the barn?"

"Yes. It was Billy's idea. He knew about the barn."

"Did you take the BMW so that you could get to Billy's grandmother's house?"

Niklas became noticeably more anxious, emitting staccato snorts through his nostrils. "We were fucking freezing, okay? We'd been sleeping on the floor at this other guy's place for a few nights, but we couldn't stay any longer because he . . . whatever! We had nowhere to go, so Billy called Annika, and she was real nice. But there were no buses and we were broke anyway, and then we saw the BMW . . . with the engine running! We didn't even need to fucking think about it. When the guy who was loading the car went back to the door of the apartment block, we just jumped in and took off."

"But if you were heading for Gråbo, then you were going in the wrong direction," Irene pointed out.

"I know. But there was a tram behind us, which meant we couldn't like do a U-turn. So I drove along Skånegatan. Thought I'd drive around for a bit . . . it was a fucking fantastic car."

A faint smile passed across his tired face, but failed to reach his eyes. Somewhere deep down inside, he had given up. He had no intention of lying. He just wanted to make sure they didn't suspect him of any involvement in the girl's death.

"Tell me about the drive," Irene said calmly.

"We . . . we drove past Liseberg, then on toward Delsjövägen. There was a cop car by the fast food kiosk . . . they saw us, and we realized they were going to pull us over. So I put my foot down and as we were passing the TV studios this old man came running along . . . He ran straight out into the road, for fuck's sake! I didn't have a chance!"

His whole body was shaking with the strain of having to relive the fatal car chase all over again. Irene had no reason to doubt his honesty. Everything he said corresponded with the facts that had come to light during the investigation.

"No, Niklas. You didn't have a chance. There are witnesses who have told us that he didn't stop, but simply carried on running without even slowing down. It was just incredibly bad luck. You were driving at high speed, and he ran out in front of you."

Niklas let out a sob. "Kleenex," he said in a voice thick with tears.

Michaela quickly produced a Kleenex out of her soft, pale brown leather briefcase. Niklas accepted it with gratitude and noisily blew his nose. Talking about the fatal accident had affected him deeply. Something told Irene that he had gone over the moment when the body thudded into the front windshield of the car many, many times. The sound of the glass as it shattered would echo through his mind for eternity even if he had tried to suppress the images.

"It's obvious that the police car in pursuit made the boys increase their speed. They naturally felt the urge to get away. We will be emphasizing this point in our defense," Michaela Lackbergh said icily.

For a moment Irene wasn't sure who the comments were aimed at, but a quick glance at Niklas convinced her that he had found consolation in his lawyer's words.

At that point Jonny decided it would be a good idea to open his mouth for the first time during the interview. "Do you have a driver's license, Niklas?"

Everyone in the room already knew that the answer was no. Irene silently cursed the ineptitude of her colleague, who had all the sensitivity of a steamroller. Niklas chose to remain silent.

"And you'd both been drinking vodka as well," Jonny gurgled happily.

"Niklas didn't say that! You don't know that for a fact." Michaela corrected him.

Jonny raised his eyebrows; it was unclear whether he was surprised at being taken to task, or whether he was genuinely astonished to find that the pretty little kitten had claws. "A little while ago he sat here and told us that his good pal Billy found a bottle of Absolut vodk—"

"He didn't say he was drinking while he was driving!" Michaela Lackbergh cut him off in mid-sentence.

"I thought he did," Jonny persisted.

"Enough! We have no interest in that discussion. We are asking Niklas for his help in the investigation into Tanya's death," Irene said sharply, glaring at Jonny.

He looked extremely put out and muttered something inaudible.

"Niklas, you know as well as I do that we don't care if you were driving without a license. It's irrelevant. Other officers will deal with that. We are looking for a killer, and you have already helped us to close in on him. I really appreciate your willingness to tell us exactly what happened, and that will definitely count in your favor," she said, giving Jonny a look that spoke volumes.

This time he had the sense to keep quiet.

"Tell me what happened after you hit the man who ran out in front of you," she said.

"I couldn't see a goddamn thing . . . the windshield was completely fucked! We panicked! I floored the gas pedal, and we took off. Billy was hanging out of the side window and telling me where to go. We turned off at the first intersection and drove up the hill . . . but I told him we couldn't fucking keep going. I nearly came off the road . . . and then he saw that little side road . . . we turned down it . . . and you know the rest." He fell silent, then trumpeted into the Kleenex once more.

"You both got out of the BMW. Poured vodka on the floor and torched it. Had you already checked out the other car and seen that the keys were in the ignition?"

"Yeah. We couldn't fucking believe it! Another car with the keys in on the same night!"

"So it was just a few minutes before you were able to drive away, leaving the burning BMW behind," Irene concluded.

Niklas nodded in response.

IRENE SWITCHED OFF the recording and gazed at her colleagues who were sitting around the conference table. The superintendent looked pensive, as did Tommy, Fredrik and Jonny. Hannu was leaning back in his chair, ostensibly relaxed, but the deep lines around his eyes gave him away. When did he last get a full night's sleep, Irene wondered sympathetically. She was also tired after the extraordinary events of the last week, but she still felt excited following the interview with Niklas Ström.

"He was telling the truth. We now know for certain that Torleif Sandberg's car was parked by the path leading down to the canoe club before eight thirty in the evening. We have witnesses: Martin Wallström and his mistress, Marika Lager. We know that the white Opel was still there when Billy and Niklas arrived at approximately nine forty."

"Muesli was run down at nine thirty-five. What the hell was he doing rambling around in the forest for over an hour? With nothing on his head and dressed so inappropriately that he ended up with frostbite? He lived just a few minutes away!" Jonny exclaimed.

"Don't you find it more remarkable that the car was parked in that particular spot?" Hannu said quietly.

"He must have seen something. Maybe he saw the actual murder . . . saw the killer hide the body in the root cellar. Torleif lay low and watched what was going on, then he tried to follow the bastard," Andersson said with conviction.

Irene felt very sorry for him. The truth was going to come as a terrible blow. But the truth cannot be disguised. It is what it is: naked and unadorned.

"He did indeed see Tanya's murder at close quarters. It was actually Torleif who killed her," Irene said.

Andersson's eyes widened, and his face flushed a deep red. Everyone in the room recognized the signs of an impending explosion.

In order to forestall him, Irene quickly added, "We have irrefutable evidence."

Then came the explosion.

"What the hell are you saying?! Are you suggesting that Torleif killed . . ." He was so agitated that he couldn't breathe.

"Here."

Irene took out a sheet of paper marked TANYA.

"I got this from Svante just before the meeting. The semen we found in Tanya's hair comes from Torleif."

Andersson sat there openmouthed, gasping for breath. His expression was mirrored on the faces of Jonny, Fredrik and Tommy. Hannu merely nodded to himself, as if his suspicions had been confirmed.

"We haven't got a result yet from the skin fragments under Tanya's nails, but the DNA in the semen is sufficient proof. Svante said we were lucky. Torleif's funeral is tomorrow, and he's being cremated. If we hadn't taken the DNA sample, it would have been too late. Svante has also charged the battery in Torleif's cell phone. It's a new Nokia with a camera, and it can also record short video clips. And replay them. Look at this."

She took out the neat little cell and flipped it open. She selected multimedia from the menu and clicked on VIDEO. She pressed the start button and held out the phone to Andersson. He looked skeptically at the small screen.

There was also sound. They could hear a young girl's wailing voice, along with the heavy panting of a man. Flickering images filled the screen.

A blonde head. Hands trying to fight back. Close-ups of a girl's naked crotch. The girl turning away. An erect penis seen from above as it moved toward the girl's pale, blurred face.

The silence was oppressive as the Nokia was passed around the table. No one commented until they had all seen the clip.

"There are stills, too," Irene informed them.

She clicked through to the first picture, and the cell did the rounds once again.

"That's enough," Andersson said.

He was breathing heavily, and suddenly his face had an unnatural pallor. His lips had lost all their color, and were almost blue. He looked dreadful, and Irene worried he was going to faint.

"I never thought . . . never . . ."

The last word was no more than a whisper.

"No. Initially we were called to the scene of the accident, where Torleif had been killed by two young car thieves. And while we were looking for them, we found Tanya's body. None of us had any idea that the two cases were connected."

"And a police officer . . . someone we knew."

Andersson looked utterly devastated. Irene understood how terrible this must be for him; on his penultimate day with the Violent Crimes Unit, his old friend and colleague was revealed as sex offender and killer. It was a tough way for things to end. He had a week off before joining the cold cases team, and he would probably need it, not least to recover from the shock he had just had.

"When did you work it out?" Hannu asked, narrowing his eyes as he looked at Irene. He still gave the impression that he might fall asleep at any moment from sheer exhaustion, but the unexpected turn of events had sparked a glimmer of interest in his expression.

"I think I started to suspect something when Anders Pettersson said that Heinz Becker had sent Tanya to see a doctor, accompanied by a trusted client. Who wasn't far from the root cellar at the time of the murder? Who could be more trustworthy than an ex-cop? And which of the men involved had we not taken a DNA sample from? Torleif Sandberg."

Andersson nodded to himself as if he was beginning to accept the facts.

"What do you think happened?" he asked.

Irene quickly thought through her reconstruction before she spoke. "It all began in Tenerife. According to my source within the police, there has been tension between different gangs for quite some time, primarily on the issue of drug dealing. One of the gang leaders, Jesus Gomez, owed money to another, Lembit Saar. Gomez couldn't pay off his debt in cash, but he had something else that Lembit Saar wanted. Contacts. Saar needed girls for the nightclub he had just opened. I'm sure there were plenty of willing girls for the club itself, but he wanted special girls for special clients. Girls who were kept shut in the rooms at the back of the club. Girls who have no voice and have to agree to anything. Girls who bring in plenty of money for their owners. The victims of trafficking. Sex slaves."

She paused to catch her breath and think for a moment. None of her colleagues interrupted her.

"Jesus Gomez got in touch with Heinz Becker, who happened to have two suitable girls who met Saar's requirements: very young, and blonde. Becker was on tour with the girls, but was happy to sell them on after they had been to Sweden. The problem was that neither of the girls had a valid passport. They had both been smuggled in. So Gomez arranged false passports, and to make sure that everything went smoothly, he also provided his right hand man, Sergei Petrov, with a false passport. He was given a new identity, Andres Tamm, and was supposed to be the father of the two girls. Under his new name, Petrov would escort the girls from Sweden to Tenerife."

"But it all went wrong," Jonny said.

"You could say that. The little Russian—Tanya—became ill. Seriously ill. She contracted an aggressive form of gonorrhea that spread through her body. Sergei Petrov was due to arrive in Sweden on Thursday, January nineteenth, to pick up the girls. On Tuesday, the seventeenth, Heinz Becker realized he was going to have to send Tanya to see a doctor. She was probably in pretty bad shape by then. For various reasons he couldn't take her himself, so either he asked his trusted client Torleif Sandberg to get the girl some help, or Torleif offered. Whichever was the case, I'm sure Becker was very grateful. He didn't want to advertise the fact that he was in the country, and that the girl was his."

"So Muesli took the girl in his car. But he didn't go straight to the doctor. He thought he'd have some fun for free first," Jonny said.

Irene nodded. "I think you're right. The images on his cell phone would certainly support that idea, along with the semen in her hair. But something went wrong. We saw her trying to defend herself in the video clip. Perhaps he lost his temper when she refused to do what he wanted. We'll never know exactly what happened, or where it happened. But we do know that he strangled her."

"Oh my God," Andersson groaned.

"What a bastard!" Fredrik exclaimed.

"I'm sure we can all agree on that. After he'd killed Tanya, he had to dispose of the body. He knew the area around Delsjövägen very well, and he knew about the old root cellar, which was no longer used. He wrapped Tanya in the blue fleece blanket that we found in his car. Fibers from the blanket match the fibers we found on her body. He drove to the little side road—or perhaps he was already there when the murder took place—in order to hide Tanya's body in the root cellar. He used an implement of some kind to break off the padlock on the door, then stowed the girl and her clothes inside. Up to that point, everything was going his way. But then his luck changed."

"That's why he was dressed so inappropriately. He never intended to spend any time outdoors," Hannu stated with a degree of satisfaction.

"Exactly. Martin Wallström and Marika Lager turned onto the side road; according to Wallström, they were parked there for almost an hour. I think we can assume that Torleif was hiding, waiting for them to leave. Obviously he didn't want to leave his car at the spot where he'd just hidden the murder victim—especially with the keys in the ignition. But he could hardly return to it or make a campfire to keep warm because the turtledoves in the Volvo would have seen him. The cold broke him. Eventually he realized he was in danger of frostbite, so he decided to head home. But instead of running along the main road leading down to Delsjövägen, he ran down one of the bridle paths. He had a flashlight with him; we know that because it was found on the sidewalk after the accident. Just before he reached the parking lot by the TV studios, he dropped his cell phone. Presumably he didn't notice; he might not have been thinking clearly because of the cold. This would explain why he misjudged the speed of the BMW as it raced toward him. Perhaps he thought he could make it across the street. But he was wrong."

"He was run down and he died," Andersson said laconically. His face had begun to regain its normal color.

"As Torleif was running down the bridle path toward the TV studios," Irene went on, "Martin Wallström and Marika Lager left the side road and drove toward Delsjövägen. Wallström saw the blue flashing lights of an emergency vehicle, which was no doubt the patrol car that had been in pursuit of the BMW, and decided to take a little detour in order to get home."

"And we know the rest thanks to Niklas Ström's statement," Tommy said.

"Yes. The one we've just listened to," Irene said.

"It was bad luck for Torleif Sandberg that Martin Wallström turned up, then sat in his car talking for such a long time. Otherwise Torleif might have gotten away with it," Fredrik mused.

"Yes. And Heinz Becker was out of luck, too. When Sergei Petrov arrived in Göteborg on Thursday to collect his girls, Tanya was still missing. Heinz hadn't a clue where she was, and he couldn't get in touch with Torleif either. We know why that was, but neither Heinz nor Sergei had any idea. Maybe they were intending to wait a while longer in the hope that Torleif would turn up with Tanya, but then they were hit by the raid in Biskopsgården. They escaped by persuading one of the builders to hand over the keys to their truck. They fled through the snowstorm; everything was going well until they came off the highway. Heinz and Sergei died at the scene, and Leili, the other girl, sustained serious injuries and is still on a respirator."

"Have we managed to identify either of the girls?" Tommy asked.

"No. We've sent out their details via Europol, and to various countries across the Baltic, but nothing so far. According to Linda Holm, the girls were probably smuggled out of Russia or Estonia. It's likely they were sold by the staff of some children's home, or by their parents. Or they might have run away themselves and fallen into the clutches of human traffickers. We may find out their true identity one day, but we may not."

"I've spoken to Varberg Hospital today. They believe Leili is brain dead. A neurologist is going to examine her this afternoon, and if that's his conclusion, they will switch off the respirator."

"God have mercy on the souls of those girls," Irene said with a sigh.

She wasn't particularly religious, but her words came from the heart.

"Amen," said Andersson.

Chapter 26

STEFAN SANDBERG LOOKED older than on the previous occasion when they had met, probably thanks to the black suit and white shirt and tie he was wearing.

"The funeral is over. I've been to the bank to sort out the final details with regard to the sale of the house in Thailand and his apartment here. So I was a little surprised to hear from you again," he said. He looked away quickly, and Irene heard him murmur, "Or perhaps not."

She decided to pretend she hadn't heard, and said, "I'm glad you were able to come in. I have some very difficult news for you."

Stefan sat motionless on the chair opposite her during the entire account. Irene told him about his stepfather's role in the murder of the little Russian known as Tanya. She wanted him to know the whole truth before it hit the headlines.

He remained silent long after she had finished. Irene began to wonder whether the shock had been greater than she had expected. After all, Stefan himself had said that he and Torleif hadn't been particularly close.

"This hasn't come as a complete surprise to me," he said eventually, as if he had sensed what Irene was thinking. "I took Torleif's laptop back to Umeå with me, along with the book on researching your family tree that was lying next to it. I thought it would be interesting to find out more about him . . . after all, I am his only heir."

He compressed his lips into a thin line and stared down at his hands, which rested on top of each other on the desk.

"There were indeed files on genealogy. And on the house in Thailand. But above all there was a huge amount of pornography. All kinds of pornography! The most hardcore, the most disgusting variations you can imagine."

He ran a hand over his face, as if to brush away the images flickering before his mind's eye.

"I'd appreciate it if you could send the laptop down to us. It could contain evidence. And we can help you to clean it if you want it back."

"No thanks. I never want to see it again." He shook his head. Then he said thoughtfully, "I always thought he was strange. I never really liked him. Mom always said he was a man with a small face."

"Interesting expression. What did she mean?"

"That Torleif was so ordinary. He wasn't the kind of person you really notice. There was nothing to make him stand out in a crowd. He was kind of beige, if I can put it that way. But if you looked more closely at him, he had his little quirks. Vegetarian. Clean living. Pedantic. Mean. And according to Mom, he didn't really have a sense of humor. A mediocre guy with a slightly odd personality. But I never thought he was capable of something like this."

"No. Nor did anyone else."

My *thanks to:*

Thomas Ekström, Superintendent with the Police Authority in Västra Götaland, LKP / Trafficking. It was extremely useful to learn what the situation in the market for sex slavery is like in Sweden today and how the police in Göteborg are working to combat human trafficking.

Leif Johansson, head of Children and Young People's Services, and Kristina Andersson, coordinator, both with the Swedish Migration Board. They helped me to gain an insight into how cases involving asylum-seeking children with no known relatives are handled.

Lena Krönström, a teacher in Sunne who is of Estonian origin. She helped me with appropriate Estonian names for some of my characters.

As usual I have taken considerable liberties with geographical facts. I do not adapt my narrative to suit the existing geography; reality is adapted to fit the story instead. All resemblance to any person living or dead is coincidental and not the intention of the author. The sole exception is Sammie, who is my own dog. He continues to remain indifferent to literary fame and takes life as it comes.

Helene Tursten

Continue reading for a sneak preview from the next
Irene Huss investigation

THE TREACHEROUS NET

THE WITNESS WHO called the police at 9:14 A.M. had been right. There was a dead body at the water's edge. The technicians had quickly gone out to Nötsund to secure the scene. After two hours' intensive work they were done, and the corpse could be removed and placed in a body bag.

Detective Inspectors Irene Huss and Jonny Blom waited patiently. Then Irene carefully examined the puffy grey face before zipping up the bag.

"Alexandra Hallwiin," she said in a resigned tone of voice.

They had suspected as much, but it still felt ineffably sad to be able to confirm that the girl was dead. They hadn't been involved in the case while the girl had simply been listed as a missing person, but as soon as the call had come in about the discovery at Nötsund, along with the information that the body was that of a young girl, they had printed out the available case notes. Jonny Blom drove while Irene read aloud.

Fourteen-year-old Alexandra had been missing for five days. According to her parents she had never shown any signs of wanting to run away, nor had she had any reason to do so now. They described her as a typical horse-crazy teenager—a little shy, perhaps. Hardworking at school, but no indication of bullying. Alexandra's teachers and school friends had backed up her parents' view of their daughter.

Alexandra's face had been all over the front pages over the weekend. She came from a well-off family, and kidnapping had been a possibility right from the start. If she hadn't been abducted, the police still suspected that a crime lay behind her disappearance. A girl who just wants to get away for a while usually tries to take some clothes and money with her, but according to her mother the only thing Alexandra had taken before she went missing on Walpurgis Night, April 30, was a wallet containing her bus pass and three hundred kronor at the most, the clothes she was wearing, a telescopic umbrella and her cell phone. Nothing else.

Alexandra had told her parents she was meeting some of her classmates in Brunnsparken. In spite of the pouring rain, they were going to see the Chalmers University of Technology's traditional annual parade, known as the Cortège. Then they were heading back to Torslanda to hang out at the home of one of the girls. She would be home by midnight at the latest. Her parents were going to a party with friends and didn't have time to give her a lift, so Alexandra said she would catch the bus into town. When she waved goodbye and walked out through the door, that was the last time anyone was known to have seen her alive.

The 6:05 P.M. bus had been full, and the driver didn't remember her. The driver on the next bus hadn't noticed her either. There were lots of young people heading into the city center to watch the parade and celebrate.

None of her friends had arranged to meet her in the park. Even the two girls who were regarded as Alexandra's closest friends had no idea what she was planning to do on Walpurgis Night. When they had asked Alexandra about her plans the previous day, she had said she would be training Prince in preparation for the show on Sunday. Since they knew how important the horse and competitions were to Alexandra, neither of them had pursued the matter.

No one could say for certain whether the girl had traveled into town on the bus. When her worried mother had started calling her cell phone after midnight, it had been switched off.

From the moment Alexandra closed the garden gate, it was as if the ground had opened up and swallowed her.

Now they had found her.

IT WAS A Labrador that discovered her. He was young and playful, and at first he was delighted to find a friend who had hidden herself so cleverly. A second later his sensitive nose registered a strange smell. Exciting, acrid, and a little bit frightening. He began to bark agitatedly, sticking his rump in the air as he circled the interesting odor, gradually getting closer. When his master called him—"Elroy! Elroy! Here, boy!"—he grabbed a scrap of fabric that was lying on the ground and proudly scampered back with it in his mouth. There was a brief struggle, but eventually Elroy let go of his trophy. The man shuddered when he looked down at the torn, bloodied black lace thong in his hands. The word SUNDAY was embroidered on the small triangle at the front, surrounded by a border of red rosebuds.

The body had been pushed into a crevice in the rocks; the murderer had piled a few branches and stones on top in an attempt to hide it.

"SO IT'S ONLY the beginning of May, and we've already had our murdered teenage girl of the summer. Along with another one, just to be on the safe side. On the same day," Detective Inspector Jonny Blom said with a sigh.

His colleagues nodded with an air of resignation. Two murders at the same time meant a heavy workload for the team, particularly in view of the fact that the gang war in the city had begun to escalate once more. It had been relatively calm on that front during February and most of March, but over the Easter weekend they had launched two murder investigations within three days. The victims were a thirty-four-year-old father of three, and a twenty-three-year-old rookie. Both had belonged to the warring factions: the criminal network known as Asir, and the notorious biker gang Bandidos.

The investigation also covered a car bomb, although only minor injuries were reported. The car had belonged to a would-be gangster who carried out his activities using the restaurant he owned as a front. Presumably he hadn't been willing to pay the price for the protection of one of the gangs, although it wasn't clear which one. Those who are willingly or unwillingly drawn into dealings with the biker gangs never talk to the police. Most people have a certain instinct for self-preservation. At the moment Asir and Bandidos were equal, with one loss each. The question wasn't *if* reprisals would follow, but *when*. And which of them would strike first.

Irene Huss was only half-listening. She couldn't get the image of Alexandra's dead body out of her mind. When she had looked at the girl's face she had noticed something that was later confirmed by the preliminary autopsy report: some kind of plastic twine had been pulled tightly around her neck. A thin washing line, perhaps. There was no doubt that they were dealing with a homicide.

The meeting with Alexandra's parents the previous day had been just as difficult as these meetings always are. During the afternoon Irene and Jonny were intending to go out to Torslanda to speak to them again, and to take a look at the girl's room. Hopefully CSI would be finished by the end of the morning.

The door leading to the corridor was open; they were waiting for their boss, Efva Thylqvist, to arrive. Her deputy would probably turn up at the same time: DCI Tommy Persson, Irene's classmate back at the police academy.

After they qualified, Irene and Tommy had both ended up in central Göteborg, and they had been colleagues for over twenty years. They had grown very close—unusually close for colleagues of different sexes. This had given rise to a number of rumors, but thanks to the fact that these rumors had been completely groundless, their friendship had survived. Before Tommy and his wife, Agneta, divorced four years ago, the two families had often hung out; they had even gone on vacation together. They had been godparents to each other's children. For eighteen years Irene and Tommy had shared an office in the Violent Crimes Unit—right up until a year ago, when their former chief, Superintendent Sven Andersson, had moved over to the Cold Cases Unit, and a new chief had taken over.

Irene and Tommy's office was right at the end of the corridor, well away from the main door. Superintendent Efva Thylqvist had decided she wanted her deputy closer to her, and after a rapid reorganization, Tommy found himself in the room next door to the superintendent. Which meant he was at the opposite end of the corridor from his old office.

"It will be nice for you to have your own space after all these years," Efva Thylqvist had said, gently placing a well-manicured hand on Irene's arm.

Irene hadn't thought it was nice at all, just lonely. She would no longer have anyone to chat to or bounce her ideas off. It had taken a great deal of self-control on Irene's part to refrain from shaking off the superintendent's hand.

That was the tricky thing about Efva Thylqvist. To begin with, everyone had a good feeling about the new chief. She had seemed friendly and genuinely interested in her new colleagues, but after a while Irene realized that her interest was mainly directed at the men. She always smiled at them, took time to have a proper conversation with them. All the guys on the team really liked her. Efva Thylqvist was an attractive brunette in her forties, with thick, shoulder-length hair. Her figure was slim but curvaceous. She certainly knew how to wear even the most severe skirt suit or pant suit; the blouses or tops she wore under her jackets were usually very low-cut, and she always wore high heels. Irene assumed this was to compensate for her lack of height. As Irene herself was six feet tall in her stocking feet, she felt like an elephant standing next to her dainty boss. They were about the same age, but Irene was slightly older. Rumor had it that Efva Thylqvist had been married at the beginning of her career as a police officer, but that the husband had disappeared at an early stage. They didn't have children, anyway. There was talk of affairs with high-ranking colleagues, some of whom had been married. Of course there was no way of assessing the accuracy of this gossip; in her more charitable moments Irene thought this was the kind of thing that was always said about women when they overtook men on the career ladder. At other times she thought it was possible that there was a certain amount of truth in the rumors. However, there was no denying the fact that Superintendent Thylqvist had led an outstanding career so far. Irene consoled herself with the thought that she was unlikely to be content to remain with the Violent Crimes Unit until her retirement.

After only a month Irene had noticed that her new boss was less and less interested in hearing her views. She hardly ever dealt with Irene personally, not even if something major was going on. She usually sent an email. On one occasion Irene had tentatively asked why she did this. Efva Thylqvist had smiled sweetly and said, "It saves me coming all the way to your office."

Any assignment that appeared to be remotely routine ended up on Irene's desk, and she had started to feel marginalized. She realized that her self-confidence had taken a knock, but sometimes there was light at the end of the tunnel, and she had the opportunity to get involved in the operational side of things. Like yesterday, when the call about the dead girl in Nötsund had come in. Then again, that was probably because only she and Jonny had been available to go out there.

Another reason why Irene was feeling lonely was no doubt because Birgitta Moberg-Rauhala was on leave. She had started reading law at the university back in the fall, and she had at least another year to go. After that she would be able to start applying for higher level posts within the police service. When they had met up for a quick lunch a month ago, Birgitta had hinted that she might carry on with her studies; she was considering training to be a lawyer or a prosecutor. Things were going well for her, and she was really enjoying the course. Her husband, Hannu Rauhala, was still on the team, and according to Birgitta he was happy to support whatever decision she made. Their son, Timo, was almost five years old, and they had decided not to have any more children. The grief had been too great after the late miscarriage Birgitta had suffered a few years earlier. As usual, Hannu hadn't said a word to his colleagues. The ice-blond man from Tornedalen had been as inscrutable as ever.

At the moment Irene was the only female inspector in the department, and she suspected that this suited Efva Thylqvist perfectly.

Just as the thought flitted through Irene's mind, the super-intendent walked in, closely followed by Tommy Persson.

"Good morning! Has everyone got a cup of coffee?"

Efva Thylqvist smiled as her gaze swept around the table. Irene noticed that she barely registered on Thylqvist's radar; it definitely looked as if she was avoiding eye contact with Irene. On the other hand, the superintendent lingered on Fredrik Stridh's handsome face. He had recently gotten married, and was due to become a father at the end of August. To everyone's surprise, the department's eternal bachelor and ladies' man had fallen head over heels for a nurse during a vacation to Barcelona the previous spring. Everything had happened very quickly after that: a wedding on New Year's Eve, the move to a larger apartment, and now a baby on the way.

Irene suddenly became aware of a strange feeling. She vaguely recognized it, and realized it had been bubbling inside her for quite some time. It took a while before she was able to identify it, but she got there in the end: rage. Pure, unadulterated rage. A second later she made a decision. Whatever happened, she was no longer prepared to be treated like an inferior being by Efva Thylqvist. She was no longer prepared to put up with that woman's disparaging attitude. It wasn't going to be easy; Superintendent Thylqvist was her boss, and she wouldn't hesitate to pull rank if she felt threatened.

Jonny Blom had placed the preliminary autopsy report on Alexandra Hallwiin on the table in front of him. Irene reached across and grabbed the pile of papers; she moved so fast he didn't have a chance to react. He glared at her and opened his mouth as if he was about to protest, but Irene merely gave him a placatory smile. The irritation in his eyes was gradually replaced by a certain level of confusion, and before he had time to speak, Efva Thylqvist took charge.

"Okay, let's make a start." She smiled and looked at Fredrik Stridh.

"Anything new on the car bomb?"

He seemed pleased to be the focus of her attention, and answered quickly. "No, but I'll be speaking to a fresh witness later today. A man walking his dog saw an older model Merc parked next to Roger 'the Hulk' Hansson's brand-new Jag. The timing is interesting; it was about eleven fifteen. Hansson left the restaurant at his usual time, just after one thirty. And as we know the bomb went off when he opened the car door."

"How serious was the injury to his foot?" Thylqvist asked.

"Only superficial. The force of the bomb was directed toward the passenger side of the car; it had probably been set up incorrectly."

"Useless bastards—they never get anything right," Jonny Blom said, just loud enough to be heard.

Efva Thylqvist managed a half-smile and turned her attention to him.

"Has anything come in on the Alexandra Hallwiin case?"

Before Jonny could answer, Irene took the initiative.

"It has. We received a preliminary autopsy report this morning; the forensic pathologist will get back to us later this afternoon with more details, but definitive information will take a few days," she said.

She glanced down at the papers in front of her.

"Dental records have enabled us to officially identify the body as that of Alexandra Hallwiin. She went missing on Walpurgis Night, and according to the report it seems likely that she ended up in the water during the first twenty-four hours following her disappearance. This means she had been submerged for approximately four days. There was a thin electrical cable wrapped tightly around her neck when she was found. The cause of death is probably strangulation. She was wearing only a black lace bra. There are knife marks on her inner thighs, around her breasts and up toward her neck. However, these are not stab wounds; it looks as if the perpetrator used a knife to inflict a series of deep scratches. Damage to the area around the anus and vagina suggests penetration with a blunt object. Even though the autopsy has not been completed, it is obvious that the body has been subjected to serious sexual violence. There are also knife wounds around the pudenda; the ME thinks the killer tried to make a pattern using the knife."

Irene stopped reading and looked up.

Efva Thylqvist was gazing at her expressionlessly. After a few seconds she turned to Jonny. "Are there still no witnesses who saw Alexandra after she left home?"

"No," Irene replied quickly, before Jonny had the chance to speak.

Without looking at Irene, the superintendent said in a

neutral tone of voice, "Jonny, you carry on with the investigation into Alexandra's death."

Then she turned to Hannu Rauhala. "What do we know about the other girl?"

"She's also been identified with the help of dental records," Hannu replied. "Moa Olsson, born September second, 1992. Fifteen years old."

Alexandra Hallwiin was exactly a year younger than Moa, Irene thought.

"She lived in Salviagatan, not far from the place where she was discovered; two and a half kilometers as the crow flies. The body was found in the forest at Gårdstensbergen; it's a recreational area with designated running tracks. But it was cold and wet the week leading up to Walpurgis Night. There weren't many people around. According to Moa's mother, she went missing the previous weekend, probably Sunday, April twenty-eighth. The mother's name is Kicki Olsson. She's been given early retirement. Mental problems, alcohol abuse. She got home at around nine on Sunday morning and doesn't remember whether Moa was there or not. But she thinks so."

"When was she reported missing?"

"On the following Tuesday."

"So she'd been gone for . . . seven or eight days," the superintendent said, looking pensive. "Who reported her?" she went on.

"The mother. I assume she'd started to sober up by then," Hannu said dryly.

"So she has a serious problem with alcohol."

"Yes. There was an older brother who died in a car accident three years ago. He was seventeen; no driver's license, drunk at the wheel. The car was stolen from Angered Square fifteen minutes before the crash. Kicki Olsson hasn't been able to work since."

"What did she do?"

"She was a cleaner at IKEA in Bäckebol."

"What about the father?"

"Out of the picture; the two kids had different fathers," Hannu explained.

"Okay, we need to check out both fathers. And find out whether the mother has a new man on the go; if so, check him out too. What does the ME say about the cause of death?"

"Nothing definite. Decomposition had set in, and animals had been at the body. Entomological samples have been taken for testing. They estimate that she'd probably been lying there for at least a week. She seems to have been sub-jected to extreme sexual violence, based on the appearance of some of her injuries. She was completely naked. The dog that found the body had picked up her panties. They'd fallen off as the killer dragged her up the hill to hide her in a crevice in the rock."

"The hill? He climbed a hill with a dead body?" Jonny exclaimed skeptically.

"A small hill, with a path leading to the top," Hannu said.

"Can you drive there?" Tommy wondered.

"Yes. There's a parking lot no more than a hundred meters from the spot where she was found, and a gravel path leading from there to the hill; it's perfectly possible to drive all the way. CSI has secured several different tire tracks. The problem is all the rain we've had since she disappeared."

The superintendent nodded; she realized this could cause problems. She gave a start as Irene suddenly spoke up again.

"It feels as if everything is a bit much right now. We've already got several ongoing investigations piled up, and now these new cases . . . I'm just wondering when we'll be getting a replacement for Birgitta," she said calmly.

"We don't have time to discuss that at the moment," the superintendent replied brusquely.

"But I think we'd all like to know where we stand in terms of reinforcements," Irene persisted.

"Robert Backman was only available for three months," Efva Thylqvist snapped.

"Yes, but that was before Christmas. We haven't had anyone in place of Birgitta since then."

You're saving money, Irene thought, making every effort not to show what was going through her mind. Thylqvist was starting to look uncomfortable.

"It's not that easy; people start taking their vacations in June," she defended herself.

"I agree with Irene. We've been under far too much pressure since New Year's, and all through the spring. We need a replacement as soon as possible."

Irene was both surprised and grateful as Tommy spoke up. By now it was clear that the superintendent was far from happy, and she couldn't hide her annoyance.

"Every department has the same problems! There's nobody available. Birgitta's leave of absence ends in August; she might be back then."

"She won't," Hannu pointed out.

And he ought to know. Even Efva Thylqvist wasn't about to contradict him. Instead her face suddenly lit up. "Oh, so she's decided to carry on with her studies?" she said in a pleasant tone of voice. "In that case we need to act in accordance with this new information."

As if you don't know that already, Irene thought. Both she and Hannu knew perfectly well that Birgitta had applied for an extension of her leave of absence several weeks ago.

The internal telephone suddenly crackled to life.

"Hello? Are you there? Superintendent Thylqvist?" said a female voice.

"I'm here," the superintendent said, leaning toward the speaker on the table.

"We've just had a call. A body has been found on Kors-vägen, walled up in a cellar. Can you send someone over to take a look?"

No one in the room moved or even blinked. They were all dumbstruck, staring at the soulless grey plastic box as if it had suddenly turned into a hissing viper.

Peter Lovesey
(England)
The Circle
The Headhunters
False Inspector Dew
Rough Cider
On the Edge
The Reaper

(Bath, England)
The Last Detective
Diamond Solitaire
The Summons
Bloodhounds
Upon a Dark Night
The Vault
Diamond Dust
The House Sitter
The Secret Hangman
Skeleton Hill
Stagestruck
Cop to Corpse
The Tooth Tattoo
The Stone Wife
Down Among the Dead Men

(London, England)
Wobble to Death
The Detective Wore Silk Drawers
Abracadaver
Mad Hatter's Holiday
The Tick of Death
A Case of Spirits
Swing, Swing Together
Waxwork

Jassy Mackenzie
(South Africa)
Random Violence
Stolen Lives
The Fallen
Pale Horses

Seichō Matsumoto
(Japan)
Inspector Imanishi Investigates

James McClure
(South Africa)
The Steam Pig
The Caterpillar Cop
The Gooseberry Fool
Snake
The Sunday Hangman
The Blood of an Englishman
The Artful Egg
The Song Dog

Magdalen Nabb
(Italy)
Death of an Englishman
Death of a Dutchman
Death in Springtime
Death in Autumn
The Marshal and the Murderer
The Marshal and the Madwoman
The Marshal's Own Case
The Marshal Makes His Report
The Marshal at the Villa Torrini
Property of Blood
Some Bitter Taste
The Innocent
Vita Nuova
The Monster of Florence

Fuminori Nakamura
(Japan)
The Thief
Evil and the Mask
Last Winter, We Parted

Stuart Neville
(Northern Ireland)
The Ghosts of Belfast
Collusion
Stolen Souls
The Final Silence
Those We Left Behind

(Dublin)
Ratlines

Eliot Pattison
(Tibet)
Prayer of the Dragon
The Lord of Death

Rebecca Pawel
(1930s Spain)
Death of a Nationalist
Law of Return
The Watcher in the Pine
The Summer Snow

Kwei Quartey
(Ghana)
Murder at Cape Three Points

Qiu Xiaolong
(China)
Death of a Red Heroine
A Loyal Character Dancer
When Red Is Black

John Straley
(Alaska)
The Woman Who Married a Bear
The Curious Eat Themselves

John Straley cont.
The Big Both Ways
Cold Storage, Alaska

Akimitsu Takagi
(Japan)
The Tattoo Murder Case
Honeymoon to Nowhere
The Informer

Helene Tursten
(Sweden)
Detective Inspector Huss
The Torso
The Glass Devil
Night Rounds
The Golden Calf
The Fire Dance
The Beige Man
The Treacherous Net

Jan Merete Weiss
(Italy)
These Dark Things
A Few Drops of Blood

Janwillem van de Wetering
(Holland)
Outsider in Amsterdam
Tumbleweed
The Corpse on the Dike
Death of a Hawker
The Japanese Corpse
The Blond Baboon
The Maine Massacre
The Mind-Murders
The Streetbird
The Rattle-Rat
Hard Rain
Just a Corpse at Twilight
Hollow-Eyed Angel
The Perfidious Parrot
The Sergeant's Cat: Collected Stories

Timothy Williams
(Guadeloupe)
Another Sun
The Honest Folk of Guadeloupe

(Italy)
Converging Parallels
The Puppeteer
Persona Non Grata
Black August
Big Italy

Jacqueline Winspear
(1920s England)
Maisie Dobbs
Birds of a Feather